A ROSE IN SPLENDOR

Laura Parker

WARNER BOOKS

A Warner Communications Company

WARNER BOOKS EDITION

Copyright © 1986 by Laura Castoro
All rights reserved.

Cover art by Bob McGinnis

Warner Books, Inc.
666 Fifth Avenue
New York, N.Y. 10103

 A Warner Communications Company

Printed in the United States of America

First Printing: June, 1986

10 9 8 7 6 5 4 3 2 1

Deirdre trembled inside.
"Kiss me again," she said.

"No, lass. There comes a price with joy and later
you might come to regret the price you'd pay."
Deirdre closed her eyes against the stark beauty of
his face. It was a dangerous moment. This was
her choice, and her responsibility. Greatly daring
she reached up and touched his face. "Kiss me
again, Killian. Please."
His hair was amazingly soft beneath the caress of
her hands. His mouth found hers, and the warm
sweetness of his tongue slipped between her lips.
She wondered if any woman had ever experienced
this flame burning within her. Kiss followed kiss,
meeting and melting until dizzy and shaken she
felt the world drop away.

☆　☆　☆　☆　☆

PRAISE FOR THE FIRST <u>ROSE</u> NOVEL—

Rose of the Mists

"Flows like a charming Gaelic folktale. Its freshness
and sensitivity will keep the reader entranced and
wanting more. Superexcellence in the field of histor-
ical romance! 5 stars!"

—*Affaire de Coeur*

"Four stars—highest rating! Reads like a beautiful,
romantic fairy tale."

—*Romantic Times*

"Quite simply a treasure of reading delight."
—*San Francisco Herald Examiner*

Also by Laura Parker

Rose of the Mists

Published by
WARNER BOOKS

This book is dedicated with love to my mother.

THE IRISH LAND
ABOUT 1700

MILES
0   50
KM
0   50

N

LOUGH SWILLY
RATHLIN ISLAND
NORTH CHANNEL
DERRYVEAGH MTS.
DONEGAL
FOYLE
LOUGH FOYLE
SPERRIN MTS.
ANTRIM HILL
BELFAST LOUGH
BLUE STACK MTS.
FINN
SWILLY
MOURNE
BANN
LOUGH NEAGH
ULSTER
DONEGAL BAY
LOWER LOUGH ERNE
Dungannon
BLACKWATER
PASS OF THE NORTH
STRANGFORD LOUGH
DARTRY MTS.
Armagh
MOURNE MTS.
Nowry
Sligo
UPPER LOUGH ERNE
CLARE ISLAND
OX MTS.
LOUGH MOY
CAVAN
Dundalk
DUNDALK BAY
CLEW BAY
LOUGH CONN
PARTRY MTS.
CONNAUGHT
LOUGH ALLEN
SUCK
LOUTH
Drogheda
TWELVE PINS
LOUGH MASK
LOUGH REE
INNY
MEATH
BOYNE
LOUGH CORRIB
Athlone
BOG OF ALLEN
LIFFEY
Dublin
Galway
SLIEVE AUGHTY MTS.
SHANNON
IRISH SEA
GALWAY BAY
LOUGH DERG
ATLANTIC OCEAN
Idrone
WICKLOW MTS.
OWN
LEINSTER
SHANNON
Limerick
Askeaton
MAIGUE
Kilkenny
BARROW
Enniscorthy
AHERLOW VALLEY
GOLDEN VALE
Cashel
BLACKSTAIRS MTS.
Ballygub (town)
MULLAGHAREIRK MTS.
FOREST
NORE
GALTEE MTS.
Clonmel
NORE
Wexford
Smerwick
Tralee
SLIEVE MISH MTS.
BLACKWATER
BALLYHOURA HILLS
SUIR
COMERAGH MTS.
DINGLE BAY
LOUGH LEANE
KNOCKMEALDOWN MTS.
Lismore
Waterford
ST. GEORGE'S CHANNEL
MAC GILLYCUDDY'S REEKS
BLACKWATER
BOGGERAGH MTS.
MUNSTER
Dungarvan
LEE
CORK
Youghal
BANTRY BAY
BANDON R.
Kinsale
SHEHY MTS.
LISCARROL CASTLE

ELEVATIONS
▲ 2,000' – 3,000'
△ 3,000' and over

PART ONE

The Flight

Ochon and ochon! when the tidings travelled forth
That our chiefs had sailed in sorrow from the
glens of the North;
Ochon and ochon! how our souls grew sore afraid,
And our love followed after in the track your
keel had made!

—from "The Four Winds of Eirinn"

Chapter One

Munster, Ireland: October 1691

"... And so, one fine morning the lass Deirdre happened upon a raven drinking calf's blood which had been spilled upon the snow. The sight arrested her. 'There,' said she to her servant, 'I could love a man with hair like a raven's wing, lips of red, and a manly body as clean as snow.'"

"Aye!" answered the seven-year-old girl who sat listening at her nursemaid's knee. "Aye, 'twill be so for me! Red lips and a fine-bodied man, 'tis what I want."

Brigid McSheehy smiled at the girl but wagged a reproving finger at her. "Ye're not to say such, lass. 'Tis unbecoming in a wee bairn. Ye know naught of men and I pray to the good Lord ye shall remain in ignorance some years."

The girl jumped to her feet, unruly corkscrews of cornsilk-gold hair bouncing at her brow. "I will not! I will have the man I choose." She perched a small fist on each narrow hip. "If 'tis today he's coming, I will have him!"

Brigid rose to her feet. The jest had gone too far. "Miss Deirdre Clare Butler Fitzgerald! 'Tis wickedness ye're speaking. Her ladyship would have me hide from me back

3

if she heard ye. I should never have begun that tale. 'Tis unfit for young ears.''

Deirdre's eyes suddenly glazed with tears and her lower lip drooped in a childish pout. ''You promised! You promised you'd tell me the story if I finished me porridge, and I did.''

Brigid raised her eyes heavenward. ''Aye, I promised, and that sorry I am that I did.'' Lady Elva, Deirdre's stepmother, had banished the tragic love story from the nursery after the child had first announced her intention of becoming like her legendary namesake in every way. Yet, Deirdre loved ''The Sons of Uisliu'' and could repeat it by heart. ''Let me tell ye the tale of 'The Dream of Oengus,' '' Brigid suggested. ''Now there's a lovely tale with a happy end for a pair of lovers.''

''I want the other, about the girl whose name I bear.'' Deirdre blinked back her tears, her flushed cheeks rounding in the beginnings of a smile. ''I'll not tell that you told me the story . . . if you finish it. Please,'' she begged softly, and placed one tiny hand on her nurse's arm. An impudent dimple puckered her left cheek. ''I promise to be good. Really.''

Brigid stared down into the child's beautiful gray-green eyes fringed with thick spikes of gold-tipped lashes and could not resist smiling back. Half a dozen years of life hardly seemed long enough for the child to have developed such artless charm, she thought begrudgingly. Yet, from birth, Lord Fitzgerald's only daughter had been able instantly to win affection from both friend and foe alike.

''Aye, well we could do with a bit of that this day,'' the nursemaid murmured under her breath. She glanced around the nursery, bare now but for her chair and the footstool where Deirdre sat. What had not been sold had been piled onto the wagons parked on the drive before the Norman fortress known as Liscarrol Castle. Within hours they would be gone, gone from Liscarrol, gone from Ireland. Forever.

Brigid caught back a sob but a sigh escaped. She saw Deirdre's eyes widen in surprise and sought to distract those sharp eyes that saw more than they should. ''We've little time left for stories, lass. Ye best go to the stables and take yer pick of the mouser's new litter.'' She held up a silencing hand as the girl began to protest. "Once we're aboard ship, I'll finish me tale, and there's a promise to ye."

Deirdre stared up into the beloved face of her nurse, noting with misgiving that the woman's usually ruddy cheeks were as white as her linen. "What is wrong, Brigid? Why does Lady Elva cry each time I ask why we're leaving Liscarrol?''

"And how should I be knowing the family business?'' Brigid answered gruffly and looked away. She had been forbidden to tell the child what was occurring.

"Is Lady Elva in the family way again?'' Deirdre persisted. "She cried all last spring before Owen was born.''

"Faith!'' Brigid whispered, coloring to the roots of her hair. "For a gently reared lass, ye've a single lack of modesty. Ye're not to think of such things,'' she admonished as she took the child by the arm and escorted her to the door.

"I will not cry,'' Deirdre pronounced. "I will laugh every day that I carry my child. You'll see. He will be as handsome as his father, but smaller, I think.''

Brigid did not even try to reason out this bit of childish logic. She simply opened the nursery door and gave the girl a gentle shove. "Come back in a trice. If I must come looking for ye, I'll be bringing me strap!''

Deirdre curtsied to her nurse but devils danced in her eyes when she looked up. "I'll come straight back, if I don't find me black-haired lad. If I do, tell Da we've gone to fetch the priest!'' She spun on her heel and raced for the narrow stairwell, taking the steps two at a time.

"'Tis a heart an' a half in that wee bairn, and there's a truth!'' Brigid murmured admiringly, going to the window to watch for her charge to appear in the yard below.

Almost at once Deirdre appeared, running across the damp grass and splashing mud on the hem of her gown. The wind tore her hair from its ribbons and lifted the thick tresses until they formed a wavy banner of gold at her back. That was the way of the lass. She disliked nothing as much as confinement. Dashing across the sodden ground was a miracle of freedom to her. How she would hate the tiny cabin aboard ship to which she would be consigned. "Enjoy it, me lass. 'Twill be yer last trip to the stables of Liscarrol."

Brigid turned away, batting back her tears, and after a long sad look about the bare room she picked up the chair and stool to carry them below stairs to be packed.

As she descended she wondered again why Lady Elva had asked her to accompany the family to France. Deirdre had already absorbed the sum of her meager education, and more. She could read and write both English and the forbidden Gaelic. Latin she had learned from her half-brothers Conall and Darragh.

Deirdre's skills were remarkable in one so young; everyone who met her remarked upon them. If she were a boy, she would soon have a proper tutor or be sent to a monastery to prepare for the priesthood. Conall and Darragh, young men both, were following their father as professional soldiers. Tradition was, the third son was given to the Church. Perhaps young Owen, whom Brigid heard in the distance bawling lustily for his mid-morning meal, would be the next Fitzgerald priest.

"I'll not be tellin' her ladyship!" a woman's voice cried from the ground floor as Brigid descended the last steps.

"Ye won't be telling her ladyship what?" Brigid asked when she spied the cook and the doorman squaring off.

Maeve, the cook, looked up, her face flushed with anger. "Sean here says there nae potatoes in the larder and nae five hams put back in the smokehouse, when I did it meself." She turned on her opponent and shook a beefy fist at the white-haired man. "Here's five hams what I'll be puttin' in *yer* larder, ye lyin' thievin' son o' Satan!"

Sean flushed but did not dodge the halfhearted swing, which went wildly astray. "God's life, woman. I swear to ye, I sent only what the master ordered. Them hams went to feed our lads at Limerick."

At the mention of the fateful battle both women crossed themselves and murmured prayers.

"Get along with ye then," Brigid said after a moment. "But ye're not to say a word to her ladyship. She's grief enough on her shoulders this day."

"Aye, that she has," Maeve agreed. "Only some is worse off than others. Ireland's good enough for those of us without. 'Tis only them what can afford the fare, hiein' off to France!"

Brigid stiffened. "Did I hear ye say a word against the folks who have fed and housed ye better than ye deserve?"

Maeve lifted her head defiantly, her double chin wagging in evidence of her well-fed state. "I gave two sons to the cause of King James. What of them, their poor bones lying in unhallowed ground, rotting till the Day of Reckoning?"

"None can tax Lord Fitzgerald for giving less than his fair share," Brigid countered. "Look about and then tell me ye do not remember how it once was at Liscarrol. The gold and silver are long gone. It put powder in yer lads' muskets. The crystal and furnishings were sent to Paris to buy shoes and blankets. Did not Lady Elva give her best jewels so that our lads marched with something in their bellies? Ye've little to complain about and much to be grateful for."

Maeve snorted. "But where did it get us, I'm asking? That coward King James is hid like a squirrel in his nest, safe tucked away in France, while our own Lord Fitzgerald claps his last rags to his back and prepares to depart from his motherland. 'Tis a sad day, this, when our own lords turn tail and run."

Brigid did not answer that sally. She herself could not quite reconcile the reasoning behind the mass expatriation of the Irish army since the surrender of King James in his war with William of Orange for the English throne. The Protestants had won again; yet, the Protestants had won before, and many native sons born and dying Catholic had remained. Why now this sudden desertion of their homeland?

" 'Tis no business of ours and certainly ye've no say in how Lord Fitzgerald conducts his affairs. Small wonder he would have his wife, small son, and daughter away for a time. There are stories about how the English are putting both women and children to the sword for no more reason than the devil's own pleasure of it. 'Tis enough reason for him to remove his dear ones."

Without waiting for a reply Brigid thrust her burdens at the footman and said, "Add them to the rest. Miss Deirdre will be back from the stables directly, and Lord Fitzgerald's give the word we're to be ready to leave when he arrives."

She turned to the cook. "Do not be gaping at me, woman. Ye've food to provide for the journey to Cork, and his lordship will not take kindly to excuses."

The cook's mouth worked open and shut a few times but no sound came out of it. Giving up, she turned and walked away.

Brigid smiled, amazed at her own temerity. Under normal circumstances she would never have dared to speak in that manner to another servant. But there was nothing normal about packing to leave her homeland.

Until she had come to Liscarrol Castle with her kinswoman, Grainne Butler, who became Lord Fitzgerald's second bride, she had never been more than two miles from her home in Kilkenny. Now, out of loyalty to her dead mistress and a sacred promise which bound her to the child, she was about to embark upon the open face of a sea she had never before seen. Crossing herself against the unknown, she stepped out into the day.

"Deirdre! Deirdre!" She clucked her tongue impatiently as she scanned the yard. "Now where has the lass gone?"

"Which shall it be then?" Deirdre questioned the orange, brown, and white tabby lying on her side as six balls of fur scrambled over her and one another, searching for nourishment.

She was alone except for the faint whistle of the breeze and the mewing of the tabby's brood, but the silence did not disturb her. The stables had been emptied months earlier as the last of the Liscarrol horses had been sent for by Lord Fitzgerald to serve his army. She had long since become accustomed to entertaining herself when Brigid was involved in other matters. The birth of Owen in the spring had divided the nurse's attention between herself and the babe.

In fact, Deirdre decided, she often preferred her own company to that of the stern but loving Brigid. Her nurse discouraged her daydreaming, and her dreams were the most exciting part of her life now that her brothers were away.

She did, however, miss her cart pony. Her father had taught her to handle the reins at the age of five, and she was allowed to drive alone under the watchful eye of a groom. Now even the young grooms were gone, some dead, others grown into hard-eyed men who followed her father, Lord Fitzgerald, a brigadier in the Irish army.

No one would tell her, but she knew that the voyage which her family was about to undertake had something to do with the war that had raged through Ireland these last two years.

Deirdre sighed. Everyone said she was too young to understand. Yet, she was not too young to understand the tears of the people of the valley when they learned that another son or father or brother would not be returning from battle. Nor was she too young to notice how fear for her father and elder brothers was eating away at her stepmother's beauty.

"If only they would talk to me," Deirdre complained to her companions.

Getting down on her hands and knees in the straw, she reached out a tentative finger and lightly poked the kitten nearest her. Instantly the kitten rounded on her finger and pounced, digging its needle-sharp claws into her flesh.

"*Ouch!*" Deirdre jerked back her hand, but the cottony-soft kitten held tight, adding the sting of its teeth to her discomfort.

"No! No!" she cried, torn between pain and giggles as the kitten clung determinedly to her. Finally she rose on her knees and shook her hand. The snap dislodged the kitten and sent it tumbling across the floor to land upside down against its mother's haunches.

"Oh, poor kitty," Deirdre crooned, instantly sorry that

she had used so much force. She quickly gathered the gray and white bundle into her palms and held it against her chest.

Unabashed by the rough handling, the kitten stood up in her hands, arched its back, and began a purring that shook its fragile body.

Deirdre tucked the kitten under her chin, enjoying the vibrations against her throat. "You're not so fierce as you believe," she told it. "You're all head and fur. Naught but a whiff of breeze would blow you away. Brigid says we'll need a good mouser, there being great rats aboard ship. But I do not think the mousies would be overly afeard of you."

Deirdre lifted the kitten to look at it, and the silver-gray cat's eyes met and locked with her gaze of soft gray-green.

Without even a whisper of wind to announce it, a huge cloud sailed before the sun, and the stable began to darken. The slipping away of sunlight did not startle Deirdre. She concentrated on the rhythmic purring within her palms and watching the kitten's vertical pupils expand from slits to ellipses of midnight black.

The prickling of her scalp was a rare but familiar sensation. She had expected a vision to come upon her for days, ever since Brigid had told her that they would be leaving Liscarrol.

Now the ground beneath her seemed to dip and sway like the deck of a ship. A journey over water. Yes, she knew that. What else? The undulation ceased, and in its stead came the pulse of hooves pounding the ground. Riders, many of them. Soldiers? She closed her eyes as her heart began to hammer in a slow but frightened rhythm. Fear had never before been a part of the dreams which Brigid refused to acknowledge as real.

When Deirdre opened her eyes the darkness did not abate. The sound of horses disappeared as quickly as it had come, but the night—if it was night—reverberated with anticipation. Gradually she realized that her kitten had stopped purring. It stood in her hands, its back arched and it claws unsheathed. It, too, was afraid.

She saw him before she heard the distant whinny of his

steed; the dark silhouette of a horseman who came riding out of the night and straight toward her.

She did not think of screaming. What good were cries when a phantom bore down on her? When he reined in his horse with a scant yard of space between them, she felt a queer mixture of emotions. Clothed in a great black cloak and hat, he was forbidding, the very tilt of his shoulders a threat.

Yet, there was strength and assuredness in him, a determination in the handling of his horse which even she, a child, could admire. When he reached out a hand to her, this faceless rider swathed in uncanny silence, Deirdre extended hers.

At once he reared back, as if afraid of touching her. "Stay away!" he roared, his voice dark, deep, and edged with unspoken pain. "Stay away in fear of your life, *mo cuishle!*"

He turned his horse and galloped away as if borne on the back of a *púca*.

"Deirdre? Deirdre, lass! Where have ye hid yerself?"

Deirdre blinked and instantly was once again inside the stable, with daylight streaming in as she knelt in the moldy hay. The kitten leaped from her hands, landed on its feet, and scrambled away as Brigid appeared in the doorway.

"There ye are!" the nurse scolded. "Did not I say ye were to come straight back?"

Deirdre jumped to her feet. "Did you see him? 'Twas a grand horseman riding a great black fairy horse!"

Brigid folded her arms across her chest, accustomed to Deirdre's spinning wild tales to divert her from her anger. "That I did not! Neither did ye. Ye were kneeling with yer eyes closed when I stepped in just now. The riders ye heard must be Lord Fitzgerald's men, and not even himself will be forgiving ye if ye keep them waiting."

Guiltily Deirdre beat the straw from her wrinkled skirts as she said, "But there was a man. I saw him." She paused and looked up into her nurse's face. "He held out his hand to me."

Brigid read the truth of Deirdre's words in her frank

gaze, and a tiny shiver sped through her. "Are ye telling me true, lass?" she demanded sharply.

Deirdre looked away. "Aye. I saw him. Real as you, he was, sitting there upon his fine horse, all black hair and wild eyes. Only I did not see his face properly. 'Twas too dark." Her eyes widened in speculation. "Do you suppose the rider was a fairy too? 'Tis said a *púca* can turn himself into a horse and gallop off to hell with any unsuspecting soul who tries to ride him. Only another fairy could control him."

Brigid blanched at the suggestion. The lass had claimed to have seen fairies before, but one never knew what to make of her stories. She was a child with a vivid imagination. As for the other, that was a matter to which few were privy and all were forbidden to mention.

"'Twas that tale I began," Brigid mused aloud. "I should've known no good would come from the telling of it. Ye drive a body to sinful ways with yer wheedling." She caught Deirdre by the arm and bent low to whisper, "Ye're not to tell a soul ye've been visited by the fairies this day, do ye hear me? 'Twould be thought a bad omen, the little people coming to see ye off."

"See me off to where?" Deirdre demanded. "No one will tell me where we're going."

"'Tis no concern of yers. Ye've a loose tongue, and these are dark days when a wrong word could hang us all. Be a good lass, else ye'll answer for it!" Brigid released the girl's arm and gave her a push. "Get back to the house and change. I'll not have ye meet his lordship in them dirty skirts, and 'tis horses for sure I'm hearing in the yard."

With Brigid on her heels, Deirdre hurried out into the day, thrilled by the thought that her father was home at last, then another thought made her stop and spin about. "I forgot me kitten!"

"Deirdre!" her nurse called in warning as the girl headed toward the dimly lit interior of the stable.

"'Twill only take a moment to find him," Deirdre called reassuringly over her shoulder. "Tell Da I'm coming. We must have a cat for the voyage!"

With a sigh of resignation, Brigid turned back to the house. Lord Fitzgerald would forgive an errant daughter. He could not be counted on to be as lenient with an absent servant.

Deirdre found the mother cat still sprawled in a slat of sunlight pouring through a crack in the wall of the stall. The yellow and white kitten she had chosen was not among the ones tussling nearby. "He's run away," she exclaimed in dismay, and turned to search the next of the empty stalls. "Kitty? Here, kitty . . . kitty . . . kitty."

The shadows lay deeper and darker at the back of the stable. As if afraid to disturb the heavy silence there, Deirdre rose on tiptoe as she neared and her call fell to a whisper. "Kitty? Psst! Puss?"

She spied the white fluff of a kitten's tail at the edge of the last stall. "There you are!" she squealed in delight and pounced upon the object, expecting to come up with her kitten. Instead, she trapped the tip of a white feather attached to a wide-brimmed hat.

Surprised, Deirdre picked it up and looked at it. It was a man's hat but not one that belonged to a servant at Liscarrol. It bore on its band a white ribbon cockade, symbol of the Irish army loyal to the defeated James II. But why was it here, stuck in the back of an unused stall?

Instinct made her drop the hat, but it was too late. Even as she turned to flee, a hand reached out of the darkness from the depths of the stall and clamped her ankle in a brutal grip.

"Scream and I'll shoot you, I swear it!"

The startled cry that had risen in Deirdre's throat died as she saw the threat of a pistol barrel materialize out of the gloom. She was afraid, certainly, but she was in her own home, and her father had just ridden in. Her attacker, she reasoned in childish simplicity, would not harm her with her father nearby. Besides, she was the daughter of a general and should be as brave as any of his men.

"I'll not scream," she said after a moment. "I'm a Fitzgerald and I'm not afeard of the likes of you!"

"There's a fierce one you are, lass," the disembodied voice answered, a brogue thickening his tone. "But I'm that desperate that it matters little to me. The soldiers in the yard—what do they want?''

Deirdre bit her lip, her confidence fading as quickly at it had come. She strained her eyes against the shadows but could see nothing more than a black-cloaked figure lying on his side. The hand wrapped round her ankle was large and blood-smeared. Finally her eyes fell on the hat she had dropped, and a little of her confidence returned.

"You're a King James man," she said.

"Aye, that I am," the gruff voice answered, more faintly this time, as if he strained for breath. "Does your house fly the standard of the Dutch jackal?"

"We do not! Me da is Lord Fitzgerald, brigadier in the service of King James."

The grip on her ankle loosened as the man sighed again. "They—they . . . did not lie then," he whispered hoarsely and then seemed to choke.

Deirdre watched spellbound as the pistol fell from the man's grasp as he coughed. The spasms racked his body and he curled up into a ball. Common sense told her run, for she was free, but fascination held her rooted to the spot.

Finally, when the racking stopped, she bent and picked up the pistol. It was a cold, heavy weapon, the same as her father's pistol.

"Careful, you'll blow your lovely nose away," the man said suddenly.

Deirdre jumped and took a step back. She had thought him dead or asleep. When he moved to sit up, she took another step backward and his hand shot out toward her. "Give it to me, lass. I'd not like to harm . . . so fair a bairn . . . but I will. . . . Give me me pistol!" he rasped.

Deirdre took another careful step backward. He was still cloaked in shadow but his harsh breathing betrayed his condition. "You're hurt."

He did not answer but with a terrible groan hoisted himself to his feet. The breeze caught at his cloak and it unfolded, billowing out like the black wings of a nightmarish creature.

Magnified by her fear and the broad sweep of his cloak,

it seemed to Deirdre that he rose to a height of ten feet and filled the confines of the tiny stall. "You're a fairy! A demon!" she cried.

Clutching his middle, he staggered into the slanted light from the open stable doors. Then, like a puppet whose strings have been snipped, his legs folded under him and he collapsed in a single, fluid movement.

Deirdre dropped the pistol and clamped her hands over her mouth to keep back a cry. He lay now in dim light and she saw that he was, indeed, a man. He wore heavy, scarred, muddy jack boots. His face was turned away and the tangle of long black hair at the back of his head was matted with blood.

Unable to resist any wounded thing, Deirdre took a step closer. Was he dead? She could not tell, for he lay so still. She moved another step closer, wondering what to do. If he were one of her father's men or only a soldier of King James, he would not have hidden himself in the home of sympathizers. No, something else had brought him here.

Deirdre glanced at the pistol lying nearby. Perhaps he was a highwayman. They were as prevalent as soldiers these days. If her father came in and found a highwayman, he would have him hanged summarily.

Greatly daring, she knelt down beside the fallen man and shook his shoulder. She felt relief mingled with trepidation when he stirred slightly and moaned under her prodding.

"If you're a thief, then you should know we've nothing to steal," she whispered anxiously. "The silver's gone and the gold plate. There's not so much as a pearl in me mother's jewel box." Too late, she realized that perhaps she should not have mentioned her mother's jewel case, for the man slowly lifted his head.

The first thing she noticed were startling blue eyes in a face drained of all color by pain. Then rapidly she noticed the dark bruises beneath his eyes, the thin scraggly beard which matched the shaggy blue-black mane of curls that fell across his brow, and the smear of bright red blood trailing from his mouth.

White skin, raven-black hair, and bloodred lips: he bore the colors of the mythical Deirdre's lover.

Deirdre jumped to her feet, her small body trembling so hard that she could barely stand. It was a fairy's trick. Hadn't Brigid warned her that the people of the otherworld did not like to be mocked? The fairies must have heard her boast of the man she would marry and had deliberately set about to frighten her by conjuring up this ghost from her daydreams.

"Do not hurt me, please!" she begged. "I did not mean to mock you. 'Twas a joke. I'll never mock the stories again, I swear it!"

The man blinked and shook his head slightly, as if he did not understand her. "Help me," he said, his voice scarcely audible.

"Aye, anything, only do not hurt me!"

He winced as he reached out a trembling hand to her. "There's the soul of Ireland in your misty green eyes."

He closed his eyes, as if musing on a far-distant thought. When his eyes opened again, his gaze had changed. There was helplessness there, and his voice was edged with desperation. "Are you, I'm wondering, as gentle and kind as your gaze?"

Deirdre nodded slowly, unable to look away from his pain-ravaged face. She had never seen a man so badly hurt, nor had she ever heard a voice like his. It wrapped her in a warmth that was both pleasing and discomforting. She reached out to take his hand and was again amazed by his strong-fingered grasp. "I'll help you."

"Dee!" came a sudden call just outside the stable doors. "Dee, where are ye, daughter?"

"Da!" Deirdre cried joyously. "No, do not move," she scolded as the stranger pushed feebly against the ground in an effort to rise. Squatting, she put a hand to his face. His skin was icy to the touch, as though he had just come out of a winter wind. " 'Tis me Da. He'll help you."

Lord Fitzgerald had spent the better part of a day and half in the saddle, leading a wretched band of war-weary soldiers on what for many of them would be their last ride through their homeland. Having signed the terms of surrender in the Treaty of Limerick a few days earlier, he, along with more than thirteen thousand other men of the Irish army, had chosen expatriation rather than submit to English rule. France promised a freedom that they would not now have here in their Irish homeland.

It was a hard decision, made worse for the families of the soldiers. As an officer, Lord Fitzgerald was one of the lucky few who had been given the freedom to carry his family with him. Most of the regular troops had been summarily herded aboard ships and shipped across the Channel without even a glimpse of the families they were leaving behind.

"Damn their English souls!" Lord Fitzgerald tossed off automatically in sympathy with his thoughts.

It was left to officers like himself to inform the soldiers' families of where their menfolk had gone. Times were hard. It would be months, perhaps years, before some families could follow their stout-hearted fathers, sons, and lovers.

As he made his way toward the entrance of his stables, he rubbed his eyes, which ached from road grit and lack of sleep. He smelled of horses, gun powder, and sweat. Beneath his dust-powdered periwig his scalp itched from flea bites. Had this been any other day, he would have ordered up a bath, a full meal, and several glasses of port before retiring for a sound sleep. Now he barely had time to gather his family together and race for the docks at Cork, where a French ship awaited them.

No doubt his famous ancestor, Gerald Fitzgerald, would spin in his grave to know that he had handed Liscarrol over to the care of a Protestant, even if he was a Fitzgerald, but his cousin Neil Fitzgerald, because of his religion, would be able to ensure that he would not lose his home. The English had promised no retribution against the Catholic families who had surrendered at Limerick, but only a fool or one too young to remember the atrocities carried out by the Englishman Cromwell would rely on such pledges.

With Liscarrol in Protestant hands, even if they were Irish Protestant hands, the government could not readily confiscate it.

A bitter vetch it was, leaving his homeland in defeat. Well, there was no turning back now. His decision was made, and if his family was bewildered and frightened, they would follow him . . . as soon as he located his only daughter.

"Dee! Where are ye, me darlin'? Why do ye not—?"

When he turned in to the stable and saw his daughter kneeling on the ground beside a fallen man, his first thought was that it was one of his own soldiers. Then reason asserted itself. His men had not been dismissed from the yard. This was a stranger. Trained to note details in an instant, he saw the jack boots of a fighting man and the pistol lying nearby. Though he lay inordinately still, the stranger's chest rose and fell with the rapidity of a man in distress.

Lord Fitzgerald's heart lurched. The outbreak of the plague had taken away thousands of souls a year earlier. War always brought pestilence and disease. Yet, here was his darling daughter trying to comfort the strange man as she would a wounded bird or lamb.

"Dee, lass. Come away. Let him be." He spoke in the calm, authoritative voice that had made many a man under his command keep a clear head in battle, but the sweat of anxiousness glazed his brow in the moments it took him to reach Deirdre and snatch her up into his arms.

"Da!" Deirdre squealed in delight as her father's arms closed around her and lifted her up high. The strength of his embrace nearly crushed the breath from her, but the pain had a joy in it that she did not mind.

"Dee, lass, what are ye doing here?" her father questioned.

Deirdre reared back from the smothering confines of his chest, her young face clouded with worry. "You must help the man. He's running from the English. They wounded him. I said we'd help him, but he's afraid. He thinks you mean to hang him, Da."

"Does he now?" Lord Fitzgerald murmured, his gaze moving from his daughter's troubled expression to the man sprawled a few feet away. Wounded. Thank God! Injuries would heal . . . or not. At least his daughter had not been exposed to disease.

He noticed now the hat and its white cockade and sighed. No doubt the man had been on the run since the battle for Limerick. Perhaps he lived nearby and could be carried home before they left for Cork.

He set his daughter down carefully. "Go fetch me the sergeant, lass. O'Conner's his name."

"But, Da—" Deirdre protested, only to be turned about by her father's hands on her shoulders.

"Do not disobey an order from yer superior, lass! Fetch the sergeant. I'll keep watch over yer wounded lad. There's a good lass," he encouraged as she started for the doorway.

When he turned back, he picked up the pistol and pocketed it before bending over the ailing man. With strong but gentle hands he turned him over. When he saw the stranger's face, Lord Fitzgerald muttered an oath. Despite the dirt and blood, there was no disguising his youth. This was no seasoned soldier. This boy with peach fuzz for a beard could be no more than seventeen.

The lad groaned and his eyes flew open. "Who . . . who are you?"

"Ye're in no condition to care overmuch," Lord Fitzgerald answered gruffly, but he cradled the young man's head against his knees. "Who are *ye*, lad, and where's yer company?"

The boy shook his head slightly. "No company."

"All dead?" the brigadier asked gently.

Again he shook his head. "Not a . . . soldier. Rapparee."

"So," Lord Fitzgerald said shortly. This was not the answer he had hoped for. A professional soldier himself, he had little liking for the rapparees, as these undrilled fighters called themselves. The countryside swarmed with irregular troops, farmers and peasants mostly, who would offer aid in one battle and then disappear before the next. Often they fought with the tools of their trades: scythes, pitchforks, pikes, and *sgians*. Some rapparees were honest fighters and defenders of their homes. Many others were nothing more than thieves and murderers who used the Irish cause as a cover for their crimes.

Fitzgerald remembered the pistol in his pocket. Pistols were rare among common herdsmen. Powder and shot were even more difficult to obtain . . . unless this lad was a highwayman.

Fitzgerald shook the boy until he groaned. "Tell me yer name!"

The boy coughed and choked, bringing a blood-tinged foam to his lips.

Fitzgerald cursed roundly when he saw the blood. After laying the boy flat he unsheathed his *skean*, threw back the cloak, and began cutting away the bloody tatters of clothing wrapped around his body.

When the last shreds of cloth gave way under his knife blade, Fitzgerald saw the dark bloody bruise that covered half the boy's right side. With knowledgeable fingers he located three broken ribs. Perhaps one or more of them had pierced the lad's lung.

When his eyes fell to the boy's waist, he blinked in surprise. Tied about his waist under his shirt was a wooden rosary and crucifix such as monks wore. Fingering it curiously, Fitzgerald pondered the reason for it. The life of a rapparee was about as far from a priestly existence as a man could imagine.

"Ye sent for me, sir?"

Brigadier Fitzgerald looked up into the ruddy face of his sergeant. "Aye, I did. We've a wounded lad here. A rapparee, by his own account, only he's slow to speak his name."

Elam O'Conner looked down dispassionately at the injured boy and said, "Will ye be having me coax it out of him?"

From the corner of his eye, and to his great consternation, Lord Fitzgerald saw his daughter step from the shadows. "What are ye doing here?"

Wide-eyed at the sight of the young man's horribly battered chest, Deirdre came closer. "Is he dead, Da?" she questioned. "He looks dead."

"No, lass, he's not dead," Lord Fitzgerald assured her.

His voice hardened as he added, "Ye were not to come back. 'Twas an order."

Her gaze shifted to the boy lying disquietingly still. "I found him," she said, as if by saying that she could reclaim him as hers.

"Aye, lass, and a brave thing it was ye did. But ye've no need to think about it any longer. We'll patch him up and have him on his way in a trice."

Deirdre looked up at her father, her gray-green eyes swimming with tears. "He thinks you'll hang him, and he hurts something fierce."

With a rueful smile Lord Fitzgerald held out his hand to his daughter and said, "If I promise ye shall see him again when he's cleaned and bandaged, will ye go up to the house and wait?"

Deirdre nodded, the agreement reluctantly drawn from her.

"That's me girl. Go now and—"

Suddenly Deirdre's father stiffened and his sergeant with him. The men exchanged glances and the sergeant nodded his head. "Damn!" her father swore.

Deirdre stared at them a fraction longer and then she heard it too—horses cantering toward Liscarrol.

"That'll be me cousin Neil," Lord Fitzgerald said.

"And the English," Sergeant O'Conner added.

"Aye. English soldiers come to see me off."

Together the two men glanced down at the boy as he stirred and began coughing. When their eyes met again, each realized that his thoughts were the same as the other's.

Regular Irish troops like themselves were under the protection of the Treaty of Limerick, but it did not cover rebels who fought the English in informal combat using ambush and surprise. Rapparees were fair game for English soldiers, to be hunted and killed like vermin.

Lord Fitzgerald shook his head even as his sergeant opened his mouth. "It will not serve, man. Look at him. He cannot escape on his own, nor can we leave him here to be discovered once we've left. I've seen too much of

English justice. Those we leave behind will be made to pay for harboring a wanted man.''

"Turn him over to them," the sergeant suggested without batting an eye.

Lord Fitzgerald did not hesitate. "I'm not a man to set the dogs on a wounded stag."

"What then, sir?" the sergeant questioned, a grin easing into his features for the first time.

"An old trick. 'Tis served well enough before," his commander answered with a wink.

He knelt and took Deirdre's face in his hands. *She is so like her mother, God rest her soul,* he thought fleetingly. Too severe of feature to be called a pretty child, he believed she would one day grow into a beauty. She was why he was willing to leave Ireland. He could watch his sons fight and die, if need be, for the cause in which they all believed. Deirdre was another matter. There was a promise made on a deathbed which he must honor to save his soul.

He smiled at her. "Lass, I need ye to go to the house and tell Brigid there's to be a man put in the priest hole. We'll be coming by way of the servants' door. Tell her that."

A smile bloomed suddenly on Deirdre's face and the effect softened her too-sharp chin and the too-high bridge of her nose. "I knew you'd not hurt him. I told him so." She threw her slender arms about her father's neck and squeezed him tightly before running toward the house.

Lord Fitzgerald turned to his sergeant.

O'Conner shrugged, offering, "I'd not wager a sum on his living out the night."

Fitzgerald nodded slowly. It was not the lad's life that concerned him at the moment. Hiding a man sought by the English authorities was a hanging offense.

While O'Conner lifted the young man into his arms like a babe, Lord Fitzgerald bent to pick up the hat with the telltale white cockade. If the mysterious young man lived, he would have to come with them to France. If he lived.

Chapter Two

Lord Fitzgerald kept watch as the sergeant lowered the injured young man to the floor in the narrow passage. Built inside the massive fireplace of Liscarrol's Great Hall, the passage could be entered only by tripping the lock that opened a door cunningly cut into the back wall.

After a quick inspection, O'Conner turned the boy on his side to ease his breathing. "I cannot be certain, but 'twould seem he took a ball in them ribs, and he's bleeding from a dozen smaller wounds."

"Do what ye can," Lord Fitzgerald answered as he held a taper to provide light. "Damnation! Where's Brigid?" he continued just before the dining-room door swung open on the nurse.

Brigid curtsied automatically to Lord Fitzgerald, who smiled as he saw the supplies in her hands. "No one saw ye?" he asked, and she shook her head. "Have me guests arrived?"

"Aye, me lord. They're in the front hall." White-faced with anxiety, Brigid glanced at the kneeling sergeant, who took her supplies, and then at the wounded man sprawled in the passage, but his face was shielded by the soldier's broad shoulders. When Lord Fitzgerald had returned to the house and ordered her to bring bandages to the secret chamber which had hidden more than one hunted priest during the days of Cromwell's terror, she had not known what to think. Yet, here was proof positive that Deirdre had found a man in the stables. Who could he be?

Lord Fitzgerald noted his servant's interest in consternation. Leaning toward her, he said, "If it comes to it, ye've seen nothing, have ye, Brigid me girl?"

Brigid's gaze flew back to his face and she shook her head quickly, her face flushing with guilt. "No, me lord. I've seen and heard nothing, and there's me word on it."

Satisfied that her nervousness was nothing more than an honest fear of danger, he relaxed. "My cousin and his English friends should not be left alone or they will begin to wonder at our hospitality."

Brigid curtsied again. "Aye, me lord. Cook's put the kettle on to boil for tea, only there's nothing to serve it in but the scullery china."

The thought brought a brief smile to Lord Fitzgerald's lips. "Liscarrol hospitality is nae so fine as it once was. There's nary a chair to be shared amongst them. Perhaps 'twill encourage them to see us off quickly."

"Aye, me lord."

"Make certain me daughter is kept away from them. She's a braw lass but her tongue gets the better of her on occasion. Keep her entertained and out of sight."

Brigid blanched and Lord Fitzgerald's sharp eyes saw it despite the gloom. "What is it?"

"'Tis Deirdre, me lord. She's in the front hall. Sir Neil asked particularly to speak with her."

Lord Fitzgerald swore a vicious oath. "Well? Why do ye stand there like a stone in a bog? Fetch her away at once!"

"Aye, me lord." Brigid turned and hurried from the room, firmly closing the door after herself.

The sergeant looked up, having firmly bound the broken ribs. "He'll hold now."

"Can he ride, that's the question," Lord Fitzgerald countered.

"Ye can't mean to take the lad with us?"

Lord Fitzgerald nodded. "Aye. When me cousin's had his fill of pacing his new home, he'll return to Dublin for supplies and furnishings. 'Twill be no great hardship for ye and a man ye trust to nip back at dark and retrieve the lad."

The sergeant's brows drew together. "If we're caught..." he began reluctantly.

"Don't be," his commanding officer answered with finality as he rose. "Report to the troops at once. I'll see to our guests. I hope to God Dee has held her tongue!"

Deirdre eyed her father's cousin mistrustfully. In his gloved hand he held out a sweetmeat, but she was much more interested in his appearance. His bushy, carrot-hair brows clashed in an absurd fashion with his black wavy full-bottom wig. In its forelock were tied tiny silk bow-knots that matched his emerald-green velvet coat. His nose was a large, bulbous affair with a spiderwebbing of veins on its blunt tip. Only his eyes, pale and slightly bulging but without any calculation or malice, were attractive to her. Yet, she clasped her hands behind her back, refusing the tempting offer.

"Thank you, sir, but no," she said softly in Gaelic. "Me da says 'tis unfitting for a lady to accept a gift from a strange gentleman."

"Gaelic!" one of Sir Neil's companions voiced in disbelief. Deirdre's gaze moved to the tallest of the three English soldiers in red coats. His was scarlet, decorated with embroidery and braid, and she guessed by his air of superiority that he was their leader. "Doesn't the chit know Gaelic is forbidden?"

Undaunted by his tone, she looked straight up at the man, who wore a modest blond periwig, and asked in English, "Why?"

He looked down at her as though she had bitten him. "Impertinence!" he snapped and turned to her uncle. "Valuable time is being wasted here. One would think *we* were the vanquished waiting upon the pleasure of our conquerors. Instead we are made to stand in wait, hat in hand, like beggars. Irish arrogance! They'll pay for it.''

Sir Neil Fitzgerald colored uncomfortably. "Captain Garret, 'tis a trying day for all of us. A little patience, I beg you.''

The English soldier smirked. "You can afford patience when you stand to gain by it." He deliberately surveyed the stripped hallway before saying, "Though one wonders at your interest in so Spartan a domicile. From what I observe, they leave you little that is of comfort, pleasure, or beauty.''

" 'Tis a lie!" Deirdre burst out. "Liscarrol is the most beautiful place on earth. 'Tis been the home of Fitzgeralds for five hundred years.''

The Englishman looked down at her, his eyes narrowing. "I believe I preferred it when you spoke heathen gibberish. At least then I was spared your plaguey poor manners, brat!''

"Deirdre, lass, are ye no better a hostess than our guests are guests?" Lord Fitzgerald questioned. His lips smiled but his eyes were hard as he entered the front hall and held out a hand to his daughter. He patted her cheek as she clasped him about the waist.

"They're horrid!" she whispered against his waistcoat.

"Aye, lass, 'tis a pity what power does to some men's judgment," he said softly. More loudly he said, "Not a week ago I saw a common English soldier strike a lady for no more reason than that she refused to yield the road to his horse. In England, such a man would have been thrown in jail or, at the very least, publicly horsewhipped for having dared the violence." He enclosed his daughter's shoulders with a firm arm, his gaze leveled on the English officer. "But we're not in England, and many a man away from home forgets his manners.''

The Englishman had the grace to blush, his neck above his collar warming to red, but that did not improve his disposition. "Your daughter is a trifle forward, Lord Fitzgerald, and my temper is somewhat uncertain these days.''

Lord Fitzgerald regarded the younger man with the barest hint of a smile. "Aye, the strain of command can be wearisome for one without the temperament for it." Turning, he held out his hand to his cousin. "Welcome to Liscarrol, Neil. I see ye prosper for all ye keep uncertain company." Gently he pushed his daughter forward. "Make yer curtsy to yer cousin, Dee, and then be off with ye."

Deirdre complied gracefully. "Welcome to Liscarrol, Cousin Neil," she said politely and, looking up, gave him a dimpled smile. "Now that we're properly introduced, 'twould be rude to turn away a gift."

Despite her deliberate use of Gaelic, Neil chuckled and produced the looked-for sweet. "A delight, you are, Cousin Deirdre, albeit a naughty one," he answered in a whisper as he handed her the treat.

Deirdre popped it whole into her mouth, afraid that the tall Englishman would somehow contrive to take it from her if she delayed. When she had chewed and swallowed it, she lifted her chin and gave the English officer a gloating smile.

"Allow me to introduce myself," the office said, ignoring the child's triumphant glance. "I am Sir Harold Garret, Baronet of Bowland and captain of the guard sent to escort your party to Cork."

Lord Fitzgerald nodded slightly, giving no ground at the man's title of nobility. To his cousin he said, " 'Tis a sad day, this. I've no accounting to ye as to the reasons, but know that Liscarrol comes into yer hands for but a short time. Take good care of it. That said, there's nothing to do but ride."

"Lord Fitzgerald, a moment." Captain Garret stepped forward to stand before the Irish lord. "We have a matter that must be attended to before you will be allowed to leave Liscarrol." When Lord Fitzgerald did not reply, the captain continued stiffly, "While I am willing to believe that neither you nor your men were involved in the incident, I must make a thorough search of Liscarrol before we depart."

"We were attacked on the road," Sir Neil offered in explanation to his cousin. "Two of Captain Garret's soldiers were killed."

"Who attacked ye and why?" Lord Fitzgerald questioned the Englishman.

"Is there ever a reason for what you Irish do?" Captain Garret challenged.

Lord Fitzgerald's lips twitched. "If ye're an example of English tolerance, then there's no reason necessary."

Captain Garret straightened, his face paling with anger. "I should remind you, Lord Fitzgerald, that you and your company are under arrest. You should know that we caught and hanged one of the ambushers. I shot the other but he got away. I mean to see that he joins his comrade. If you will help me in this matter you will be treated with the utmost kindness and accorded the freedom you earn."

"As yer prisoner I would have none," Lord Fitzgerald answered. "But ye're neither my jailer nor my superior, and I will not submit to a search of my private possessions without express orders from your superior."

For the first time Captain Garret smiled. "is there, perhaps, good cause for your reluctance? A man in your position should care little what happens to the property he deserts."

For the first time Lord Fitzgerald became aware that Deirdre still stood beside him, watching and listening. He turned to her. "Go upstairs to yer nurse, Dee, and do not come down till I come for ye."

Deirdre nodded, not quite meeting her father's eyes. But when she turned away she gave the Englishman one long last look of enmity. He was responsible for the injured man lying in the priest hole. At last she understood why her father hated the English, for the anger roiling in her breast made her want to scratch and bite the officer.

"If you wish to be difficult, I can see to it that your family is delayed indefinitely at the barracks in Cork," she heard the Englishman say as she hurried up the narrow winding stairwell. "I'd not care to have my womenfolk subjected to the indignity. Will you allow the search?"

"Search anywhere ye please! And may ye find the Devil himself at the end of it!" Deirdre heard her father answer as she reached the top.

"We will, sir. And when we do, we'll hang him!"

The skin on Deirdre's arms puckered and she shivered

in fright as she stood on the landing. They would hang him! The English would hang her stranger!

She glanced up the stairwell that led to the nursery and then back down. Unlike her father, she did not believe that the English would fail to find the priest hole.

Her stranger could not be the murderer. He was the embodiment of a daydream come to life. Somehow, without her willing it, she had conjured him up. But who would believe her? Certainly not the silver-eyed English officer. Perhaps not even her father, who refused to listen to her tales of fairies and disturbing visions. Childish fancy, he called them. Yet, the man in the stables was real enough.

"I must do something!" she whispered to herself, and, seizing a candle from the hall sconce, she hurried toward the servants' stairwell, which was a back way into the Great Hall.

Pain was the only definable sensation within Killian MacShane as he regained consciousness. The pain was excruciating. It crushed his lungs and radiated out to numb his arms and legs. He was helpless against the stabbing that caught him unprepared each time he drew a breath. Tears pricked his closed eyes. No. He would not cry. He had witnessed and suffered too much to shame himself with the cowardice of tears. If he was dying, perhaps it was best. This sliding down into the red seafoam of pain flooding him was not so difficult. Then, at last, it would be over.

Yet, even as he gave up to the rich dark agony, his body resisted, coughing to eject from his lungs the fluid that threatened to choke him.

"Shh! You mustn't make a sound!"

The cool small hand that touched Killian's cheek and then pressed against his mouth surprised him and disturbed the rhythm of his spasm, and his coughing stopped as his eyes flew open. Looking down at him through the dimness were a pair of serious sea-green eyes set in a child's face.

Deirdre smiled as she saw his eyes open. In the flickering light of the candle she held, he did not seem nearly as frightening or as huge as he had in the stables. Not that it mattered. Perhaps, if she protected him, the wee folk would in turn protect her family.

She began awkwardly petting his sweaty cheek. "You must hide yourself, fairy. The English have come."

Killian blinked, unable to fathom her speech. Who was she, this child awash in a sea of golden crisp waves? He tried to lift his head but pain shot through him again, making giddy eddies in his brain and muddling his thoughts.

Where was he? Nothing in the dimness looked familiar. The curved walls were of stone and had no windows. Was he in prison? If so, what was a child doing with him?

Gradually his attention wandered back to the child bending over him. "Who are you?" he whispered.

"Shh! English!" She looked up as footsteps sounded in the room overhead.

When they faded, she bent close to him and said, "You're a fairy. I know it because I conjured you. Only I didn't mean it. Save yourself and remember that I was the one who helped you."

The last thing he thought he could do was move, but suddenly the child at his side began shoving him.

I must be mad with pain, Killian thought as the girl shoved ineffectually at him. It was not possible that she thought him a spirit. Perhaps *she* was the fairy. 'Twas said fairy women were golden-haired and as tiny as children. If only his head and chest did not hurt so badly he might be able to sort things out.

"I mean you no harm. I can prove to you I'm a friend of the wee folk," Deirdre exclaimed in excited tones that her whisper scarcely muted. Reaching up, she began unfastening her bodice.

"There!" she cried, leaning over until her shoulder was only an inch above his nose. "You see? I've been kissed by the fairies!"

Before Killian's blurred gaze swam a red mark no bigger than a ha'penny. It rode the crest of her small round shoulder. Why she should show it to him he could not imagine.

Deirdre pushed him again. "Please leave! They'll hang

us all if they find you!'' she whispered thickly as tears roughened her voice and filled her eyes.

Through the thick mist of pain her words struck a rational chord within Killian. Yes, the English soldiers would certainly hang the men of this household if they found him hiding here. He could not do that to them, to the child, who had offered him aid.

Rousing himself with a strength he had not expected to possess, he rolled from his side to a sitting position. The bandages held, though piercing pains robbed him momentarily of breath.

''Aye! Flee!'' Deirdre encouraged, pulling on his sleeve as though she could lift him single-handedly.

Killian sucked in air and hoisted himself to his knees, moaning softly when he would rather have cried out his agony. The room began to spin slowly but he fought the vertigo. ''Where . . . do . . . I hide?'' he whispered.

Deirdre stood up beside him as the clatter of more boots entered the Great Hall beyond the hidden door. ''Don't you know?'' She looked around wildly, half-expecting an exit magically to appear, but the flickering candlelight revealed only roughhewn walls. The room was barely seven feet deep and three feet wide. It was not meant to house a man for more than a few hours.

Air!

Deirdre looked up and saw the black cavern of the air vent in shadow behind a protruding boulder in the ceiling.

There was another way out of this hiding place, one long forgotten until she had stumbled upon it while playing by herself several months before. It was an air shaft. She had found she could climb it by putting her back against one side and bracing herself with hands and feet on the other. As agile as a monkey, she had climbed its height to find that it led to a false bottom in an upper-floor room. When Brigid found out about her discovery, she had blocked the exit and forbidden Deirdre ever to use it again. But if Deirdre could climb it, so could this man.

She grabbed him by the sleeve and pointed. ''Up there! You must climb up the shaft.''

Killian raised his head and looked at the narrow opening

and knew he would never have realized that it was there if not for the child. Even so, he doubted he could rise to his feet, must less climb the shaft. Yet, he had to try.

Deirdre watched him place one foot under himself, her heart hammering so violently within her chest that she was certain it would become audible. He was sweating; it ran down into his eyes and pasted his thin beard to the hollows of his face. When he tried to rise, he began to shiver, his face graying with the strain.

"I cannot!" he muttered through clenched teeth and collapsed back onto his knee.

"Aye, you can!" Deirdre whispered urgently. After leaning her candle against the wall, she reached out to place his right arm about her shoulders. "Try again. Hurry!" she commanded, using her father's authoritative tone of voice. She could not say precisely why, but, perhaps because she had willed him here, she knew she could make him do as she bid.

Killian accepted her support to please her and found to his great surprise that she was the anchor he needed. The ceiling was too low to allow him to stand upright. Raising his left arm, Killian felt for the opening and measured its diameter with his hand. It was less than three feet across. He knew that even if he were not injured he could not hoist himself high enough off the ground to enter the shaft and get a purchase with his knees and feet.

"I can't . . . make it, lass."

"You can with help," Deirdre said softly. Before, she had used a chair drawn in from the dining table, but now they did not have that luxury. Without a word, she dropped to the ground, tucked her knees under her chest, and balanced herself with her hands.

Killian stared at her as though she had lost her mind. He could not use her as a step stool. His weight would break her back.

"Hurry!" Deirdre hissed just before the candle flame guttered and left the passage in utter darkness.

Killian did not move. The sudden darkness had cost him his sense of equilibrium and the swirling void made him feel like a man on the edge of a precipice.

"Take your boots off," Deirdre encouraged, growing impatient with the stubborn man. "I've borne Ian O'Casey on me back and he's twice the size of you." When he did not answer, she felt around in the dark until she found his feet.

"Lift," she directed, and when he did, she tugged the first of his boots off. When the second was removed, she pulled on his leg to direct him to her. "Climb! Now!"

Suddenly, boot steps sounded again, this time much nearer.

Deirdre swung her head toward the hidden doorway. Someone had come into the dining room. Before she could encourage him again, she heard a scraping at the hidden door. They had been found.

Killian, too, realized that they were about to be discovered, and his instinct for self-preservation took over. He ripped a piece of cloth from his tattered clothing and stuck it between his teeth. Once more he reached for and found the shaft. Gently he felt for the child with his toe.

"Brace yourself, lass," he whispered and placed his foot on her back. If he was careful and did not tax her too long, perhaps she could hold his weight for a moment. There would be only one chance.

The scraping ceased and was replaced by the *whack* of a gun butt or an ax against the stone doorway.

Killian hoisted himself up into the shaft with a lunge meant to take some of the weight from the child beneath him. The impetus launched him hip-high into the flue, and he slammed his back against the wall as his left hand shot out to brace him there. Stars exploded behind his eyelids as pain jabbed him like a knife blade, but his cry was muted by his gag.

For a moment he hung suspended, his muscles quivering and seeming to melting under the pressure of his weight. Then, miraculously, he felt her hands direct his feet to her shoulders and she supported him from below.

"Climb!" called the childish voice from the darkness below.

If it had not taken too much effort, he would have thanked her, but all his concentration was upon following her orders. It seemed to take hours, years, to move an inch, yet she stayed beneath him, pushing and supporting him until he had one knee braced against the cold damp stone.

A little more, he told himself. Just a little more and he would be out of sight. His back was being rubbed raw by the wall and he could feel a trickle of what might be blood or sweat down his flanks. Straining until he thought his eyes would pop out of his head, he lifted his loose leg up and pressed it against the wall. There, he was stuck, wedged in like a peg in a hole.

A moment later he was prodded in the behind. "Take your boots," she called up to him. "And do not move!"

Killian caught his boot tops between his thighs and pulled them up, too exhausted even to speak, much less to move.

Lord Fitzgerald had thought he could restrain himself by visiting his wife's rooms while the English searched his home, but when he heard the work of axes in the Great Hall he lost his temper.

"What on God's earth do ye mean, demolishing me property?" he cried as he strode into the room where two English soldiers were applying axes to the back of the fireplace.

Captain Garret looked up with a satisfied smile. "We're searching, as you so graciously gave us permission to do."

Lord Fitzgerald clenched his fists. "I did not give ye permission to pull me house down about me ears! Cease that at once!"

"Forgive me, but I cannot," Garret replied. "Your cousin was kind enough to recall that there was once a hiding place behind this wall. A priest hole, he tells me."

Lord Fitzgerald raked his cousin with a blighting glance. "Ye've a queer memory, cousin. Ye're in error."

Sir Neil mopped his brow with a handkerchief and then smiled uncertainly at his cousin. "You will remember that I once spent a summer here when we were children. We played behind there." He pointed to the fireplace. "Your father found us after hours of searching. We had tripped the lock and could not get out.''

Lord Fitzgerald nodded sharply. ''Aye. Me father blistered both our behinds for the lark. I'd have thought the memory would have dampened yer interest in the place.''

Captain Garret turned back to his host. ''Have you perchance learned the method to open it?'' He indicated the fireplace. ''My men and I are tired and anxious to be away to a place that offers the basic amenities of civilized life. If you cannot help us, I am ready to resort to gunpowder.''

A muscle began to twitch in Lord Fitzgerald's face. ''Ye bloody bastard!'' he snarled and took a step toward the English officer, who drew his pistol.

.''I would regret shooting you, Lord Fitzgerald, but I will do it without hesitation if I perceive myself in danger from you. You may cooperate or not, but I will see behind this wall before I leave here today.''

Lord Fitzgerald hesitated, not because he feared being shot. He might be willing to take a ball in the shoulder if it would prevent the wall from opening, but it would not do that. There was nothing left to do but bluster his way through this. ''Ye'll pay for every bit of damage ye've done, see if ye don't!'' Without waiting for the officer to put away his gun, he walked purposefully to the fireplace and reached for the head of one of the ornate andirons. When he twisted it, the latch set into its base made a audible *click*, and a small stone door inside the fireplace opened a crack.

Captain Garret looked slightly bemused when Lord Fitzgerald turned to him. ''So simple. I suppose your servants were unaware of it. I threatened one with hanging, yet none of the others would confess to its existence. If not for your cousin's timely memory, ye might have lost an able servant.''

''Some men believe there are things worth dying for,'' the Irish lord answered darkly.

''And surely things worth living for,'' Captain Garret finished and nodded at his men. ''If you should be hiding a criminal, I can't promise—''

The scream that erupted from the depths of the fireplace brought the soldiers to alert as they grabbed for their muskets and Captain Garret drew his pistol. A second later the door swung open with a loud scraping as Deirdre burst into the room.

"Da! Da! Do not let them kill me!" she screamed as she launched herself into her father's arms. Giving up to the panic that had been choking her, she pounded her father's chest with small hard fists. "Hide me! Hide me! The English will kill me, they'll kill us all!" Twisting and kicking, she sobbed hysterically until lack of breath made her collapse against him.

Amazed to find Deirdre in the hole and as frightened as he had ever seen her, Lord Fitzgerald could only think that something terrible had happened in the attic while he had been pacing his bedroom floor, refusing to follow the English about like a guest in his own home. Anger showing in his eyes, he said, "What did ye blackguards do to me daughter that she's hid herself where she might have died?"

As surprised as his Irish host, Captain Garret could think of no good answer. "We—we did nothing. I haven't seen the scamp since she left the front hall." Badly startled by her tirade, he turned to his men. "Did any of you see or speak to the child?"

Deirdre hiccuped a breath, twisted about in her father's arms, and pointed at the captain. "He's a devil! He roasts children for his supper. He'll roast me if I don't hide!"

"Dee. Deirdre, me darlin' girl," Lord Fitzgerald crooned against her ear, trying to calm his distraught child with the stroke of his hand. When she quieted to a whimper he turned to the captain. "There'll be no more of this! Ye've had yer fun. Ye've stirred up me household and frightened me daughter half to death. We'll be lucky if she doesn't come down with brain fever behind it. I hope ye're satisfied. But, whether or no, 'tis enough. Ye'll leave me home or I swear I'll shoot ye meself, and the treaty be damned!"

"Perhaps you've seen enough, captain?" Sir Neil suggested.

Captain Garret looked from Lord Fitzgerald to the opening within the fireplace. "Do you see anyone?" he asked the soldier nearest the secret door.

The man ducked his head in briefly and then looked back. "No, sir. Nothing."

"I see." The English officer surveyed the father and daughter, unable to still the niggling doubt that something was amiss and yet knowing that he had proceeded as far as his authority permitted under the circumstances. If he continued the search and no man was found, he would be shown to be an even greater fool that he was at present. If this were a plot to embarrass him, the livid look of rage on Lord Fitzgerald's face proved that he had no knowledge of or part in it.

"Very well," he said shortly. "Return to your posts, men, and see that you are prepared to ride immediately." He then turned stiffly to his host. "For the inconvenience, I apologize. I trust you will be ready to accompany me to Cork within the hour?"

Gently rocking his still-crying child, Lord Fitzgerald stared at the Englishman before speaking. "Here's me hope for ye, captain. That one day ye'll have a daughter of ye're own. When ye do, then every time ye gaze on her ye'll think of this hour and remember, and that'll be me revenge."

The curse was mild enough but even so the hair lifted on Captain Garret's scalp. He bowed stiffly. "An hour, Lord Fitzgerald. We'll wait in the yard."

Lord Fitzgerald watched without emotion as the Englishmen filed out of the room. Only when Brigid hurried in, closing the door behind herself, did his daughter stir in his arms.

"Me lord! I've lost Deirdre. She isn't— Oh! There ye are, and me that worried about ye!"

Deirdre lifted her head from her father's shoulder and amazed him with a bright smile. "I had to save him, Da. He's up the air shaft," she whispered, and motioned toward the hole.

"He's— But how?" Lord Fitzgerald exclaimed.

"I gave him a boost, on me back," Deirdre answered as she wiggled to be free.

A series of expressions crossed Lord Fitzgerald's face, among them wonder, disbelief, and pride. "Ye did that? Ye might have been shot!"

Deirdre put a finger to her lips. "I wished him here. I do not know how to wish him away. The English would have hanged him."

"Wished him—?" Lord Fitzgerald shook his head. "Dee, lass, what are ye saying?"

"The black-haired lad . . . I wished for such a man just this morning. I told Brigid all about it. Well, he's come, and one day I will marry him."

To humor her, her father said, "Oh, aye, lass. He's every father's wish for his daughter's husband. He's a murderer and wanted by the English."

Deirdre paled. "Ye'll not betray him?"

"Of course not," he answered quickly. " 'Tis not an Irishman among us I'd turn over to the likes of Captain Garret. Only ye must be brave a little longer. Go now with Brigid and change yer dress. And when ye have, ye must ride in the carriage with yer stepmother and wee Owen and never, never mention to them what happened today. Will ye swear it?"

"I swear." Deirdre cast a last look at the priest hole. "Will I see him again?"

Lord Fitzgerald gave his daughter a long, considering glance. She was young, but she did not behave as a child. In many ways she was uncannily mature, and romantic enough to have taken a fancy to a handsome face, and he had no doubt that the lad scrubbed up to good effect. The fact that she had risked her life to save this stranger would join them in a bond that was better broken at once. Deirdre was his pride and joy. He would allow no common rapparee to steal her affections.

His face grew more serious as he grasped her by the shoulders and knelt before her. "If a thing is meant to be, lass, it will sort itself out. Do ye believe that?"

Deirdre bit her lip. "Ye're going to send him away."

"Aye, for his protection and ours."

"If 'tis meant to be, 'twill sort itself out," she repeated wistfully and turned to take Brigid's hand.

"Send Sergeant O'Conner to me," Lord Fitzgerald ordered the nurse.

When he was satisfied that he was alone, he stepped into the priest hole and peered up into the vent. "Are ye still alive, lad?"

"Aye," came the groggy reply.

"Hold steady, we'll have ye out in a trice."

Killian did not reply. His muscles were locked in tortured spasms that would not have been worse than results on the rack, he decided. A few minutes later, hands reached up for him, supporting his spine and feet, and he relaxed, slipping out of the shaft as easily as a babe out of a womb.

When he had been laid on his back, he saw a stern, weatherbeaten soldier's face above him. "Where is she?"

"Who?" Lord Fitzgerald questioned innocently.

"The lass," Killian whispered.

"Lass? There's no lass, lad, nor has there been. 'Tis only two Irishmen determined that the English won't hang ye this day."

Killian shut his eyes. So, it was a dream after all. Or had he been pixied by the fairies?

"Find a crate to put him in," Lord Fitzgerald ordered his sergeant. "He'll become another bit of baggage." When the soldier was gone, he reached out and touched the cross hanging at the boy's waist. He would take the lad to Cork, perhaps even sail him to Calais. But that was all he would do for him.

As for Deirdre, she would forget, as they all must. Ireland and its misery would soon be behind them.

PART TWO

The Exile

I know how men in exile feed on dreams of hope.
—Agamemnon

The Wild Geese shall return, and we'll welcome them home
So active, so armed, so flightly,
A flock was ne'er known...
—Eighteenth-century Irish poem

Chapter Three

Nantes, France: Summer 1702

"You mistake my intentions entirely, mademoiselle. I beg a single kiss. That is nothing!"

"Nothing?" the young lady questioned, her cheeks coloring above the flirtatious lace of her fan. "Are then my kisses nothing to you, monsieur?"

"*Mais non*, mademoiselle!" the young Frenchman answered. "I assure you, there is nothing further from the truth. In my ardor, my haste to offer my most solemn and heartfelt adoration of your beauty, I misspoke." The young man smiled his most beguiling smile. "From you, a kiss would mean everything," he added in a husky undertone.

"Everything, monsieur?" the lady repeated in a scandalized tone that belied the laughter in her eyes. "If a kiss is 'everything,' how, I wonder, does a lady of your acquaintance escape complete corruption? I have heard it said that a kiss is but an overture. If it is the entire opera, then I dare not sing even a note for you."

"Mademoiselle," the young man countered, his voice quavering as his defeat drew closer. "A kiss from you would knight my soul, a token of greater value I cannot imagine.''

The lady regarded him skeptically. ''Claude, am I to consider you less a wit and considerably less a lover than your face and form advertise? I have heard on good authority that there is a certain sort of lady who, granting a gentleman her kisses, will grant him much more. If you tell me you have not received such bounty, then I must wonder about your ability . . . or your honesty.''

''*Non*.'' She stepped away from him and shrugged elegantly as he reached for her. One sleeve of her pink silk gown slipped in delightful abandon down the curve of her shoulder until she caught it and lifted it back into place. ''I am afraid I must deny myself the most tempting offer of your lips, monsieur.''

She turned to face him, her smile still hidden behind her fan. ''For, you see, I am not quite convinced that you would think me the most wanton of creatures in going against your own advice.''

''Advice?'' he questioned in bewilderment. ''I gave no advice contrary to my desire to kiss you.''

''Did you not? Did you not say that a kiss means everything? If not in fact, then in intent, you implied as much. We are not strangers, Cousin Claude, else we would not be permitted to be here in my father's garden without a chaperon. Haven't you guessed? It is a test.''

She suddenly lowered her fan and allowed him the full benefit of her radiant smile with the dimple in her left cheek. ''A test, Claude, and we have passed! Brigid! Brigid! You may come out now. We are to be trusted!''

''But—but!'' Claude protested, only to fall silent as the formidable figure of Brigid McSheehy appeared from behind an elephant-shaped shrub in the topiary garden. In the ten years that he had made cousinly calls upon the Fitzgeralds he had never lost his awe of the black-clad Irish servant who treated her mistress like a naughty child of eight rather than the beautiful young woman of eighteen she had become.

Ignoring the gentleman as she approached, Brigid said in Gaelic, ''Aye, ye've passed a test ye knew was in the making. Little enough honesty to be found in that, Miss Deirdre. If I were ye, I'd be more concerned that me brothers were cleaning the mud from their boots this very minute, without a sister to give to give them a proper greeting.''

"Conall and Darragh? They're home? Truly?" Deirdre cried in delight. At her nurse's terse nod, she turned back to her companion. "They're home, my brothers have returned from Cremona," she explained in French. "Oh, monsieur, it's wonderful! Da will will be so pleased! I must go. Forgive me!''

To the young man's astonishment, she grasped him lightly by the shoulders and placed a quick, hard kiss on his mouth before running toward her house with skirts lifted.

Brigid's eyes narrowed on the young Frenchman, disapproving of the show of affection her mistress had given the man, who was clothed in a beribboned habit and red-heeled shoes. The mass of golden curls that framed his pleasant but weak face were not his own but those of a full-bottomed wig. He was nothing like the broad, clean-limbed lads of Ireland who grew their own thick heads of hair. He might be a nobleman and a Fitzgerald cousin, but he was no man for her Deirdre. "M'sieur Goubert," she said finally in badly accented French and turned toward the house.

Claude bowed slightly before he could stop himself. Immediately he resented her all the more for making him feel so intimidated. After all, he was Claude Goubert, the Comte de Quentin.

He cast a doubtful glance over his shoulder at the Fitzgerald residence. He did not need Brigid's reinforcement to know that he was not the Fitzgeralds' choice as a husband for Deirdre. The fact that the Fitzgerald brothers were back in Nantes might be pleasant news for Deirdre, but it did not bode well for his own campaign to win her as his bride.

The Fitzgeralds gave little consideration to the fact that they had lived their first years in France on the Gouberts' largess and that the house they rented was part of the

Goubert estates. It was quite extraordinary. These Irish cousins whom his father had welcomed as émigrés to Nantes eleven years earlier walked the streets as if they owned them and looked every man in the eye as an equal. They lived for battle, honor, and reckless daring. It never ceased to amaze him that this family of loutish soldiers had produced the perfect, radiant confection of loveliness that was Mademoiselle Deirdre.

"Mon Dieu!" Claude murmured in astonishment as he remembered Deirdre's kiss. He touched his fingers to his lips. For more than two years he had waited in anxious anticipation for the moment when he would first kiss her. Now it had happened, in a most unexpected manner and without the satisfactory results he had hoped for. Yet, the soft impression of her mouth burned sweetly enough for him to remember it. He might not yet have won Cousin Deirdre as his bride, but she was not indifferent to him.

Who knew what the summer might bring? Now that she was at last home from the convent school where she had spent the better part of the last four years, she would be easier to court. There would be parties aplenty to celebrate the season, chances to dance with her and talk with her and dazzle her with his intense love.

"Alors, I must contrive to win her heart soon," Claude murmured as he strolled away. After all, he had waited patiently for her to grow into womanhood, and the waiting had been more than worth it. She was exquisite, a beauty quite without compare. She was the darling of her family; they denied her nothing. If she chose to love him, nothing and no one would gainsay her.

Gazing down from the second-story window of her home, Lady Elva Fitzgerald shared the young Frenchman's concerns as she watched her stepdaughter's headlong race toward the house. It was she who had contrived the tryst between Deirdre and Claude Goubert in hopes that Deirdre's interest in the young man would decide her father in favor of the match. After all, the Gouberts were distantly related to the Fitzgeralds, and a marriage would cement those ties. Yes, she suspected that Deirdre's haste had nothing to do with the young Frenchman. Due, no doubt, to Brigid's meddling, Deirdre had learned that Conall and Darragh had arrived.

Lady Elva turned back from the window, two vertical lines marring her usually smooth brow. Despite her husband's unconcern, she thought it unseemly that a lass should hold her brothers in greater esteem than she held any of the eligible young men vying for her attention.

"They're home, lady!" Lord Fitzgerald announced loudly as he opened the door into his wife's room without the formality of knocking. "The lads have returned this very moment. Will ye not come down to greet them?"

The frown instantly disappeared from Lady Elva's face. "Aye, m'lord." As he turned away she glanced down at his legs. Instead of a stout calf to match his left, a mahogany stump protruded from the right leg of his breeches. Before she could reconsider she said, "Should we not wait for the servants to bring up the litter?"

Lord Fitzgerald swung around. Beneath his short military wig his ruddy complexion had darkened. "Crippled I may be, but I'm nae an invalid. A cane has done me these last months, and ye know it!"

Lady Elva flushed in embarrassment before his anger. A full year had passed since the amputation, but he hated every reminder of the infirmity that kept him in Nantes while his sons took their places in the Irish Brigade fighting for the Bourbon King, Louis XIV. She was not like Deirdre or her husband's sons. They always knew what to say and do. They treated him no differently since his illness. Yet, why could he not see that her concerns and fears were as genuine as their hearty, devil-may-care attitude toward him?

"I apologize for—for the impertinence, my lord," she said softly.

Lord Fitzgerald muttered an oath. Once again he had rebuffed his wife when a smarter man would have held his tongue. Though they had been married fourteen years, he often treated his third wife more like a second daughter. Deirdre had more spirit than Elva and possessed a more mature sense of the world. Yet, Elva was his wife. 'Twas not her fault that his leg pained him with special intensity this day. As he made painful progress across the carpet toward her, he shut from his mind the annoying *clump* and *thump* that his cane and stump made as he walked.

When he reached her, he lifted a hand and patted her cheek. "Och, lady. Have ye not known me long enough that ye cloud up at the first sound of thunder?

"That's better," he continued with an approving nod when she smiled uncertainly. "Ye've nae changed a whit since that day I married ye. There's still springtime in yer lips and cheeks. Ye've more the look of a lass than the matron and mother ye are."

The reminder of Owen made Lady Elva blanch. Instantly Lord Fitzgerald wished he had held his tongue a second time. Not a man to mince words, however, he continued. "Aye, there's pain for me, too, in the loss of Owen. He was the lad I would have offered to the Church. The ways of the Almighty are a mystery, and not ours to question."

Lady Elva shook her head. " 'Twas not God, 'twas the swine fever that took me son."

"And hundreds of other sons and daughters," Lord Fitzgerald added. "The epidemic took the youngest and best of the region. We might have lost Deirdre, too."

Lady Elva bit back the words of reproach that flew to her lips. Her husband was a good man who cared for all his family, but Deirdre was another matter. Deirdre touched him to the quick. Had she been a jealous woman, she knew, she would have grown to hate her stepdaughter for having usurped a vital portion of her husband's love. Yet, she did not hate Deirdre. There was in the lass a kindness of spirit and a natural generosity that prevented jealousy from taking root in those who knew her. Deirdre had wept the longest and most bitterly over Owen's loss.

Lord Fitzgerald saw pain move through his wife's expression. "Elvy," he whispered roughly against her ear as he reached an arm about her waist. "We'll nae be stopped by a loss."

He looked down significantly at her waistline and Lady Elva blushed. He had hopes, as she did, that she would soon become pregnant again. The loss of four unborn children had not dimmed her desire to give him more sons. Perhaps they, unlike Owen, would be like their stepbrothers Conall and Darragh, unafraid and adventurous.

Given new hope by her husband's desire, Lady Elva squared her shoulders and smiled. "Shall we go below, m'lord?"

Lord Fitzgerald grinned. "Aye, that's me lass. Starved as I am for news from the front, there'd be half a regiment of Irish soldiers under this roof before dark if I had me say."

Lady Elva slanted a lively glance at her husband. "I shudder at the thought of so many booted feet tramping our carpets. Would the patter and chatter of bairns not be better?" She shook her head at his hopeful expression. "I was thinking 'twas time your sons looked toward marriage. 'Tis certain Deirdre's thoughts run in that direction." Her husband's expression turned to surprise. "Deirdre's showing an uncommon interest in le Comte de Quentin. They were walking in the topiary garden a little while ago. I sent Brigid after them, and I wouldn't be surprised if she came upon a pair of cooing doves. Innocent kisses, of course," she added hastily at her husband's lowering brows.

"There's nae such a thing as an innocent kiss. Ask any man!" he pronounced. Then he shook his head, smiling once more. "Deirdre will nae have him. She'll have none but a full-blooded Irishman. I would nae fret over the new Comte de Quentin. She'll nae encourage him above an afternoon."

Lady Elva accepted her husband's arm, saying, "If 'tis a Irishman she must have, then 'tis time to look for him. She's no longer a wee lass. Deirdre should be thinking of marriage."

Lord Fitzgerald frowned slightly. "Aye, perhaps 'tis so." It was a question he had considered often in the months since his enforced idleness. Deirdre needed a husband's protection, but what man was good enough? Since childhood she had sworn to marry only an Irishman who would take her back to Ireland. Though many in his regiment talked longingly of returning home, nary an

Irishman to his knowledge had returned to his native land. To the contrary, more young men than ever before were deserting Ireland for the promises of freedom and wealth offered by service in the armies of the Catholic countries of Europe. Ireland offered no future for its native sons. Only in foreign lands were they able to rise in wealth and station.

Lord Fitzgerald cast a proprietary eye about his wife's comfortably appointed room. His courage and valor in the service of Louis XIV had earned him the French gold which made this luxury possible. Their home in Nantes was better furnished than Liscarrol Castle had been in his lifetime.

Deirdre was not the only one who felt the pull of the old country, but she was not practical. She could not know the danger and heartbreak that would greet her return. Perhaps Elvy was right. Perhaps it was time for Deirdre to fall in love. If she wedded an Irishman who made his home in France, she would give up her obsession with her homeland.

He ignored the feeling of having, by his thoughts, betrayed a promise. The pledge he had made Deirdre's mother had been in another time and place. He was being practical. Ireland was no longer home to the Fitzgeralds. The lass could not go back. The promise could not be kept.

His eyes twinkled as he turned to his wife. "I'll ask me sons about the younger officers in the brigade. There should be a man of passable face and form to satisfy Dee. We'll host a ball. We've done naught since she returned from the convent. 'Tis time the lads had a chance to look her over."

"And she they," Lady Elva added.

"Put me down, put me down! You're wrinkling my gown!" Deirdre squealed, her protests diluted by laughter as she was passed from brother to brother and swung high over their heads.

"You're still a bairn! Where's your height, lass?" Darragh teased when he had set her back on her feet. Though Deirdre was not tiny, her brothers towered head and shoulders above her.

Taking delight in stressing the difference, Conall clapped a broad hand on the top of her head. "Aye, I have it! You're growing the wrong way. She's a half a head shorter than when we left, is she not, brother?"

"That's the truth of it," Darragh declared in laughter. "In another year they'll have you back in swaddling, lass."

"You're a pair of beasts." Deirdre knocked Conall's hand from her head. "Look at that," she complained as a lock of hair fell into her eyes. "You've ruined me coiffure."

"Serves you right for being disrespectful to your elders," Conall answered.

"Coiffure?" Darragh mimicked. "*Ma foi, la belle mademoiselle, elle est sans coiffure!*"

"Your French is abominable," Deirdre snapped, "and you've the manners of an ill-bred Gael. Little wonder there's nary a bride between you. Who'd have you, I'd like to know?"

The brothers exchanged glances. "Aye, well, there was a certain sloe-eyed beauty in Milano—"

"Conall! Darragh! Ye've taken the devil's own time coming home!" Shaking off his wife's arm, Lord Fitzgerald started down the stairway, biting off a pained sigh that escaped him as he put weight on his wooden leg.

"Look at ye, tricked out in yer finery! A pair of ungrateful curs, ye are, keeping yer father waiting these months for news. Ashamed of ye, that's what I am!"

His sons laughed heartily, giving no indication that their father's grimace of pain affected them, nor did they move to offer him aid. Preening like a pair of peacocks, they turned this way and that to show off the brilliant green velvet coats they had stopped in Paris long enough to have made.

"Da! You're up and dressed," Deirdre said in frank surprise before she could stop herself. When her father frowned in disapproval of her reference to his invalided state, she said, "Your sons are scarcely worth the honor. I for one intend to take to my bed until they've gone. Just look what Darragh's done to my hair!"

"At least you can be proud of Conall," Darragh replied

as he reached for the arm of his brother's coat. "See there? He's wearing a new stripe on his sleeve. Of course, 'tis nothing compared to the stripes on his back."

Lord Fitzgerald's eyes blazed, his pain forgotten. "Ye've been whipped? Who'd dare whip an officer?"

Darragh's lips twitched as Conall glared at him. "I doubt the gentleman wielding the riding crop had the wits about him to search for Conall's coat, what with me brother presenting him with the respectable target of his naked buttocks." Chuckles sputtered from him. "Of course, he might have been distracted by his wife sprawled so invitingly beneath!"

"Darragh!" Lord Fitzgerald roared, taking the last few steps in an angry stride. "Ye're nae to speak of such things beneath this roof, and certainly not before the lass!"

"Aye, Darragh," Conall agreed as he turned to wink at his sister. "There's no telling what evil thoughts a wee lass the likes of Dee might fall victim to were she to learn that her brother is the wiliest of rogues and a devil with the ladies."

"So, it's conceited ye're getting, is it!" Lord Fitzgerald turned to Conall and looked him over, noting with satisfaction that, despite a year of warfare, his elder son looked strong and fit. " 'Twas more likely the poor lass thought she was answering to the devil for her past sins!"

"M'lord, please," Lady Elva protested softly at her husband's elbow.

"Oh no, do not stop them," Deirdre pleaded with an impish grin. She knew she should have been shocked by the crude remarks, but she was not. She had heard worse tales told within the convent by young daughters of the French aristocracy. "How am I to learn the ways of men if I am never to hear them speak of their adventures?"

"Ye've nothing to gain from the hearing of some tales," Lord Fitzgerald advised her. "As for the ways of men, have ye learned nothing from young Goubert? Ha! Ye thought I knew nothing of yer interest in the Frenchman."

Deirdre shook her head, dislodging another curl. "I've nae interest in Monsieur Claude. He's nice enough but not one to win the heart of an Irish lass."

Conall groaned, smacking his brow with a hand. "Have you nae given up that tiresome tune? 'I will wed none but a man with Gaelic blood running hard in his veins!'" he mimicked his sister's voice. Reaching for his brother's arm, he linked his own through it and glanced up coyly into Darragh's face. "'Faith, a brawny Irishman! Och, ye great beast! Aren't ye the very lad for me!'"

Darragh shoved his brother away in irritation but laughter got the better of him as Conall fluttered his lashes at him and made noisy kissing sounds. Lord Fitzgerald joined his sons' laughter, leaving the Fitzgerald women to exchange exasperated glances.

"I do not see the joke," Deirdre said tartly. "The pair of you refuse to wed when any half-dozen French mademoiselles in the city would have you."

"But that's just it, lass. When any half-dozen women will have me, why should I settle for one and make the others miserable?"

Deirdre smacked her brother's hand away as he tried to tweak her nose. "Boastful braggart! I do not know why I was glad to see you when you treat me no better than this."

"Now, Dee," Darragh began. "Would you have no feelings for brothers who've ridden hard these last days to bring you a gift from Paris?"

"From Paris?" Deirdre's eyes widened. "You've been to Paris?"

The brothers exchanged glances. "Only long enough to purchase a few wee trinkets for the women in our lives," Conall answered.

Lifting fallen curls from her eyes, Deirdre peered through the open doorway. "I do not see a wagon. Where are all these trinkets, you fickle-hearted souls?"

Conall was about to reach into his pocket when Darragh caught his eye and nodded meaningfully at their father. Lord Fitzgerald had begun to perspire and the hand on his cane trembled under his weight. Conall lifted his hand from his pocket. "Have a heart, lass. We've ridden till we're near dropping."

"Of course! Forgive me," Deirdre replied contritely. "Come in and sit. We'll have ale and cakes."

Darragh turned to his father. "You're looking thinner, old man."

"I am, am I?" Lord Fitzgerald challenged.

"Aye, I agree," Conall replied. "Once I despaired of lifting you. But now, well . . ." He grinned wickedly as he advanced on his father.

"Keep yer distance!" Lord Fitzgerald warned softly, lifting his cane.

"Afeard I cannot only lift you but carry you away?" Conall's grin widened.

"Not when I've finished with ye," his father replied. "Keep back! Keep—" Lord Fitzgerald's voice failed in astonishment as his son bent and hoisted him up across one shoulder.

Lady Elva gasped in horror but Deirdre caught her by the sleeve and said, "I'd like to see you carry Da the length of the hall." She, too, had noticed the strain in her father's face.

"Aye!" Darragh seconded. "Carry Da into the salon and tuck him into his favorite chair, as easy as you please."

"What do you say, old man?" Conall challenged. "Are you too frail for such games?"

"Old and frail, I could still be the death of ye!" Lord Fitzgerald countered as he lightly struck his son with his cane. "Ye began this mischief, finish it. If ye can!"

"Do not look so worried, lady," Deirdre whispered. "Darragh and Conall would lose an arm each before they hurt Da."

Lady Elva gazed worriedly at her husband as his sons jostled him down the hall. "He is worse. Did you not notice? Do his sons not see it? Why am I the only one who sees the pain in his eyes?"

Deirdre bit her lip. "You're not the only one, ma'am. But what are we to do? Conall and Darragh humor him, 'tis true. Yet he allows himself to be carried by them. When is the last time he called for his litter chair?"

Lady Elva turned a surprised gaze on her and Deirdre

reached out and hugged her stepmother. "Do you think them heartless, lady? They're nae so cold as it would seem. With the pair of them for company these next weeks, plying him with brandy and tales, Da will sleep like a babe and wake with a smile. You'll see."

Lady Elva sighed. "You're right, of course. Will I never learn to see good in the rough ways of men?"

Deirdre nodded. "'Tis a most peculiar goodness, to be sure. Cousin Claude confided to me that he finds the Irish a mystifying race." She smiled coyly. "He confessed that he once feared that I would grow up to have Conall's height, Darragh's breadth, and Brigid's temper."

Lady Elva eyed her stepdaughter. "You are quite taken with Monsieur le Comte."

Deirdre shrugged airily. "He remembers me as a wild, barefoot lass with a brogue thicker than my skull. I cannot help teasing him now that he looks at me with eyes as wide as those of a lad who's spied an unwatched pie. I daresay his fascination will wear through soon. But enough of that. Conall and Darragh promised us gifts from Paris. I will not let them forget so quickly."

Lady Elva linked her arm through Deirdre's. "Your father has decided to hold a ball. I believe he intends to show off his eligible daughter."

"Da should think better than to present me as a piece of marriageable goods," Deirdre replied tartly.

Lady Elva nodded, approving of her stepdaughter's maidenly reluctance. "If you are not eager for marriage 'tis only because you've had so little time to consider it. A lass is never complete until she's a woman wed. A ball would bring every eligible man within twenty leagues under your eye. You may change your mind then."

Deirdre turned her face away before her stepmother saw her amusement. Lady Elva used every opportunity these days to hint and prod her with the idea of marriage. "Who would entertain you, were some great brute to hie off with me?" she questioned lightly.

"I, above all, would be the most happy were you to find a husband," Lady Elva answered.

Deirdre turned an astonished gaze on her stepmother.

"Is it so very difficult having me home again that you'd marry me off to the first acceptable man?"

A deep red blush suffused Lady Elva's neck and cheeks. "Deirdre, you must know I'd never think ill of you. To think that I—I . . ."

Deirdre turned and quickly hugged her. " 'Tis only teasing, I am."

Lady Elva fine brows arched in confusion. "You were teasing? Ah, of course," she said contritely.

Deirdre bit her lip. Lady Elva was a dear sweet lady but sadly lacking in a sense of humor, while the Fitzgeralds possessed that trait in abundance. When she married, her husband would have to be a man of wit and spirit. *Oh, Lord! I'm beginning to think like Lady Elva!*

When they entered the salon, they found Lord Fitzgerald comfortably ensconced in his favorite chair, his injured leg raised on a stool. His sons flanked him, Conall pouring wine into a glass while Darragh unfolded a map drawn from his pocket.

"What is the news? Has Adair been promoted?" Lord Fitzgerald prompted when he had taken the wine.

"You'll not be believing the half of it, sir," Darragh answered. "We sketched out the campaign as we remember it. Let's begin with that."

"This is no place for us," Lady Elva suggested, aware that war would be the talk of the afternoon.

"I would rather they carried the latest sketches from Parisian seamstresses," Deirdre agreed in feigned sympathy for her stepmother's feelings. In reality she was eager to hear each and every tidbit of news from her brothers. During the past six months since her return from convent school, she had been driven nearly mad by the tedium of Lady Elva's secluded life. The only thing that had kept her cheerful was the knowledge that her brothers would soon return. Now they were here and she was to be dragged away like a child.

"Lady Elva is right," Conall concurred, deliberately ignoring the silent plea in Deirdre's eyes. "We've much to discuss that would not be proper for young ears."

"But, the presents—you promised!" Deirdre protested.

"Is that the wail of greed I hear!" Darragh said, chuckling. "Patience, lass, we're back for more than a day."

"More's the pity," Deirdre exclaimed lightly. Ah well, she told herself as she turned away from the salon, there would be other times to listen to Darragh and Conall. "Come, lady, we'll not be drawn into their merry war talk."

"The excitement of the morning has quite exhausted me," Lady Elva confided when they had stepped back into the hallway. "I'm positively light-headed. I believe I would rather lie down than study sketches just now. Do you not find the air a trifle stuffy?"

Deirdre glanced sharply at her stepmother's flushed face. Often of late Lady Elva had complained suddenly of light-headedness and overheating. There might be many causes but she hoped it was the one that would bring back her father's triumphant smile. Siring another child would do that.

Deirdre flashed her brilliant smile. "Lady, would you mind if I returned to the garden for a little while? The day is so beautiful that the thought of remaining inside distresses me."

"Shouldn't you— Wait, lass," Lady Elva called as her stepdaughter sped away. "You've forgotten your hat!"

Not looking back, Deirdre called, "I won't be long, I promise!"

She pushed open the front door before the surprised doorman could aid her and swept past him and down the front steps. Once the warmth of midsummer struck her face she drew a deep sigh of relief and smiled. She was free for the moment. After a quick glance back at the house, she started toward the garden path.

Under the warmth of the midsummer sun every blade of grass was intensely green. In the trees birds bickered and warbled. Beneath budding shrubbery insects sang and chirped while bees droned softly, darting in and out of the lushly petaled blossoms.

Without consciously choosing it, Deirdre followed the

path through the rose arbor. Her skirts scattered the pink
rose petals that had drifted down from the tangled vines of
ancient roses. Here in the shade, cool air had collected,
bringing with it from the garden the heady perfume of
pungent jasmine and spicy pinks. Lady Elva often used the
example of the gardens to illustrate what a lady should be:
serene, beautiful, and with just a whiff of wit to tantalize
the senses.

Deirdre chuckled. Now that she was extolling the virtues of marriage, perhaps Lady Elva would choose the
cabbage patch as an illustration. *The married state is like a
cabbage garden: one's life is neatly arranged in rows of
duty and responsibility, the promise of a child lurks behind
every plant, and the tiny annoyances of life are like cut-
worms among the leaves.*

"Not I," she murmured. Lady Elva's good intentions
and her family's tolerant indifference to her own desires
would not deter her from her one goal in life: to return to
Liscarrol Castle. She would do nothing that did not forward her return to her home.

"So then, here ye are, lass."

Deirdre whirled about. "Brigid, have you nothing better
to do than to sneak about spying on me?"

For a moment Brigid did not answer but let her gaze
skim with loving pride over the lass she had raised. Nae,
Deirdre was no longer a lass; she had grown into graceful
womanhood, just like her mother before her. The strong
features that once had overwhelmed her childish face were
now proportioned and softened by the womanly fullness of
her mouth and the open friendliness in her soft green
eyes.

She was not a great beauty, though few saw less than
perfection when they experienced the swift charm of her
smile. The quicksilver flash of her soul lit up any room she
entered like lightning on a storm-dark night. It was that
smile, her mother's smile, that had beguiled Lord Fitzgerald
into marriage a second time. When Deirdre found the man
of her choice she would win him, even against his will,
just as her mother had. Even so, there were dark times

ahead for the lass. The predictions at her birth had promised glory or tragedy. Only Deirdre herself would deter-
mine which it would be. The time was coming; the signs
were beginning to show themselves.

"Why do you stare at me, Brigid? I'm not ill."

Brigid blinked in surprise. "Yer hair's untidy and yer
skirts are mussed. Ye should go in and change. Fancy what
the foreigners would say to see ye so."

Deirdre smiled indulgently. Brigid never thought of
herself as a foreigner, rather she regarded the French,
whose land this was, as such. She reached up and gathered
her hair in her hands. "Perhaps I should bend to fashion,
after all, and use powder. Cousin Claude is too polite to
mention my lack of formality, but just last week Honorace
was kind enough to point out that a good clipping, poma-
tum, and powder would bring under control my willful
horse's mane."

Brigid snorted. "There's nae a horse in all of Ireland
that would not think itself lucky to sport as fine a mane as
yers. As for clipping, I'd sooner see ye bald than fleeced
like a sheep!"

Deirdre laughed. "You do not understand the finer
points of fashion, Brigid. 'Tis dreadfully gauche to
have hair as long as one's arm and as thick and unruly as sheep's wool. 'Tis not even a fashionable
color."

Brigid pursed her lips in annoyance. Deirdre's hair was
willful, that was true, but its waves were like spun gold
crackling with captured sunlight.

"Once ye were not so quick to scorn yer blessings." A
bemused smile crossed the nurse's face. "'A lass with
twisted yellow hair and beautiful green eyes. Foxglove the
color of her cheeks, and wine-red her lips. She will
become a tall, beautiful, long-haired woman whom queens
will envy.'"

"Brigid! You've not repeated the story of 'The Sons
of Uisliu" in many years. What calls it to mind today?"

Brigid answered softly, "'Tis a scent the air. Have ye
thought what it must be like at Liscarrol? 'Tis midsummer.
In swift cool streams the salmon are running, and the

briars are full of slick-skinned blackberries. There'll be herdsmen *booleying* in the mountains, and in the valleys foxglove is blooming.''

Deirdre nodded. "Aye, I've thought of home. When I'm alone I think of little else." She looked at the older woman. "They've changed, you know. Conall and Darragh are not like me. They no longer talk of returning home."

" 'Tis only for ye to be remembering, lass, and never forgetting. Ye were born of an ancient line, there's O'Neill blood in yer veins. The others do not have it. 'Tis what sets ye apart."

Deirdre shook her head. "Once I thought I was destined to be someone special, but I do not feel it anymore, not as I did when I was a child. Do you remember?''

Brigid looked away from her. How could she forget the dreams that had come to a wee lass too young to know their import?

"I suppose I should be grateful the nightmares stopped," Deirdre continued. "Still, sometimes I think that those dreams were more real than not. They made me feel alive. I seemed to know when something of great importance was about to happen. Strange. I wonder what became of them."

"Are you troubled by dreams now, lass?" she asked quietly.

"Nae, Brigid. 'Tis only that I'm so confused and I cannot name the cause. Lady Elva urges marriage, but surely marriage should wait until I've found the cure."

"Perhaps marriage is the cure," Brigid offered gently, but relief flowed through her with the knowledge that Deirdre was not eager to wed.

Deirdre shook her head. "No marriage for me today. I've indulged my wayward emotions enough for one day. It must be Darragh and Conall's return that sparks my perversity. I'm jealous, 'tis all. They pat me on the head and give Da their entire attention. There, 'tis said. I should be sent to bed without my pudding." She smiled again, her soft green eyes suddenly bright with guile. "You won't do that to me, will you, Brigid, not when there's gooseberry tart for dessert tonight?"

"Get on with ye!" Brigid chided, giving the younger woman a gentle shove. "Ye've not changed a whit since ye were a bairn."

Deirdre sobered instantly. "I know you care for me, and you worry more than you should."

"We'll be knowing that when ye're settled, won't we?" Brigid answered obliquely. "As for yer brothers, why do ye no slip into the study, quiet as a mouse, and settle in a corner to listen? They cannot mind that."

The light of hope flared and died in Deirdre's face. "Lady Elva expects me to help her choose new fabric."

Brigid's broad pale face became mobile at last. "Och, well, I can at last understand yer fears. 'Tis monstrous hard, her ladyship is, to be heaving such a burden on yer young shoulders. I wouldn't be at all surprised to learn next that she's banished ye to work in the scullery."

Deirdre smiled at herself, for indeed she did sound petty. "Oh, very well. I will go up to her for an hour. But then I will slip into Da's study and listen to the menfolk."

Brigid watched Deirdre hurry toward the house, the girl's ankles showing where she had lifted her skirts. "The lass may be nearly a woman, but she's a bit yet to learn what life holds in store for her."

She touched the tiny flint stone that hung from her neck by a string looped through the natural hole in its center. It was a witch-stone, symbol of the Ever-watching Eye, said to protect one from dreams.

Every night since their arrival in France she had tucked this stone under Deirdre's pillow and the child had slept untroubled by the bewitchment of dreams. As a *bean feasa*, a wise woman, she knew the words to make the stone obey her command.

The magic of the stone was losing its power. Though Deirdre had denied it, Brigid saw signs in the girl's restlessness that the dreams were returning. There were other signs, too, things that only Brigid had been chosen to see.

The charm's power was failing. It was an omen, a warning that it was time for Deirdre to return to Ireland, and Lord Fitzgerald must be made to accept it.

Chapter Four

Deirdre gazed fondly but enviously at her brothers as they sat at the evening meal. Next to them in their emerald brocade coats with gold brandenburgs and lace-edged cravats, she felt like a dowd in her pale yellow-sprigged muslin gown. Nor did her coiffure compare in grandness with theirs. But about that, at least, she felt less ungenerous.

Her eyes darted toward and then away from Conall's hair as she hid a smile behind her hand. Officers of the military did not wear formal wigs but shorter campaign periwigs. As Irishmen proud of their red heads, Conall and Darragh had always worn their own hair curled and tied back with a black ribbon. But tonight, for their family's entertainment she suspected, her brothers appeared at the dinner table sporting enormous blond full-bottomed wigs. The hair rose in peaks on either side of a center part, then cascaded in a mass of curls and ringlets over their shoulders to the middle of their chests.

"Do I see you smiling, Dee?" Darragh asked as he saw her amused gaze, which her hand did not hide.

She lowered her head. "I? Nae; that is, I'm only thinking of a certain biblical tale."

Lord Fitzgerald exchanged glances with his daughter,

his own blue eyes merry. ''Could it be that yer brothers' tales of derring-do have put ye in the mind of a great warrior? King David, perhaps?''

Deirdre nodded. ''I *was* thinking of a warrior. Samson!''

Her parents joined in her laughter, as did Darragh and Conall. ''Were you thinking, mayhaps, we should be shorn?'' Conall questioned.

''I'd say by the expensive look of the garments ye're sporting that ye've already been fleeced by the Parisian merchants,'' Lord Fitzgerald rejoined.

As more laughter flowed around the dinner table, a warmth settled in Deirdre's chest. Perhaps she had been wrong earlier. Perhaps things were not so different after all. She smiled at her father, glad to see that laughter had filled his cheeks with color and eased the pain-etched lines about his mouth.

'' 'Tis only our poor attempt to show you what you miss by not traveling to Paris,'' Conall offered when the amusement subsided. ''Lady Elva could see the sights. And a visit to Versailles would do our country-mouse sister a bit o' good. There's nothing to compare with it in my travels of the world.'' He leaned near Deirdre, who sat beside him. ''Not even Ireland has gardens to compare with those of the French kings.''

Deirdre shrugged, refusing to rise to the bait. ''If Ireland does not have it, then, nae doubt, 'tis not overly worth possessing.''

''Spoken like a true daughter of the old sod,'' Lord Fitzgerald pronounced, lifting his wineglass. ''*Slainte!*''

''*Slainte!*'' his family seconded and gladly drank the toast.

''Here's to a return of Ireland to the safe lawful keeping of her own,'' Darragh offered when the first toast had been drunk.

''There'll be a din to wake Saint Patrick himself,'' Conall replied. ''The sound of pipes and drums and the sweetest music of the harp as was ever heard inside Tara's walls.''

''Aye, and soldiers the like of the mighty Fian of old.

Then there'll not be an Englishman left to tell the tale of their defeat!" Lord Fitzgerald joined in.

"Soon! It should be soon!" Deirdre declared, as much carried away as her menfolk. " 'Tis time for the Wild Geese to return and fight for their own!"

"When will you be returning, Dee?" Conall questioned blandly as he set down his goblet.

"Returning? To the convent?"

Conall smiled. "Nae, *cailin deas*." He winked at his father. "What I'd like to know is when will our fierce warrior sister be setting sail for Ireland?"

Though she guessed what was coming, Deirdre's cheeks flamed. Yet, she was not a Fitzgerald for nothing. "Were you thinking of accompanying me, Conall? 'Tis said the land is poorly in need of good stock. Another bull would not go amiss."

"Deirdre!" her father exclaimed, taken aback by his daughter's pertness.

"Do not scold her, Da," Darragh said. " 'Tis the influence of bad company that's to blame. The poor lass has been cooped up for four years with the daughters of French aristocrats. 'Tis little wonder she thinks constantly of breeding. Have you not yet found a man for her to wed?"

Lord Fitzgerald snorted. "None would have her. They fear the sharp edge of her tongue."

" 'Tis not true," Deirdre answered, her pride smarting. "Le Comte de Quentin finds me quite acceptable company."

"Monsieur le Comte, is it?" Conall asked. "Once he was 'Cousin Claude' to you. But of course, he was a mere lad and you were all brambles and petticoats. Now he is Monsieur Goubert, le Comte de Quentin, thanks to his merchant grandfather's good fortune in landing the only daughter of an impoverished aristocrat."

He leaned back in his chair and lifted the cloth to look under the table. "I see the good sisters have put you to the habit of wearing shoes, but I wonder that they left you with the habit of dressing your hair like a haystack. As la Comtesse de Quentin, you will need to do better."

Deirdre smiled sweetly at him though the barb stung

her. All her life she had hated her wild wavy hair. "'Twould seem I'm destined to marry a poor but honest Irish lad who's not so afraid of the English that he fights every battle but the one he was born to meet."

The table fell silent and she immediately wanted to take back her words but she could not. Her father's scowl had returned, his thick brows knitted low over his nose. She glanced at her brothers in appeal but they had suddenly found their dinners fascinating and were busy over their plates.

"Ye always were a lass to speak her mind," Lord Fitzgerald said into the uncomfortable silence. "There's no need to task yer brothers with such harsh accusation. 'Twas I who made the choice to leave Ireland."

He indicated the length of the table before them with a sweep of his hand. "Life in France has been good to us. There's meat and bread and wine before ye, and more luxury than was available at Liscarrol since before that bloodthirsty Roundhead Cromwell set foot in Ireland."

Lord Fitzgerald's face grew fierce when he spoke of the English ruler, for he was old enough to remember much more than did his children. "There comes a time when every man knows he's fought his best and the day is lost." His frown deepened as he remembered that dark time and his lips thinned into a determined line. "I'll nae apologize to any man for what I've done!"

Deirdre stared down at her fingers laced tightly together in her lap. What could she say? *I'm sorry* seemed so inadequate. Before she could even utter that weak expression of her mortification she heard Darragh say, "Well, I, for one, am grateful."

Deirdre lifted her eyes, amazed that her brother would deliberately make things worse by heaping more coals on her head. Smiling reassuringly at her, he continued, "I am grateful to know that the good sisters of the Ursuline convent have not convinced the lass that all she need do is smile prettily and cozen a man to earn a husband."

"Aye," Conall said, winking at her. "Perhaps 'tis nature's way of protecting her beauty. As for Ireland, you're welcome to me share of it, Dee. There's more to keep me in France than ever.''

"I see a lady's fine hand in the writing of that declaration," Darragh suggested in a lazy drawl.

Conall shrugged. "There's a lass or two I've managed to keep out of your view, thank God."

Darragh's smile widened into a grin as he turned to his sister. "If 'tis a fighting man you want, I've the lad for you. He'll arrive before the end of the week. If he cannot fill your heart's desire for a brawling bruising soldier, then none can."

Deirdre was intrigued. "Is he Irish?"

Darragh loosed a guffaw. "Is he a man, you might as well ask!"

"Well, I am asking," she persisted.

Conall leaned forward, his eyes moving from his brother to his father and back. "I thought we agreed to ask Da first."

Darragh grinned. "Curse you for a timid soul, Conall. There's no harm in a visit."

Lord Fitzgerald put down his fork, his sharp eyes watching Darragh. "Who is it ye invite that yer brother quibbles at the thought?"

Darragh leaned back in his chair and folded his arms across his chest. "What name have the dispatches from Italy been full of lately?"

"Dillon!" Deirdre responded instantly.

"Burke!" Lady Elva offered more slowly.

"Do you read nothing but the generals' names?" Darragh said disapprovingly. "There's many a brave man whose memory goes wanting, if that's true. Think again, what name keeps returning to the roster of battles won and honors received? He's not a great noble such as Dillon or Burke. Some say he was spawned by the Devil himself. He certainly fights the like. 'Tis not for his piety that some men call him the Avenging Angel."

"MacShane!" Lord Fitzgerald rose so suddenly that he nearly overset his chair. "Ye've invited MacShane here? Without my permission?"

Lady Elva was on her feet instantly, forcing her sons to

rise with her. "My lord, please!" She turned to her stepsons. "What have you done? Who is this man? Och, never mind. You will simply withdraw the invitation." She looked pleadingly at first one, then the other. "If he's not due to arrive before the end of the week, there's time to ride out and meet him. Offer him some excuse that will save him embarrassment. You'll do that, will you not?"

Darragh crossed his arms, his eyes hard on his father's face. "'Twas time you told us, Da, why you hold MacShane in such disdain when the soldiers of the Wild Geese consider him the pride of the brigade. What is between you?"

Lord Fitzgerald shook his head. "He's nae welcome in me home. That's an end to it."

"But why, Da?" Deirdre questioned, her curiosity piqued beyond containing. "Did this MacShane insult you?"

A muscle twitched in Lord Fitzgerald's lower jaw as he looked at his daughter. "This is no business of yers, lass. Go to yer room at once."

"Da!" Deirdre cried, stung by his reprimand.

"Why do you not tell the lass the story you told Conall and me?" Darragh suggested.

"Aye, I'd like to know why you would deny hospitality to a famous soldier, and an Irishman at that," Deirdre declared.

Lord Fitzgerald turned a savage look on his daughter. "Ye'd like to know, would ye? And who, I'm wondering, gave ye the right to question yer father?" He reached for his cane and waved it menacingly. "Go to yer room! Go at once, before I send ye back to the Ursulines!"

Conall's hand closed over Deirdre's elbow. "Come, lass."

"Aye, go, Deirdre," Lady Elva encouraged. "I will send Brigid to you with tea."

"Ye'll do no such!" Lord Fitzgerald roared. "As for ye, lass," he continued, pointing his cane at Deirdre, who stubbornly held her ground, "ye'll leave my sight this minute or I shall damage more than yer pride!"

Deirdre flinched at his barrage of words but she did not flee. "I will go, Da, but I think you've been entirely unfair!'' With an accompanying swish of her skirts, she turned and marched from the room with Conall at her elbow.

Lord Fitzgerald reseated himself when his son and daughter were gone and swallowed his glass of claret, struggling to control his temper. When he looked across at his wife's white face he knew he had acted badly, but the name MacShane had startled him. He smiled reassuringly at her. ''Ye're much too lenient with the lass. She's been so long among the arrogant French that she thinks she's become one of them. A night without a meal will not damage her overly.''

Deirdre allowed Conall to steer her up the stairs but she was far from cowed. When they reached the second floor she came to a halt, all but tripping her brother. ''Da's never, ever threatened me before!'' She turned to Conall and, blinking back tears of hurt, demanded, ''Who is this MacShane?''

Conall scowled and put a finger to his lips. After a brief glance back down the hallway, he beckoned her toward his room.

The doors of his apartment opened onto a magnitude of disarray that appeared to have been weeks in the making but had been achieved in the few hours since his return. Two huge trunks stood open in the center of the room, spilling their contents of clothing and papers over the furnishings and floor.

Ignoring the disorder, Deirdre lifted a map from a suspicious pile and discovered a chair.

Conall hurried over to lift the remainder of the chair's contents and then waved his sister into the seat.

''Who is this MacShane?'' Deirdre demanded impatiently. ''And why did you invite him here, knowing Da's feelings?''

''Patience, lass.'' Conall seated himself after unearthing a second chair. Instead of speaking, he braced his elbow on his knee, dropped his chin into his hand, and stared off into space.

In an effort to control her curiosity, Deirdre drove her fingernails deep into the palms of her hands. "MacShane?" she prompted when she could no longer bear Conall's silence.

Suddenly he smiled and the corners of his eyes crinkled in a pattern exactly like his father's. "I should have known any hint of mystery would whet your appetite. MacShane always turns the lasses' heads, though he does not seem to hold them in so high a regard."

"He does not like women?"

Conall gave her a disapproving glance. " 'Tis unladylike of you to inquire, lass. But, as you did ask, he's a man, as much as any." A teasing smile lifted his mouth. "Whose business is it, I say, if he chooses to deny himself the more tender pleasures? I suspect 'tis his convent upbringing which formed his character."

"Convent?" Deirdre replied in surprise.

"Aye, convent." Conall shrugged nonchalantly but his gaze never left his sister's face. "Some say he's the misbegotten child of a nun, but I know for a fact that his mother had simply retired to a French convent before his birth."

"He's French?"

"Nae. MacShane's blood is as Irish as his name. His mother came as a widow to France and birthed her son inside convent walls before taking the veil. The lad was reared in a monastery." Conall looked away with a sly smile. "A priest, that's what he was meant to be."

Deirdre waited five seconds before saying, "Until . . . ?"

"Until that idiot William of Orange invaded Ireland," Conall finished. " 'Twas enough insult to raise dead clansmen from their graves. 'Tis not surprising that righteous anger sprang a courageous lad from the confines of monastery walls to defend his land."

"A warrior priest," Deirdre said wondrously.

"A damn fool lad with no schooling in the ways of war and less sense than heart, that's what Da called him— them!' " Conall glanced nervously at his sister. He had nearly given away more than he intended, but Deirdre seemed not to notice. "There were many green lads running amok in ninety-one," he added. "They were the first to run into the thick of battle and the first to die. Da said 'twas bad for morale—green lads bleeding their life's blood at your feet while a man was trying to separate an enemy's head from his shoulders."

"Not to mention the strain it put on the poor lads," Deirdre added, then flushed at the callousness of her statement. She shook her head in bewilderment. "Even if what you say is so, it does not explain Da's dislike of MacShane now. MacShane is a skillful soldier, if the dispatches are to be believed."

Conall nodded, satisfied that his sister's reasoning was as sound as his own. "Da is a man with a long memory. Perhaps you will better understand Da's feelings when I tell you that MacShane once saved Da from the maw of death."

"MacShane did that? When?"

"Oh, 'twas little more than a month before a land mine took Da's leg. Our regiment was caught in a cross fire. Da had ordered the lads to fight their way through when enemy fire cut us off. MacShane's regiment had been fighting beyond the hill. Suddenly, he was amidst us, and his quick action brought Da down before a cannonball could take his head off. A rare scolding Da gave the lad, too, for the impertinence."

Deirdre stood up. "I should have known you would not tell me the truth."

"Sit down, Dee, or I'll be forced to stand; and, God's truth, missing me dinner is all the gallantry I'm in a mood to serve you this day."

Deirdre's anger dissolved. "Oh, Conall, I forgot about your dinner!"

He caught her by the waist and brought her to sit on his left knee. "I like contrition in you, lass. 'Tis as becoming as your anger."

Deirdre lifted her chin haughtily but the dimple in her left cheek appeared. "You're entirely too arrogant, brother, and if you will not tell me the truth, I will seek out Darragh. He will answer my questions.''

"I have not lied to you," Conall replied. "Da's dislike of MacShane is as much a mystery to me as it is to you. 'Twas like he'd seen a ghost when MacShane appeared in the thick of battle. If there were words between them, I did not hear them. Da would not discuss it, nor would he thank MacShane for saving his life. Since then, Darragh and I have fought beside MacShane, yet he's said nothing of the incident. It does make a man curious."

" 'Tis hard to believe that an untrained lad has made so grand a name for himself in the brigade.''

"Well now, lass, MacShane is not a lad any longer," Conall replied, a new look in his eye. "As for untrained, you'd not think him born for anything else were you to see him in battle. I've seen him and he's a beauteous thing to behold. Fierce and ugly, without mercy and without fear, 'tis a superb fighting animal he is. Och, for the days when men stood shoulder to shoulder in battle with nothing between them and the enemy but the swing of their axes!''

"I should think it rather windy for such immodest display," Deirdre replied, remembering stories told to her of how their Gaelic ancestors had fought in the nude. "Do not tell me MacShane shames his enemies in like manner?''

Conall's chuckle rumbled through his chest before it reached his lips. "The lassies would nae mind, would they, Dee?''

Deirdre hid her face in his shoulder, glad that he could not see her blush. "So, the man's a brute, and ugly as sin. 'Twould seem there's little to interest me in his visit.''

"Aye, there's little in MacShane that would interest a convent-reared mademoiselle. He'd frighten you to death. Eyes like flame, he has, twin fires of blue-white light that seem to illuminate a man's soul. He's a man more men would measure themselves against if they did nae fear they'd be found wanting.''

Deirdre lifted her head. "You sound as though you admire him.''

Conall nodded. "Aye.''

Deirdre regarded her brother for a moment, reading the

truth of his answer in his eyes. It surprised her. Conall and Darragh held few things in esteem besides their family and their faith. MacShane must be extraordinary to so charm two seasoned soldiers. "So. When may we expect this warrior paragon?"

"Not later than Friday."

"Then he will be here for Cousin Claude's soiree," Deirdre mused. "What will you say to Da? Will he change his mind about MacShane's visit?"

Conall's ruddy face became serious. "Da's ailing. Could be his candle's burned low. No, hear the truth, Dee," he counseled as Deirdre opened her mouth to protest.

"It grieves me to see the old man hobbling about like a three-legged dog. Truth, I believe he would rather have died than be left behind each time Darragh and I return to battle. He's a warrior and should have died as such."

Conall paused and smiled suddenly. "Yet, the good Lord's left him here these many months to torment his children, and so we deserve! Still, there comes a time when a man should put his house in order, and so it is with Da. He will see MacShane. And whatever there is between them will be resolved."

Deirdre did not reply because there was nothing she could add. Her father was ill, his strength ebbing. She knew it as well as did her brothers. She only hoped that Lady Elva might linger a little longer in happy ignorance of the fact. " 'Tis up to us to make him comfortable," she said mostly to herself.

She rose from her brother's knee and surveyed the room's disorder. "Where's Gildea?"

"Gildea, damn his black heart, has deserted me!"

"Poor Gildea," Deirdre murmured sympathetically, for she knew her brother's valet was rarely in the wrong when the two of them had been quarreling. "What has the poor man done this time that made you leave him behind?"

"I? Leave him? Never! Oh, the cunning of the idler. He deserted me, he did, and for a Parisian flirt of doubtful parentage!"

Deirdre's eyes lit up. "Gildea's in love?"

"Wedded and bedded!" Conall eyed his sister with a

jaded expression. "Truth, I thought you had him so tightly rolled up in your skirts that the lad would rather slit his throat than look at another colleen."

Deirdre made a face. "That's no pretty thing you say about me."

Conall chuckled. "When you always rise to the bait, how can I resist?" He glanced about the room as though seeing it for the first time, and his gaze was sheepish as he looked up at Deirdre. "Perhaps one of the maids could . . ."

"Lady Elva will have none of that, not with your reputation with servant girls," Deirdre answered. "I will send up one of the footmen to look after you."

"But they know nothing of keeping a gentleman's person," Conall protested.

Deirdre's dimple deepened. "And neither do you, Conall Sheamus Fitzgerald. You need a wife to keep you, though I doubt even a bride would look fondly upon this disaster."

Deirdre walked to the door, turning back only when she had reached it. "What will you say to Da?"

Conall shrugged. "MacShane's been invited. 'Twill not be said a Fitzgerald was inhospitable to a guest."

Deirdre doubted her father's hospitality, but she was equally certain that MacShane would not be turned back from their door.

"If you leave your door off its latch, 'tis fair certain you shall be visited by the fairies this night," Conall said and mimed eating.

Deirdre smiled at him. "Thank you, brother."

When she was gone, Conall heaved a sigh of satisfaction. He had baited his hook well. Deirdre was breathless with anticipation over MacShane's visit. He and Darragh were in agreement that Deirdre should marry. With Da ailing, it was only a matter of time before the burden of the Fitzgerald women became theirs. With Deirdre wed, they would have fewer worries. MacShane was their choice; and, though the man himself did not know it, he had become their prize candidate in the marriage market.

Of course, if Darragh had not pushed the matter with Da, they might have been able to plan better. As it was, they would have to deal with their father's wrath until MacShane arrived.

'Twas time the old man saw reason. "MacShane's the man for Dee," Conall said aloud and was answered by a rumbling belly. "But first there's a meal to be eaten."

Deirdre struggled with the last of the lacing at the back of her gown as Brigid entered the bedroom. "Oh, good. I cannot reach the last. I really should have my own maid. After all, I am a young lady, and all young ladies of means have their very own personal maids."

"Some young ladies of means are *mature* enough to have a maid," Brigid answered sourly as she came forward to help her charge. "But the likes of ye, lass, who tests her da's temper to its limits, needs a nurse."

Deirdre laughed. It was an old joke between them. Brigid was more than a servant, not to be turned out or demoted. She acted as Deirdre's maid but it was well understood that she did so out of affection.

"There ye are, and ye'd best hurry to bed. Lord Fitzgerald is stomping about below, roaring like a wounded stag."

Deirdre swung about as she pulled her gown from her shoulders. "So you've heard the commotion. Do you know why Da dislikes this MacShane?"

Brigid did not alter the bland expression on her full face, but Deirdre thought she saw a flash in the woman's eyes. "I know nothing of it. But, if his lordship dislikes the man, so do I."

"Blind loyalty is for fools and soldiers," Deirdre said peevishly. "I did not think you took orders well."

"Lord Fitzgerald is a man worthy of blind belief," Brigid said flatly and reached to lift the fallen gown from the floor.

Deirdre turned toward her vanity and began pulling the pins from her hair. As she reached to place a handful of them on the tabletop, she glimpsed her right shoulder in the mirror. She twisted about even more until the full shape of her birthmark came into view. It was bright red and the exact size and shape of a rosebud.

One of the fairies' own. Conall had spoken of the fairies a minutes earlier, but it was Brigid who had first spoken to Deirdre of the otherworld when, as a child, she had been distressed by the birthmark.

"Do you still believe I was kissed by the fairies?" Deirdre asked softly when she saw Brigid's reflection above her own in the mirror.

Brigid smiled and the smile transformed her into a woman younger than the six and thirty that she was. "Aye, lass, I'd swear to it."

Deirdre ran a finger lightly over the mark. "'Tis a curious thing, this mark. Sometimes I forget it's there. Other times I believe 'tis the thing that links me to Ireland, the thing that will not allow me to forget that I should go back."

Brigid unfastened Deirdre's petticoats. "Aye, 'tis a reminder, but there's something more important that should remind ye." She tapped her chest. "'Tis the heart, lass."

"Why, Brigid, you sound positively sentimental." Deirdre turned about to face the woman. "You're not too old; you should think of marrying."

"I've not met a man who could call Brigid McSheehy his wife and be proud of it."

Deirdre frowned. "Who would not be proud to love a woman such as you?"

Brigid had already turned away and was folding a petticoat. She did not answer for so long a time that Deirdre thought perhaps she had not heard the question, but finally the nurse said, "I made a bargain, a vow, a long time ago that nothing would persuade me to neglect me duty. Men come and men go. None of them tempted me to forget me vow."

Deirdre considered this. "So, there have been men?"

Brigid looked up, a secret smile on her lips. "Ye're young, lass. One day ye'll understand that the traffic between a man and a woman need not be bound by vows of marriage or promises. There, I've shocked ye, as so I should. Go to bed and dream of the man *ye'll* wed."

Half an hour later, with a comfortable purloined portion of Conall's supper in her stomach, the candle blown out, and the curtains drawn, Deirdre lay in bed staring up into the dark. She would not dream. She could not remember dreaming since she had come as a child to France. Yet, she did think of the great and ugly MacShane who would come riding up to her door in a few days' time.

"I hope he's not so monstrously ugly that I cannot be civil to him," she murmured sleepily.

The wind whistled in the trees, bending and snapping their tips like flags. The wind struck the dull gray surface of the water, whipping it into mare's tails. The wind soared and on its back it carried leaves, bits of grass, and the pungent odor of ancient past. Higher still, dark gray clouds scudded on its invisible shoulders. And in its wake the whistling, singing, keening wind carried the thunder of hooves.

They appeared out of the misty morning air like a black speck on the green sea of grass. As they neared, rider and horse drew more distinct until the black cape whipping high over the horse's rump revealed the muscled thighs of a horseman.

They swept down the long slope into the valley where she stood waiting as she had every night of her life.

Her heart beat so loudly in her ears that she could no longer hear the thunder of hooves.

When he reined in before her, she could not turn away, could not move, could not deny him. She lifted her arms.

He raised his arm to fend her off. "Stay away!" he cried, his words snatched by the wind and sent keening down to the sea below them. "Stay away, in fear of your life, *mo cuishle!*"

*   *   *

Deirdre sat up in bed. What had awakened her? She could not remember. For a long moment she listened in the dark, but she heard nothing but her own heartbeat.

Brigid stood in the hallway, her candle snuffed by a pinch of her fingers.

"What happened? Why do ye nae go in to her?"

Brigid turned readily toward the sound of the man's voice, though his features were indistinguishable in the gloom. "She'll come to nae harm. 'Twas but a dream."

"A dream! Ye said she did nae dream."

Under that cover of dark Brigid clasped the tiny witch-stone that still hung about her neck. This night she had deliberately kept the charm from beneath Deirdre's pillow to see what would happen. The dream had returned, as she had known it would. "The signs are growing stronger. The time is coming for the lass to return to Liscarrol."

"No! No! I forbid it!"

"Ye cannot forbid the wind nor the tide . . . nor fate, Lord Fitzgerald."

Chapter Five

As Killian MacShane stood wrapped in his cloak at the edge of a copse, he watched the rising sun with indifference. It was just the beginning of another day, a day he would have to live through as best he could. No different, no better than any of the days he could remember. If not for the dream, he would be sleeping still. *If not for the dream*.

The corners of Killian's mouth lifted slightly in a self-mocking smile. He would have slept through many other nights if not for the dream. It would not let him rest. It had mocked and teased him these last eleven years. Not even life in the belly of a galley ship had earned him dreamless sleep. He never knew when it would strike and so could not prevent it. Only in waking and waiting for the dawn could he keep himself free.

Were it a terrible nightmare, he might shake free of it. Were it an omen of his death, he would meet it bravely. Were it a memory of past grief, he would outlive it. It was none of these. It was a childish dream, a dream of fairies and magic and goodness and beauty. It had haunted him until his spirit was weary with yearning for what could not be. Yet, it would not leave him.

The blue-gray mist over the field drifted past, scored pale yellow where the first rays of dawn filtered through it. Even as he willed it away, wisps of the dream, like the seeking fingers of the mist, wrapped themselves about his mind until, for an instant, the dream was with him once more.

The face that haunted him was the face of a child and yet it was not. With tangled curls the color of ripened grain and wide gray-green eyes as calm and deep as peace, she sought him out, beguiling him with the promise of peace and belonging. *Something of his own*. That was what she represented. In all his twenty-eight years he had never possessed anything of his own. And yet, in the darkness of night, a creature of dreams aroused in him a need for love so strong that he feared her.

Killian tossed his head, an unconscious gesture that flung a lock of black hair from his eyes, and then rubbed his brow with a gauntleted hand. That was his guilty secret, a thing he could not reveal in a confessional where he freely admitted the deaths he had caused on the battlefield, his lust, his weaknesses. This longing for the love of a phantom was too foolish a thing for a man of his age to admit, even to himself. That was why he awakened whenever the dream came over him. He was too ashamed to submit to its seductive pleasure.

The snort of his horse momentarily attracted his attention. The war horse was all he had left to show for his years of service in the French army. His superiors had not believed he would simply walk away. After all, he was a hero. It was of little consequence to him. In the end, they could offer him nothing that he wanted or needed. They had need of a man with his skill, they had told him, and that had made him smile as he walked away.

All his life, people had had a need for his talents. He was an efficient soldier. He killed cleanly, swiftly, and reliably. They would miss his ability to defeat the enemy, but none of his comrades knew or cared for Killian MacShane, the man. They feared him. He saw it in their eyes and knew that they had heard the exaggerated tales of his birth and upbringing. In the beginning, he had enjoyed the awe those tales inspired, but now he realized that they had only isolated him. He had had enough of killing. He had had enough of loneliness. From now on he would work to fill the need within himself to possess something of his own.

He raised his head as the sun's corona edged above the horizon. By midday he would arrive in Nantes.

"Nantes." Killian said the word aloud. Perhaps it was his journey to Nantes that had prompted last night's dream. That, and the prospect of meeting Lord Fitzgerald again.

Killian's frown deepened as he mused over the confrontation before him. In some mysterious way, the beginnings of his dream were bound up in his chance encounter with Lord Fitzgerald many years before. He had been only a lad then, a wounded, frightened boy who had seen the worst that war could offer in a homeland that was not his birthplace. And for his trouble he had been betrayed. Aye, he would begin at the beginning, with Lord Fitzgerald of Liscarrol Castle.

He wrapped his cloak tighter about himself. As for the dream, its effect would fade with the rising sun. It always did.

Southern Brittany was a low flat land, little of which was readily amenable to farming. It was on the coast that most Bretons made their home, and their livelihoods came from the sea. Nantes, on the banks of the Loire near its confluence with the Atlantic, was a center of trading where sailors and fishermen rubbed shoulders with the rest of the world. In good times, the streets of the city were lined with folk selling their catch. In bad times, it was filled with men offering their services for any price. Yet, good times or bad, the streets were filled with the disconsolate: the beggars, the lame, the abandoned.

Killian held his gaze above the milling throngs as his horse threaded a path through the streets. It was midsummer, the catch was going well, and the city prospered. The stink of fish and mussels and crabs filled the narrow, humid lanes as vendors cried out their wares.

"M'sieur! M'sieur!"

A tug on his pants leg made Killian look down into the filthy face of a child not more than twelve years of age. The urchin tightened his grip on Killian's leg as he extended a grimy hand. "*Un peu sous, m'sieur! Pour Mama et les bébés! Un peu sous!*"

The coin was in his hand before Killian checked himself. The child's dark hair was matted to his brow by mud, and the corners of his lips were crusted with oozing sores. Only his eyes were bright, so very bright and sly.

Deliberately, Killian bent in the saddle and wiped one corner of the child's mouth with his gloved hand. The sores smeared, coming off on the leather covering his thumb. His eyes narrowed as he raised his glove for inspection. Fake. A bit of grease, flour, and fish blood had been fashioned into a very realistic resemblance of pox boils.

As the beggar turned to flee, Killian grabbed him by the collar. The child shrieked in alarm as he was lifted from the ground and hauled across the man's saddle.

"Liar! Thief! Charlatan!" Killian growled in French, punctuating each word with a slap of his hand against the child's buttocks. "Tell . . . your . . . mama . . . to . . . put . . . you . . . to . . . honest . . . labor!" With a last rough shake, he set the urchin back onto the cobblestone street.

"*Merde! Bâtard!*" the child yelled as tears made clean tracks on his dirty cheeks. When the man bent toward him again, he jumped back with a yelp of fear. The man did not reach for him a second time.

Killian opened his hand, palm up, and tossed a few coins at the boy, saying, "Use this to start your new life."

Startled but recognizing the flash of money, the child grabbed them from the air, then turned and ran, spewing filthy words over his shoulder.

A crowd quickly gathered to assail him with well-wishes and to plead for further generosity, but Killian ignored them, quietly urging his horse past them.

"*Gom!*" Killian muttered when he had made his way

onto another street. What had he thought to accomplish by making a spectacle of himself? Why had he not simply ignored the child? The boy was a professional beggar. No passerby would reform him.

He knew the answer. Despite the brutalizing forces of the last twelve years, the desire to make right the wrongs of this world had never left him. Once he had believed that those feelings represented a calling to the Church, but no longer. Now he distrusted the urgings that moved within him, for they left him vulnerable and he could not afford vulnerability. One mistake, one unguarded moment, and a soldier might become a corpse. How could he help others when he could barely keep his own body and soul together?

The duchesse would laugh at him when he told her of his foolhardiness this day. It was a grandiose, empty gesture unworthy of a man of sense and practicality. She would offer him wine, kiss his mouth, and laugh at his honor, his chivalry, his belief in right. Then she would wrap him in her arms and thighs and, for a short while, make him forget that he was a fool. He should have gone to Paris.

No, not Paris. The duchesse had need of his talents again, or so she had said in her most recent letter. But he had had more than enough of the duchesse's brand of work. More than the others, she had used him for her own ends, and more than of any other he had a need to be free of her.

The summer sun shone brightly on the port city. Ships dotted the river Loire like horseflies on the surface of a pond, their sails tightly furled and their rigging swaying to the pitch and roll of the water. He paused on the quay, his eyes searching out the name of one ship—the *Cygne*—but she was not there. With a sigh, he turned back from the harbor. Once he had loved the sea, and as a boy he had thought he might run away to join the navy. More foolish dreams. The reality had been worse than a nightmare. Dreams. Always dreams.

Without stopping to ask directions, he wound his way back from the harbor, out of the narrow lanes, and once more into the countryside toward the more prosperous

portion of the town. He knew where to go though he had
never been there before. He knew much about the Fitzgeralds.
He had made them his business this last year. The Fitzgeralds
were Anglo-Irish nobility. Six centuries earlier their ancestors had been among the Norman conquerors of Ireland.
Some had remained, intermarrying and becoming "more
Irish than the Irish," as the English had learned to their
dismay. The present Lord Fitzgerald owed much of his
success in France to family ties dating back to his Norman
French connections with the de Quentins of Nantes. There
was a daughter fresh from the convent and more than
likely promised to the new comte.

*He will take her to court and perhaps she will find favor
with Le Roi Soleil and her success will be made*, Killian
mused cynically.

With French coins in their pockets and French blood
mingling in their veins, the Anglo-Irish Fitzgeralds would
soon forget their Irish homeland and their heritage. The
only loyalty remaining in them was their preference for
their countrymen. 'Twas said that any Irishman in need
could count on finding shelter, at least temporarily, with
the Fitzgeralds. Yet even that was a lie, as he had learned
to his own detriment.

Killian's thoughts drifted as he rode across the grounds
of a modest estate. Butterflies danced above the carpet of
green, their bright wings opening and closing with lazy
flashes of yellow, blue, and white upon the dew-drenched
lawn. The beauty of the day pleased him and he reined in.
The morning was silent but for the chatter of nesting birds
in the trees.

For a moment he closed his eyes. How tired he was,
how weary of riding. In the distance the beckoning shade of
a chestnut tree was too much to resist. What difference
would an hour's rest make?

The moment he leaned back against the tree trunk he
was asleep.

The galloping hooves sounded softly in the damp thick
grass. Had he not been so recently at war, he doubted he
would have heard them until the rider was much nearer.

He was on his feet in an instant. A blink of an eye later he was hidden behind the tree trunk, his pistol drawn.

The horse and rider rode along a tree-lined lane across the meadow from where he stood. At first they were too far away for him to judge much. The steed was a big dark roan with a deep chest and heavy hooves, a war horse. The rider was slight, perhaps a groom who had been sent out to exercise his master's steed. Nothing threatening in that.

As Killian tucked his pistol back into his belt, the horse and rider suddenly swerved off the path and into the field of butterflies and sunshine, and he realized that this was no groom on the horse's back. A girl rode the huge animal.

She rode astride, her feet bare of slippers, yet she had a commanding grip on the horse's reins. She wore a plain dark blue gown, and a long tangle of bright golden hair flew out behind her like a windblown flame. As he continued to stare, the sound of her laughter, clear and sweet, rose above the thudding hooves.

"Go! Go, Lachtna!" she cried, digging her heels into the flanks of the sweating horse.

Horse and rider galloped past just feet from the tree by which he stood, splashing through the shallow stream that bordered the near side of the meadow.

For a moment Killian stood transfixed. Her cheeks pinkened by exertion, her eyes wide with pleasure and quite green, the girl's face had borne a strange, unearthly familiarity. That blend of strength and sweetness was worthy of a saint . . . or a dream.

Hers was the face of his dream!

In the time it took him to snatch the reins free of the tree and mount up, Killian realized how absurd his thoughts were. She was no ethereal spirit. No doubt she was some stablehand's daughter stealing a ride from one of her master's steeds. Yet, she could not be French, for she had spoken in Gaelic. An odd ripple of excitement sped through Killian as he urged his horse after the pair. Spirit or flesh and blood, he must find out for himself.

Deirdre did not turn to glance over her shoulder when she heard the approach of a rider. At dinner the night before, Darragh had bet her ten francs that she could not ride his charger, bareback, the length of the estate without a tumble. She had accepted at once with an eye toward improving the stakes. That was why she had set out an hour earlier than their agreed-upon time, leaving behind a note challenging Darragh to double or nothing if she returned astride.

Darragh had agreed that she could ride the course alone, at her own pace, but it seemed he had ridden after her. With a firm pressure on the reins, she turned the horse with surprising ease.

"A fine brother you are, that you don't trust me!" she challenged the approaching rider.

At once she realized her mistake. The rider was not Darragh or any other member of the Fitzgerald household.

The man was wrapped in a dark cape, though the morning was warming under the late June sun. His head was bare, and his long black mane, too carelessly waved to be a wig, moved on his shoulders with his horse's gait.

"Good day to you, lass," the stranger said in Gaelic as he halted his mount a few yards away.

Deirdre stared at him, offering him no words of greeting or challenge. His face, permanently blushed by the sun, was stern. His features were not those of a gentle man or a good-natured one. Black brows slashed the broad forehead and his bold nose and jutting chin spoke of a belligerent nature. Yet, he was not ugly. Of singular beauty were the bright blue eyes regarding her.

For an instant, recognition flirted with memory. He was familiar, yet . . . surely she would have remembered meeting such a man before.

Gaelic was a tongue rare in France, despite the daily influx of Irish who had escaped across the sea. The man was a stranger. There was determination in his posture and a tense readiness that made her wonder at his intent. Her gaze moved uneasily to the butt of the pistol outlined beneath his cloak. A port city was open to the freebooters of the world: sailors, adventurers, pirates, and thieves. That was why she always carried a skean in the left sleeve of her gown when she went out riding. Her right hand moved to grip the hilt of it and draw it free.

The stranger's expression altered subtly into the suggestion of a smile as he casually flung back his cloak to expose his black coat and breeches. He lifted his arms high. "I will not harm you. You speak Irish. I heard you call your pony Lachtna."

"He's not a pony!" Deirdre responded indignantly, then blushed instantly. He had tricked her.

"Would you be in the employ of Lord Fitzgerald, by any chance?" he asked.

Deirdre did not allow surprise to stampede her into speech this time. She glanced at his upraised hands and a little of the tension went out of her. At least he was not bent on robbery.

She reached down to flick away a branch that had caught in her skirts. When she looked up again she saw that her gesture had drawn the stranger's gaze to her bare ankles and feet.

"Have ye nae seen a lass's feet afore?" she asked in an exaggerated brogue as she twitched her skirts lower.

"Aye," the stranger answered, his lilting voice deep and caressing. "Aye, that and much more, lass." He raised his eyes slowly to hers, and Deirdre felt her pulse quicken. "Truth, you look too young to know of love's diversions, but your blush says 'tis not so!"

Deirdre stared at him, struck once more by the intensity of his blue stare. It was too much to bear and she shifted her gaze to the blue-black waves on his shoulders.

Who was he? He did not wear the soldierly green of the Irish Brigade. More likely he was a refugee looking for work. Whether refugee or soldier, she knew she should not be talking with him. She had flirted with danger quite enough for one morning.

"That way lies the Fitzgerald place!" she offered with a pointing finger and suddenly kicked Lachtna into a gallop.

Killian watched her flee, a rare smile touching his lips. He thought of himself as a man untouched by mortal comeliness, but he could not take his eyes off her. Dirty bare feet and a smudge on her nose had not diminished her beauty, for it was not that kind. There had even been a dusting of gold freckles on the bridge of her nose.

She was a real Irish lass, flesh and blood. No wonder he had mistaken her for a figment of his dream world. The pleasurable sensation surging through him was not altogether lust, and yet there was enough in it that he could not resist following her, albeit at a tactful distance.

Deirdre did not glance back over her shoulder to see if the stranger followed her. That would be encouraging him and she knew it. Yet, after several seconds passed and she did not hear the sound of his horse, disappointment eddied through the relief that washed over her.

She had allowed him to believe that he had frightened her into headlong flight, which is exactly what he had done.

"Shame on you, Deirdre Fitzgerald!" she muttered as her cheeks stung.

He was not the first handsome man she had encountered. To the contrary, he was not handsome at all. He had not even smiled. Perhaps he had bad teeth like Sean, the groom's eldest son. That would explain why he had not smiled. What lass would find foul breath and rotted teeth fascinating?

There was in his forbidding expression something aloof, judgmental, and altogether critical. It was as if he had seen through her blushes and known her to be a silly young lady enjoying a flirtation with a stranger. He reminded her of the parish priest of Liscarrol during Lent. Each year the priest fasted for forty days until his cheekbones stood out in gaunt relief and his skin was gray. Only the fire of fanatical belief blazed in his eyes.

The stranger's eyes held that same fierce light. Yet, self-denial did not seem an attribute of a man who so casually mentioned that he knew much more of women than their bare ankles. Nor was he gray-faced and gaunt. His complexion, burnt by the sun and wind, was not red like her brothers' but golden. The contrast made his eyes seem lit from within.

No matter, she preferred a man of greater breadth and width, like Darragh or Conall. Even in the saddle she judged that he was not as tall as her brothers. Indifferent in height and thin, that was what he was.

Well, perhaps not thin; the stranger was sinewy. In fact, what little she had seen of him was rather nicely formed: long thighs, broad shoulders, and a flat belly behind the butt of his pistol. He was arrogant, self-assured, and . . . and . . . and quite the most magnificent man she had ever encountered.

When Deirdre realized that her thoughts had once more circled back to ones of admiration, she could not help but laugh at herself. She had been dazzled, that's what she had been, and was too proud to admit it.

With a sniff of self-disgust she rubbed the end of her nose to dislodge a fleck of mud that Lachtna's hooves had kicked up. It was just as well that she had not revealed who she was. She looked like a rude country girl in her oldest gown.

When she glanced back over her shoulder the stranger was gone, vanished. Yet, an image remained with her of the tall, black-haired, blue-eyed Irishman.

Out of nowhere a sudden chilling breeze sped across the meadow, lifting the edge of her skirts and raising goosebumps on her skin.

She shook her head, dismissing the disquieting shiver that traveled through her. He was a man, only that, and not a very polite one.

All at once she remembered her bet with Darragh. If she did not return soon, she would lose.

With a slap on the horse's rump she cried, "Go, Lachtna! Go!" and they galloped off toward home.

When she reached the north lawn of the house, Deirdre saw her brothers standing on the drive, Conall's red head easily discernible in the sunlight. She did not slow Lachtna until she was upon them, and then she slid from the horse's back with a crow of triumph.

"I did it! I won!" she cried breathlessly, tossing the reins to Darragh.

Instead of the chiding she expected, Darragh's eyes grew round at the sight of her. "Dee, what happened? Were you tossed?"

She looked down. Her skirts were muddy and damp. She could feel the sweat running in rivulets down her back and between her breasts, pasting her bodice to her skin. She looked anything but ladylike, and she had never felt more alive. During her convent years she had been allowed to ride only sidesaddle on a pony within the nunnery walls.

With a grimy hand she pushed back the strand of hair sticking to her brow and smiled widely. "You did not say I could not exert myself in the effort to win, and that I've done."

Darragh shook his head. "You've ridden without a saddle, and Lachtna's not accustomed to that. You could have been killed!"

Deirdre shrugged, vaguely annoyed by his tone. "Once you'd have applauded me, now you scold me."

"Now, Dee," Conall inserted on his brother's behalf. "You know we're proud of you. Allow a brother to show a proper concern for his sister."

Deirdre knew that none of the men under Conall's command had ever heard so conciliatory a tone from him. Even so, it was Darragh who had scolded her and it was from him that she wanted an apology. Turning away, she began stroking the long smooth column of Lachtna's neck. "'Tis a fine, beauteous horse. I cannot remember a faster ride. I wonder how I should spend my twenty francs."

"Only half that sum," Darragh protested. "And how am I to know you kept the course, with no one watching?"

Deirdre looked up. "Calling me a liar, are you?"

"Never that," Conall broke in. "'Tis just that there's no way of telling whether or no you kept the course."

"I did more than that. I rode astride, without boots. Darragh owes me double the bet!" Deirdre added with a glint in her eye.

"Now that I did not agree to," Darragh answered, drawing her note from his pocket. "You did not give me a chance to say yea or nae. Ten francs, 'tis all I bet, and the loss of that is not yet proved.''

"Cheat!" Deirdre declared in frank disgust. "Give me the reins and you'll see who won!"

"Whoa, lass." Conall grabbed his sister about the waist when she would have tried to remount. "There'll be a rematch in the morning when Lachtna's rested and Darragh's temper has cooled.''

"There's naught the matter with my temper," Darragh answered, but his face was flushed.

"Nae, there's nothing wrong with his temper, 'tis stinginess ailing him," Deirdre taunted.

"Stingy is it? And me the one who brought you five pairs of silk stockings and a novel from Paris.''

"Children, children," Conall chided between chuckles, only to have his siblings turn on him and snap in unison, "Shut up, Conall!"

"Perhaps I may be of service," a man's voice offered behind them. The three Fitzgeralds swung toward the rider in surprise, for they had not seen him approach.

Deirdre gave a guilty start as she recognized the man. He had dismounted, and where his cloak gaped open she saw not only the pistol in his belt but also the gleam of silver from his sword scabbard. Pistols and swords were both signs of a gentleman; why had she not thought of that before?

"The lass kept a murderous pace, you have my word on that. I followed her from the meadow near the stream and she never dismounted nor slowed her pace.''

"MacShane!"

Darragh strode forward to clasp the stranger in a bearlike hug. "MacShane, I should nae be surprised that you've appeared without a sound. 'Twas the same stealth that made the Spaniards believe you dealt in witchcraft.''

Killian subjected himself to Darragh's intimacy but he stuck out his hand to Conall before that brother could envelop him in an embrace.

"Captain MacShane!" A grin split Conall's face as he pumped the man's hand. Then, giving in to greater sentiment, he clapped him soundly on the back. "Your visit has been eagerly anticipated."

Killian looked up at the great house before him and then back at his hosts. "Anticipated or dreaded, as one waits for death or the tax collector?"

"The tax collector, of course," Conall volunteered without hesitation. "Yet, the brigadier has sworn that you'll be made welcome, be you the devil himself."

"I can imagine the devil would be more welcome," Killian murmured as his gaze moved to Deirdre, who still stood by Lachtna.

Conall followed his gaze, frowning as he took in his sister's damp-streaked skirts and dirty bare feet. She looked like a street urchin. Then his eyes blazed as a thought struck him. "Och, well now, about the lass." He bent to whisper in MacShane's ear.

Deirdre felt herself coloring as the whispery breath of her brother's unheard words filtered toward her. She could not hear what Conall said, but the leap of life in MacShane's blue eyes assured her that it was pure mischief.

When Conall raised his head with a chuckle, MacShane stared at her, and the look in his piercing eyes set Deirdre's blood racing. This was the famous MacShane, the man her brothers had told her tales about for the better part of a week. This was the man many believed to be in league with the devil, a murderous warrior without mercy or weakness. And he was looking at her with an intensity that she suspected he reserved for his foes.

Her instinct for self-preservation made her take a hasty step back when he moved toward her, and she saw his black brows lower over his strangely light eyes. When he stood before her he reached out and put a hand under her chin to lift her face to his.

"I did not mean to frighten you in the meadow, lass. I'd not harm so lovely a creature."

Deirdre stared up at him, fascinated as much by his touch as his gaze. He was not at all what her brothers had led her to expect. He was daunting with his black garb and stern face, that was true, but he was not the battle-scarred ogre they had described.

"You're not ugly at all!" she blurted in surprise.

The frank wonder in her voice pierced Killian in an unguarded place. The stable master's daughter, Conall had informed him. His guess had been correct. What he had not guessed from his meeting with her, and what Conall had added, was that she was *slow-witted*.

His gaze moved over her bright golden hair wildly tangled in corkscrews. And her eyes. Had he ever seen eyes so fine? A forest of gold-tipped lashes surrounded eyes so green a gray they reminded him of the misty waters of a lough. Aye, she was very like the face in his dream. Such waste of beauty, he thought with a surge of anger against nature's cruel joke.

Deirdre watched his expression darken and alarm sped through her.

Killian's hand fell to his side as he saw fear reflected on those misty-emerald depths. "Tell her I mean her no harm," he said to Darragh. "Is she so dimwitted that she cannot understand even that?"

Dimwitted? Deirdre's eyes narrowed as she spied the gleam of mischief in her brother's eyes. She took a step toward Conall. "You told the man my wits wander?"

"Now, Dee. A stable hand's feeble-minded daughter, that's how you look," Conall replied before laughter got the better of him.

"Conall!" she scolded, and then raised her arms as if she would embrace him.

She smiled at him so sweetly that Conall knew something was about to happen but he could not puzzle it out before she balled her fists into small hard knots and struck him hard on both ears.

Caught off guard by the unexpected blow, he yelped like a schoolboy as Darragh's unsympathetic laughter rang in his ears.

Without a glance at the man called MacShane, Deirdre grabbed her skirts and fled toward the house on bare feet.

"Am I to understand that the lass is related to you?" MacShane inserted quietly into Darragh's laughter and Conall's muttered curses.

"In a manner of speaking," Darragh murmured, deciding not to spoil his brother's jest.

"Aye, the she-devil's name is Deirdre," Conall added. "Though for the life of me I cannot understand why she is not named *Faolan,* for at times she is more like a wolf cub than a lass."

"Welcome to Nantes, MacShane," Darragh said, mirth twitching his lips. "You'll nae be bored in the Fitzgerald household."

"No, I do not think I will," Killian murmured as he gazed at the door through which Deirdre had fled.

"Idiot! Dolt! Fool!" Deirdre slammed the door and marched to the center of her bedroom. How could Conall have played such a nasty trick on her? And she—she had had no better sense than to walk right into the baited trap.

She turned to look at herself in the mirror above her mantel and the reflection confirmed her worst fears. Bedraggled and mud-smeared, her hair tumbling about her shoulders like the remains of a haystack after a high wind, she was every inch a lamentable picture.

"You're a sight, lass, and make no mistake about it," Brigid offered from her chair by the window where she sat hemming a gown.

"You'll never guess what Conall and Darragh have done to me."

"Aye, I know. I saw it all from this window. And that ashamed I am that ye allowed them to best ye, and with company watching," Brigid answered sourly.

"Then you did not see the last. I knocked the wind out of Conall. Calling me a dim-wit, I should have—"

The ridiculous scene her words painted made her put a hand against her mouth to still the laughter that threatened to erupt. She had been acutely embarrassed before a guest. She had every right to be angry. Yet, the specter of herself planting a fist on either side of Conall's head would not fade, and amusement got the better of her.

"We have given our visitor a rare picture of ourselves as rag-mannered, brawling nobles," she said when her laughter subsided.

"Aye, the Fitzgeralds always were ones to prefer a dog-and-pony show to proper genteel pursuits," Brigid said as she came forward to help Deirdre out of her dirty clothing.

"Did you see him, the one they call MacShane?"

"Aye," Brigid mumbled.

Deirdre shrugged elegantly. "He's not at all what I expected. For a fierce warrior the likes of which Darragh and Conall described, I thought he would be taller and broader, with a dozen wicked scars."

"Handsome is as handsome does," Brigid replied obliquely.

Deirdre closed her eyes the better to recall the details of his strong, hard face. "I suppose he's pleasant enough for a woman's tastes. Black hair, blue eyes, 'tis a combination I'm partial to myself." Strangely, she felt a trembling inside her. Blue eyes. Black hair. Why should those words seem fateful? She could think of no reason. "He stares. His eyes seem to see through a body." She shook her head. "I do not believe I like his stare."

"Sure'n he should have them eyes put right out, seeing as how Mistress Fitzgerald doesn't approve," Brigid replied.

"I did not say I do not approve, precisely," Deirdre countered. "Perhaps 'tis not so much that I do not like his eyes as that they disturb me. 'Tis like looking at a reflection of oneself bared of all pretense and comeliness." She shivered delicately. "'Twas like the feeling I had as a child, you remember, when I thought the fairies visited me."

Brigid's expression sharpened. "There's magic in the man?"

"Magic? Oh no." Deirdre looked away from her nurse's sharp eyes. She was betraying far too much interest in the man. "'Tis only that MacShane wields a very pointed gaze. I wonder that he carries a sword. Surely he can carve his victims at will with that razor-sharp stare!" She laughed, pleased with her joke.

"Is he man enough to carve up a plump partridge named Miss Deirdre Fitzgerald, that's worry enough for me."

Deirdre stepped out of her gown as it fell to her ankles. "You need not worry. After our introduction, I doubt he will ever think of me as anything other than a dirty, spoiled child."

"If 'tis so, then shame on ye," Brigid replied. She bent down and picked up the discarded gown, shaking her head as she spied a rip in the hem. "A lad likes his lass to have a bit of sparkle in her, and ye've given him nothing to set his heart upon."

"Perhaps he'd prefer this display." Deirdre pirouetted about the room, her petticoats lifting in a swirl to show slim ankles, strong shapely calves, and the neat indentation of dimpled knees.

Brigid clucked her tongue in disapproval.

Deirdre flung herself across her bed and rolled onto her back, tucking her arms behind her head. "Oh, Brigid, do not pout. I have no designs on the forbidding MacShane. Conall said he was once bound for the Church. Perhaps he keeps his priestly vows."

Brigid did not reply. She had seen no more of Killian MacShane than a second-story window would allow, but that was enough to convince her that he was not a man much given to thwarting his desires. A tall man with powerful shoulders, he had stood in the Fitzgerald yard and appraised the house as though he had come to purchase it.

"He's come for something, and that's a fact!" she muttered.

Deirdre glanced about the dining hall in disappointment. "What do you mean? Did you drive him away, Da?"

"Aye, I might have, had he dared show his face to me," Lord Fitzgerald grumbled from his place at the head of the table. "Yer brothers, like scared rabbits, hied off with MacShane before I got a look at him." He eyed his daughter suspiciously. "Is that a new gown?"

Deirdre touched the lace at the neckline of her new

rose-silk gown and said, "This? Da, you never remember which you've seen and which you haven't."

Lord Fitzgerald nodded absently. It was true that he never paid much attention to his daughter's gowns. What he paid attention to was the modiste's bill. "Well, 'tis a very pretty picture ye make, lass, and sorry I am there's none to see it."

Deirdre took her place at the table feeling defeated in a battle she had not fully realized she was waging. "Where did Conall and Darragh take him? 'Tis like them to prevent me from amending my wretched impression of the morning."

"They've gone to Nantes, whoring, nae doubt," Lord Fitzgerald grumbled. "I do not expect them before morning."

Lady Elva smiled at her stepdaughter. "There'll be another, better time to make a good impression."

"MacShane's no man to impress, now or ever," Lord Fitzgerald said. "I'll nae have his like eyeing me daughter. Ye're to keep to yer room when he's about."

"Da!" Deirdre looked from her father to her stepmother and back. "Is the man so much a brute that you fear he will snatch me out from under the nose of a Fitzgerald man? If 'tis so, I'd best wed an army, and quickly, for there's no protection to be had under this roof."

Lord Fitzgerald snorted. "Ye best be wed to yer supper before yer tongue snatches it from ye."

Deirdre picked up her fork. Her father's mood was unalterable where MacShane was concerned. It made her all the more determined to learn what it was about the man that he mistrusted and feared.

"He is a most polite young man," Lady Elva offered into the silence of the meal. When Deirdre glanced at her in surprise, she added, "He was most solicitous in offering his sympathies upon learning of the weakened wits of my daughter."

"*Wirra!* The lad's mad!" Lord Fitzgerald answered.

Deirdre hid her smile with a spoonful of soup. So, MacShane had learned the truth, or part of it. The summer was beginning to show promise. MacShane might not be an ogre, but two minutes in his company had convinced her that he would not be an easy man to know . . . and there was nothing she liked so much as a challenge.

Chapter Six

Fey crouched in a midnight-dark alley on the waterfront of Nantes and waited until the last of the footfalls died. Safe. For a short while. In the morning Darce would come looking for his little beggar, the wicked iron buckle of his belt flashing in the morning light.

No, that was wrong. Darce would never come looking for anyone again. Darce was dead.

Fey cringed, remembering how that buckle had gleamed in the lantern light as Darce had swung it. Sniffling back sobs, Fey reached back to rub one of the many welts that belt had raised. Uncertain whether the sticky substance was sweat or blood, Fey sniffed it. Blood.

"Damn Darce's rotten black heart to hell!" Fey muttered and angrily wiped away new tears. Who would have expected gold to be among the coins a stranger threw a beggar's way?

Fey pulled the ragged shirt from the abused skin and shivered. Darce had not believed it. Darce had been certain that Fey had cut the purse of an aristocrat, something that Darce strictly forbade because theft was a hanging offense.

"Beg your livelihood, do not steal it!" Darce always

warned the ragamuffin children he protected from the workhouse.

Fey was only one of many whom Andre Darce had tutored and then sent into the streets to beg from passersby. Each child kept one-fourth of whatever he begged. In exchange Darce gave him a dry warm place to sleep, an evening meal, and protection from the workhouse and the other beggars who vied for key positions on the streets. They all feared Darce and left his brats alone. In spite of the occasional flare of Darce's brutal temper that earned the offender bruises, Fey had had little to complain about.

The girls Darce kept did not fair as well. By the age of eleven, they spent most of their hours on the street after dark. The boys' lives were the better part . . . until now.

"Base-born bastard off a pock-ridden whore!" Fey mumbled in Gaelic without conscious thought. Gaelic had been the language of Fey's mother, but she had died when Fey was eight, and life in Brittany had taught the Irish child that French and Breton were better languages for begging in France. So, too, had Fey learned the value of new ways of dressing and acting, ways that no one had uncovered.

With dark hair cropped short and wearing breeches and a shirt, everyone who saw Fey assumed that they saw a young boy. That was not surprising. After four years of the masquerade, barring an incident or two when the call of nature had nearly given her away, Fey had ceased to think of herself as a girl.

Yet, the time of hiding was coming to an end. And then what? Life in the streets as one of Darce's whores? No, not Darce's whore. Darce was dead.

"Should have hid the gold," Fey murmured. Instead, as always, Darce had been offered a fair share of it and Fey had lost it all. Every beggar in Nantes knew of the peculiar turn of mind that made Darce dangerous. 'Twas said a child was never seen again once he had crossed Darce. It had done Fey no good to protest that the gold was not stolen. Darce had not believed it.

When the buckle had first bitten into Fey's skin, she had scarcely believed it. There had been beatings before, but not with a force that tore skin. When Fey realized that

Darce would not stop but was bent on murder, she had done the only thing possible and pulled her dagger in defense.

Fey wrapped her thin arms about her bony knees, wishing she could shrink into a tiny speck and disappear before daylight. Yet, there was total resignation in the sigh she uttered. Flight was useless. There was scarcely a sailor or pub owner who would not recognize her. It was one of the drawbacks to life with Darce. When they learned that Darce had been murdered, none of the townspeople would hide her. They would seek out Darce's murderer, and when they did, Fey would die.

Fey gave short consideration to hiding aboard a ship but dismissed it. The worst time of her life—other than this night—had been during a short excursion aboard a ship where seasickness colored every memory of the voyage. No, even a slit throat was preferable to that tortured living death. So, she must wait to die, all because the foolish generosity of a well-to-do stranger had ended in death.

"Served the bastard right!" Fey continued as the desire for revenge flowed in warming pulses through her bruised body. If she ever found the stranger who had tricked her with gold, she would drive the sharp length of her blade through his liver, too.

Fey suddenly shot to her feet. If she was to die, she would not die easily or as a coward. She had perhaps five hours before daylight, time enough to find a new hole to hide in.

Killian felt more alive and less angry with the world as he and his companions followed a meandering street through the dockside of Nantes. It was nearly daybreak. The brandy humming in his veins would soon claim him in sleep. Only the promise of a clean, louse-free, goosedown mattress awaiting him at the Fitzgeralds kept him from dismounting and taking a bed in one of the boardinghouses they passed.

He glanced at Conall and Darragh, who rode ahead of

him. Darragh dozed as his horse walked a familiar path. Their loquaciousness had been drowned by spirits and for that Killian was grateful. The Fitzgerald brothers shared one of the more lamentable qualities of their countrymen: they loved the sound of their own voices. For hours he had been subjected to story after story until it was all he could do to keep from deserting their company and the tavern. To ease his frustration he had drunk far more than he was accustomed to doing.

Killian smiled in the darkness. He felt a fluid ease in his body and mind that was all too rare. Spirits usually left him in the mood to sermonize. Well, he had done his sermonizing that morning, on the streets of Nantes. The young scoundrel had no doubt accounted himself blessed to have earned five gold francs for nothing more than a thrashing.

What a fool he had made of himself. He had tossed away the coins without glancing at them. Five gold francs! That would teach him to act in the heat of righteous anger. "A costly lesson, to be sure," he murmured.

The *clip-clop* of their horses' hooves made the only sound on the street as Killian momentarily closed his eyes. Immediately the image of gray-green eyes and bright wheat-ripe hair stirred behind his lids. The thought of her stirred him more deeply than he had expected. She was lovely, like a rare marsh orchid sprouted suddenly in the midst of a bog. The fact that her beauty was marred by a wandering mind made him unaccountably sad.

Yet, he was too experienced in the ways of the world to wish her different. Had she her full wits, doubtless the lass would trade on her good looks. If guile were added to that loveliness, she would be a hardened flirt, an aspiring courtesan worthy of a king. It was just as well that her feeble mind kept her from knowing the power she might possess over men. Perhaps it was God's grace given to a lovely fragile spirit. Still, it was bitter to contemplate.

Suddenly there was a movement across his path. It might have been nothing more than a cat's paws on the sandy lane, but then again . . . Killian reined in his horse as the others went on ahead.

A shadow moved, ejected from the gloom of a doorway with unexpected speed. It was much too thick and brief to seem human, but Killian did not wait to find out whether it was a ghost or his imagination. His right hand reached for his pistol as his left hand shot out to grasp at the wind. He did not encounter empty air. His fingers closed hard and tight on a small fist flashing a blade. The fist twisted in his. Killian held tight, muttering a curse as the blade pricked him in the arm.

Bending from the saddle, he expected to face the man who had dared to attack him, but when he looked down into the gloom he saw nothing. If not for struggling hard within his grip he would have doubted that anything had happened, for the Fitzgerald brothers were riding ahead, the only sounds in the lane made by their horses.

"Damn!" Killian felt the blade prick him again, this time in the thigh. In anger he wrenched up his prize and found himself dangling a boy by the arm. For the second time this day he had been accosted by a child. He tucked his pistol back into his pocket and with his free hand jerked the knife from the boy with a vicious twist.

The boy yelped but Killian was too angry to care. He stuck his face close to the child's and said in French, "What a place is this, that children plague men!"

"Let go of me, ye great stinking whoreson!" came back the tear-choked reply in Gaelic. The boy kicked and twisted as he dangled by his captured arm.

It was too dark to see, but a feeling of recognition stole over Killian. Throwing a leg over his saddle, he dismounted without releasing the child. Then, looking back down the lane, he spotted a lantern's glow at the far end. Without saying a word, he dragged the boy toward it.

"Wait! Where are ye taking me? Stop! *Peste! Merde!*" the child cried, only to be silenced by a box to the ear.

"Yell again and I'll choke you and have done with," Killian answered in Gaelic. Immediately the boy ceased struggling.

The lantern was posted at the corner near the entrance to a pub. A couple stood within its glow but they were occupied in an embrace and did not give heed to the man and boy who came toward them.

"You, ratling, who are you?" Killian muttered as he swung the boy around to face him.

Recognition was swift. Even with the mud and fake pox boils washed off, he knew it was the beggar boy he had met that morning. Now a smooth child's face looked up at him, marred only by a mutinous anger in the large, luminous dark eyes.

"You!" Killian spat as fresh anger surged through him. "Did you not steal enough of my gold this morning?"

He paused thoughtfully as his gaze switched to the knife he had wrested from the child. When he looked once more on the cherub-sweet face twisted now in pain and fear, his eyes were wintry.

"Did the gleam of gold whet your appetite for more? God! What a greedy little savage you are. You did not count on being caught, did you? Well, I hope you'll remember what you got for your trouble this morning, for I mean to give you again a generous measure of the same!"

The boy's dark eyes did not even blink as Killian raised his hand. If anything, they seemed to welcome the expected violence. The child did not plead or beg. There were no false tears or sobs. Killian's hand halted in mid-stroke.

"Well, have you nothing to say for yourself?"

The boy did not move or speak.

Killian took in once more the soft contours of the child's face, almost too pretty to be a boy's, and then the emaciated body. Only then did he notice the shredded shirt and the suspicious dark stickiness seeping through the tatters.

He spun the boy about and swore under his breath at the sight of the many vicious bloody welts visible through the ruined shirt. "Who did this to you?"

"Darce."

The boy said the name as though Killian should know it. "Why did Darce do this?"

For a moment, naked fear blazed through the boy's composure. Killian was familiar with the many faces of fear and realized that the child was near blind panic. Then the expression changed and the childish features hardened into a mask of violence. "Because of ye!"

Despite the fact that he held the dagger and had the child in a viselike grip that precluded his doing any harm, Killian's blood chilled. The rage in those childish eyes was mature beyond reckoning.

"Your master or father, or whatever the fiend's connection, beat you half to death because of me, *bouchal? Raumach!*"

"MacShane! We though we'd lost you!"

Killian looked up in annoyance to find Darragh and Conall riding toward him. In the last moments he had forgotten their existence.

"What have you there?" Conall peered down at the two people under the lantern. "A lad, is it? Did he throw himself under your horse's hooves? 'Tis an old trick to gain your sympathy. Do not be taken in." He drew his pistol and aimed it at the boy, but he was so drunk that the barrel wavered back and forth until it came to point at Killian's chest. "Away, rascal, afore I end your miserable life!"

"I'll thank you to put that away before you blow my head off," Killian said coolly. "I can handle one wee bairn with murder in his heart." He shook the boy roughly by the collar as he tried to twist free. "Not so fast, *bouchal*. What's your name?"

Fey hesitated. From the moment she had launched herself at the tall stranger, nothing had gone as she had planned. Chance and outrageous luck had brought her to the tavern where the three Irish nobles were drinking. At first she was not certain that this was the same man who had thrashed her and then given her money. Then she saw the man's eyes, the bright piercing blue depths, and knew that he was.

As she had waited, hiding in a corner and listening, her desire for revenge had changed into the more practical one of theft. With money she could buy passage on a coach out of Nantes. He had money. She would take some of it. But nothing had gone as she had planned and now she was trapped.

Fey gazed up into the angry face hovering above her and suddenly felt very much a child in an adult world. There was violence in that face but no cruelty. Perhaps it was the man's eyes, Fey never reasoned it out. She knew only that the child inside her responded to the mixture of rage and pity and sympathy that lurked in those blazing light eyes. That, and the lilting Irish brogue that flowed from the man.

"Oh, sir, have pity!" Fey flung herself against the man's chest and dug her broken-nailed fingers into his arms. "Save me! Please save me! They'll kill me, they will!"

It was a ploy and Killian recognized it as such, yet the child's bloody back was proof enough that he told only a partial lie. And the sobs racking the thin body were genuine. Against his better judgment he put an arm about those frail shoulders and heard himself say, "I don't believe this performance, but 'tis late and I'm more drunk than I prefer to be. Until I'm of a better frame of mind and can sort this out, you will come with me."

Fey did not protest when she was picked up and carried back to the man's horse. Her battered skin burned like hot coals, and her anger dissolved into fear as she remembered Darce's throat washed in a scarlet flood. If she went with the stranger, at least she would be in a place where Darce's friends were not likely to search.

Killian felt the child's shiver and an unwanted tenderness blossomed in his chest. He held no illusions about the ruffian's being a good child or a pleasant one, but the accusation that he was in some way to blame for the welts on the child's back had made it impossible for him simply to walk away.

"He's coming with us, then?" Darragh questioned, too filled with ale to have understood anything of the last moments.

"Aye." Killian climbed into the saddle with the boy in his arms. A moment later he swung the cloak from his shoulders and tucked it about the child as he would have swaddled a babe. "Lie still, *bouchal*, or I'll tie you across my horse's flanks."

"Me name's Fey," she offered in a tiny voice.

"Fey? What sort of name is that for an Irishman?"

Fey did not answer but huddled deeper in the warm folds of the cloak as the man urged his horse forward. She was safe for the moment. Perhaps her luck was changing, but she was cautious by nature and her secret was better kept until she knew this man better.

"What will you do with the bairn?" Conall asked when they had dismounted before the Fitzgerald residence.

"The stable will do well enough for the likes of him," Darragh offered.

"I'd rather the lad were where I could keep an eye on him," Killian answered as he scooped the sleeping child from his saddle.

"You mean to tuck the brat in your bed covers?" Conall shook his head in amazement, then groaned as the effects of the liquor reeled through his brain. "I'd as soon sleep with a wolf cub."

"If he'll not conduct himself civilly, I've a length of rope that will secure him to a bedpost until morning. Good night."

By the time Killian had climbed the stairs to his room, he knew that the child in his arms was no longer asleep. His dead weight had lightened into a tense bundle of expectancy. He did not blame the child. They were strangers and neither of them trusted the other.

Killian dropped his bundle into a chair and stood back, folding his arms across his chest as the child struggled to disentangle himself from the cloak. Finally the dark head emerged.

Fey's eyes widened as they took in and valued every inch of the large, lavishly furnished room. She had heard that some men lived like kings, but until this moment she had never guessed what that phrase meant. Now, confronted by silk tapestries and bed curtains, fancy carpets from the

East, and lavish furnishings, she could only gape. "Is all this yers?"

Killian followed the child's greedy gaze to the silver-and-gold cigar box on the table nearest the chair. "As it happens, none of it is, and I'll thank you not to touch a single item in the room. I'm certain you claim thievery as well as beggary as an accomplishment." He pulled the child's weapon from his belt and turned it over in his hand. "I will not concede to you the appellation of murderer, for you do it so poorly, *bouchal*."

Despite the man's bantering tone, Fey blanched at the mention of murder. In fact, she had accomplished that act with surprising ease.

Killian studied the small boy wrapped in his cloak and remembered that this was a child, after all, and in obvious need of some sort of mothering. "Are you hungry?"

Fey's head shot up. "A pint of ale would nae come amiss!"

"Ha! You gave yourself away then, I'd say. You're an Irishman—uh, Fey. Fey, what sort of name is that?"

Fey lowered her head, the long sweep of her dark lashes brushing her cheeks. "Me mother was thought to be a bit queer in the head. When I was born, she claimed 'twas a fairy's trick, for she never lay with any man. '*Twas the work of fairies, the gift of this fey creature in me bed.*' That's what they told me she said just before she died. The Fey part stuck."

Laughter, coming unexpectedly from the sober-faced man, startled Fey.

"So, you're a changeling," Killian said when his laughter subsided. "Well, 'tis a good tale, not the best I've heard, mind, but a good tale. So tell me, Fey, where do you live?"

Fey lowered her head. "Nowhere."

"Come, everyone lives somewhere. The gutter? The sewer? A brothel, perhaps. Nae, you're yet young for some vices, but I dare swear that will change." Killian looked about, the dampening effects of the brandy beginning to supersede his interest in the foundling. " 'Tis late, *bouchal*. Sit quietly in that chair while I stretch out for a short while." He turned toward the bed and then looked back over his shoulder, his gaze hard. "You'll not run away?"

Fey shook her head.

"Nor steal a thing?"

Again the head shake of denial.

Killian shook his own head. It was the height of madness to trust the child. A few quick strides brought him to his door, where he turned the key in the latch and then pocketed it. When he had discarded his boots, jacket, and vest, he lay back on the inviting softness of the feather tick and fell instantly asleep.

Fey watched the sleeping man for several minutes before curiosity brought her to his bedside.

Darce had taught her to judge a man at a glance, for in a moment's hesitation an opportunity could be lost. There was a streak of perversity in this man; she had seen it at work twice this day. It showed itself in his face. His gaze was hard, uncompromising, ruthless . . . but not cruel. The high forehead and straight nose were those of a thoughtful, educated man. Darce said that when a man took time to think, he lost an opportunity for action, but it did not seem overly to hamper this man.

When she came to the mouth Fey grinned. Softened now in sleep, it betrayed a man of sensitivity and deep feeling, things that he kept hidden from the world in his waking hours. She did not fault him for that.

Satisfied by the inventory, Fey moved on to other things. Where it spread upon the pillow, the man's black hair shone in the candle's faint light. Fey picked up a strand. The cool smooth tress slipped easily through her admiring fingers. Men were not the only things Darce had taught her how to judge. She knew the quality of silk and laces and many other items of contraband. This gentleman's head of hair was of the very best quality and would fetch an excellent price on the wig market.

Fey banished the thought. She doubted the man would sell his hair. He was a gentleman. As for stealing it . . .

Fey looked about until she spied her skean sticking out of the man's waistband. With a thief's touch she slipped it

free. Then, with a last guilty look at the blue-black head of
hair, she tucked the skean inside her waistband. She would
not steal from the man who, perhaps, had saved her life.

Fey turned away from the bed, her eyes seeking a
window. If she kept to the country lanes and traveled by
dark, she would escape.

The window opened with little noise, and a stiff sea
breeze greeted Fey as she climbed out onto the ledge. The
second-story perch did not faze her. She pulled the window shut behind herself and, grasping with fingers and toes
a perch in the house's stone facade, began a slow descent.
In less than a minute her feet touched the ground.

She was turning away from the house when the distinct
aroma of toast and cinnamon reached her. She paused in
mid-stride as her empty stomach twisted in hunger. How
long had it been since she had eaten? At least a day. Darce
had not given her a chance to consume her only meal of
the day.

Almost against her will, Fey retraced her steps until she
spied a candle's glow behind the shrubbery to her right.
Squatting, she peered through a crack in the window and
down into a kitchen. Not a yard from where she crouched
lay three thick slices of toast topped with sugar and
cinnamon. From a steaming cup nearby, the rich dark
smell of cocoa arose.

Fey clutched the windowsill, near swooning with delight
as her mouth watered in anticipation. A quick look confirmed that no one was about. Ten seconds, that was all it
would take to steal the bread. The cocoa, alas, would have
to be left behind.

The basement window was much more shallow than
those of the upper stories, but Fey was small and adept at
fitting herself into small places. She squeezed through the
opening and landed, catlike, on her feet. The bread was in
her hand, its buttery surface slicking her fingers with a
warm golden drizzle, and then the taste of cinnamon
tingled her tongue.

"Did I forget my manners, or did you forget yours,
young sir?"

The hand that fell on Fey's shoulder carried the weight

of capture. Fey flung the toast away, a sob of regret catching in her throat as she whipped out her skean and turned to face the discoverer.

"Well, that's a fine way to treat my breakfast," Deirdre said in a voice that did not betray the fear that flooded through her at the sight of the weapon. She deliberately looked away from it. "I suppose that piece was a bit overly brown. But this one is perfect." She picked up a piece of toast and held it out to the ragamuffin child before her. "Would you care to sample it?"

Fey did not move, too astonished by the young woman to say or do anything. Dressed in a white gown, her head wreathed in the halo glow from the candle sconce on the wall behind her, the lady appeared as ethereal as an angel. The flame struck golden sparks in the masses of hair falling over her shoulders. And her voice—was there any other tongue for an angel to speak but Gaelic?

Deirdre wet her lips, prepared to begin again, for surprise had prompted her to speak Gaelic when, of course, the child was surely a Breton. "You are lost? I see that you are hurt. Would you like a cup of cocoa?"

Fey slowly shook her head, surprised that the angel would change languages. She very much wanted her to be an Irish angel, if angel she was. Perhaps she was the angel of judgment sent to hear a confession of her sin of murder.

"I killed a man," Fey said in Gaelic, the words tumbling out of their own volition. "He tried to kill me but I drew me skean and slit his throat."

Deirdre took a backward step. The Fitzgerald house was not isolated, and they often had wanderers at their door begging for food. Occasionally a thief would break into the larder. The sight of the small beaten child had won her heart instantly, but the talk of murder frightened her. If the child was mad, Deirdre was in danger.

"Who did you kill, child?"

Fey shook her head, tears threatening her. She felt her courage dissolving like salt in warm water. "I did nae mean to kill him. Only he kept hitting me, again and again, and I knew he would kill me!"

The last came out in a wail of regret, and then sobs

shook her thin shoulders as the blade fell from her hand and clattered across the stone floor.

Deirdre picked up the weapon and placed it on a nearby shelf. She did not move toward the child but waited patiently until the hard sobbing eased. When the child raised his head from the crook of his arm, the enormous brown eyes awash with tears that stared back at Deirdre were the most beautiful that she had ever seen.

"Why, you're pretty enough to be a lass!" she exclaimed in surprise.

Fey's chin lifted. "In a pig's eye!"

Deirdre smiled. This was no lunatic but a very frightened child. "I suppose you're a highwayman in the making. What is your name, brigand?"

Fey did not answer immediately. The lady had moved away from the candlelight, and though she was quite pretty, the effect of an angel was diminished. Her face was very pale with fright and there was a smear of cocoa at each corner of her mouth. "Who are ye? Will ye set the servants on me? Will they string me up?"

"So many questions," Deirdre answered mildly. "Will you not help me finish my breakfast? I have a bargain with Cook that I may make toast and cocoa as long as I am gone from her kitchen by first light, and I distinctly heard the cock crow just now." She reached for another slice of toast and offered it. This time Fey grabbed it and stuffed it into her mouth.

Deirdre moved purposefully to the pot on the fire and poured cocoa into another cup "This will help the crumbs go down. I always think cocoa is the very best way to clear the throat, do you not agree?"

Fey looked at the dark surface of the cocoa as if staring into witch's brew. She had smelled it in taverns on occasion and watched the gentry sip delicately at it in the yards of coaching houses, but in all her life she had never had a cup of cocoa for her own.

Guessing the child's thoughts, Deirdre lifted her own cup and blew lightly across the surface. She took a tentative sip and smiled at the troubled dark eyes watching her.

Fey needed no further encouragement. If she was to hang for murder, she would die with the memory of a full cup of cocoa in her middle.

As the child drank, Deirdre pondered what she should do. She was certain that if she left the room, her young thief would vanish. Perhaps she should simply sit with him and wait for a member of the household staff to find them. If she called for help, the boy might panic and hurt himself or someone else.

"Did you climb in the window? Clever lad," she murmured and rose to close the escape.

As she reached the latch, a shadow slipped past the open window followed by the sound of boots. She rose up on her toes and saw a man standing with his arms on his hips staring up at the second floor of the house.

"MacShane!" she whispered in horror and slammed the window. There was one man whose leniency she could not count upon. He was known to be a terror, unforgiving, without mercy. Conall had told her so.

The sound of the closing window drew Killian's attention to the lower part of the house. At last he spied the telltale slit of light pouring from the basement window, and immediately he suspected what had happened.

Only moments after he had fallen asleep a guilty conscience began to plague his peace. He had not even looked after the boy's wounds. When he finally awakened to an empty room he was not surprised. What had he done, after all, to win the boy's trust? Even his horse had been led to a dry stall, rubbed down, and given water and a pail of oats by a conscientious groom. So, of course, Fey had gone in search of food and found a kitchen window off the latch.

He rejected the idea of following Fey's sewer-rat entrance into the kitchen. He was much too big, and the child would likely escape while he tried to wriggle through the small window. He went back inside and, following his nose, found the kitchen stairs. The sound of voices surprised him as he reached the doorway. If Fey had been caught, Killian would have to apologize to the Fitzgeralds for bringing a thief into their home. His expression grim, he stepped into the kitchen.

"But that sounds like marvelous fun, Fey! Perhaps one day you will show me how it's done. Will you have another piece of toast before Cook comes in? I—"

Fey shot to her feet beside Deirdre, her eyes trained on the doorway. With a calm that belied her racing heart, Deirdre rose to her feet, her gaze steady on Fey. "Now, whoever it is, you're not to worry. This is my home. No one will hurt you."

"I would not lie to the lad. There's more than one who would find thievery a hanging offense."

Deirdre whirled about at the voice. "MacShane!" she whispered in undisguised alarm. As if a specter from her worst nightmare, he stood in the doorway, black hair loose about his angry, tight face. He had removed his jacket and, she noted inconsequently, his black shirt was open at the throat.

Killian's gaze moved from Fey to the golden-haired girl who stood beside the boy. It seemed that Fey had found a coconspirator. Despite his anger, it was not dislike that made his gaze linger on her for a moment. Each time she caught him unprepared, surprising him by her resemblance to his dream. Yet, she was real and all too innocent to know in what danger she stood. "You should know better, lass, than to allow thieves to steal from your father. As for the lad, he'll answer to me."

"He's yours?" Deirdre asked wondrously.

"In a manner of speaking," Killian answered. "He's a black-hearted wretch with no scruples and no manners; but when I'm finished with him, he'll think better of stealing so much as a nap."

Deirdre blanched, remembering the vicious welts on the boy's back. She drew in a quick angry breath and said to Fey, "You must believe me, he'll never lay a hand on you again!"

She looked up at Killian. "I have heard of you, sir, yet it did not prepare me for your vicious nature. To batter a child so that—that his body bleeds—" She broke off, astonished by the rage pouring through her veins.

Killian listened to her in disbelief and exasperation. Evidently, anger loosened her tongue and chased away her vacant stare. Perhaps she was not as backward as people believed, only shy and skittish. "Go fetch your father, lass, and have him bring with him a whip from the stable."

A lifetime of chicanery had taught Fey the value of playing upon the pity of others. Her small hand fastened itself about Deirdre's. "Don't let him beat me, miss!"

Killian's mocking gaze met Fey's sly look. "Your cozening days are finished. The lass won't save you."

Deirdre swallowed the lump of pity that rose in her throat. The child was clearly frightened out of his wits. "He's no thief. I gave him the cocoa and bread."

Killian raised his eyes to the girl, noting how absurdly lovely she looked in her rumpled bedclothes. The thought annoyed him. This was none of her business. She should still be abed. "Stand aside, lass."

As he took a step toward them, Deirdre thrust Fey behind her. Where had she put the boy's skean? She spied it above the cupboard. Too late, she realized that MacShane's gaze had followed hers. He reached for the weapon and pocketed it.

Frantic, Deirdre reached for the bread knife that lay on the table and raised it menacingly. "Stay back! You've beaten the lad enough. Have you no mercy?"

Killian paused, taken aback by her words. "You cannot think—? I did not beat the boy! Damnation! Ask him. Ratling, who beat you?"

Fey considered her answer. The lady, silly wench that she was, was prepared to believe any evil of the man. Yet, the lady was an unknown quantity. Her bravery might not last. The man, at least, had proven himself to be fair as well as wrathful. Fey flashed a cherubic smile at the tall angry man. "Ye did nae beat me, but I'd nae give a sou for the future."

Deirdre looked down at the boy, her eyes searching the young face. "You need not be afraid to tell me what really happened. He will not beat you again. My father is Lord

Fitzgerald, and he will have MacShane whipped from the door if I ask it.''

Killian went cold inside. No one had ever dared threaten him quite like that in his life. Whip him from the door? Did she think she defended an innocent?

He took a step toward her, his face tight with anger. ''The lad's name is Fey. I plucked him from the dockside of Nantes a few hours ago. He had drawn his skean and was displaying a curious desire to slip his steel between my ribs. I have yet to ascertain why, but I shall.''

He advanced another step. ''But for my foolish sympathy for a beaten ratling, he would not be here now. I offered him the comfort of my room for the night. He has repaid my hospitality by stealing away and breaking into the kitchen.''

The third step brought him within arm's length of Deirdre, and he saw that his method was effective, for her eyes were wider than he would have believed possible. ''I had Conall Fitzgerald's permission to bring the lad here, but I now believe that his advice of putting a pistol ball through the lad's head might have been the better answer!''

Deirdre's mouth went dry as the man's blast of anger scorched her, but she was not a Fitzgerald for nothing. She had been weaned on the blustering of men. ''Why, then, did you not follow that admirable advice?''

Killian made a violent movement with his hand, and Deirdre flinched; but she did not put down the knife or release Fey. A grudging respect for her bravery moved within him, and then suspicion followed it.

''You are Lord Fitzgerald's daughter, are you not?''

''I am,'' she answered, and her voice surprised her with its composure. ''And, I assure you, I'm as sound of mind as I am of limb.''

A familiarity with Darragh and Conall Fitzgerald made his complete understanding swift, and he reddened in spite of himself. He had been made the butt of one of their jokes. Lord Fitzgerald's daughter was not weak-minded or slow. She must think him as simple and gullible as he had believed her to be.

A spark of impish mischief in Fey's dark eyes warned

Killian, and he reached out to grab him as the lad tried to dart past. Shaking him like a dusty rag, he said, "You're a young devil with no pretense to manners."

"Skelping him about is a certain method to rectify the matter, I'm sure," Deirdre answered.

Killian looked up, annoyance replacing his chagrin. "Can you do better? And give me that damned knife before I slap you as well!"

Deirdre hesitated as his brilliant blue eyes bore down on her. Every instinct told her that this was defeat, but that very realization sparked her anger. How dare he, a stranger, enter her home and order her about! She would not yield her weapon to him. Instead she placed it gingerly back on the table beside the bread loaf. When she raised her eyes to his once more, she felt flushed with triumph. "You know nothing of children, 'tis plain to see."

Killian resisted the urge to shake her as he had shaken Fey. "What do you suggest, m'lady?"

Deirdre folded her arms across her bosom, aware at last that she stood in her bedclothes. "I would begin by stripping the lad of those rags and bathing his back. You'd do as much for your horse."

"My horse deserves it," he muttered, though he had had the same thoughts moments earlier. "As for you, ratling, I'm of a mind to send to Nantes for the authorities."

Having watched the battle of wits between the two with no more interest than for her chance to escape, Fey now perceived the wisdom of her choice. The lady might have courage on her side, but the man called MacShane had the power. Fey smiled a smile to do an angel proud. "I do nae care if ye beat me, sir, only do nae turn me over to the authorities. They'll string me up, sir, that they will, for nothing more than being a motherless hooligan Irishman!"

Killian mastered his inclination to smile and gave Fey another rough shake. "Beat you, can I? At my leisure? Unconditionally?"

Deirdre reached for the knife a second time but Killian's

hand shot out and captured her wrist. "As for you, Mistress Fitzgerald, I won't strike you, though, by God, you've given me more than enough cause."

"You're hurting me," Deirdre protested, but she did not try to twist free of the fingers wrapped around her wrist.

Killian released her, surprised that he had touched her. He had meant only to snatch the knife out from under her grasp. The sound of footsteps in the corridor outside the kitchen further disconcerted him.

When the Fitzgeralds' cook walked into her domain she was brought up short by the sight of Lady Deirdre in her bedclothes confronting a tall black-haired man with a ruffian boy in his grip. Yielding to motherly instinct, she grabbed a chair and charged the stranger with a yowl of fury.

Killian stepped easily out of the woman's path and plucked the chair from her grasp with a neat twist. The farcical elements of the moment were not lost on him. As the cook turned on him, her cap askew and her face a portrait of affront, he succumbed to the amusement that he had been holding at bay.

Deirdre stared in amazement as the masculine laughter filled the kitchen. With his head thrown back and his face split by a smile, MacShane's hard features were transformed into handsomeness. When he looked down at her, it was as though another, younger man stood before her, his vivid blue eyes softened and warmed by a very human emotion. Without reasoning it out she smiled back at him.

Killian sobered instantly, for the servants who had been following the cook thronged in the doorway, their faces avid with excitement. "You will excuse me, Mistress Fitzgerald. Bow to the lady, ratling, we're off."

After the most brief of nods to Deirdre, he turned and strode out, pushing Fey before him by the scruff of the neck.

"Whoever was that gentleman, m'lady?" Cook whispered.

"That was no gentleman, that was MacShane," Deirdre answered, as nonplussed as the cook.

Chapter Seven

Back in his room, Killian poured water into a porcelain basin from the matching pitcher and splashed handfuls of it onto his face. It was dawn; and though he had had little sleep, he was in no mood to rest. Beside the basin lay a clean linen towel, its hem embroidered in tiny pink rosebuds. He ignored it, wiping his face on the sleeve of his shirt. No doubt Lady Deirdre would be horrified, he mused, but such amenities were rare in a soldier's life. He had long ago become accustomed to using whatever was handy and often to going without. Hunger, abstinence, poverty, and self-denial were part of a soldier's life.

A thought struck him. Those criteria were also a part of a priestly existence. Until now he had not considered that, but it seemed that he had changed one life of privation and solitude for another. The boy destined to become a priest had become instead a professional soldier. Instead of saving men's lives, he had spent the better part of the last ten years taking them. There must be some moral there, but he had no time to consider it now.

He turned his head to look at Fey, who stood in the middle of the room shifting his weight from foot to foot. The child's wary expression altered immediately, becoming blank and smiling, toadying in nature. The change irritated Killian, and his voice was more harsh that he intended. "Well? You might as well tell me why you ran away, though it will not prevent your punishment."

Fey's cherubic smile widened. " 'Tis not what ye think, m'lord. 'Twas only the powerful gnawing of me innards that drove me to the kitchen. The smell was too much a temptation, with me having no supper nor likely to get any."

Fey came forward, head lowered in the manner of a cowered animal. "I would nae blame ye if ye was to beat me. 'Tis what I deserve. Only, I will nae be able to work so hard afterwards, what with the stripes on me back already."

Her expression changed to one of hope. "Would ye nae consider beating me a day or two from now, when I'm better? I'd be good to ye, if ye'd let me. There's things I know could make a man happy to have me."

When MacShane did not answer but continued to stare at her with an unreadable expression, Fey's smile faltered. What could she do to make the man want to keep her? Should she reveal the truth—a truth not even Darce had guessed? Fey's translucent lids lowered as her voice dropped to a husky whisper. "I know how to make the gentleman below stairs stand tall. I know how to please ye better than them pox-ridden whores of the streets!"

As Fey's small hand reached out to touch the placket of his breeches, Killian recoiled as before a hot poker and shoved the child away. "Good God!" he whispered coarsely. "A catamite! Is there no end to your infamy?"

"I did nae . . . mean to . . . anger ye," Fey said in quick gasps that ended in dry sobs. "Twas only . . . I wanted to please ye."

The raw edge of Fey's voice tightened the knot of anger in Killian's stomach. He was not a puritan, but the boy's proclivity for depravity was straining the limits of his tolerance. Yet, what could he expect from a lad he had picked up on the docks?

His expression remained hard but his voice was mild as he said, "I apologize for striking you. 'Tis not your fault that you're steeped in every sort of devilment known to mankind. Did your master send you to ply that trade among sailors?''

Fey's face did not alter.

Killian swore under his breath. "How old are you?''

Fey shrugged, the old sly gleam returning to her eyes. "I'm small for me age. I can be ten, or eight if ye'd like.''

Annoyance flashed in Killian's face. "What I want is for you to be yourself, if you can remember who that is.''

"I'm eleven . . . I think.'' Fey's face grew thoughtful. A moment before, she had been about to reveal the truth about herself, but it seemed inconsequential now. "What's to become of me?''

Killian's black brows lowered even more. "How should I know? Oh, I'll not have you hanged, if that's what worries you.''

Fey eyed the man before her in frank appraisal. "Ye will nae beat me?''

"I may take the flat of my hand to your britches if provoked,'' Killian amended.

A quick grin lit her face. "Then I will stay with ye!''

"No.'' Killian shook his head. "You cannot do that.''

"I'm strong, and wily. I could cook for ye, clean for ye—''

"Steal for me?'' Killian interjected softly.

Fey's eyes widened, and then her lovely smile blossomed full. "Ye're having me on!''

"Aye, that I am. I'll string you up myself if ever I catch you stealing again!''

His voice had taken on a menacing edge but Fey did not back away this time. "Ye'll have me, then?''

"No, *bouchal*.'' Killian dug into his pocket, pulled out his purse, and emptied half the coins into his hand. "Take this and find yourself lodgings at an inn on the main highway to Paris. Buy yourself a bed, a joint of lamb, and a bottle of ale. When you get to Paris, ask for the apartments of the Duchesse de Luneville. Say that MacShane sent you. You'll be given work there, and perhaps one day we'll see each other again.''

Fey listened in polite silence, her eyes averted from the

gleaming gold. She had no intention of leaving this man. If she stayed with him she would not be put on the street to beg or endure merciless whippings or days of starvation.

Yet, Fey was too steeped in the greed and avarice of men not to suspect that she would need to offer him something in return for his generosity. But what could it be?

With the jaded vision of a street urchin surveying her prey, she gazed at the tall strong man. He was splendidly made, handsome and virile—her hand had briefly touched strong evidence—but one never knew about a man's tastes. "Do ye nae like the ladies, m'lord?"

"My name's MacShane," he answered shortly. "I prefer women. Ladies are terribly tiresome to woo."

"I shall keep that in mind," a cool voice remarked from the doorway behind them.

"I knocked twice," Deirdre said as she advanced into the room. "I heard voices, so I did hesitate, but water cools quickly in the morning air and the boy should scrub while it's hot." She turned to nod at the pair of servant girls who followed her, one of whom carried a pair of steaming kettles and the other an iron washtub from the laundry.

"I brought the child a fresh pair of britches and a shirt. They belong to the stable master's son."

The slight emphasis she put on the last words was not lost on Killian, but he only rested his hands on his hips, amazed at the change that had taken place in her in so short a time. Dressed in a wine-red manteau, her hair caught up off her neck and covered by a small linen cap, she appeared a very proper young mademoiselle. Killian's gaze flickered to her feet. She even wore slippers.

Aware of the hard blue gaze on her, Deirdre crossed the room in a slow, elegant glide to deposit on a chair the clothes she carried.

When MacShane had disappeared with the child she had not known what to do. She could scarcely have run after them and demanded to know what he intended to do with the boy. Nor had she thought it wise to wake her family and bring them into this odd business. Her father did not like MacShane. He would put the darkest of interpretations upon MacShane's involvement with the child who had broken into their kitchen and drawn a knife on her. Then she had hit upon the idea of bringing the child fresh clothes and bandages. It was the perfect excuse to go to MacShane's apartment, and the child was badly in need of someone's attention.

She had hurried so to dress that she had torn one of the new Parisian silk stockings Conall had brought her. But MacShane would not know that. Neither would he be aware of the rapid tattoo of her heart nor see the tremor of her knees beneath her morning gown. This was her home. MacShane could not say or do anything to prevent her from looking after the child.

She turned to him and held out a small stoppered bottle. " 'Tis horse liniment. O'Grady swears by it as a panacea for every kind of abrasion."

MacShane did not reach for the bottle but continued to stare at her.

Undismayed by his rudeness, she turned to Fey. "Have Captain MacShane put this on your back when you're bathed. 'Twill sting, but you're a brave lad and can bear it. O'Grady used it on my scraped knees whenever I took a tumble as a bairn. When you are dressed, come down to the kitchen for breakfast. Cook is expecting you."

Without a backward glance at MacShane, Deirdre walked out of the room followed by the two Fitzgerald servants.

Killian stared at the empty doorway. Lord Fitzgerald's daughter had just flirted with him!

Fey, too, had been impressed by the lady's composure. "She's nae afraid of either of us," she murmured a little in awe.

"Then she should be!" Killian grumbled and turned to the child. "Well, *spalpeen*? There's your bathwater. Faith! You reek of fish and dung."

Fey looked at the tub of steaming water in horror. She could not undress before him without revealing her secret. "Ye cannot mean me to step in there? I'll boil." She began backing away. "I won't do it!"

Killian caught Fey before she reached the door and

hauled her kicking and screaming toward the washtub, peeling away her clothing as he went. "You will bathe, my lad! Hold still! I won't—! *Mille murdher!*"

Fey slid out of the big man's embrace, her face pale with alarm. "I was going to tell ye, I swear it!"

Killian stared at Fey, his eyes moving slowly from the child's face back down the length of the young body. "You're nae a lad! You're a *lass!*"

Fey grabbed her torn britches from the floor and held them before her naked loins. "I never said I was a lad. 'Twas ye who called me that!"

"You let me believe, *ma girsha*, didn't you?"

Fey's eyes flickered toward the bed and away. He was very angry with her, but perhaps she might still be able to persuade him to keep her. She lowered the garment she held, a forthright look in her dark eyes. "I said I'd be good to ye, I meant it! I'd do anything for ye. *Anything!*"

Killian lifted a hand only to lower it again as the child before him flinched. "I'd not take you for all the gold in Nantes harbor, you thieving, lying little whore!"

The accusation stung her as none of his other words had. "I'm nae a whore! I do not like the trade."

Killian's voice was wintry. "Have you tried it?"

Fey shrugged, hugging the scraps of cloth tighter against her thin frame. "A lass has little else to offer. But a lad can beg on the streets. He can sweep up in shops, run errands. With a protector he can keep shy of the worst sort that would force themselves on him."

The anger washed out of Killian as Fey summed up her life and her reasons for masquerading as a boy in those few sentences. "How long have you been on your own?"

"Four years." Fey gave a shuddery sigh as her muscles relaxed. It was hard to remember to trust this man when she had not trusted anyone for so long. "I did not think it made much difference, me being a boy. Only now..." She looked down at her chest, where only the most discerning gaze would realize that breasts were beginning to bud.

"Aye, we must do something about that," Killian murmured, looking away. "Get in the tub, la—lass, and do not tell me that you'll drown. When you're clean, put on the clothes the lady brought you. They'll do for now.''

"Ye'll keep me?'' Fey cried as Killian headed for the door.

"I'm not in the habit of cosseting bairns!'' he answered unhelpfully.

When the door shut behind him, Fey collapsed on the floor and gathered herself into a tight ball. There were no sobs this time. The emotions careening through her were too strong for tears. MacShane would not rape her or beat her. And there was the lovely lass who had fed her, brought her clean clothes, and promised her more. Perhaps she had died, after all. Perhaps Darce had beaten her to death and she had found heaven at last.

Deirdre had paused at the top of the stairway after sending the maids below, her heart beating so rapidly that she knew the agitation showed in her face and gave away her feelings. She was elated, exhilarated, triumphant: all because of the flash of interest she had spied in MacShane's blue eyes. It had not been flattering or particularly admiring . . . but it had been passionate.

That look had caught her utterly by surprise. Yet, why should it have? She had been raised in France in a season when all women could expect to be admired, flattered, and constantly pursued. She knew that ardor was but a polite mask for lust. If MacShane had no better manners than to reveal his baser instincts to her, it did not follow that men like Cousin Claude did not have those instincts. She had lived in a household dominated by men too long not to know better.

That was what excited her—that, and something more. He was a stranger, yet those hot blue eyes were hauntingly familiar, as something remembered from long ago. If he had smiled again she would have remembered, she was certain of it.

A tiny pinprick of pain began between her brows, the same annoying pain that had awakened her during the night. She put a hand to the point between her brows and massaged the spot. Why should thoughts of MacShane always make her head ache?

When a door in the hall behind her opened, she swung about, embarrassed to have been caught daydreaming.

MacShane strode toward her, head bent in thought. When he realized who stood in his path, he checked his pace as if annoyed.

Deirdre waited patiently for him to speak. After all, he had ignored her moments before. He ran both hands through his long, uncombed hair but it was in lamentable disarray. His shirt was spotted where water had dripped from his face, and he had not yet taken a razor to his beard. Black stubble contoured his hard jaw and set off the lines of his wide firm mouth. All in all, he looked the part of the remote, ill-tempered Irish soldier whom her brothers had warned her of, but she could not forget the sound of his laughter. It had echoed through the kitchen and startled her with the unexpectedness of its warmth. He was unlike any man she had ever known before, and that in itself was intriguing.

"Is your father awake?" he asked without preamble. "I must see him."

"Good morning to you, too, MacShane," she answered with a polite nod. So much for flattering looks!

The frown puckering his brow faded but his expression remained austere. "Aye, my manners are wanting. Good day to you, Lady Deirdre."

Deirdre smiled until her dimple was on full display. His gaze was on her once more, hard and unwavering. This time there was no passion in the blue eyes, only the curious, steady gaze of a man sizing up a problem. "Da will not be about for hours yet, sir. 'Tis scarcely dawn. We may be country mice but we keep city hours. Perhaps I can help you."

Killian glanced back down the hall. " 'Tis a terrible vice of mine, imagining that I can cure the world's ills when there's drink warming me veins," he muttered.

Deirdre followed his gaze. "Does your problem concern the child? I am quite good with children."

Her coolness annoyed Killian. What had happened to the wild-haired lass with dirty bare feet who had ridden light-as-the-wind on the back of a seasoned campaign horse? Where was the wildcat in night clothes who had drawn a bread knife on him to protect a street urchin whose crimes included murdering his employer? The poised, serene creature before him was not the sort a man would confide in nor was she the stuff of a man's dreams from which he awoke aroused. She was a lady fit only for gentlemen who visited gilded salons and scented gardens. Well, he was no gentleman, and she might as well learn it.

" 'Tis no matter for a lass," he said curtly.

Deirdre's pleasant feelings evaporated. She had been dismissed. "Then do not allow me to detain you." She turned and started away before she remembered her own manners. "When your temper has improved you may find my father in the stables. 'Tis his custom to ride at midmorning. Bring the lad with you. I'm certain Da would like to meet him."

"The lad's a *she*."

Deirdre turned about and said, her voice cool, "Do not mistake me for a fool, sir. I have seen the child."

Killian regarded her steadily, his eyes narrowed. "Aye, and what you saw was a lass."

"How can you expect me to believe you when—" Deirdre's voice faltered as the sound of splashing water was heard from the end of the hallway.

Killian regarded her now with a stare of undisguised amusement. "I may be rude and ill mannered, but I know when I'm looking at a lass's quim."

Blood stung Deirdre's cheeks. Even Conall and Darragh would not have used such language in her presence. "You've nae manners, MacShane!"

The grin that had teased Killian's mouth disappeared. " 'Tis why I'd prefer to deal with your da. 'Tis your own meddling that brings you into my affairs.

"I'm a soldier, nae a courtier," he added as he approached her.

When he was only a foot from her he placed his hands on her shoulders, and the pressure of his touch betrayed the latent strength he possessed. He stood so close that she discerned for the first time several tiny white scars crisscrossing his brow and the regular pulse beat at the base of his throat. He leaned toward her, and for one wild moment she thought that he would kiss her.

"You've a way of walking, lass, that puts a man in mind of earthy pleasures. But if your virginal conscience shies at the thought of ravishment, if you need soft words and fancy manners, find yourself another."

Deirdre took a hasty step back, breaking the warm contact of his hands. The insult was so outrageous that she could not at first find words with which to answer him. *Find herself another, indeed!* He had seen through her cool manners and knew she found him attractive. What's more, he found it amusing; no, he found *her* amusing.

Deirdre straightened her shoulders and fitted him with her haughtiest stare. He would not get the better of her. "Mind your manners, sir! I am not afraid of you, nor is ravishment likely to happen beneath my father's roof."

The threat had no visible effect on MacShane. He simply crossed his arms. Yet, his mouth was less hard as he said, " 'Tis a relief to know it would not be ravishment, lass, yet I trust to your father's good name that you'd come to me a virgin."

Deirdre gasped. "You—you're ill mannered, rude, arrogant, and quite offensive, Captain MacShane!"

Killian nodded. " 'Tis a fair beginning for an insult, but you end too soon, lass. You should call my friendship with your brothers into account, remind me of your own considerable consequence, and perhaps even question my parentage. Aye, and you should not give me the advantage of my rank. It spoils the effect." Quite to her surprise he smiled at her. "But I own, I do like you in a hot rage, lass. That I do."

"You're mad!" Deirdre replied.

"That's the way of it. Now stamp your foot. You do know how?" he added carelessly.

Nonplussed, Deirdre could only stare at him.

"You've not the eyes of a termagant," he said thoughtfully. "They're as green as a *slieve* in summer."

He must be mad, Deirdre thought again. What else would explain why he insulted, bullied, taunted, and then flattered her in turns? She turned away, afraid of what he might say or do next. "The child Fey will be removed from your care immediately. I will see to it myself. She may come to my room until my father decides what is to be done with her."

Without waiting for his reply, Deirdre walked past him toward his room.

Killian followed at a leisurely pace, more than a little pleased with himself. He had routed the prim mademoiselle and awakened the wolf cub beneath Lady Deirdre's exterior. What had Conall called her? *Faolan*. Aye, he liked *Faolan* better than "Lady Deirdre."

When Deirdre opened the door, Fey stood in the middle of the room scrubbing herself dry with the rose embroidered hand towel. Deirdre had only a momentary glimpse of the girl's naked loins before Fey looked up in horror and covered herself, but one look was enough.

Fey's gaze flew to MacShane as he appeared in the doorway. "Ye gave me away!"

MacShane nodded at the furious girl. "Aye, I did. And what's more, Lady Deirdre has offered to be your guardian henceforth."

Fey sucked in a furious breath. "Ye said ye would nae send me away! Ye said ye'd let me stay! Ye black-hearted, whore-mongering—"

"Shut up, brat!" Killian spoke quietly but his words struck through Fey's vitriolic speech.

Deirdre cast him a furious glance. Could he not see that the child was more alarmed than angry? She moved toward the young girl. "Do not be frightened, Fey. My name is Lady Deirdre. This is my father's home and you are welcome here."

Fey did not even look at Deirdre. Her whole concentration was upon the man before her. A ripple of emotion crossed her face and was followed by another more violent one, and then she began to tremble. The trembling turned into convulsive sobs as she flung herself against Killian.

"Please! Please! I'll do anything! Do nae leave me! Please!"

Killian brought his arms about the girl's slight frame, his hands encountering the sharp jut of her shoulder blades beneath her skin. Her anguished tears reminded him of how as a boy he had often lain alone in the dark monk's cell and cried out his own loneliness and despair. He had been a charity orphan, yet he had been clothed, sheltered, and wanted because he had shown the scholarly aptitude needed to become a priest. How much more terrible it must be for a child of the streets. Fey was all he suspected and possibly more, yet she was still a child and needed protection.

"I will not abandon you, lass, even if I must leave you behind." He cupped her chin in his broad palm and lifted her face from his shirtfront. " 'Tis my word on it, *girsha*."

Fey stared at him for a long moment and then nodded. "I—I did nae mean to cry. I never cry," she said defensively, wiping the dampness from her face.

Killian looked across at Deirdre. "Your father is certain to be pleased when he learns that his daughter is cosseting a street urchin."

Deirdre flinched at the sarcasm in his voice. Did the man never do anything but cut up people with his gaze and voice? "I will not tell him, not yet."

Killian's expression soured. " 'Tis a bairn's game, lying to her elders. If you will not, then I will tell him."

Deirdre considered her dilemma. What could she say to her father that would make him sympathetic? She looked down at the shivering, naked girl who had wrapped her arms about Killian's waist, and as her eyes lingered on the long, vicious welts on Fey's back fury leaped within her. Some monster had done that to the child. Fey deserved to be protected from further abuse.

"I will tell Da the truth," she said crisply, all doubt gone from her mind. "Oh, he will bluster and confound us with terrible oaths, but Da will not send the child away."

"You've more faith in the power of your father's clemency than I," Killian rejoined.

"How do you know my father?" Deirdre questioned.

"Ask your da," Killian answered curtly. He reached down and unlocked Fey's arms from his waist. "Go and dress, lass. Lady Deirdre can not introduce you to her father in your nakedness."

"But—" Fey protested.

"MacShane is not deserting you," Deirdre interjected. "He is visiting here for a few days. That will give you time to become accustomed to us."

Fey's canny gaze moved from one to the other. "If I do nae like this place, ye will give me money for Paris, as ye promised?"

Killian's gaze grew distant but he nodded. "Aye."

Satisfied, Fey smiled. "Then I'll stay a bit."

"Ye're telling me I've hidden a thief and murderer beneath me roof this night and did not know it?"

"Hardly, Da. The child came with MacShane and—"

"MacShane!" Lord Fitzgerald thundered. "No doubt the man brought the murdering bastard into me house to slit our throats as we sleep!"

Deirdre looked pleadingly at Darragh, who sat at the breakfast table with a glass of brandy in one hand and his head in the other. "Tell Da that you agreed the lass could come here."

Darragh groaned and opened his red-rimmed eyes a slit. "I had naught to do with it. MacShane had a lad by the throat, 'tis all I remember. Oh, and Conall offered to put a ball in his gizzard."

Conall, equally under the aftereffects of too much drink, nodded cautiously but did not speak.

Deirdre turned away from her brothers. There was no help to be had from them. "We speak of a child, a small battered lass! If you saw her, Da, you would not turn her out."

"What I doubt is that MacShane himself did not beat the bairn and bully her into this pretense, for God only knows what purpose," her father answered.

Deirdre sucked in an angry breath. "That is not true!"

"Softly, lass. Your father will begin to believe that I've corrupted not only a poor helpless orphan but the rest of his household as well."

Lord Fitzgerald lifted his eyes toward the doorway and saw that a tall man in black filled it. "MacShane."

"Aye, Killian MacShane at your service, my lord."

Killian came forward slowly, aware that the entire Fitzgerald family watched him. It amused him to be the recipient of Lord Fitzgerald's attention.

Lord Fitzgerald eased back in his chair, his usual frown of pain replaced by the squint of a seasoned campaigner sizing up his enemy. "What brings ye here, MacShane?"

"Justice," Killian answered quietly.

"Och! I've heard the tale of the lass that was a lad and of the murdering she's done. Were it not for me daughter, I'd be turning the pair of ye out!"

Killian turned to Deirdre. "Forgive me for doubting you, lass. I had thought that no one could persuade a man of your father's nature to go against his own mind."

"She's not done that," Lord Fitzgerald answered. "She's soft-hearted, but she's not a fool. If Dee says there's worth in the bairn, I accept it."

"And if Lady Deirdre says there's worth in me?" Killian invited.

"She's not seen enough of ye to know," Lord Fitzgerald returned testily, "and I mean to see to it that she remains in ignorance."

"I would be pleased if you would stop speaking of me as though I am not present," Deirdre said impatiently. "Do sit down, MacShane."

"Nae, lass," Killian answered, his gaze never leaving her father's face. "Your father and I have business that does not need a meal between us. I will wait upon your pleasure."

"In the library," Lord Fitzgerald announced and pushed back his chair. "And there'll be no waiting upon me. Yer appearance has curdled the eggs and cream."

He rose to his feet and reached for his silver-headed cane. "Come along then. I've the morning before me and I mean to have ye gone before then." He turned and began walking toward the door, his stump and cane making their familiar tattoo upon the floorboards as he walked.

For a long moment Killian did not move. His bright blue gaze was fastened on the wooden stump that protruded from the man's pants leg.

"He lost the limb last year," Deirdre offered under her breath.

Killian turned sharply, unaware that she had come to his side. "He is ill but he will not admit it," she continued. "Deal harshly with him, if you must, but clear the air between you."

"What do you know of the matter between us?" Killian asked coolly.

"Nothing," Deirdre lied.

"I do not believe you."

She shrugged. "What I know is not enough to satisfy me."

The corners of Killian's lips turned up slightly. "Then I believe that you know nothing."

Rebuffed once again, Deirdre simply turned away. Almost at once she turned back, but he was striding toward the doorway through which her father had disappeared.

"What will come of it?" Darragh asked his brother.

"When Da's in a mood, there's no telling what will be said," Conall replied.

"What should be said?" Deirdre demanded.

"I wish I knew, lass, I wish I knew."

"Men!" Deirdre muttered, adding a profane word under her breath. "I'd best go and tell Lady Elva that Da is speaking with MacShane."

"Do not be led astray by way of the library," Darragh called after her. "Da would not care for it."

Deirdre did not answer, for that was exactly what she intended to do. Without a pause she turned toward the library. She could not very well barge in and perch herself upon a chair. Neither man would allow that. Yet, there were ways of listening without being seen.

She smiled as she entered the gallery that flanked one wall of the library. As a child she had clambered over every inch of the old French chateau, and one of the things she had learned to her delight was that this house was very like Liscarrol, with unexpected corners, bowers, and even a hidden alcove behind the tapestries that lined the gallery.

After a quick look over her shoulder to be certain she was not seen, she gathered her skirts and slipped behind the huge tapestry of medieval knights and ladies dressed in their best for a day of falconing.

It was dark behind the tapestry and she had to feel along the dusty length of the wainscoting to find the latch. The string-loaded catch gave way under her nimble fingers and a panel yawned open, its depths darker than the gloom of the alcove in which she stood. Dust tickled her nose but the faint sound of voices drew her into the dark. With a finger under her nose, she leaned forward and pressed her ear against the bare paneling of the library wall.

Chapter Eight

Lord Fitzgerald lowered himself painfully into the chair behind his desk. Killian noted the maneuver with interest. Lady Deirdre was correct: the old man was not well. The thought did not please him.

When he had put his cane aside, Lord Fitzgerald braced his hands on the edge of the desk and said, "Why have ye come here, MacShane?"

"Did you so dread my coming?"

"Dread has nothing to do with me feelings about ye, lad," Lord Fitzgerald answered shortly.

"Then dislike, perhaps?" Killian suggested, but Lord Fitzgerald did not reply. "For myself, I feel a bond with the Fitzgeralds. After all, I owe you my life."

"Ye repaid that when ye saved mine," Lord Fitzgerald answered stiffly.

"And you hate every reminder of it," Killian returned pleasantly. He looked down at the man's cane propped against the desk. "You might have done better to reconsider offering me a captaincy in your brigade two summers ago. I might have saved you that."

Lord Fitzgerald bristled. "Ye upstart braggart! I've thirty years as a fighting man to me credit. 'Tis longer than ye've been alive!''

"True, but it does not change the present. Your fighting days are over, and your sons are little comfort while they ply their trade hundreds of miles away. You should marry your lovely daughter to a man of sound Irish stock. She would breed you an army of grandsons that you could command to your heart's content.''

Lord Fitzgerald leaned forward in his chair, his canny eyes hard on the younger man. "Me lovely daughter, did ye say? And would ye be putting yerself forth as a suitor?''

Killian seemed to consider this possibility but his face darkened suddenly and he gave a tiny shake of his head. "Nae. She'd not consider a man without a 'm'lord' to his name. I'm a commoner. There was a time when a man's clan name was enough to make him the equal of kings. Now the name MacShane gains me little respect.''

"A man who can trace his ancestry back to the great O'Neills of Ulster can claim himself an equal at my table any day,'' Lord Fitzgerald maintained.

The pretense of indifference left Killian's face and voice. "I've known you for a tyrant and a traitor, m'lord. Do not tell me that a gimpy leg has turned you sentimental!''

Lord Fitzgerald heaved himself up by his arms, ignoring the pain stabbing through his leg. "No man speaks to me like that in me own home!''

"What will you do, have me ejected by lackeys, for, by God, you cannot do it yourself!''

His face crimson with rage, Lord Fitzgerald reached for the pistol that he kept primed in his desk drawer and laid it on the desktop. "Tis as ye say, lad. I cannot flog ye. A ball in the chest will have to do.''

Killian glared at him. "Aye, that's more like it. Only a coward keeps a pistol ready in his own home. How many other ghosts do you fear, old man?''

"Is that yer last word?''

Killian smiled his contempt. "I won't be done until you've heard me out.''

Lord Fitzgerald nodded. "Have yer say and then get out."

"I will tell you a story, m'lord. You know the ending but not the beginning. It began in ninety-one with the siege of Kilkenny. Did you once know the O'Dugans of Ballyvourney? Sean O'Dugan was my cousin. We fought at Kilkenny. Oh, we did not fly an English king's banner, but we took the part of James over William because we were Irish and full of hope. We were both seventeen and as green as any grass the Good Lord ever saw fit to raise from the earth. When the battle was lost, we were not offered amnesty. Unlike you, m'lord, we had to run and hide and fight our way home. We were rabble, we were rapparees."

Lord Fitzgerald shook his head. It was an unfortunate turn of events that he could do nothing about then or now. "Formal treaties are for formal armies."

"So they said," Killian answered. "But I am not finished. Sean and I were within five leagues of home when soldiers loyal to William of Orange appeared. The sight of an Orange banner was more than Sean could endure. I told him it was madness, two against twenty, but there was blood in Sean's eyes. He'd lost his father and two brothers at Kilkenny. You know the rest of the tale."

Lord Fitzgerald frowned. "Yer cousin was captured and hanged by the English, but you escaped and hid in my barn."

As if the threat of the pistol had vanished, Killian braced his hands on the desk, leaned forward, and thrust his face into the old man's. "Could you not find pity for a lad who'd taken shot? Did you think me less than a dog because I was a rapparee, a commoner with no title or wealth?"

"What gibberish do ye speak?" Lord Fitzgerald demanded. "I saved yer life, did I not? Took ye in, hid ye, and all the while knowing that if the English found ye, my womenfolk would have been imprisoned and I hanged."

"And yet you took the chance. Why? 'Twas common knowledge that Liscarrol had been stripped of its wealth.

Were you sharp to the ways of making money for a fresh start abroad?''

Killian gave the room a careful appraisal before looking again at Lord Fitzgerald. The lines of his face, made harsher by his anger, seemed hewn of granite. "I've heard the French pay well for galley hands. Was that why you saved me, to sell me as a galley slave for a few pieces of gold?"

Lord Fitzgerald snatched up his pistol. "'Tis a lie! I've never traded with slavers, and that's God's own truth. Do nae make me kill ye, lad. 'Twould be a waste.''

Killian held his gaze as he reached into his pocket, withdrew a paper, and tossed it on the desk. "Read the answer to your lies, old man.''

Lord Fitzgerald lowered his pistol and picked up the paper. After a start of surprise, he read steadily to the end. When he was done, he raised his eyes. "I know nothing of this. I saw ye as far as Calais. There were French soldiers recruiting Irish lads for service. I signed ye up. 'Tis what I did meself once I'd settled me family.''

"This bill of sale carries your signature," Killian maintained, his light eyes burning in his sun-darkened face. "Do you know what they do to a man condemned to the galleys? He's bound hand and foot in chains with five other men to a fifteen-foot oar. They shave you; hair, beard, even eyebrows.''

He touched the spot where a thin white scar angled up from the black wing of his eyebrow. "I learned not to object after the first time. We sat in our own filth for weeks at a time, a loincloth to cover our nakedness. One day the overseer killed the man next to me, beat him to death. I never knew his name. He never spoke to me. After that there were four men to do five men's work.''

Lord Fitzgerald's color had faded. He was a campaigner, knew more of the atrocities of which men were capable than most, but the life of a galley slave was anathema to a man of his ilk.

"I had nothing to do with that, lad." He sat down heavily. "They promised me ye'd be given a place in one of the Irish divisions.''

Very slowly Killian rolled up each shirt sleeve and presented his wrists. "Shackles take no time at all to rub a man's wrists raw."

Lord Fitzgerald nodded slowly, his gaze lingering on the welts of scar tissue that encircled those strong wrists before he raised sad eyes to MacShane's face. "As God is me witness, I never knew."

Killian absently began to rub the healed skin as if his wrists pained him still. "My desire to murder you kept me alive for the six months I rowed to Egypt and back."

"How did you escape?"

Killian's voice was dangerously low as he said, "Does it matter? I escaped. Anger's a powerful motivation, and I used it to my advantage. There are people willing to pay handsomely for men with unsqueamish natures. The nobles of the French court, for instance, have use for men like myself."

A bleakness crept into the older man's face. "You became an assassin?"

"Nae, not an assassin." Killian's smile was not pleasant. "A noblewoman hired me as her personal guard. She paid me well and I stayed in her employ until I learned many trades."

"I'll not say what I think of a man who's kept by a woman," Lord Fitzgerald observed censoriously. "Yet ye did not remain, and I suppose that's to yer credit." He watched MacShane closely as he said, "I'm innocent of yer charges."

"Are you now? If you are not guilty of selling me into bondage, then why did you not want me here?"

"Only a fool fails to recognize an enemy, though he may not know the reason," Lord Fitzgerald responded cautiously. He was not about to reveal his reasons for fearing MacShane's presence in his home. "But I am curious. Why have ye waited this long to confront me?"

Killian turned away and began pacing the room. He did not know the answer. Or perhaps he did. Perhaps he had never really believed Lord Fitzgerald capable of such treachery. And yet, had the man confessed his guilt just now, Killian would have done nothing. It no longer mattered.

Perhaps it had never really mattered. So why had he come to Nantes? Was it because the invitation had come at a moment when he had broken with his past and knew not where to seek his future?

He stopped before the mantel and gazed up at the gilt-framed portrait of a lady. She was black-haired, her green eyes tilted up at the corner, and about her red mouth played the most provocative smile he had ever seen. It was not Deirdre, and yet there was something familiar in those wanton features. His gaze lingered on the red mouth, imagining it as Deirdre's, and he felt a familiar but rare stirring in his loins.

"'Tis Deirdre's mother," Lord Fitzgerald offered in the silence. "Lady Grainne was the second of me wives."

"A beautiful woman."

"A woman the like of her is better dreamed of than attained," the older man answered heavily.

"Do you dream, my lord?"

The question surprised Lord Fitzgerald. "No more nor less than most."

"Have you never had a dream come again and again, plaguing your nights until wakefulness is preferable to dreamful sleep?"

Lord Fitzgerald looked up sharply, his voice roughened by an odd emotion as he said, "Dreams are for bairns."

"Have you not dreamt of the day you will return to Ireland?"

"'Twas all that kept me alive those first years here in France," Lord Fitzgerald answered guardedly. "But a man of sense learns to give up useless dreams."

"Aye," Killian echoed softly. So he had told himself over and over for eleven years. But Lord Fitzgerald was wrong. Senseless dreams held a power more persuasive than reason.

"I have a dream that haunts me. Liscarrol was the place where I first dreamed it."

The thud against the paneled wall behind him made Killian turn from the portrait to Lord Fitzgerald, who still sat behind his desk. "Did I startle you, my lord?"

His thoughts distracted by the sound that had come from

the gallery beyond the library wall, Lord Fitzgerald did not answer immediately. Were they being spied upon? "I do not know what ye mean," he muttered finally.

"Do you not? Then you are fortunate." Killian turned back to the portrait but his thoughts were full of the lady's daughter. Was this Deirdre as she might be if love came her way? Or was it his imagination again playing tricks on him? When he had first set eyes on Deirdre he had thought her a figment of his dreamworld come to life. Now he saw her in a portrait that only vaguely resembled her. Perhaps it was that he wanted the answer to his dream to be found here.

Killian turned and walked forward to stand before Lord Fitzgerald once more. "I have one question more. The day I came to Liscarrol and hid in the stables there was a lass there, a young girl with hair the color of flax. Who was she?"

Lord Fitzgerald felt as if his collar had suddenly tightened. "There was none but ye when I found ye. Me sergeant put ye in the priest hole. When we came to fetch ye ye were babbling, out of yer mind with pain and fever. Ye must have dreamed her. Fever will do that to a man."

Killian was silent. He risked a great deal in exposing himself to this man's ridicule, yet he knew he was not a lunatic. He had seen and talked with a real person.

"Why should I lie?" Lord Fitzgerald asked a little desperately.

"I do not know," Killian said slowly. "I'm a man who believes what he can see and touch. I saw the lass. I touched her. She bore a rose birthmark, here, on her shoulder."

Lord Fitzgerald's heart thudded heavily in his breast. "I saw no lass."

Killian saw a tremor of anxiety in Lord Fitzgerald's face and knew that the man lied. "If you will not help me, then I must seek my answers elsewhere."

Lord Fitzgerald said nothing as MacShane turned and left the room. What could he say—that he knew the answer to Killian's dreams because his own daughter had had a part in them?

"Nae!" he muttered low, but an old fear crept into his mind, one that he could not thrust aside.

It had been a long time since he had thought of the days following their flight from Liscarrol. The trying voyage from Cork to Calais had become a nightmare once Deirdre fell ill. She dreamed constantly, crying out for the black-haired lad she had saved from the English. He was her gift from the fairies, she had said. She would have him or die.

Lord Fitzgerald sighed, feeling every one of his fifty years. He had refused to have MacShane brought up to her for fear that if the lad died Deirdre would go mad. Even so, the dreams had worsened, making her feverish, until even Brigid had despaired of her life. Once they reached Calais even the local priests had shied from the seven-year-old lass who called upon the powers of the otherworld to produce the boy. They said she was possessed.

The hair lifted on his neck as the memories assailed him. He was a God-fearing man if not a pious one, and the powers of the otherworld lay heavy on his conscience. Desperation had driven him to relent his stricture against magic, but it was Brigid who resorted to her *bean feasa* charms to protect his daughter.

The witch-stone had done its trick and it was then that he knew that Deirdre's dreams were not holy things. They were the work of spirits, of fairies, of the otherworld.

He leaned forward, his eyes riveted on the portrait he hated but could not destroy. "Ah, Grainne, ye cursed me with a burden over which I've nae power!"

In a moment of passion one summer's day so long ago he scarcely remembered it he had abandoned himself to forbidden love, and Deirdre, her body and spirit tainted by the mark of the otherworld, was the result.

He had married Lady Grainne Butler to save her from censure, but he had disliked from the first her wild talk of spells and magic and the changeling child to which she hoped to give birth. Once pregnant, she had no longer any desire for him. She cared only for the child in her womb, a female child, she declared, who would bear the mark of her legendary ancestress Meghan O'Neill Butler.

He had almost been glad to lose Grainne in childbirth,

for he considered her talk to have stemmed from madness and feared her influence over the babe. But for one thing, his world would have returned to normal. Just as Grainne had predicted, Deirdre was born with the bloodred rose birthmark of her ancestor, the mark of the otherworld.

Few knew of it. The mark was well hidden. Brigid was the only one who knew the full story of the legend of the rose birthmark, but he would not allow her to speak of it to him. There had been no indication that Deirdre was anything but a normal child until the incident involving MacShane.

Afterward, he had wanted nothing to do with the magic that had saved his daughter's life, yet he had believed Brigid when she told him that France was an alien place to which Gaelic spirits would not travel. Deirdre had overcome the spell of madness, and under Brigid's watchful care she had grown into womanhood untroubled by dreams.

"Brigid!" Lord Fitzgerald murmured. He must warn Brigid before MacShane questioned her. Deirdre must be kept away from MacShane. If she was not, he might reawaken Deirdre's nightmares and bring her to ruin and madness.

Lord Fitzgerald clasped his hands together and bowed his head. "Lord, I've done me best to shield me daughter from the pull of the spirits. I will nae lose her now!"

The sun was warm on her bare head but Deirdre did not mind. The feel of her mount's long, elegantly shaped muscles bunching and relaxing beneath her made her wish the ride would last forever. The breeze stroked her hair free of its confining pins and tugged back her riding skirt until the white ruffles of her petticoats were visible about her ankles. The salty tang of the sea, present whenever the wind was from the southwest, stung her nostrils and slicked her cheeks. In the distance, flashing silver-gold between the tall reeds, was the river Loire. The river was as close as she could come to the sea on a moment's notice and the sea was where she longed to be, for beyond it lay Ireland, and Liscarrol.

She dismounted from her sidesaddle perch in the shadow of a tree. Lifting her skirts, she began to walk across the grass to the riverbank.

Sunlight dazzled her eyes, turning the water's surface into a mille-faceted mirror. As she neared the bank the thick blanket of grass tapered off into short tufts, coarse and bleached at the tips by sun and water. Here and there wild flowers of pink and red and blue clung tenaciously to the tips of windblown stalks. She paused to collect a few of them, braiding their stems together until she had made a ringlet of wildflowers, which she slipped on her wrist.

The air smelled of warm grass and the faint odor of fish. Birds cried in the distance, the sounds rising and falling as they swooped toward the water and away. Far out on the glistening surface of the broad river bright-hulled fishing vessels bobbed beneath their wings of canvas. All about her in the near-silence of the warm summer day was peace and solitude. Yet, inside, her thoughts tumbled and tripped over one another. Only away from the house, with no one to disturb her, could she consider the many questions that her eavesdropping had brought to mind.

The shouting between her father and MacShane had been easily heard. She doubted that anyone in the house was in ignorance of the angry words that had passed between them. The talk of dreams, however, had been in lower, more secretive tones.

MacShane had spoken of a dream he had had at Liscarrol. It had so astonished her that she had caught the toe of her slipper and struck her shoulder against the dividing wall.

In horror she had listened to the noise reverberate through the tiny room. Surely her father had guessed that someone was listening in the secret chamber. Guilt had sent her scurrying for her riding clothes and a swift mount. To have been caught eavesdropping would have been bad enough. If MacShane had accompanied her father she would have fainted in mortification.

Standing now in the full sunlight, feeling its warmth, she could dismiss MacShane's accusation that her father had sold him to the French as a galley slave. Her father would never ever do anything so traitorous and cruel. Yet, her father was wary of MacShane; she had heard caution in every word he had spoken. What could he have to fear from the man?

"If only I had heard more," she murmured.

One thought circled round and round in her mind, casting shadows of unease with each wing beat. MacShane had been at Liscarrol. When?

The faint rapping at her temples was a long time making itself felt. It stole over her as softly and silently as the clouds above spreading thin cool fingers before the blaze of the sun, dimming its beauty and heat. Gradually sunlight faded into the golden haze of a cloud-banked sky. The river's brilliant surface dulled, glazed brown and green with purple undertones, like some rare dark opal.

Anticipation shivered through her, and she looked back across the distance to where her horse stood cropping grass beneath a tree. The gentle, insistent drumming at her temples increased, throbbing just at the edge of pain.

It was then that she caught sight of a man lying in the grass.

He lay propped on one elbow, his coat discarded on the grass and his long legs stretched out before him. The breeze rippled in his long black hair, feathering it over the shoulders of his shirt. His head was turned toward the river and his profile revealed the strong somber face of Killian MacShane.

He had not seen her, she knew, or he would not expose himself so casually to her regard. Always before she had had to endure his harsh scrutiny as she looked upon him. Now, lost in his own reverie, he seemed completely accessible, the quietude of the day reflected in the supple ease of his body. There was something frankly sensual in his easy, relaxed pose, a compelling grace that drew her toward him.

As she neared, he picked up and began nibbling a long blade of grass. The bow of his smile deepened and then split, revealing the even rows of his teeth. She was startled to feel that smile blossom inside herself, unfolding upon some hidden warmth that until now had lain undiscovered within her. When he turned his head to find her standing over him there was no amazement in his face.

"My lady," he said and extended a hand to her.

She heard his words as if from afar. The day suddenly gusted cooler, and haze gathered on the surface of the river as though it were dawn, not midday. She extended her hand to him, pleasantly shocked by the firm warmth of his fingers closing over hers.

"I expected you," he said softly.

She blushed, remembering her part as spy an hour earlier. "I did not follow you."

"I know," he answered, exerting pressure on her arm to pull her down beside him. "I've been waiting for you."

"How did you know where to find me? I do not usually come this way."

He did not answer, merely smiled at her in a way that fed the fragile blossom inside her. When he pulled her down beside him, she did not resist. When he released her she instantly missed the warmth and strength of his touch.

To her surprise, the grass was slick with dew, its texture unusually luxuriant beneath her hands as she spread her skirts to cover her ankles. It was springy and supple, the rich deep green of springtime.

"Why do you frown, *acushla?*"

Deirdre raised her eyes to his face, struck once more by the beauty of his eyes. They were clear and vivid blue against the golden skin stretched tightly over his cheekbones. He smiled at her, and because the smile would not be denied, she smiled back. "Do you always wear black?"

It was a forward question, one too personal for a lady to ask a gentleman, but he seemed not to mind. " 'Tis a noble color."

" 'Tis no color at all," she answered. A portion of her mind recoiled at her breach of manners, but another part, the part that was in control, urged her on. "Black is the absence of all color."

"A philosopher, *acushla?* If black is not a color, then what color is a moonless night? What color is your deepest fear? What color is the soul of a man who has lost all he loves best?''

"You are in mourning?''

"Aye.''

She looked for any sign of sorrow or sadness in his face but she could not see past the quiet intensity of his gaze. "Did you lose someone very dear to you, your wife, perhaps?''

"That question is unworthy of you, *acushla,*'' he answered.

She looked away, faintly annoyed by the amusement in his tone. In the distance, on the river, mist now obscured all. Even as she watched, the tops of the trees on the opposite bank disappeared and mist rose to form ragged peaks like those of the tumbled granite mountains of west Munster. The drumming inside her head which had abated when MacShane touched her returned.

A shudder passed through her and she looked quickly away. "Black is the symbol of bitterness, emptiness, coldness,'' she challenged.

"As a child had you no liking for licorice? Does not blackness fill every unlit place? Is not the warmth of burning coals stronger than that of the flame?''

He had bested her with her own words and she knew it. "You have the better of me, sir. I stand corrected.''

His laughter startled her. She never expected so rich or powerful a voice of mirth from this man. The years fell away from his face, and the lines of tiredness and bitterness and sadness disappeared. When he looked at her again, there was nowhere to look but straight into the cerulean fire of his disarming gaze.

"I thought you were a dream, all these years a dream,'' she confided shyly.

"I was,'' he said, rising from his elbow to sit. His words were low and deep, the lilting brogue recalling another time and place. When he reached out a hand to touch her, she knew she should draw back; but there was no place to go, no other place she wished to be but here, with him. He gathered a windblown curl into his palm and crushed it, smiling as it sprang back and jumped from his hand.

He was so close that she could see the pulse beating at his temple and the few silky black hairs that rose above the open collar of his shirt. His hands moved to her shoulders and his palms were warm, the only warmth in a day gone suddenly gray and damp. Behind his black head the sky was pewter. A faint drizzle had begun. Droplets trembled in his hair and clung to the long curve of his ebony lashes.

"It's raining," she whispered in surprise.

"Nae, lass, 'tis only a soft kiss of the old sod," he answered. His gaze lowered at last from hers and fastened on her mouth.

"I have dreamed of you," Deirdre heard herself say and wondered if the words were true.

"I, too, have dreamed," he answered. "I dreamed of a winsome lass with unruly golden curls and sea-green eyes. She was a wise and brave and strong woman who saved my life."

Deirdre shook her head. "I am not the lady of your dream."

Disappointment flickered in his eyes. "Are you not, lass?"

The drumming in her head doubled in intensity and Deirdre sighed in pain. "I do not know," she said, shaking her head from side to side. "I cannot remember." Yet, she did know, not why or how, but that she had been there in his dream.

"Shh, *acushla*, do not weep," he said softly, drawing her closer until his cheek rested against hers. "I did not mean to make you cry."

Deirdre drew back from him. "Why, why have you come here?"

He grew very still and suddenly she was frightened. She had asked a question to which she did not want the answer. She looked down. "No, do not tell me."

He lifted her chin until she was forced to look once again into his eyes and read the answer that she both feared and desired.

She knew that he would kiss her. She drew a quick breath, tried to make her mouth less tremulous than it was . . . and failed.

She failed, too, to prepare herself for the feel of his mouth on hers, the warm hunger and sweet fire of a kiss unlike any she had ever known.

The kiss deepened and the drum of pain within her was replaced by the thunderous pounding of her heart. He tasted of green grass, and she shivered deep inside to the languorous stroke of his heat-drenched tongue across her lips.

When at last he lifted his head, she could not draw breath and kept her eyes closed against the devastating effect of his kiss.

"What's this, *acushla,* have you never been kissed before?"

Deirdre opened her eyes to his gentle laughter and thought of Cousin Claude and the half dozen other young men who had dared press their mouths briefly to hers.

"No, I do not think I have," she answered with wisdom of her new knowledge of a kiss.

"Good," he answered and pulled her to him again.

They lay in the grass a long time, his mouth on hers, his hands on her shoulders, one long black-clad leg thrown across hers as though he feared she would flee. But Deirdre had no desire to move an inch, unless it brought her closer to him.

Finally, he rose away from her and lay back on the grass beside her and they both stared at the misty day about them.

"I did not know that kissing could be like this," Deirdre admitted after a few moments, too timid to turn and look at him.

"Like what, *acushla?*"

"Like fear and joy, Christmas Day and its anticipation all rolled together."

"Aye, 'tis like that, *acushla.*"

She smiled to herself. "Why do you call me 'darling'?"

From the corner of her eye she saw him roll onto his side to face her. "What could you have me call you? *Madilse?*"

My love. Deirdre trembled inside. "Kiss me again."

"No, lass."

Confused, she turned to him and met his serious look. "You'd nae like it if I kissed you again."

"Why?" she whispered, already suspecting what his answer would be.

"There comes a price with joy, and though I do not think you'd be sorry now, later you might come to regret the price you'd pay."

Deirdre closed her eyes against the stark beauty of his face. It was a dangerous moment.

"Aye, dangerous currents tug at your skirts, *madilse*," he said quietly, as though she had spoken her thoughts. "Only the bravest venture into the strongest currents. Ladies do not set sail upon strange seas."

Deirdre opened her eyes and once again met his gaze. She had heard of lands to the south where the sea was a deeper blue than the sky, where green and sapphire currents ran together in a warm flood of beauty. She felt the tug of those currents as she gazed into his eyes and she wanted nothing more than to launch herself upon that sea tide in his eyes and go where he would take her.

"You think me a coward," she whispered.

He touched a finger to her cheek and then traced the sensitive bow of her upper lip. "Nae, I do not think you a coward. The lass of my dreams would dare anything if her heart ruled that it be so."

She understood at last what he meant. This was her choice, and her responsibility. Greatly daring, she reached up and touched his face. "Kiss me again, Killian. Please."

He did not kiss her at once. He continued to trace her mouth with a callused finger, and the strange, spellbinding motion sensitized her skin until the sweet abrasion became a torment. "Please," she whispered raggedly and hoped that he would not laugh at her.

He did not. His face was unsmiling as she opened her eyes. There was a new tenseness in him; it carved caverns beneath his cheekbones and intensified his eyes, which were shaded by a heavy fringe of black lashes. He was as expectant and perhaps as wary as she of the moment that yawned before them.

And then they were past it, leaping the precipice as his mouth found hers.

Deirdre felt the burden lifted from her and joyously flung her arms about his neck. His hair was amazingly soft beneath the caress of her hands. The warm sweetness of his tongue slipped between her lips and she wondered if any woman had ever experienced this low sweet flame that began burning within her.

Kiss followed kiss, meeting and melting until she no longer knew when one replaced another, until they left her dizzy and shaken. His hands framed her shoulders as he lifted and rolled her over, carrying her with him until she lay over him, chest to chest, belly to belly, and thigh to thigh.

With gentle insistence he tugged off the jacket of her riding habit and then found the lacing at her back. The cool river breeze stroked her back as he parted her gown. She kept her eyes on his, drawing courage from his intense gaze.

He smiled at her, but there was no amusement, no glibness at her expense. He lifted her off and onto her knees beside him and sat up himself. Then he was pulling the gown from her shoulders and she found that she could no longer look at him. She leaned forward and embraced him, hugging her body so close to his that the gown could fall no further.

"Now, *acushla?*" he questioned softly. Then he sucked in a quick gasp and his fingers tightened on her right shoulder. "The rose!" he whispered, and bent to place his lips against the red mark.

The flame leaped within her as the fiery heat of his mouth touched her cool skin. His lips moved from her shoulder to her neck as his hands slipped her gown lower, leaving their scalding impression. And then he lowered his head and took a nipple gently between his lips.

Deirdre shut her eyes, making a soft murmuring sound deep in her throat as his tongue coaxed unnameable sensations of pleasure from her flesh. Tears rose to her eyes with the strangeness of the feeling he stirred deep inside her. He was a wizard, a magician who brought her a joy too profound to give speech.

The world dropped away, day becoming twilight, summer rolling back to spring. As he laid her back in the dewy grass, she breathed deeply of the air about them and knew she would remember always the smell of grass and mist and the scent of his body.

He moved more swiftly now, pulling the gown from her hips and then stretching out to cover her with his own naked length.

His skin was smooth; and as she rubbed her hands over his chest and shoulders, she wondered why she had expected a man's skin to be hard and callused like his hands.

Yet, one part of him was hard, and hot, and pulsating with the urgency of the life within him. When he touched her with that life, slipping it inside her, it took her breath away; and she thought she would die well quit of the world in that instant.

But he was not yet done. The strangely gentle yet hard urging of his body on hers demanded a response she did not believe she possessed. Despairing, she twisted her head from side to side.

He caught her face in his hands and, bending, placed his lips on hers. "Open to me, *acushla*," he said against her mouth. "Feel my joy within you. Take from it. Make it your own."

And she did. Wave after wave of pleasure broke over her, flooding her from breast to belly with sensuous joy. MacShane's strong body rode hers with superb skill, urging her again and again to the unutterable ecstasy of fulfillment.

Afterward, he rolled over and pulled her tight against him, hugging her head to his shoulder. He did not speak again and she was too content and too awed to do so. After a moment the finger tracing the lobe of her ear stilled and his breath deepened, and she knew that he slept.

All about them it was cool and dark, and yet inside herself she was warm and content. She did not think she had ever been so alive, so awake within her skin.

It came as a distinct shock when an insect tickled her

nose and a sneeze sent her bolting upright and she realized that she had been asleep.

The sun was beating down on the riverbank, the grass hummed with insects, the river's smooth surface reflected all the bright light and color of the summer day . . . and MacShane was gone.

Deirdre jumped to her feet, stunned to find herself alone. She was dressed just as she had been when she left home, the lacing of her gown as tight as Brigid had made it. Her anxious gaze ranged across the open field until she saw the silhouette of her horse still grazing under the tree where she had left him. The mist was gone, the clouds, the rain. The crisp tough grass crunched beneath the tread of her feet.

As she hurried toward her horse, her heart racing wildly, she began to cry. She had dreamed it, had dreamed it all, the day, the rain . . . and MacShane.

Deirdre pushed open the door to her room, her mind full of what she had dreamed, and was brought up short by the sight of a young girl sitting at her vanity.

Gowned in pink taffeta, the girl was tugging a brush through her short, dark curls. When she caught sight of Deirdre's reflection in the mirror, she turned about and Deirdre found herself gazing into enormous, luminous dark eyes that belonged to Fey.

"How could I have ever mistaken you for a lad?" Deirdre remarked in wonder as she came forward.

"I'd as lief ye had," Fey muttered, a mutinous expression creeping into her features. "As for that pisspot ye call a nurse, I've a thing or two to say about her." She stood up and cast the brush aside. "Look at what she's done to me!"

"You look lovely," Deirdre said.

"I look like a prize pig on market day." Fey tugged at her waistband. "Old pisspot took me breeches and trussed me up in a corset. Under these skirts me arse is as bald as the day me mother whelped me. I cannot go to Nantes dressed the like. Some swab would have me off me feet and his prick betwixt me legs afore I could cross the street!''

''I suppose so,'' Deirdre murmured distractedly. ''Where is Brigid?''

''Old pisspot? She's gone to get a bar of soap. Says I need me mouth washed out. Does she do that to ye?''

''Not very often,'' Deirdre answered, determined not to allow the girl to make her laugh, for it would only encourage her outrageous behavior. *Old pisspot*! How vexed Brigid must be.

Deirdre pulled off her riding jacket. ''I must change in a hurry. Since Brigid's not here, will you unlace me?''

Fey complied reluctantly and when she was done, Deirdre stepped out of her gown and scooped it up, flushing guiltily as she spied grass stains on the hem. It was a dream, she reminded herself, but a sudden warmth gathered in her middle at the very reminder of what she had dreamed. She did not feel very confident about facing Brigid at the moment, and the woman was certain to cluck at her about the stains.

''Ye've ruined that gown,'' Fey remarked.

''Aye. Brigid will be furious,'' Deirdre responded.

Fey watched Deirdre cross the room in her petticoats, sizing up her narrow waist and full hips and bosom. Having had time to think about MacShane's betrayal of her, Fey had come up with the only answer that made sense to her. MacShane lusted after the lady. Fey's mouth tightened ominously as she speculated on the reasons for the grass stains on the lady's gown. Perhaps he had already helped himself.

''Were ye out riding with MacShane?''

The name so startled her that Deirdre bumped her head on the armoire as she spun about. ''What did you say?''

Fey's expression soured. ''He has eyes for ye, I saw that the minute ye was together. He should give ye a rare old time, being as he's that well hung.''

All the color drained from Deirdre's face. The child's speech was as appalling as her innuendos.

Fey's expression hardened as she observed the lady's

distress. She had guessed right. "I should have said ye were out riding MacShane, and from the looks of it, ye didn't waste clean sheets when the grass would do as well."

"You have no idea what you're saying," Deirdre replied dry-mouthed.

Fey shrugged. "Ye've the look of a tupped ewe, that's what I know."

"You impudent little guttersnipe!" Deirdre exclaimed indignantly.

"MacShane's a man, and a man must have his pleasures." Fey stroked her hands down over her still-flat breasts until they rested on her hips. "I'm nae so prettily made as ye, but I've seen other lasses get udders and hips as they grow. Once I'm rigged, MacShane will look at me the same."

Deirdre turned away from the lustful gleam in the girl's eyes. Fey was only a child. She could not possibly know what she said. And yet...

Deirdre turned back, her skin tingling with alarm. "Did MacShane say something to you? Did he tell you that he had lustful—?"

"That he did not!" Brigid closed the door behind herself and came forward. "I've already questioned the lass, and she told me Captain MacShane did nae lay a hand on her. I checked. Though God only knows how, the lass is still intact."

"Brigid!" Deirdre said hoarsely, wondering how much the nurse had overheard. "You're back."

"That I am." Brigid stared meaningfully at Fey. "And I've a fat bar of soap for a dirty mouth. If ye'd leave us, Miss Deirdre, the lass and I have a spot of business to see to."

"Ye damned bawd, and with cold fingers into the bargain!" Fey cried. "Ye'll nae lay hands on me again!"

Though defiant, Fey paled as Brigid advanced on her. Lady Deirdre she did not like, but Brigid she feared because the woman did not fear her back. She treated her like a child and for that she hated her. "Miss Deirdre's just changing after a bit of a tumble," she said suddenly, her dark eyes full of guile. "MacShane had something to do with it."

You damned little sneak! Deirdre thought as Brigid turned to stare at her. The girl had successfully turned Brigid's attention away from herself. "Fey is teasing, Brigid. I rode quite alone." She turned and lifted the nearest gown from the armoire, hoping Brigid would be satisfied.

"He's a dangerous man, is MacShane," Fey continued. "I would nae go far with him, Lady Deirdre. 'Afore ye know it, he'll be showing ye the way of the blanket hornpipe, and have ye thinking 'tis proper."

"*Ochone!* Ye dirty-mouthed little slut!" Brigid cried. "I'll scrub that filth out of ye, see if I don't." Shaken out of her customary self-possession, she grabbed Fey by the hair and dragged her toward the basin.

Terrified, Fey fought back, kicking and scratching, even butting the woman with her head. But Brigid was strong and larger and held on grimly to the twisting, thrashing girl.

"Brigid, Brigid, please," Deirdre said desperately. She had suffered a similar fate at Brigid's hands when she was ten. Fey would lose, and though she deserved it Deirdre could not stand to see the girl hurt again.

Brigid looked up blankly from her struggle. "Not to worry, Miss Deirdre. I've sorted out worse cases."

Deirdre smiled her best smile. "Surely you might allow her this one mistake." She glanced pleadingly at the girl. "Fey will promise to be as docile as a lamb after this, won't you, Fey?"

Fey jerked free of Brigid and stumbled back a few steps, breathing hard. She did not agree, but neither did she deny Deirdre's words.

Reluctantly Brigid placed the bar of soap on the wash-stand. "'Tis against me better judgment," she said with a last hard glare at Fey. "So, I'll be taking up the matter with Lord Fitzgerald."

When she was gone, Deirdre turned to Fey. The girl had turned a pasty gray shade. "Oh, Fey, I'm sorry!" She threw her arms about the girl. "We mean you no harm. You'll never be beaten here, I promise you that."

Fey struggled out of Deirdre's embrace, her face white but her eyes hard as stones. "I'm nae afraid of a beating. I've took worse than she can give!" She doubled up her fists and was glad to see Deirdre back away. "Ye'll nae keep me here against me will. When MacShane leaves, I'm going with him. And when herself comes back, I'll be ready for the old pisspot."

"Do not call her that!"

"I'll call her what I like. And call ye what I like, come to that!"

Deirdre knew she could not allow the girl to best her. She dropped her gown and balled her hands into fists. "My brothers taught me to fight when I was a lass. 'Tis certain I'll remember something of it."

Fey blinked in amazement at the lady before her. "Ye would nae strike me?"

"I'll try very hard to if you strike me first," Deirdre said determinedly.

"MacShane would nae like it," Fey said less certainly.

"Aye, he would not. So what shall we do, bloody each other's noses or decide that we must be friends? Even Brigid can be made to forget her anger."

"Who?" Fey questioned blankly.

"Old pisspot," Deirdre replied, and turned quickly away to keep the child from seeing her smile. She picked up her gown and stepped behind an ornate screen to dress. "I'm going to visit my stepmother. You stay here!"

Fey stood irresolutely, her fists still clenched. If she struck the lady, what would MacShane say? He would not like it, of that she was certain. As for the lady herself, she was not at all what Fey's notion of a lady should be.

"She's that mad!" Fey exclaimed after a moment and turned away in disgust.

Chapter Nine

"I thought you'd deserted us," Conall greeted as Killian rode into the stable yard. "You were gone some while, MacShane. Did the ride clear your head?"

"Aye, of some things," Killian answered and swung his leg over to dismount. Mostly he had allowed the fatigue of a sleepless night to overcome him in the shade of a tree near the Loire. His talk with Lord Fitzgerald had left him dissatisfied, but thoughts of a very different nature had kept him company until the slanted rays of the sun fell across his face and awakened him.

"I'll not ask how your conversation went with Da. I heard a good measure of it, as did the rest of the house," Conall informed him. "I will tell you that Da has been in a rare mood since."

Killian did not answer directly. His mind had been too full of other thoughts these last hours. He noted Conall impatiently flicking his riding crop against his leg. "Are you riding out?"

" 'Twas my intention. At breakfast Deirdre made me promise to accompany her to see our cousins, the de Quentins, but the mad lass rode out earlier in the day and has yet to finish dressing."

"Perhaps she had another appointment to keep," Killian said quietly as he turn his horse over to the care of the stable boy who appeared at his side. Without haste he added, "Is the Comte de Quentin a particular friend of Lady Deirdre's?"

"Cousin Claude has always doted on the lass," Conall agreed, his expression bland. "Lady Elva believes that he will offer for her, though Dee will not have him."

"Can you be certain? The gentleman is a comte."

Conall laughed. "That's how little you know our Dee. She'll have only an Irishman, she will. She's sung that tune these last eleven years till our ears are weary of the ditty."

"But a man of property and noble birth—"

"Gains no advantage with our Dee." Conall cast a speculative eye on his guest. "You show a rare interest in the affairs of my sister."

"The Fitzgeralds do not tread softly in their new homeland," Killian answered coolly. "Much is heard of you, and gossip is always of interest to your fellow countrymen."

Conall considered this. "Aye, 'tis so. But I'll not have any man or woman speak ill of Dee."

"There's no disrespect in wishing a lass luck with a man of wealth and title," Killian answered, though he was reluctant to pursue the conversation. "Most mothers dream of such a match."

"Ah well, that's the rub. There's no mother to matchmake for Dee. Lady Elva does her best but she's not even a match for Dee." He chuckled at his own wit. "Now Dee's mother, there was lady a man might prefer for his bride."

Conall looked about to be certain they would not be overheard and then leaned closer to Killian, a grin on his broad face. "A witch she were, or so they say. For all Lady Grainne was noble born, there was a wantonness in her the likes of which I've never seen before or since. Black-haired she was, and red-mouthed. I was all of twelve but I knew I was a man when she walked within me view." He made a rude gesture with his hand and chuckled. "Da always was a man for the lasses. Dee's the result. *Wirra!* The poor soul did not last. She gave up her life birthing Dee. 'Tis Brigid, Lady Grainne's kinswoman, who's reared the lass.''

Conall paused to stroke his chin, his merry blue eyes darting away from and then back to Killian's somber expression. ''I know what you're thinking: why's he telling me the story of Dee's birth?''

He rested a hand on Killian's shoulder. ''I've had it in me head for a year or more that you should meet our Dee. She'll not be easy to win, but you'd not have it any other way, I'm thinking.''

Killian's expression grew remote. ''I'm not the man for the lass.''

Conall grinned. ''Many a man has made that hopeless vow concerning a lass.''

''And a few have meant it.''

Conall dropped his hand from MacShane's shoulder. ''Well, then, you best be warned that Dee is not a lass to be trifled with. Do not give her false hope. I've seen in her eyes a certain partiality for you. She's a stubborn, willful brat at times; but she has heart and spirit, and I'll not have her hurt.''

''A man cannot always spare a lass's feelings,'' Killian said, ''but I promise she'll not know grief on my account.''

Satisfied, Conall nodded. ''Then I'll warn you away from her nurse, Brigid, only because I've a liking for you. She's not the way to Deirdre, in any case. She's calls herself a *bean feasa*, with her charms and such. Be careful that you do not arouse her suspicions. Ah, here comes the lass, and dressed like she's going to a ball.''

As Deirdre entered the stable yard she gave a final tug to the black silk kerchief that held her lace fontange in place. She had chosen her blue taffeta gown with its tight bodice and low neckline because it made her feel beautiful. Yet, when she recognized the man who stood beside Conall, she suddenly felt less certain of herself. ''Captain MacShane,'' she said in surprise.

''Lady Deirdre,'' Killian returned quietly with the smallest of bows, something she had not seen him do before.

''Have you been riding?'' she asked politely, though she

knew the answer. His face glistened with sweat and his black clothes were dusty.

"Aye, down by the river."

Deirdre's throat constricted. MacShane had been to the river. Had he seen her lying asleep in the grass? The fact that he could not possibly have guessed her dreams did not keep a blush from rising in her cheeks. The dream was too fresh, too vivid, to be easily forgotten. What would he think if he knew she had dreamed of him, had dreamed of lying in the cool grass beside him, of lifting her mouth again and again for his kiss? Would he be glad, or would he ridicule her as always?

She would never know because she could never tell him. The lover of her dream had been nothing like the hard, unreachable stranger before her now. His face was closed to her, his mouth a straight, unemotional line.

Killian said nothing. He had no words for the serene creature who stood before him. Only in anger or when she forgot that she was a lady did he feel free to speak his mind to her. Had he known beforehand that he had been invited to Nantes to be paraded before her like a prize bull, he would never have come. For, against his will, she did stir him. When he looked at her he saw his dream made flesh and the yearning to hold her, to love her, nearly overwhelmed the reality of their situation.

She would be shocked, appalled, insulted to know what thoughts he had had as he lay daydreaming on the banks of the Loire. He had dreamed of her lying in his arms, pliant and eager for the caress of his hand.

His gaze dropped briefly to her daring neckline and an unexpected surge of desire jolted him as he lifted his eyes to her face once more. How warily she regarded him, her soft sweet mouth trembling with emotion. It was as if she suspected him already, could read his mind.

He looked away. "Until later," he said to Conall. "My lady," he added with a sketchy bow before striding toward the house.

"The gathering at the de Quentins," Conall called after him. "Ask Darragh about it. You're invited."

"He's invited?" Deirdre questioned in amazement.

"Mind your manners, he'll have heard you," Conall admonished, but MacShane did not turn back.

Deirdre blushed. "I meant no insult. I only meant that MacShane would not seem to possess the proper dress."

Deirdre turned to Conall and saw anger and hurt reflected in his expression. He was dressed informally. The only decorations on his dark blue coat were the lace frills below his turned-back cuffs and a small lace cravat. Instead of the accepted black-heeled shoes of a gentleman, he wore boots and spatterdashes that reached to his knees. His head was free of a wig and crisp red curls bounced about his shoulders.

"I'm not a courtier the likes of Cousin Claude," Conall said stiffly. "Nor is MacShane a man to sport ribbons and powder. But then, the lass who would win him wouldn't want him powdered and rouged."

"No, I think not," Deirdre agreed, remembering how she had imagined his raven-black hair blown by the wind and the smooth silken feel of it under her fingertips. Patches and wigs would not suit the man of her dreams who had lain at his ease among wild flowers and grass. That man had been a part of the land, an earthy pagan element among his own kind. Which was the real MacShane? Would she ever know?

Bemused, Deirdre smiled at her brother and that smile gave away more than she knew.

Conall grinned back at her. She had betrayed a little of her feelings for MacShane. Because MacShane did not fancy a bride, it did not follow that he would not have one. Many a man had come reluctantly to the altar.

Half an hour later the Fitzgerald coachman turned onto the drive before the de Quentin chateau and the carriageway was abuzz. From the tall front windows, new additions to the centuries-old facade, the light from hundreds of tapers shone upon vehicles of every description.

"You did not tell me 'twas to be a grand affair," Conall grumbled as he reached for his tricorner hat. "I would not have come!"

"Cousin Claude's invitation said it was to be an intimate affair," Deirdre answered, as much surprised as he.

Conall snorted. "A man with this many intimates has no friends at all. But then there's a merchant for you."

"The Gouberts haven't been merchants for at least two generations," Deirdre reminded her brother.

"Aye, but they remind the countryside of their heritage with such vulgar display. Mind you, there'll be more meat at supper than the Fitzgerald household sees in a week."

"They are our cousins," Deirdre reminded him.

"Just barely, and only because some foolish de Quentin noblewoman with a soft head to match her heart fell into bed with a French captain named Goubert. Amazing what French francs will buy. Now the Gouberts are the de Quentins, properly titled and all. The last comte, rest his soul, was the veriest old pirate who ever lived."

"You are harsh in you judgment of all who are not Irishmen," Deirdre teased.

"Aye," Conall concurred. "Come, lass, there's Cousin Claude dancing in his red-heeled shoes for want of a glimpse of you."

Deirdre glanced up the stone steps of the house to discover that Conall was not far wrong. Claude Goubert, le Comte de Quentin, waited just outside the open doorway, a breach of protocol that was certain to be discussed as fireside gossip by his nobler-born guests when the evening was done. He was splendidly attired in a pale blue satin coat whose nipped-in waist and wide skirts accented his slender figure. Tiers of lace cascaded from his lawn cravat, and his sleeves had been split rather than cuffed to reveal blue satin ribbons at his elbows and wrists. Pale blue silk stockings and a tall cane trimmed with a matching bowknot completed his attire.

Deirdre's spirits sank a little when he nodded at her, a singular greeting that she would rather have done without. He was making no secret of his infatuation with her. Overt displays of tender regard were all the fashion, but she did not like being the center of attention. Suppressing a sigh, she gave Conall her hand.

"Have we come acourting?" Conall whispered waggishly in her ear as they climbed the steps.

Deirdre shot him a sideways glance of pure enmity.

"Why do you not go back to war where you belong, Conall? The pastimes of genteel folk are well beyond you."

"Mademoiselle Deirdre," Claude greeted her warmly as she reached the top of the steps.

"Monsieur le Comte," she returned pleasantly and extended her hand. To her relief, he did not salute it but simply held her fingertips for a moment.

"But we are too formal," Claude said. Gazing into her face, he exerted the most subtle of pressure upon her fingers. "We are *en famille,* cousin. Will you not call me Claude?"

Deirdre smiled. "Very well, Cousin Claude."

"Cousin Claude," Conall seconded boisterously and offered his hand.

The Frenchman reluctantly released Deirdre's hand to clasp her brother's and winced as the huge ruby on his ring finger was crushed into his skin by a strong grip. "Cousin Conall," he murmured. Retrieving his mangled hand as quickly as possible, he turned again to Deirdre. "But where is your papa? I most particularly wished him to be here."

Deirdre leaned close to him, as if she had some secret to impart, and said, "Papa is feeling unwell this evening. Yet, had he known what a grand evening you had planned, I'm certain he would have struggled from his bed to attend."

In the dazzling moment of having the lady of his dreams so close, Claude did not notice Conall's snort of amusement. He stood that moment in awe of the glorious beauty of Deirdre's daring décolletage.

"Mademoiselle, my prayer to God is that your father's health improves *instanter.* But, as you're here, I must confess that my happiness is complete." Deirdre retrieved her fan from its ribbon about her wrist and flicked it open. "I, too, am pleased. Will you not give me your arm, cousin, before those who stand waiting behind us become less pleased and return to their carriages?"

"More likely they'll trample us over! Damme, if that

isn't the smell of roast venison in the air," Conall grumbled in Gaelic as they entered the house.

An hour later Deirdre sank gracefully into a petit-point chair beside Conall, plying her fan with an uncommon amount of energy. "Do not say it, you devil."

"What should I not say?" Conall questioned in all innocence, but his grin was as broad as ever.

"That I have somehow brought this upon myself," she answered tartly.

"I would not say that precisely," he replied and offered her his cup. " 'Tis only canary, and plaguey poor stuff that is for a man with a thirst!"

Deirdre took a long sip, luxuriating in the feel of cool liquid sliding down her throat. The Gouberts' intimate gathering included fifty guests, most of whom had made it their business to engage her in conversation meant to extract the extent of her interest in their host. It had taken all her skill at conversation to keep them guessing.

"Better?" Conall prompted. "Good. Then I will say that you had best keep a place or two away from Cousin Claude at supper. He's been gazing at you the evening long as though you were his favorite dish. Put a spoon in his hand and he may not be responsible for his actions!"

"Cousin Claude would never do such a thing," she said stiffly but her eyes twinkled. "I might upset his elaborate toilette."

"Paint on a man!" Conall muttered. "May the devil himself come to fetch me to hell the very hour I paint me face like an aging jade."

"I'm told 'tis all the rage at court," Deirdre answered. "There are those who japan their faces from cheeks to chin. Besides, I am quite taken with his face patch. 'Tis a unicorn?"

"Puts me in mind of a pregnant cow!" Conall said in a voice loud enough to be heard but, thankfully, not understood because he spoke Gaelic.

Amusement got the better of Deirdre, and she retreated behind the shelter of her open fan.

Satisfied to have raised her spirits, Conall patted her hand. "Well now, there's a certain lady who's been making eyes at me the evening long. I should relieve the poor lass's suspense.''

Deirdre followed his gaze. ''That's Madame Perot,'' she whispered. ''Her husband is away in Spain, I believe.''

''So much the better,'' Conall muttered, adjusting his steinkirk.

''She's married,'' Deirdre repeated.

Conall turned on her a surprised glance. ''Lass, sometimes I forget how innocent you are. A married woman bereft of her husband is a gift of fate, to my way of thinking. 'Tis easier to tip the scales in me favor if she's missing a man's arms already.''

''That's infamous!'' she whispered in genuine shock.

'' 'Tis life. Do not judge so harshly what you do not understand, lass.''

Before she could answer him, Conall rose and strode off toward the place where Madame Perot sat. In consternation Deirdre watched him make an elegant bow with his leg extended.

''*Bodach!*'' she murmured. He was much too big and broad for courtier's gestures but it seemed not to matter. Madame Perot smiled at him, rose from her seat, and accepted the arm he offered. It was not until they reached the doorway leading from the salon that Deirdre realized someone had come to stand beside her.

''Mademoiselle. At last.''

Deirdre felt the muscles of her face stretch into an automatic smile. ''Cousin Claude. Do join me.''

With a sweep of his hand he adjusted the skirts of his coat and sank gracefully onto the chair Conall had occupied.

''You've outdone yourself, cousin,'' she said, feeling the need of her fan again. ''You may be justifiably proud of the evening.''

''Just to be beside you, to breathe the air that you do, *chérie*, makes me the proudest and most content of men.''

There was an earnestness in his fair face that made Deirdre's heart ache. *He will propose,* she thought, and found the idea not repugnant but simply unwelcome.

''Are we not all a merry group?'' she said absently to keep the silence from growing too full. As the small orchestra began a country tune she smiled in genuine delight. "Are we to dance, too? Oh, Darragh will regret having missed this evening. He does love to dance."

"But he is here," Claude replied.

Eagerly Deirdre searched the crowd of gaily dressed guests. When her eyes came to rest on the man who entered the doorway, she went utterly still.

"What is it?" Claude questioned, puzzled by her reaction. "Mademoiselle?"

Deirdre turned to look at her companion. "You seem to have another guest, cousin. Will you not greet him?"

Claude looked toward the doorway and saw a tall man dressed severely in black, wearing his own black hair waved about his face in a style half a century old. "I do not know this man," he said in annoyance.

"It is Captain MacShane, our houseguest," Deirdre informed him.

Claude rose reluctantly to his feet. Etiquette had demanded that he invite the Fitzgeralds's guest, but he had not expected the man to accept. He turned to Deirdre, *"J'ai regrets,* cousin, that I must leave you a moment. I will return, with your permission."

Deirdre nodded him away and then lowered her gaze, concentrating on the open fan in her lap. It was her favorite accessory. Painted upon the delicate vellum stretched over sticks of mother-of-pearl was a miniature of Liscarrol. Darragh had commissioned the fan in Paris for her sixteenth birthday. She stared at it, smiling at the French artist's whimsy which had placed a topiary garden at Liscarrol's left and an artificial pond in the foreground. Neither of those existed at Liscarrol. But every detail of the house itself was correct. The massive gray walls of the Norman castle held a dominant place in the middle of the painting.

"That bored are you, lass?"

Deirdre looked up with a smile. "Darragh, I did not think social evenings much to your taste."

Darragh sat down beside her. " 'Tis true," he admitted freely in Gaelic. "I've little fondness for French society. I prefer me air perfumed with horse manure and the green grass."

Deirdre agreed. The press of sweating bodies coupled with an abundance of perfumes and powder scents had nearly overwhelmed her. "I suppose one becomes used to it after a time."

"MacShane agrees with me, but I thought he could do with a bit of entertainment, seeing that Fitzgerald hospitality is not at its most charming."

Deirdre looked up again in spite of her resolve to keep her eyes from MacShane, and another shiver of anticipation sped through her. He looked splendid in his severe costume of black. He was conversing with the comte in French, the deep murmur of his voice reaching her beneath the rustle and chatter of the room.

"What's the matter, Dee? You look sickly of a sudden."

Deirdre took a deep steadying breath. " 'Tis much too warm in this corner. Take me out onto the floor, Darragh. I want to dance."

Darragh came to his feet instantly, concern showing on his face. "You should not have come. 'Tis not the season for indoor affairs. Your Frenchman is mad."

"He's not mine," Deirdre protested as she took his arm and they moved to the center of the floor.

"Have you told him so, lass?"

"I have tried," Deirdre murmured, curtsying as the dance began.

"I know how to put it to him in a way he'll not forget," Darragh grumbled.

"You would make a corpse of him and that's hardly necessary. In the whole world he's the only gentleman willing to pay me court. I must guard my sole suitor lest I become known as a spinster."

Darragh nodded solemnly. "Aye, 'tis there in your eager gaze, lass, that you're too desperate by far for a husband. Do try to curb your impatience, you're running the lads away."

"Wretch," Deirdre responded, but laughter bubbled up in her as it always did in her brothers' company.

When the dance was done Darragh relinquished her to

an elderly gentleman and he, in turn, bowed to a younger man to partner her for the third set of dances. Finally Darragh claimed her again, twirling her about the floor with more gusto than grace.

Through it all she heard MacShane's voice and knew when he was closer or farther away, but she did not look up. She did not need to. It was as if her ears and skin had taken on a new keenness of detection because she had denied her eyes. She heard him flatter Claude's sister, Annabelle, felt his bright blue gaze on her repeatedly as the dancing progressed, and each time she wondered if and when he would speak to her.

Now, as Darragh spoke to him, turning MacShane's head her way, she took a deep breath and raised her head.

"Mademoiselle Deirdre," he said softly.

"Captain MacShane," she replied and offered her hand. He lifted it in the quickest of salutes, his lips hovering a scant space above her fingertips. The pure black sheen of his hair reflected the light of the hundreds of candles which illuminated the room, and she had the absurd impulse to tell him so. Instead she said, "I am delighted to see you."

His look disconcerted her, for it seemed to suggest that she had done a very reckless thing by admitting her pleasure at his presence. "Do you dance, captain?"

She had not meant to say that, she had meant to say something that would divert him from his intense contemplation of her face. "If mademoiselle wishes," she heard him say.

With her heart pounding in her chest she took the hand he offered and followed him out onto the gleaming marble floor.

She wondered why Darragh did not stop them. Surely he must see that she was much too pleased, too expectant and happy with the invitation for it to be proper for them to dance together. Yet, when she turned and looked up into MacShane's arrogant face, she knew why she had acted too rashly in suggesting the dance.

To touch him, if only this once, that was what she wanted. Did it really exist, the answer to these wild sweet urgings of her body, or was that kind of guilty pleasure found only in the dreams of silly young women who fell asleep on riverbanks during lazy summer days?

The music was a country air, a tune that would find no enthusiastic audience in Paris, and many couples left the floor. But MacShane smiled at her, and her reluctance vanished as they took up the measure.

Conversation was expected no matter how she felt, and so Deirdre said, "You are a dancer, captain, so few soldiers are."

"I'm a Gael, my lady, and few of us are less than what pleases our lasses," he returned in a bored drawl that Claude might have used. It was a wicked mimic, and she did not miss its significance.

"*Touché*, captain. I should know better than to bandy words with a man of the sod." As they made a turn about the room she added softly in Gaelic, "Was Cousin Claude polite to you?"

"I've never treated an enemy so well," Killian answered blandly.

His choice of words amused her. "You've scarcely met. What could cause you to be enemies?"

Killian shrugged. "You are right, of course."

His oblique answer further intrigued her, but she was wary of matching wits with him. "Where will your travels take you when you leave Nantes?"

"To Paris, in the morning."

She looked up, startled. "So soon?" Instantly she recovered. "Och, we must be poor hosts indeed."

Killian did not answer. Until the moment she asked him he had made no definite plans. Now that he had received satisfaction of a sort from Lord Fitzgerald, there was nothing to keep him in Nantes. If his curiosity was piqued to learn whether the absurdly lovely lass by his side bore any resemblance to the wanton of his riverbank daydream, then it must go wanting. Perhaps he was more like other men than he had thought. The insistent press in his loins was becoming an embarrassment and a trial. For the first time since arriving at the Fitzgeralds', he thought of the duchesse.

They continued in silence another set of steps, Deirdre's

heart pounding from anxiety and her head swimming with the heat. MacShane must not go away, not yet.

Deirdre moistened her suddenly dry lips. Words trembled on her tongue. She did not want him to go away, not while they were yet strangers. Why were the words so difficult to say? They rang in her ears yet she could not speak them. Suddenly the room's candles brightened, their light blinding her. She blinked twice and MacShane's blue eyes came into focus, staring down at her with the same intensity that so daunted her. She reached out to him, her hand curling tightly on his sleeve. "Lead me from the floor, captain," she whispered breathlessly. "I am fatigued."

"Of course, mademoiselle." He led her to a chair beside an open door, and when she was seated, he signaled for a cup of punch from one of the servants. "Mademoiselle must drink this; it is cool and your cheeks are flushed," he said smoothly in French.

She took the cup, grateful that he thought nothing out of the ordinary had occurred.

"Cousin Deirdre, are you ill?" Claude questioned with great concern in his voice as he reached her side.

"She is fatigued," Killian answered flatly.

Claude looked up at the plainly dressed man. "Perhaps you should have noticed this earlier and not subjected her to the strenuous exercise of the dance."

"Please!" Deirdre said more loudly than was polite. "I am exhausted; my head aches abominably, and I need fresh air."

"Dee, lass, you'll be stamping your foot and holding your breath next," Darragh said without concern as he joined them. "She's a rare temper when she's tired."

Claude nodded politely. "Of course. Cousin Deirdre, may I offer you my accompaniment for a turn about the garden?"

"She should go home," Darragh answered for her.

"But of course." Claude bowed to Deirdre and offered a slight nod to her brother, but his eyes were cold as they met MacShane's. He did not, however, allow his feelings to overrule his manners. "Would you care to indulge in a

game of chance, monsieur? There are several gentlemen so
engaged in the library.''

"No, monsieur,'' Killian answered absently, his eyes
hard on Deirdre's pale face.

"Then you'll be coming with us,'' Darragh cut in
swiftly.

Deirdre rose to her feet only to find MacShane's arm
offered before Darragh's. She took it, trembling as he
pressed her hand against his side. When they entered the
front hall, Darragh suddenly stopped, planting his feet like
a bull. "I'm that mad! I forgot to fetch Conall! See to my
sister.''

Too late Deirdre realized that Darragh was leaving her
alone with MacShane. She looked about a little desperately,
but no other guests had chosen to leave before supper was
served. The absurd desire to cry seized her, but she willed
it away. She could not say why she was do afraid. What
harm was there in a moment shared? "So you go to
Paris,'' she heard herself say, her voice sounding strained
and faraway.

"Aye.''

He bit off the word, leaving her no entrance to further
conversation, but her tongue would not be stilled. "I've
heard that Paris is beautiful in autumn but too warm in
summer. Nantes is lovely in summer.''

Deirdre closed her eyes when only silence answered her.
She wished she had said nothing, wished she had stayed
behind in the ballroom, wished that she were not standing
alone in the foyer with a man who made her tremble.

"Why must you leave?''

He reached out for her; and before she fully understood
the reason, she felt the stunning surprise of his mouth on
hers.

It was not the kiss she had dreamed.

There was nothing subtle or sweet about the savage heat
of his mouth. He engulfed her. His hands found her waist,
pulled her tight between his spread legs, and then rose
again until his thumbs hooked under the soft fullness of
her breasts.

For an instant she was too amazed to resist. When she

did try to push him away, somehow the hands she raised in protest found anchor on his neck; and the breath she expelled in anger became entangled in his. He drank in her mouth, dragging a heavy breath of air in with it and then, to her complete astonishment, his tongue flickered across her lips.

It lasted only a moment, the feelings and sensations slipping away almost before she could record them.

Suddenly cool night air flowed between them.

Killian stared down into her sweet face with eyes still closed and lips still parted in invitation and felt a curious tug of emotion which he could not name.

"I did not mean to do that." His heavy voice was strangely husky. "But then, surely you've been kissed before, lass."

Deirdre opened her eyes, her wonder reflected in pupils so wide her green eyes appeared black. "Nae, I do not think I have," she whispered.

"Then 'tis a lesson you're certain to repeat," he answered and broke away. "Goodbye, *acushla*."

She did not really see him go. He simply walked out of the door and melted into the darkness of the night.

Chapter Ten

Deirdre dozed on the carriage ride home, wedged comfortably between Darragh and a very unhappy Conall, who had seen his well-warmed desire for Madame Perot come to nothing as his fraternal duty to see his sister home intervened.

"One of us would have done as well," Conall grumbled.

"Two of us are better," Darragh answered. "Unless I miss me guess, the house will be full of intrigue this night. Two pairs of eyes are better than one."

"Intrigue?" Conall scoffed. "You speak nonsense."

" 'Twas not nonsense I spied in MacShane's eyes. 'Twas lust, brother, a need so great he nearly gave himself away."

His interest piqued, Conall glanced at his sleeping sister and then said, " 'Tis come to that already, has it? Damn quick, it was."

Darragh shrugged. "Did I not say MacShane was the lad for our Dee?"

"Aye, incessantly. Still, I had me doubts. MacShane was reluctant, and our Dee, while pretty enough, is not so much a wanton that a man's prick rises at the sight of her."

"Watch your speech, brother!" Darragh cautioned.

Conall smirked. "Why should we not speak the truth? You can be certain 'tis lust that moves MacShane to seek a woman, the same as any other man."

"And that, brother, is why you've come home with me."

"He would not!"

Darragh grinned, his teeth gleaming in the darkness. "Maybe aye, maybe nae. 'Tis up to us to make certain he does not have a moment in which to seduce the lass."

"Perhaps," Conall said, " 'twould not be so bad a thing, were it to happen. They've had nary a moment alone, and Da is not so fond of MacShane that he will come easily to the point of making him a son-in-law."

"Aye. Da will curse and swear and threaten until he's blue in the face, but you're forgetting Dee. She has Da wrapped neatly about her finger. He'll bluster, but he'll conceed to the wisdom of seeing his daughter wed." Darragh nodded to himself. "I would not be surprised to learn Lady Elva's in the family way again. Dee needs a man to take care of her, too."

Conall glanced at Deirdre's sleeping face. "Do you think we rush the matter? After all, Dee's had little enough time to consider MacShane. The choice should be hers."

"Curse you for a soft-headed man!" Darragh said irritably. "Blind was it you were to them on the dance floor? 'Twas some rare sight. MacShane watched her like she was the first lass he'd ever set eyes on, and him in the discovery of his manhood. And she behaved no better, trembling and skittish as a filly with the first smell of a stallion in her nostrils she was."

"As bad as that?" Conall asked mildly.

"Aye, 'twas a miserable display," Darragh groused. "Shocked I am that even a Frenchman should allow such doings in his home."

"Then 'tis settled. Who'll broach the subject of marriage with MacShane?"

For the first time neither man had a ready answer. They looked at each other and then down at Deirdre.

"Nature taking its course would not be so terrible,"

Conall ventured softly after a long pause. "There's you and me to look after her best interests. A blind eye, if it comes to it, might serve us well. MacShane will do right by her, I'm thinking."

"Aye. 'Tis no surprise to most when a young bride makes the mistake of birthing her first bairn a wee bit early," Darragh answered and resettled himself. "As we all know, the others are sure to come at decent nine-month intervals!"

"Was it a fine evening then?" Brigid asked as she drew Deirdre's gown over her head.

"Aye," Deirdre answered sleepily. "I danced with half the male company, including MacShane."

"And how did that please ye?"

Deirdre avoided the woman's eyes. "He's a fair dancer, for a man so unfamiliar with civilized things."

"Some dancing's less civilized than other dancing," Brigid replied. "Turn this way and I'll have ye out of that corset in a trice."

Deirdre did as she was told, glad to be able to turn her back on Brigid, for she had a question to ask. "MacShane tells me that he once visited Liscarrol."

"Did he now?" Brigid said noncommittally.

" 'Twas in ninety-one. Do you remember him?"

"Those were dark times, lass. Many a stranger came and went, and so much the better that we forgot they did."

"He should have been difficult to forget, what with his black hair and bright stare," Deirdre offered as bait.

"He could nae have been more than a bairn himself. 'Tis oftimes surprising to see what nature refines from dross," Brigid countered.

Deirdre turned around as she was freed from the corset. "Are you certain you've never set eyes on MacShane before?"

"I'd nae swear to it," Brigid replied in a manner that brooked no argument. "Hurry into bed, lass, afore ye catch yer death."

Annoyance rippled through Deirdre's expression. "Mac-Shane came to Liscarrol the day we left. He and another lad had been chased by English soldiers and the English had captured and hanged his friend. How can you not remember that?"

Brigid looked at her charge, her eyes oddly bright. "How would ye be knowing of such things, lass?"

"Da told me," Deirdre lied, crossing her fingers behind her back. "Now do you remember MacShane's visit?"

"Aye, I remember it." Brigid hesitated. "What do ye remember, lass?"

"I?" Deirdre frowned in confusion as she slipped off her remaining petticoats to stand in her shift. "You know I remember nothing of those days. Da says 'tis because of the fever I caught at sea."

"Aye, we said that," Brigid said quietly. "But memory is a tricky thing. It often comes galloping back, given the right mount."

"Is MacShane the right steed?" Deirdre asked glibly as she scrambled into bed.

"Maybe aye, maybe nae," Brigid replied. "Go to bed, 'tis no time for chatter."

"If only I could remember," Deirdre murmured, and it suddenly seemed very important that she should. When she had danced with him she had done so with an indefinable sense of elation and trepidation. When they conversed they had teetered on the brink of something of great importance; she had felt it. But then he had spoiled it by his boorish behavior and his careless kiss. She was a lass from whom he had snatched a token, nothing more.

She glanced at Brigid, who picked up her hair brush. Perhaps she should tell her a little of her dream.

"MacShane asked me if I had saved his life. 'Twas so strange a question. He spoke of fairies and magic."

The crash of the perfume bottle surprised Deirdre, for Brigid was seldom clumsy. "You're butter-fingered this night, Brigid. Brigid? What's wrong? You're white as a sheet!"

Brigid did, indeed, feel as though her blood had frozen in her veins. She looked down at the shattered glass oozing the oily expensive perfume but it was the play of the candle's flame upon the crystal shards that held her spellbound. The light danced, colored gold, green, red, and blue, upon the sharp edges until a pattern began to form.

She heard Deirdre's voice faintly, questioning and calling her name, but she could not draw back from the trance.

She was not a strong *bean feasa*. The years away from her homeland had weakened her powers even further. When as a child her family had sent her to learn the uses of her power, she had not progressed well. She could scarcely remember from day to day the recipes for elixirs and potions. She forgot the names of herbs and their uses. By accident her mentor had discovered that bright light reflected from a shiny surface drew her into a trance and in those trances lay her powers.

Brigid closed her eyes and slipped down into the cool colors.

Reds and blues, gold and greens played about her. Each facet of color held the image of a face, like portraits in frames. As they shimmered past she recognized two of them. Deirdre stood enveloped in a brilliant red flame, the man called MacShane in a sapphire glow.

But there were others dressed in old-fashioned garments whom she did not recognize. One was a beautiful black-haired woman surrounded by deep emerald light. Entrapped in a golden halo was a golden-haired gentleman with a face so perfect that Brigid caught her breath. And then she knew, knew who the strangers were and what the vision meant.

The colors winked in and out until the red and sapphire flames outshone the rest. Blending, they became a single amethyst tongue of light.

"Brigid, are you all right? Brigid, please, answer me!"

Brigid opened her eyes to find Deirdre's anxious face hovering over her as she lay sprawled on the carpet. "Aye, lass," she mumbled, still trembling from the vision.

"You fainted. I'll get Darragh."

"No! Call no one, lass. No one!" The numbness began to drain from her body, leaving behind a weariness that always plunged her into an unnaturally long and deep sleep.

She reached out and grasped Deirdre by the wrist, her grip strong enough to make the girl wince. She struggled to rise and with Deirdre's help pulled herself into a sitting position. "Water," she said.

Deirdre hurriedly retrieved a goblet from her nightstand and brought it. "I think I should call someone. You look pale as death."

Brigid took the cup and noisily gulped the contents. When she had drained it, she raised her head, her pale blue eyes bright with knowledge. "Hear me, lass, and do nae ask questions." She pulled in a long, slow breath. "The man called MacShane, he's the one we've waited for. He's yer way back to Liscarrol!" Her head drooped in weariness. "I almost did nae know in time."

Nervous laughter trembled on Deirdre's lips. "The one? A husband, do you mean? A fine husband he'd make, being so mannerless and rude. No, thank you, I prefer to be courted."

Brigid swallowed, her tongue feeling thick and lifeless in her mouth. "Ye must go to him. he will know what to do." She closed her eyes, seeking the phrase that would send Deirdre to MacShane's room. "Raven's-wing black, a complexion as pure as snow, and a scarlet spill of blood." She looked up. " 'Twas ye who saved MacShane's life. Ask him, lass. Ask him!"

"I saved his life?" Deirdre rose, Brigid's words echoing in her head. She put a hand to her temple, the tolling becoming tiny hammerings of her pulse. She wanted to remember . . . and yet she was afraid.

"Go to him!" Brigid cried. "Go!"

Deirdre turned and ran out the door.

As the door slammed shut behind Deirdre, a long, weary sigh escaped Brigid. "He's your mate, lass, the one the fairies sent ye." She closed her eyes, missing the small shadow that crossed the room and then silently disappeared out the same door.

*   *   *

'Twas you saved MacShane's life! 'Twas you! 'Twas you! 'Twas you!

Deirdre ran down the hallway with those words ringing in her ears. If that were true, why had no one told her? Why would they want to keep from her this act of bravery?

Did MacShane know?

Deirdre came to a halt at the end of the hall, confusion swamping her. She hugged her body with her arms. She was shaking, shuddering like an autumn leaf under the first gust of winter. The headache, absent since MacShane's kiss, had returned.

Her memory was returning but the recall was not yet complete. What were the missing threads that when woven into the spiderwebs of reverie would make whole cloth? She needed to talk to her father, to make him explain what she could not remember and what others would not tell her.

Round and round her thoughts spun until the darkness before her seemed to heave and shift. For an instant she thought she was mistaken, but then a long black shadow detached itself from the rest at the opposite end of the hall and moved toward her.

She took a backward step, pressing a hand against her mouth to still the cry that catapulted into her throat. Even as she recorded the phantom, it changed shape, taking on the contours of a man. MacShane.

He turned when he reached the landing, only a few yards from where she stood, and on a silent tread descended the stairs. She waited, watching until he lifted the bolt from the front door and went out.

There was the man who knew all the answers to all of her questions.

That single thought sent her down the stairs after him. She was not afraid of the dark. She did not hesitate to open the door and go after him. Only when the dew-slicked stones of the front steps chilled her feet did she remember that she was dressed only in her shift.

She looked about, searching for him, and saw his long shadow, made sharper and more black by the moonlight, slipping behind the tall shrubs that lined the path to the rose garden. Even before her decision was complete, she was running across the moonlit grasses silvered by dew.

When she reached the arbor she paused again. Moonlight streamed in milky-white slants through a canopy of briers, making a houndstooth pattern on the paving. Disappointment knifed through her. MacShane was not here.

He stepped out of the shadows slowly, and this time she was able to quell the fear that raised the hair at the nape of her neck.

"MacShane?"

"Aye."

He came forward, moonlight silvering his black hair. "What are you doing here, lass?"

His voice, dark and edged with unwelcome, made her timorous. She said nothing.

"Were you looking for me?" He spoke softly and slowly, the annoyance gone from his voice.

"I saw you leave the house," she said.

She saw the sudden tensing of his body. He lifted his head as though he heard a noise she could not hear. For the space of three heartbeats he did not move, and then his body relaxed and he said in the same low voice, "I could not sleep."

"I—I thought you were leaving."

She seemed to feel him smile, for his face was in shadow. "I am a solitary man but I do not skulk away like a thief. I was restless."

He looked up at the midnight sky. "They tell me I was born on such a night. Perhaps 'tis Samain's light that draws me out with the tide in my blood."

"Samain?" Deirdre repeated in a near whisper. " 'Tis a pagan name for the moon."

"Aye. Sometimes a man feels more the pagan than the Holy Ghost within him. There are many thoughts a man may think only in the dark of night."

"Of places he's been and seen?" she asked cautiously.

"Of things he has done or failed to do, of battles and regrets . . . and desires."

"You hunger for a return to war?"

He sighed. "Nae. I'll not return to the battlefield again. I've grown weary of war. A man who lives for battle lives only to die. It is a never-ending thing, an animal that lives by feeding upon itself. Ah, a riddle. 'What is it that grows by devouring itself? War!' "

The air between them vibrated with his gentle humor, and she spoke only to break its harmony. "You could fight a battle that has a useful purpose."

He smiled again, she sensed it as a breath of air upon her skin. "What war would that be, lass?"

"The war to free Ireland," she answered promptly. "It would be an honorable war, a holy war, a righteous war."

"Such passion, *acushla,*" he answered with amusement roughening his voice. "And who would fight this battle with me?"

"All Irish lads with heart in them. The Irish Brigade!"

This time his laughter had a sting in it. "Lass, you're not such a fool as to believe that the Wild Geese desire defeat at the hands of the English? The Irish are tired of defeat. We go where we may win wars."

"Do not speak for the others," she answered heatedly. "Are you a coward, then, that you dare not face the possibility of defeat?"

"Perhaps," he answered quietly.

"Then you're not a true Irishman!"

"Hush, lass. We are not so far from the house that our voices would not bring the curious."

He held out a hand to her. In spite of her anger, she took it and allowed him to drag her back into the shadows beside him. "Better," he said.

Her eyes were growing accustomed to the dark and she saw as he gazed down at her the silver-white moonlight captured in his eyes. She shivered as his arm grazed her naked shoulder. He was no longer shadow but warm skin and firm muscle.

"Are you afraid, *acushla?*"

"Why do you call me 'darling'?" she whispered, almost afraid of her own voice.

"Do you not like it? Faith, but you're a hard one to please." Silent mirth shook his shoulders, brushing him against her once more, and she gasped at the touch of his elbow upon the tip of her breast.

He stilled. "You should go back to the house."

"Why?"

"If you do not know the answer to that, lass, then you most definitely should go in."

She knew the answer, but the desire to provoke him made her brave. "Because you might kiss me again?"

His silence was electric.

Deirdre pulled away, ashamed of her reckless words. What a foolish, ill-chosen thing to say. The strong fingers which captured her wrist startled her.

"Do not go yet. Stay a bit with me."

His arms came about her as she turned back to him, his hands finding her waist as her cheek sought the pillow of his chest. "Aye, 'tis better like this," he whispered against her hair as his hand came up to lightly stroke her curls.

His gentleness astonished her. Before, there had been only harsh words between them. Had the reminder of a single kiss wrought this change in him?

"You are small, *acushla,* no more than a child."

"That is not true," Deirdre whispered. The tremulous excitement in her had no part of childish fancy. "I am a woman."

"A woman does not protest a man's flattery," he answered. "A woman smiles prettily and is smug in the knowledge that a man finds her winsomeness lovely."

"Then I am smug," she murmured shyly against his shirtfront. Beneath her cheek his heartbeat was slow and steady, while inside her chest her own thumped a lively rhythm worthy of a jig. "How is it you know so much of women, captain, when 'tis said that the 'Avenging Angel' has little use for womenfolk?"

She felt him tense and immediately regretted the words, but his voice was quiet as he said, "Who told you of my battle name? Ah, your brothers, though I wonder that they spoke of my prowess—or lack—in more delicate matters."

She turned her face into his chest but he would not let her hide there. He took her chin in his hand and raised it, bending deliberately to set his lips on hers.

It was a kiss so unlike the first that she felt no alarm, only a sense of inevitability and joy. Little more than an hour earlier she had been shocked by his touch. Now the warm sweetness of his lips persuaded her that there was much in this difficult, contrary man that could not be simply or easily discovered. And, that she wanted to discover it all.

Almost reluctantly his mouth lifted from hers, hovering a moment as the tip of his tongue lightly stroked the shape of her upper lip.

"It seems we've done this before . . . but this is not why you followed me, *acushla*, is it?"

Deirdre stood a moment with her chin propped by his thumbs and her cheeks cradled in his fingers. No, this was not why she had followed him. She wanted to know the truth about their first meeting.

"You are shivering." His hands left her face to touch her shoulders and then travel down over her back to her hips. "*Acushla*, you're all but naked!"

The shock in his voice made her skin burn where his hands touched her, their heat branding her through the thin barrier of her shift. She tried to break free but he brought her tight against him once more.

"What a clumsy fool you are, Killian MacShane!" he murmured and bent to kiss the top of her head. "Are you angry with me, lass?"

Deirdre shook her head, too confused by his nearness to understand her feelings.

Without completely releasing her, he slipped off his coat and wrapped her in it. His warmth, trapped within the velvet folds, surrounded her and Deirdre accepted it gratefully.

When he bent and picked her up she was startled. "What are you doing?"

"Taking you back inside."

"No! No, you mustn't do that," she whispered. "We must talk, now, where no one will hear us."

He held her a moment longer and she saw that the hard lines of his serious face were in place again. "It must be very important to you."

"It is," she whispered.

"Then we will talk."

"Put me down."

MacShane hesitated, as if he would not comply, but then he lowered her to the ground.

When her feet touched the path she held on to his shoulders to steady herself. The solid warmth of his body was amazingly comforting and she wished suddenly that she had not asked to be freed.

She was glad for the gloom of night because it hid her chagrin. "I know where we may talk. There is a hunting lodge at the end of this path. No one will find us there."

He did not speak, but she sensed a change in him, as if he doubted the propriety of her suggestion. Flushed with expectancy, Deirdre pulled on his hands. "Come! Please!" He followed her.

The night was cool, but in the breeze lingered the warmth of the day perfumed with the odor of lavender, roses, and honeysuckle. Overhead a bat swooped, the flap of its leathery wings a sudden sound in the silence. They crossed a small wooden bridge and then a field toward a small house which had once offered hospitality to hunting parties or shelter from the rain to a rider. She had not been there in years but knew that it was neatly maintained as part of the de Quentin estates.

The night seemed to beckon them, Deirdre thought. The moon itself laid out their path in a broad white avenue of light that ran in a straight line to the place they sought.

When the small dwelling came into view at the edge of the forest, the aching hunger that had been in Deirdre's blood since the moment of his kiss vanished. She held the hand of a stranger; a complicated, contrary, and lonely man.

To her surprise, the hard, warm hand in hers trembled slightly, and she knew that he was not as remote and indifferent as the rest of her family believed. She knew that if she asked him he would tell her the truth about their first meeting eleven years before. And, if Brigid was right, in that telling lay the answer to her future.

"Shall we go in?"

Chapter Eleven

Once inside, Deirdre moved away from MacShane, her path lit by moonlight filtered through the open door. Her bare feet, damp from the dew, left imprints on the wooden floor as she walked in. A huge table dominated the small enclosure and she walked over to it and pulled out one of the chairs. "Will you sit, captain?"

"I prefer to stand," Killian answered in a faintly amused tone. Now that they were truly alone she chose to resort to more civilized behavior.

" 'Tis a lovely night," Deirdre said, endeavoring to bring something of ordinary conversation between them. She had his attention but she did not know where to begin.

"Aye, a fair night and a soft breeze and the smell of rain in the air. Now that we've covered that, should you not get on with your questions, lass, for 'tis weary I am of your reluctance."

Deirdre turned to him. The moment of tenderness between them had passed. He lounged in the doorway with his arms crossed, the night's light silvering his hair and honing his profile to razor sharpness, and she knew she dealt once more with the MacShane the world knew, a hard man, abrupt and distant. "I know that you once came to Liscarrol many years ago. I heard you and Da speak of it.''

"You listened at the keyhole," Killian said without apparent surprise.

"Aye, in a manner of speaking. There's a room behind the gallery tapestries that shares a wall with the library. I went there to listen."

"The Fitzgeralds have an uncommon fondness for secret places," he murmured. "So what did you hear, lass?"

"Enough that I wanted to learn more."

"And have you?"

"Aye. Brigid told me this night that 'twas I who found you in the stable all those years ago," Deirdre answered quietly.

Killian was suddenly alert. "What's that you say?"

Deirdre shook her head. "I was ill for a time after we left Liscarrol, and my memory of those last days deserted me. I remember nothing, and yet it troubles me that I cannot remember. Do you not think it strange?"

"Perhaps," Killian answered guardedly. "Perhaps your feelings are hurt that you've never been properly thanked by me?"

"Of course not!" Deirdre replied. " 'Tis only that Da has never mentioned it, and I do not believe Conall and Darragh know anything about it." She moved toward him, her hands lifted unconsciously in pleading. "Will you not tell me the full story?"

"Why?"

Deirdre stared up into his hard face. "Why not?"

Killian looked down at her and a shudder of desire traveled through him. He raised his hand to touch her face but did not do so. He had touched her once this night. He must not do so again. He was leaving in the morning. It was better to leave her in ignorance of his feelings. "If you listened to your father and me, you know as much as I," he said finally.

"Was that all?"

Killian frowned. "What more should there be?"

"You spoke of fairies."

"Did I now?" he answered in a hushed voice.

Apprehension danced along Deirdre's spine. "You spoke of a dream which haunts you."

Killian was silent.

Deirdre looked away. It was difficult to put into words the feeling that had come over her when she heard his confession. "I, too, once dreamed. As a child I believed the fairies came to visit me. 'Tis a common belief for an Irish child. Brigid scolded me about my talk of fairies and dreams, but I think she enjoyed my wild tales."

The chill of the night swept through the door, a brief gust that raised goosebumps on her skin, and she pulled MacShane's coat tighter about herself.

"There was one dream, I do not remember it now, but it was more a nightmare. I remember that it made me cry."

"What has this to do with me?"

"I do not know." Deirdre shrugged. "I suppose I thought that a man of your experience and worldliness would not mention a dream to a stranger unless it meant a great deal to him."

Killian was silent a long time. "You are not a fool, lass. Forgive me for ever having insulted you on that account."

Deirdre moved toward him. "Then your dream was of great importance to you? Would you tell me, does it have something to do with me?"

He looked at her, thinking that she was never more beautiful. Here in the moonlight, she was the image of the fairy woman who haunted his dream and made him ache with longing. Were they the same? Almost, he could believe that they were.

"I will tell you what I remember of that day at Liscarrol. I remember a wee lass in a soiled gown with yellow curls tumbling down her back. She chased kittens in the hay. When she discovered me I was so frightened that I drew my pistol on her. But she was brave as well as fair. She did not scream nor run. She offered me protection as one of King James's men."

His voice, low and exceedingly sweet, seemed to move inside Deirdre and become a part of her, painting pictures in her mind of things that she had not recalled in eleven years.

"When your father came the lass went away," he continued. "I wanted her to stay, to talk to me, to make me less afraid." His voice was as dark and mysterious as the night. "When she looked at me I did not fear dying. She had eyes the color of a mist-shrouded lough in the winter when its green still depths hold nature quiet in expectation of spring. I would have died for her, killed for her, done anything to keep her with me!"

The violence of his words made Deirdre shiver; but the remembered feeling of love for the wounded stranger which had lain dormant so long burst full upon her, and she knew then the source of the dream at the riverbank. She had dreamed of this man, of the feel of his hands on her skin and his naked body pressed hot and heavy against hers. The desire had been with her from the moment she had seen him riding toward her, so familiar and yet unknown. "I remember," she whispered.

Killian did not hear her. He was caught up in memories dark and painful. "I do not remember anything more until I awakened in a cave."

"The priest hole," Deirdre corrected. "I—I remember." She turned to him with a smile of triumph. "I was there with you! After Da went away, I came to be with you. I was afraid that you would disappear because the fairies had brought you to me, and I had not been gracious about it."

She paused, astonished by her flood of memory. "I remember it all. I had been listening to Brigid tell the tale of Deirdre and Noisiu. I often boasted that I, too, would marry a man who bore the colors of the raven's wing, snow, and blood. When I found you, black-haired, white with pain, and red with blood, I thought 'twas a fairies' trick to repay me for my bragging."

Killian's heart began to pound in slow heavy strokes, but nothing of his agitation sounded in his voice. "What else?"

Deirdre pressed a hand to her brow. "Let me think. The English had come to escort us to Cork. They demanded to search the house. Mother of mercy, why has no one told me, helped me remember? I came to the priest hole and helped you hide. I even made myself into a step stool to aid your climb into the air shaft.''

Killian reached out and grasped her by the arm. ''Do you mock me, lass?''

His grip hurt her but Deirdre was too elated to care. ''Mock you! I tell you, I remember. I cried when Da told me that I could not see you again. I begged him, told him I should be with you, that you belonged to me, that . . . I loved you.''

Killian released her and moved back out of the moonlight into the shadows. ''I thought I dreamed those moments in the priest hole.'' Yet even as he said it he knew that he lied. He had always held on to the foolish hope that the lady of his dreams did in truth tread the earth and that he would one day find her. That was the real reason he had come to Nantes to see Lord Fitzgerald, a reason he could not even admit to himself until now.

Deirdre looked at him with joy in her eyes. ''What you say you felt for me all those years ago, I have felt since you came here, but I could not understand the cause. From the moment I first saw you, you were familiar to me. Now I know why.''

Killian did not answer.

''Tell me about your dream. Is it only a memory of that day?''

Killian stiffened. Dare he finish his tale and risk her ridicule? ''As a child you say you believed in fairies. I never did. But in the priest hole of Liscarrol a fairy woman came to me.'' He hesitated. ''She bore the mark.''

''What mark?'' Deirdre asked, her heart trebling its pace.

''She had a red rose on her right shoulder,'' Killian answered in challenge.

Without a word Deirdre slipped his coat from her shoulders and stepped into the slat of moonlight. With trembling fingers she lowered the strap of her shift. ''The mark of the fairies,'' she whispered.

Killian grasped her shoulder, turning her so that the mark could be clearly seen. '' 'Twas you!''

''Aye,'' she answered shakily. '' 'Tis I you love.''

Killian stepped back from her. It was not possible. And yet, he knew that it was. The possibility had become reality, but with every heartbeat he knew a dread so great that his skin shrank against his bones. He had been raised in preparation for the priesthood, and he understood the temptation of unholiness and that it was imperative to shy from that which smacked of magic. The lady before him spoke the words of his dream which he had confided to no one. He did not fear any mortal, but he would be mad not to be in awe of the power of the *Daoine sidhe.*

"I knew that you were special," Deirdre said, unaware of the transformation in MacShane. She raised a hand to her lips to still the joyous laughter that trembled there. "But for Darragh and Conall we might never have met. A clumsier pair of matchmakers would be difficult to find. Yet, they have succeeded beyond their expectations, have they not?"

She reached out to him but MacShane did not move toward her. "Am I too forward, captain?" she teased. " 'Tis happiness that makes me bold."

"I will not wed you, lass."

Deirdre wet her lips. "I am making a fool of myself, talking and talking. 'Tis your prerogative to do the courting, I know, but I am not some vain mademoiselle who needs the wooing."

"I will never wed," Killian added flatly.

"But you love me."

"Do I?"

Deirdre regarded him steadily and felt within herself a certainty that nothing, not even his protests, would shake. He was a challenge, she had understood that from the first. Yet there was a recklessness awakening in her that had been dormant too long to be denied its resurgence of life. She was not afraid. "Aye, you've loved me without knowing 'twas I."

Killian moved toward her. "When you kiss me I feel a need here." He took her hand in his and drew it down to his groin. Deirdre tried to pull away but he pressed her hand against the turgid heat of his manhood. "Do not fret, lass. 'Tis what happens to a man when there's a woman about he lusts after. That's what I feel for you.''

Deirdre jerked her hand away, and he freed her with a mocking chuckle.

"You want to be loved," he continued cruelly. "I would love you, lass, if you'd let me. I would love your body and make you feel what you do not yet know is possible.''

Ignoring her struggles, he caught her about the waist and leaned down until his lips were nearly against hers. "I would make you moan with joy. I can nearly hear you already. Is that a sigh of fear? I think not. You sigh for fear that I will not kiss you. You beg me to kiss you now, but in the morning . . . ah, in the morning.''

He drew back from her. He had been deliberately cruel. She frightened him, offering herself as though she did not care what happened. He was weak, felt the pull between them, the temptation. To take what she offered would be so easy.

Deirdre felt hot tears on her cheeks. "Why? Why do you spurn my love?''

"Lass, you do not know the emotion. Not yet. But you are ready. And if I were a little more ruthless or depraved I would enjoy showing you the way of it.''

His words struck at her like hard sharp stones until she felt battered. But anger was welling in her, too. He had cut up her newborn dreams before she had fully realized them, and the hurt made her brave. "Then show me!''

"No.''

"Are you a coward as well as a bully?" she hurled at him. "My brothers say you do not care for women. Perhaps 'tis true that you are unnatural. Perhaps you nurture disgusting depraved thoughts. You will not touch me, whom you say you have loved unknowingly for many years. And yet you spoke of tender passion for a child of seven. What are you? What are you?" she echoed as tears clogged her throat and squeezed off her voice.

He said nothing, but in his eyes there was a hunger that fed on the silver-white moonlight so fierce and naked that Deirdre knew the instant she had won.

"Please," she begged softly, not knowing why she was so desperate. "Please love me!"

In his strength he did not snatch what he desired from her. His hands moved slowly toward her, giving her every opportunity to escape. Even when he touched her face, cradling it, his caress entreated rather than demanded her acceptance, and she never knew whether he drew her or she leaned toward him, her face lifted and her lips parted, to receive his kiss.

As his mouth lingered on hers she felt a sudden dizziness, a rush of warmth that enveloped her from head to toe, and she knew that her dream beside the Loire had not lied to her about the power of this man's kiss. But that was not enough. She wanted it all, wanted to know if the promised glory of loving him was as real.

She did not shy from the hands that loosened the ribbons of her shift, nor did she balk when he slipped it from her shoulders along with his coat. She welcomed the touch of the night air that cooled her feverish skin, for when he turned his eyes on her she thought she would ignite like kindling. She knew that he saw her well enough, could judge her size, her contours, her foolishly naked body.

"You are beautiful," he said simply, and no other words could have sounded more happily in her ears. "Though you will hate me and yourself for the weakness soon enough, come and let me show you how it is done, *macushla*."

She took his hand and knelt down beside him and then she was in his arms, his wonderful strong warm embrace that eclipsed the last of her doubts and fears and offered kisses sweet as midsummer honey and headier than spring wine.

She did not know the exact moment when he laid her down, but suddenly she was on her back, his velvet coat her bed as he bent to her.

His hands caressed her and pleasure ran like water over her skin. Abandoned to a will of its own, her body answered her inexplicable need with desire that surged in wave after wave out to her belly and hips from the throbbing center of herself until she trembled like a purring kitten.

Her hands were clutched to his back but she yearned to return to him a measure of her joy. Shyly her hands stroked down over his shoulders to his waist and back, slow deliberate strokes that firmly pressed the satiny smooth skin, the curious hard welts, and the taut muscles.

In answer she felt the same curling pleasure ripple through him, from his spine down to his hips, and he moaned in the same inarticulate need.

She floated in a dark world of flesh and sensate pleasure as ancient and mysterious as time. Her breasts undulated like waves under the play of his hands, rising and falling in a sea of tactile delight. And yet she sensed that there was more.

When he lifted himself from her she whimpered at the loss and opened her eyes to call him back. But then she saw why he had moved. Very slowly he opened his breeches, shoved them down his thighs and stepped out of them. He stood over her naked and still.

In the moonlight his body was like marble, smooth, firm, and pale. His black hair was darker than night, and then her eyes lowered in wonder to that part of a man she had never seen before. It amazed, delighted, and shocked her all at once. Her gaze flew back up to his face, and she knew that he was looking at her, waiting for her reaction.

Drawn by a need greater than her shyness, she sat up and reached out, her fingers brushing the fine dark hair of one leg. She felt a shudder ripple over his flesh and knew that he was as vulnerable as she. Coming to her knees, she ran her hand up the bulging muscle of his calf and across to the top of his thigh. Spreading her fingers, her thumb brushed the tip of him

He groaned as if in pain. All at once he was on his knees beside her, pushing her back onto his coat. He covered her cool skin with the heat of his own, enveloping her from mouth to feet. His kiss soldered them together, obliterating the separateness of their natures.

His hands continued to caress her as he gently prodded her knees with one of his, crooning words she did not fully understand but that made her pliant, vulnerable, and trusting in his gentleness.

The moment of union surprised her. She had not known what to expect, had not even in her dream understood this stretching of oneself to fit the design of other.

"Deirdre . . . love!" he whispered harshly, then dragged his mouth back to hers, and she knew then that this was right. This was what she was born for, to love this man . . . in this manner . . . forever.

Afterward they lay side by side facing each other, their lips barely touching, her leg pulled up across his waist and he still within her.

"I love you," she whispered, the words a breath expelled into his mouth.

"You do not know me," he answered.

"I have loved you since I first saw you at Liscarrol," she answered and was astonished to find the words true. She thought briefly of the dream that had brought them together, of the magic of a world older than that of Christianity, and wondered if they were blessed or cursed by this loving.

"Cursed," he answered, and she did not ask him why he spoke that word.

Killian reached out to trace her face with his fingertips, memorizing each curve and hollow. He had never expected to find his dreams made flesh. He had been a man haunted, night after night, by the dream of a lass with a sweet mouth and eyes that held a promise for him alone, and a fiery brave spirit to match the yearning of his own.

Deirdre Fitzgerald was not what his dream had portended. She was frighteningly young and innocent, not a fighter but the cosseted daughter of a nobleman. Aye, she set his blood aflame and then drowned that ardor with the satin-cool touch of her body; but was this moment only the consummation of the passion he had carried like a hair shirt these last years? Or was it more? Had he found love?

Perhaps what she believed was true, that magic had brought them together. That was reason enough to be wary of the emotions snaking through him. Any man with sense avoided trafficking in magic. Magic was a double-edged sword, exacting a price for its glory. He was between worlds, cut off from his past and his future uncertain. How could he be certain that any feeling within him could be trusted? He had longed for something of his own, but Deirdre Fitzgerald was not any man's for the taking. She was a lord's daughter.

Deirdre felt him pulling away from her, his thoughts retreating even as he continued to stroke her. "What is wrong?"

"This," Killian answered.

"Why? Perhaps we have been wicked this night, but I love you. I will make a pretty confession before we marry, but I cannot say in truth that I regret a moment of this sinning." Deirdre rubbed her cheek against his shoulder as the thought made her smile. "If Da will not agree to the marriage I shall tell him that I shall bear him a bastard grandson in nine months' time. You do not know how stubborn I can be. He will give in."

"Aye, *acushla*, I believe you could make the seas obey you, but your father would be right to forbid the marriage." He bent and kissed her quickly. "I can offer you nothing. I resigned my commission in the brigade before I came here. I cannot house you or clothe you or feed you. What I own I carry on my back. I am no proper suitor for a lady."

Deirdre smiled up at him. "If you think to frighten me away you will not. I do not need fancy gowns and extravagant furnishings. As for meals, I'll have you know we ate nothing but porridge and potatoes that last year in Ireland, and I will happily do so again if Liscarrol is my home."

"Liscarrol?" Killian questioned with a frown.

"Aye. It has been promised me from childhood as my dowry," she answered. "So, you see, you need not worry about where we shall live. We, my love, shall live in a castle."

Killian shook his head in wonder. A castle in Ireland and marriage to a lord's daughter; her proposed future sounded like the stuff of fairytales. "We'll see," he grumbled and lowered his head to kiss her.

Deirdre gripped him tightly between her thighs when he tried to pull away. "Not yet," she begged. "Can you—will you not love me again with your body?"

She felt him stir inside her even before he kissed her and knew that he would.

Pain was the only definable sensation within him as Killian opened his eyes to the darkness. The dark tide of agony washing over him did not surprise or frighten him. It would pass as it always did.

Yet, even as he gave up to the bloodred tide of pain, his body resistèd, coughing to eject fluid from his lungs.

"Shh! You mustn't make a sound!"

The cool small hand that touched his cheek and then pressed against his mouth stilled the spasm of his coughing as it always did. With a smile Killian opened his eyes. Looking down at him, her childish face awash in a sea of crisp golden waves, were a pair of serious gray-green eyes.

She smiled at him and petted his sweaty cheek. "You must hide yourself. The English have come."

Through the mist of pain her words struck a rational chord in him: Aye, the English soldiers were after him.

The child stood up as the clatter of boots was heard beyond the hidden door. She grabbed his sleeve and pointed. "Up there! You must climb up the shaft."

"I cannot," Killian answered, too weak to rise from his knees.

"Aye! You can! You must save yourself. I'm a friend of the wee folk," she exclaimed and began unfastening her bodice. She leaned over until the red birthmark on her shoulder was exposed. "You see? I've been kissed by the fairies."

Killian held his breath. He knew what would happen next. The face of the child before him wavered in the torchlight, blurring and then redefining itself into the mature features of a young woman. The face that had haunted him for so long was Deirdre's.

Killian caught his breath sharply as she leaned toward

him, beckoning a kiss with moist, parted lips, her bodice slipping down to bare the full globes of her breasts. The swift jolt of desire in his loins overrode the pain of his wounds. He had never dared touch her before, had always awakened himself with the guilty knowledge of his lust. This time he reached for her and brought his mouth down on hers.

He did not hear the heavy pounding that broke through the door. He was lost, drugged to all sensation but that of her kisses and the undulations of her warm velvet skin under his hands. She was snatched from him without warning. For an instant her face remained before him.

"Save yourself! Save yourself!" she shouted at him. "You must go away or we will die!" Her cries became piercing screams of terror as she was dragged away by red-coated soldiers.

With a roar of rage Killian tried to rise, but his body would not obey his command. The more he fought, the heavier his body became, until he lay sprawled helplessly on the floor with her cries ringing in his ears.

Sweat oozing from every pore, Killian sat up with a start. The stillness of the night surrounded him, but the galloping of his heart filled his head with sound. Where was he? Instinctively he reached for the skean he always kept by his side, but his hand met instead the soft flesh of a woman's thigh.

He turned his head sharply to find Deirdre lying on the floor beside him, her naked body sprawled invitingly in sleep. He touched her, half-fearing that she was not real. The warmth of her skin made him sigh with relief.

He rested his head in his hands and was amazed to discover that his fingers trembled. The dream. The dream had changed. Always before he had awakened with the frustration of thwarted desire. Never had he awakened to the sickening anxiety of loss that now roiled in his belly.

She is gone from me forever.

The dream was gone and it would never return. He

could not say why or how but the feeling was unshakable. It was over.

Killian raised his head and turned to gaze down into Deirdre's sleeping face. How to tell her? Could he tell her?

He stood and began dressing. He did not think of what he should say or how he could make her understand that he must leave. He would not even try. For a single night he had believed that he had attained his heart's desire. Now he understood that the circle of fate that had had its beginning at Liscarrol eleven years ago was complete this night with their union. In time Deirdre would realize it herself, but he could not remain until then. If he did he might not ever leave her.

The woman-child of his dreams had beguiled him with the promise of a real love. Yet, the dream was gone and the reality was that Deirdre was not for him. He was an impoverished mercenary, a man who lived by his sword and wits. If he swept her away now, with the ecstasy of their lovemaking blinding her to the realities that lay ahead, he would be no better than a thief stealing his bride. Deirdre deserved better than he could offer. Let her remember this night of his love, for he had nothing else to give her.

Fey waited impatiently in the shadow of the hunting lodge until gray fingers of light stretched across the sky. MacShane had lain the night with Lady Deirdre. She had heard their sighs, their whispers and moans of joy, and had finally stopped her ears with her hands as jealousy raked her. She knew something of the ways of gentry and that marriage was expected to follow coupling. MacShane was bound to marry the lady. And, when he did, he would have no further use for her.

Fey sniffed back a tear. She was done with crying. Yet, it seemed wholly unfair for a lady who had so much to take from her the one benefactor who could have made her life easier.

The sight of MacShane in the doorway surprised her, for

she had heard no one stir inside. Yet there he was, fully clothed. He stood staring at the dawn, his head lifted to catch the breeze, and Fey felt a stirring deep inside her unlike any she had ever before experienced. It was more an ache than a pleasure, and she wondered fleetingly if she was sickening. But then he glanced back into the darkened interior, and the ache inside her twisted, sharpening the pain, and she realized that the source of her ailing was MacShane.

She thought he would go back in or that the lady would come to him but neither thing happened. After a long pause, MacShane walked out into the dawn, his stride long, rapid, and purposeful.

Fey waited until she was certain of his direction and then she rose from her hiding place and hurried after him.

She was surprised to see him enter the Fitzgerald house through the front door. After what had occurred during the night, she expected him to sneak back inside. She smirked as she thought of Lady Deirdre still sleeping in the lodge, unaware that her lover had deserted her. So, MacShane was not so different from the other men Fey had observed over the years. Once lust was satisfied, they all sought their own company above the woman's.

She hesitated to go in after him. There had been much movement in the house the night before. The strange incident in Lady Deirdre's room when Brigid had succumbed to a fit had almost made her feel sorry for the old thing, almost. They had completely forgotten that Fey had been given a bed in the alcove behind the dressing screen. They did not know that she had heard their strange conversation of dreams and fairies and magic.

Lady Deirdre did not know that she had been followed, that there were others, too, abroad, and that Fey was not the only one to spy on the lovers in the rose garden.

When she had realized that Lady Deirdre's brothers had followed the pair, she had nearly cried out in warning to MacShane. But, curiously, the men had not challenged MacShane, nor had they intervened when the two kissed. They had simply disappeared back the way they had come, and she would swear she had heard their laughter on the breeze.

Fey gazed at the second-story window of the room that belonged to MacShane and was rewarded with the flicker of light that signaled he was inside. Her eyes moved down the line of windows but all the other rooms were in darkness. After a moment's thought, she grabbed two handfuls of the tangled vines that cleaved to the house and began to climb.

The knock at his window surprised MacShane until he turned and spied the shadow dancing upon the window panes. When the window was opened, he reached out and grabbed Fey by the arm and lifted her into the room. "What do you think you're doing hanging about like a monkey on my windowsill? God's death! You're naked!"

Fey pushed down the hem of her nightgown, which she had tied about her waist to aid her climb, and then fixed him with a withering glare. "I came to say goodbye."

"Now?" Killian asked in faint annoyance. "*Geersha*, I'm too weary for games."

"Aye, and so ye should be, with no sleep and plenty o' night's work behind ye."

MacShane slanted a sharp gaze at the lass. Her dark hair was slick and damp, her bare feet muddy. Her face was lightly crisscrossed with scratches like the ones she might have received had she crawled through thorned bushes...*rose bushes*. "You followed me. Damn your eyes, you little sneak!"

Fey held her ground but her knees trembled as his anger rolled over her. "I do nae care what ye done. ye could have swived and buggered the lot of Fitzgeralds and I'd nae care." She paused to sniff back a suspicious sob. "Ye once offered me money. I'll be taking it now."

MacShane had had little experience with women, children in particular, but he did recognize jealousy. That emotion played over the lass's face, giving away the source of her animosity. That she had followed them and knew what had occurred did not bother him as much as what she had overheard. "Why did you follow us?"

Fey shrugged, an obstinate look filling her eyes. "I did

nae follow the lady. I followed ye. I won't stay here. I'm going away.'' She looked about and noticed for the first time that MacShane's saddlebags were lying open on the bed and that they were full. ''Ye were going away! And ye weren't going to tell me, were ye?''

MacShane debated lying and thought better of it. ''Aye. I am going as I told the lady I would.''

''She knows ye're going and she will nae stop ye?'' Fey asked in frank disbelief.

Killian was silent.

A quick grin split Fey's face. ''Then I'm going, too. 'Twill nae take me a minute to dress.''

''No.'' Killian grabbed Fey's arm as she hurried toward the doorway and spun her effortlessly about to face him. ''No, lass, you cannot come with me.''

''Why?'' Fey demanded. ''Because of her?''

''No, because it would not be right. You don't understand and I don't expect you to, but some things cannot be, no matter how badly you may want them. When that happens, you must learn to accept it.''

''Would she nae agree to wed ye?'' Fey's eyes narrowed suspiciously. ''She wanted ye badly enough. I heard her mewling for ye, panting like a bitch in heat. She wanted ye then, and I cannot believe ye did not service her until she had her fill.''

''You've a gutter tongue, lass. 'Tis none of your business what passed between the lady and me.''

Killian reached out and caught her lightly about the neck, but the pressure of his fingers at her throat made Fey go utterly still. ''You're not to tell a soul what you heard or saw or suspected of the night's events. Is that very clear?''

Fey had thought this man capable of violence but not cold-blooded murder. Now as she stared up into his eyes silvered by violence, she knew that she had misjudged him. Unlike Darce, who had bullied and struck out in indiscriminate rage, MacShane 's anger was a very real and specific threat. He would snap her neck if he thought it necessary to protect the lady, and in that Fey read the beginning of the end to her own hopes and plans. MacShane loved the lady.

"If she means that much to ye, I'd nae harm her," she choked out.

The words brought the beginnings of a smile to Killian's lips. "You mean that, do you?" Fey nodded reluctantly. "Then you can be of help to me, if a help it is you want to be."

"Anything!" Fey said too quickly, for she saw the flash of amusement in his eyes, a flash that changed the silver back to blue.

"You must overcome your inclination to offer a man 'anything,' lass." He reached into his coat and withdrew Fey's skean. "Lady Deirdre will not be pleased when she learns I've gone. I would not have her do anything foolish like try to follow me. If you're as clever as you'd like me to believe, you should be able to keep her from doing just that."

"I could tie her up, or hide her away for a few days," Fey suggested with a sly smile.

"And have that pair of Irishmen brothers of hers on your heels? No, lass. You must be more clever and subtle than that."

Fey pondered the thought. "Aye, I'll think on it. When the job's done, where am I to find ye?"

"That's just it, you're not to follow me either." He frowned as she started to protest and Fey fell silent. "You've a rare opportunity in remaining with the Fitzgeralds. There's Lady Deirdre, who will be kind to you because you will remind her of me, and lasses can be amazingly sentimental about that sort of thing. You'll have the run of a grand house and servants to see to your needs. You may even learn to be a lady from Brigid, if you so desire."

All of this appealed to Fey but the last. "I'll nae have that old pisspot spit on me!"

Killian smothered a laugh. "'Tis up to you. Do you prefer the alleys of Nantes to this?"

"Only a fool would," Fey answered reasonably.

"Aye. And you're not a fool, *geersha*."

The shrewdness left Fey's face as Killian lifted his

belongings from the bed, and she was once more a lass of eleven. "Ye've done well by me, and me with nothing to offer ye in thanks."

Killian turned and smiled at her. "You may repay me by remaining here and learning all they can teach you. When next we meet, you'll be so grand a lady you will not even nod to a common soldier the likes of me."

"That's a lie!" Fey protested and launched herself against him. "That's a lie! Please! Please take me!"

"Shh, *geersha*, you'll wake the house." Killian bent to pry her arms from about his waist, but when he had freed himself she grabbed him by the neck and jerked his head down as she rose on tiptoe to put her lips on his.

Killian held still under her kiss, for to pull away would have wounded her beyond enduring. Finally, her grip slackened and her mouth moved from under his. Her eyes were bright in wonder and then the light dimmed and she pulled away from him and spun away, hunching her shoulders in defense. "I'm sorry," she mumbled.

He straightened and looked down at her, his expression bemused. What could he say that would not further shame her? "Are you telling me you're sorry that I do not please you, lass?"

Fey looked back over her shoulder, her whole heart in her eyes. "Nae, ye please me fine."

"And you me," he replied. "You've a great deal to offer some man, lass. Keep yourself worthy of him."

"I will," Fey whispered as she watched him stride to the door and disappear through it. She would do anything to win his affection.

After a moment she ran to the window and stood watching until, ten minutes later, she saw a dark figure on horseback appear in the field behind the stables. She watched him until he was a speck and her tears dissolved it.

Even before she opened her eyes, Deirdre knew that she was alone. For a moment she pretended that she was waiting for Brigid to arrive with her first cup of chocolate. Brigid would enter, draw open the draperies on another perfect morning with buttery sunshine and the hum of bees and the scent of flowers, and she would wonder what the day held for her. Lady Elva would want to plan the ball they had talked of. Perhaps they would talk of a guest list, of who should come and who should be omitted. She would mention Cousin Claude's gathering and Monsieur Orsiney's horrid table manners.

Deirdre's sigh ended in a sob. No, she would do none of those things this morning.

She had awakened at dawn to find MacShane gone. Even as she hurried to the house she knew that she was too late. She felt his loss as an ache inside herself, an emptiness that had nothing to do with bodily hunger. His room was empty, his horse and saddle gone. He was gone and she did not know why.

She closed her eyes to prevent tears from slipping down her cheeks, but they would not be checked. MacShane had gone without explanation or the reassurance that he would return. There was no one she could turn to, no one in whom to confide. Thankfully, Brigid had not yet awakened. If Brigid knew what had happened during the night, she would go to Lord Fitzgerald.

"No," Deirdre whispered to herself. She would tell no one. For whatever reason, MacShane had left her. She would not trap him by a false cry of rape.

She stood at her bedroom window hugging his coat to herself. It was all she had left of him. She would one day have more.

"You belong to me," she whispered to him though she knew he could not hear her. She would not believe that he was gone forever. During the hours of the night they had forged themselves as one, and nothing, not even MacShane himself, would be able to break that union. Brigid said that he was the man for Deirdre and she believed it.

Until MacShane came she had had only one passion in her life: Liscarrol. Now there were two.

"I will have them both!" she told the dawn.

Chapter Twelve

Paris: January, 1703

The alehouse called The Fair Lady was less than its
jaunty sign proclaimed, Killian decided as he watched a
thin film of grease float on the top of his fourth whiskey.
The smoke-filled air choked him and the greasy smell of
sizzling sausages made his stomach heave in protest. If not
for the fact that he waited for someone he would not have
remained. The tavern was one of the few meeting places
for Irish expatriates in Paris, a place whose clientele dealt
in the usual ale, women, and smuggled goods . . . and
contraband of a very unique kind: Catholic clergymen
bound for Ireland.

Killian waved away the servant girl who smiled hopefully at him in expectation of an order or a proposition. She
was not as loosely laced as the two other serving women,
whose breasts had strained free of their bodices, much to
the delight and temptation of their admirers. She was
younger, too, with real color in her fair cheeks rather than
the painted kind. Still, he knew her favors could be bought
cheaply and would be before the end of the night.

The waiting did not improve his mood, which had

darkened steadily as the day progressed. It seemed a man could not earn an honest living in Paris.

Killian smiled wryly. Honest labor. The position he had lost to another had been purchased away. He would have done the same had he possessed the funds. Without position and backing he would get no appointment he desired. So why, then, did he not take the position offered him by the duchesse? Smuggling was a very lucrative business and the company no worse than that of most soldiers. She had even promised him a free hand.

The thought made him laugh, and those at a nearby table turned to stare at him, but Killian did not care. The duchesse did not give free rein, as well he could tell them, and a more dangerous benefactor he could not imagine.

When a man slid into the chair beside him, Killian did not immediately lift his eyes.

"Will you not greet a man who's come this distance to see you?" the young man at his elbow asked in Gaelic.

"I'd not have come a foot in this direction had I known you would be late, Teague O'Donovan," Killian returned sourly. "Faith! Could you think of no other place?"

"Are you afraid the lasses cannot see your ugly face for the smoke?" Teague rejoined. "They always see what they like, even when it's covered with a fortnight of whiskers."

"Three days' worth," Killian amended, still glaring at his drink. "Now that you're here, it may be that a man can get a proper drink. I swear they store their sausages in their whiskey barrel. Look at my cup."

"Aye, 'tis a miraculously dirty thing," Teague agreed. "Like your coat and breeches. Och! Killian, have you run yourself to ground at last?"

Killian lifted his gaze, giving his companion a lazy perusal that made a slow smile spread over his face. "Ah, Teague, lad, you're sporting a fine white lace collar. Are you not afraid they will nae serve you, being a priest and all?"

"Keep your voice down!" Teague admonished as he pulled his cloak closed, "or would you have my vocation known far and wide to the company? There are always spies about.''

Killian shrugged, wondering idly how much whiskey he had consumed in the past three hours. His head ached but not enough to blot out all thought, and that was what he was after. He reached for the tumbler and downed its contents in one fiery swallow. When he opened his eyes again, Teague was watching him closely. ''What do you gape at, Father? Have you never seen a drunkard?''

''Aye,'' Teague answered softly. ''I only wonder that you've fallen so far, Lucifer.''

Killian's laughter startled those nearest them, but after a curious look the company of soldiers and hangers-on returned to their concerns. '' 'Tis been some while since I thought of those days, Teague. You always were afraid that the devil would come and snatch you away from the monastery, while I was afraid he would not. Well, we both got our wishes, you're a priest and I'm . . . I'm one of the fallen ones.''

Teague smiled. ''You're not fallen, you're lost, and there's a difference, Killian.''

''Ah, priestly advice.'' Killian leaned forward suddenly. ''Do not preach me a sermon, Father, I'm too drunk to heed it and not drunk enough to be polite about the hearing of it.''

''Ah, here she is!'' he cried, grabbing the young servant girl about the waist as she passed. ''Smile prettily for the man, lass. He has a certain fondness for Irish lasses, haven't you, Teague?''

Teague nodded politely at the young woman, but his fair face reddened beneath his thatch of red-blond curls.

''You'll have to do better than that with the lasses if you mean to go abroad as a common man,'' Killian said and pushed the young girl into Teague's lap. ''A schoolteacher is a handsome catch, to many a mother's mind.'' He grabbed Teague's hands and pulled them about the girl's waist as she balanced on the young man's knee. ''There, you've got the way of it. Irish ladies will have you to tea, those that can afford it. Those who cannot will find excuses to stop you and pass the time of day. But the forward lasses are the ones that will bear watching." He winked at the girl. "They're the ones who'll steal kisses from unsuspecting schoolteachers."

Before Teague could realize her intent, the girl twisted about, threw her arms about his neck, and kissed him hard on the mouth.

Teague stood up, spilling the girl from his lap as he jerked her arms from his neck. Too flustered to speak he stood silently as Killian's laughter once more rang through the tobacco-filled room. "You should not—" Teague began, only to remember to extend a hand to the girl on the floor.

"If ye've no liking for kissing, 'tis nae a reason to treat a lass that rough!" she said, ignoring his offer of help as she rose. She jerked at her skirts and pulled her bodice up to hide one rosy nipple that had popped free. "And ye, ye're nae better than he!" she said, wagging a finger at Killian.

"Aye, 'tis so," Killian agreed as he lazily fished in his pocket for a coin. When he found it he tossed it at her. "But I pay better."

The girl's blue eyes widened in interest and she laid a small hand on his shoulder. "Well, a lass can take a joke as well as the next. What else would be to your pleasure, sir?" The look she gave him was not mistaken by either man.

For an instant Killian wavered. Why not? What prevented him? Certainly not any concern for the duchesse's feelings. She had none. More than likely she had found other company this night, as she had many other nights these last months. The barmaid was pretty, reasonably clean, and young. After a few months in this place she would be much less of all three.

The throbbing at his temples made him curse and shake his head. He needed to be far more drunk than he was to still the ache, and in that condition he would be of no use to either himself or the girl. "Nae, another time," he said and reached for his cup. "Fill this, lass, while you look for another to fill you."

The girl's mouth tightened at his crudity but she pocketed

the coin and took his cup. She turned to his companion to make the same offer, but then her gaze fell upon the collar and cassock revealed by the man's open cloak. Realizing that she had kissed a priest, she fell back a step and crossed herself before she turned and fled.

Embarrassed, Teague snatched his cloak closed and reseated himself. "If 'twas your aim to revolt me, Killian, then I will save you further trouble by saying that I am revolted. What has become of you? Baiting priests is a lad's game."

Killian looked at his monastery companion between narrowed lids. "Is that what you think I've done? I merely wished to illustrate a point, Teague. You've grandiose plans of smuggling yourself into Ireland, of going among the deprived and poor, the weary and thirsty souls in need of the Word and the Mass."

Teague nodded solemnly, the light of righteousness shining in his face.

Killian looked away as he continued. "And how will you go? As a schoolteacher, newly sent from Scotland? 'Tis an old ploy. You have no guile, Teague. You could not handle the moment with the lass just passed. How do you expect to deal with priest hunters who'll be alert to your weaknesses? They've had years to sharpen their traps and snares."

Killian looked up at his friend with sorrowful eyes. "It would be simpler to do as many others have done. Hide in holes, in bogs. Keep your presence a secret, while you can, and when at last you're caught, accept the transportation back to France and know that at least you tried."

Teague shook his head. "If I'm caught, I'll return."

"You'll be caught again, and the law is quite specific on the point. Hanging, drawing, and quartering, I believe, is the punishment of the second offense." Killian reached for the drink the girl had set before him and swallowed it in a gulp. "'Tis not how I would wish to remember you, Teague, a dismembered corpse. If you must tend an Irish flock attend these good folk." He waved a hand toward the assembled company.

Teague smiled at him tolerantly. "I will go. You've

known me half my life. When my family sent me to
France to study I did not speak a word of the language. I
thought I would die from loneliness until we met. Even so,
you know returning to Ireland is all that has kept me a sane
man. Well, now I'm ordained. I must return home and
serve as my vows direct me.''

''You'll go home and die,'' Killian mumbled. The
whiskey had struck his empty stomach like a hammer on a
cymbal, and his body vibrated with the shimmering warmth
that preceded a loss of conscious thought. ''Go home and
die! Why plague me with its anticipation?''

Teague watched his companion a moment longer before
he wet his lips nervously and said, ''There is a reason I
asked you to meet me here.'' He leaned forward until he
was nearly stretched across the table. ''You're correct
when you say I'd be no more than a bairn among wolves.
But you, Killian, you'd be a wolf among wolves.''

Killian smiled benevolently. A wolf among wolves; he
liked the sound of it. But what was Teague talking about?
He was no priest. ''I am no priest.''

''No, but you're a soldier, and Ireland is as much in
need of temporal as spiritual emboldening.'' He lowered
his eyes. ''I am much a coward, Killian, but you've
always had the heart of a lion. Had you listened more to
the call of your vocation, you might be sitting here in my
place.''

''I did listen, lad,'' Killian countered, wondering how
much longer Teague would sit beside him with that fair
innocent face that made him seem half his twenty-eight
years. ''I was called to slaughter France's enemies, and that
I have done in abundance, on any and all occasions until
my hands are red. I have lived war until I am weary of it.''

Teague gripped his wrist. ''I knew that you were weary
of your life, Killian. I felt it! 'Tis why I wrote you. You
need a mission, something holy and worthy of your best
effort.'' His voice fell to a whisper. ''You have been much
in my prayers when I have needed guidance. Again and
again you came to my thoughts as I knelt and prayed for
the strength to do what I must. Finally I realized what the
Holy Mother was telling me. I need your strength to help

me in this sacred mission. Come with me to Ireland. I leave tomorrow night, and there's funds enough to pay your passage. Come and do the Lord's work, Killian!''

Killian shook off Teague's hand and stood up, his head feeling as though it floated a foot above his shoulders. ''Bad cess to you! I am no confidant of priests. You could do no worse in choosing a Reformation minister as your companion. I cannot help you. I cannot help myself!''

He turned and lurched out through the doorway, uncaring that people turned to stare openly at him. His head no longer ached. It no longer felt attached to his body. But the reflexes of years of training never leave a man.

As he entered the dark crowded lane, he felt a hand brush him, a wandering hand that sought his money purse. Without pausing in his stride, he grabbed the offending member and bent back its fingers until they snapped and the would-be thief screamed in pain and vanished into the night.

No one came near him after that. Indeed, the crowd parted before the tall black-haired stranger whose blue eyes burned too brightly in his tight, angry face.

Charlotte Maria Yvette Mont Clair, the fifth Duchesse de Luneville, eyed her late dinner companion balefully. Only Killian MacShane would have dared this gross insult to her sensibilities. Not only had he failed to appear on time, he had failed to appear at all the four preceding evenings. He sat now in his street dirt, his black hair matted and uncombed, his cheeks unshaved, and his head held in grimy hands. Worst of all, he smelled of the tavern. His breath was a hot expulsion of whiskey fumes that ruined the delicious aroma of her dining table.

As her slim fingers, bejeweled with sapphires and gold, toyed with the ivory-handled fruit knife beside her plate the duchesse contemplated what she should do. Once she would have had MacShane thrown out for such audacity. She would have ordered him taken into the stables and chained there until his drunkenness wore off. When she felt he had suffered enough, she would have sent footmen to wash, shave, and dress him before they escorted him to her bedchamber.

The duchesse smiled, making a thin curve of her small pink mouth. On those few occasions when he had suffered the consequences of her wrath, he had been contrite afterward, offering her in the form of urgent lovemaking a little of the secret desperateness that ruled him.

She never knew whether he received in equal amount that which he so generously gave her. She suspected not. She sensed that he held himself in reserve.

In the nine years she had known him she had been tormented and frustrated by that part of himself that he always held back, kept detached, a secret shut within an inner shell that nothing could touch. The search for the key to MacShane's inner self was one of the few challenges she felt worthy of her pursuit. As a woman, it tantalized her. As his lover, it beguiled her into forgiving him over and over.

She raised her eyes to the doorway where a pair of footmen stood in attendance. Their sapphire-blue livery with golden embroidery momentarily diverted her attention. They made a handsome contrast to the sky-blue wall panels and pink marble pilasters of her newly redecorated room. Even the Duchesse de Montage had remarked upon her choice of pale pink silk draperies which added to the drama of the chamber. *Oui*, she was quite pleased.

She turned to MacShane to urge him to praise her latest project, but one look at him erased the thought. She doubted that he realized where he was.

''*Mon cher*, you must burn that horrible coat. It smells of—of the bourgeois!''

Killian lifted his head from his hands and winced as the light of two dozen tapers struck his eyes. He must have dozed, he thought, for he did not remember returning to the *hôtel de Luneville*. Yet, as he raised his eyes he saw the duchesse in all her splendor regarding him with displeasure.

As always, she was robed in sapphire cloth, velvet on this winter evening. About her throat and wrists and cascading from her ears were elaborate diamond and sapphire jewels. Sapphires winked on every finger of every hand. Nothing, however, could detract the observer from the face of the duchesse herself. It had once been a beautiful face. Much of the skin was still flawlessly smooth and lily white, which made the disfigurement all the more hideous.

From her left temple a long puckered scar jagged wickedly down across her eye to the middle of her left cheek. The eye itself was covered by a jeweled patch which sported a single five-carat sapphire of the deepest blue in its center.

"I will tolerate many things, *mon cher*," she said sweetly. "Gross negligence of one's person and insufficient care for my feelings are two things I will not abide." Unconsciously her hand had risen to her left cheek, where she traced the scar made nearly invisible by rice powder. "You should be horsewhipped. Shall I see to it?"

"Whatever pleases you, duchesse," Killian answered indifferently.

"Then I believe I should order it done, but for the fact that you would enjoy the pain too much." She laughed delightedly at his baleful glare. "I know you well, MacShane. You are too vain a man to mask your handsomeness in that most vile garb and fill your head with the piss that passes for spirits among the commoners. Unless," and she leaned forward to touch his hand. "Unless, *chéri*, you seek to punish yourself."

She sat back with a look of distaste. "*Merde!* Can you never forget your years in the monastery? What imagined sins do you seek to redress? If you must suffer then do so, *mon cher*, with a little elegance."

Her hand curled against her scarred cheek in the gentlest of caresses. "Shall I introduce you to those who know how to exact exquisite pleasure from pain?"

Killian looked away but not before she spied a glint of something—interest or disgust?—in his eye.

"I, myself, do not indulge in the madness of the flesh that yearns for pain before the pleasure of Venus can be achieved. Yet, it is popular enough in certain circles. What do you think, *mon cher?* There are ways, I'm told, of deriving the ultimate humiliation of one's soul without so much as a loss of a single drop of blood or the turning of a hair.''

Her hand fell to cover the jewels decorating the deep décolletage of her bodice, trembling slightly as she imagined him writhing in the ecstasy of some perfect agony delivered by an expert hand. A delicious tremor began in her middle and sped to her groin as she considered the acts of debauchery which might drive him to such frenzy that he lost control and revealed his innermost secret self. She must be there, to comfort, to pleasure, and to master once and for always this difficult man.

"I know of one place where nothing will be denied you. Shall we go there, *chéri?*" she whispered in a husky betrayal of her emotions.

Killian shook his head, freezing his expression to keep from revealing the revulsion he felt. He had known the duchesse a long time. Yet, he had only to look at her to be reminded that she was a decadent creature at heart, a woman capable of giving herself on a whim to her stablemen or exacting a grisly revenge for some slight upon her person. She was the rare lady who wielded the power of her dead husband's fortune, a proud and predatory aristocrat who obeyed no law but her own, and it was that her pleasure was the law.

"Ask Henri to accompany you," he mumbled. "I am in no mood for the circus."

The duchesse's gaze slipped sideways to the doorway once more, where the taller of the two footmen stood, his handsome swarthy features powdered as pale as her own. It was no secret that Henri was one of her lovers. Occasionally, Jean, the second footman, joined them in her bed. But it was Henri with his broad back and his bullish proportions that she preferred when Killian was absent.

"Are you jealous, my Irish stallion? You may have your place at a moment's notice, provided you bathe and shave, and beg my forgiveness."

Killian raised his head. She was very angry; it glittered in her one good eye. If he was not careful she would, indeed, have him horsewhipped. He rose and bowed low. "A thousand pardons, duchesse. With your permission—"

"You will sit down!" she cried, her voice like a whip. "Fool! Charlatan! Do you think I do not know that you—" She paused, her attention turned to the footmen. "You! Out! both of you!"

When they were gone she turned back to MacShane, who swayed on his feet. "So tell me, my stallion, what has gelded you?"

Killian nearly smiled. If only she knew how far she was from the truth! "I prefer the seductive kiss of brandy these days."

"You prefer the stupor of forgetfulness," she replied. "Do not mistake my interest for sympathy. I have seen you at your worst, *mon cher,* and that is when you are most dangerous. I have not forgotten the day we met." Her smile lifted her enameled brows on her lineless forehead. "It is rare that a lady has so revealing an opportunity to judge the worthiness of a prospective lover."

Killian shook his throbbing head. "Must we speak of the past?"

"*Oui,* we will speak of it because it pleases me. And you will sit because it pleases me, *n'est-ce pas?*"

Killian dropped back into his seat, not out of fear but because to remain or to leave was a matter of indifference to him.

The duchesse saw his indifference and was pleased. She did not want him bested or afraid. Too many in her circle of acquaintants feared her. Her staff did as she bid out of terror. Only MacShane remained intractable. His courage had first drawn her to him.

She had gone to Calais nine years earlier to survey a ship she intended to purchase. She had offered the beggar nearest her a purse as she alighted from her carriage. It was not until he stood up and tossed the purse of money back at her that she had turned to look at him. His back still oozed blood from a recent beating, but his legs and shoulders were strongly muscled. His face, though filthy, was well made and his loincloth fit tightly a most pleasant bulge. But it was his sapphire eyes, so much like her own, glaring impotent rage, that had made her purchase his freedom.

"Do you remember what you called me?" she asked in amusement.

They had played this game of remembrance too often for Killian to feign ignorance of her thoughts. "A dissolute aristocrat with more money than honor, more pride than piety, and more beauty than heart," he answered dully.

"*Oui*. It was those last words that won your freedom from the galley ship," she answered softly and raised her hand again to her scarred cheek. No one had called her a beauty for such a long time. And then, a mere commoner, the lowliest of slaves, had called her beautiful. "'Tis strange, I knew you meant what you said. I would have given twice, no, twenty times what it cost me to buy you!"

"You have since been repaid," Killian reminded her.

"*Oui*." Her fingers encircled the inch-and-a-half jewel-encrusted orb which had been added to her necklace and she lovingly rubbed it. Inside the orb was the eye of the man who was responsible for the loss of her own. "You are stubborn and proud, *chéri*, but I will always forgive you because you paid me back in a way that gives me pleasure each time I am reminded of it."

She had seen the passionate heat that fired his eyes that first day and had known that he would be useful to her in many ways. She was not surprised when he did not accept her invitation to her bed at once. He had suffered much and was too proud to admit even that need.

And so I waited until both your back and your pride healed. And then you came to me, mon cher, you came! As he would again, when he had exorcised his latest demon.

"I have received news at last of the *Cygne*," the duchesse announced in an abrupt change of topic. "She was nearly boarded by a British man-of-war off the Cornish coast. Her *capitaine* escaped only by throwing half my cargo overboard to increase his speed."

Killian looked across at her, his interest snared at last. "What fool captain took his ship along the coast of Cornwall? Was he not aware that all ships leaving the Irish coast put out to sea?"

"All smugglers," the duchesse amended genially. "As

to my *capitaine,* I have it on rumor that he carried more than my trade in my ship's hull.'' Her fingers tightened into a fist over the gold orb as she said, ''I will not be bested or made the dupe of any man's folly!''

Killian did not ask what had become of the foolish *capitaine;* he knew that by the duchess's order the man was dead. ''Who will captain the *Cygne* next?''

''I have a generous offer for a loyal man, one who knows the language and the people of Ireland. You.''

The last word chilled Killian's blood. He knew her. The disfigurement of her beauty had followed an incident that was true to her nature. The trauma of the scar had refined her spirit into that of a heartless predator who thrived on danger, intrigue, and triumph. They kept an uneasy truce because she had not yet bested him. He knew what she expected of him and in that they had both been satisfied . . . until recently.

''I will not go to Ireland for you.'' He said it quietly and waited.

The duchesse considered his words. Few times in the past had he refused her requests. ''I am thinking of taking up the African slave trace,'' she mused aloud, her eye on his face. ''The profit is better than in the Irish wool market, and the English are less bothersome. Perhaps you would prefer to command the ship which I am considering purchasing. It is anchored in Nantes.''

''I would not,'' Killian answered.

''Do you not like Nantes? *Mais oui,* I remember. You spent less than a week there last summer. I have heard that it is a rural, backward place. *Ma foi!* I do not think I shall go, then.''

''You have considered traveling to Brittany?''

The duchesse lifted a gilt-edged envelope from the salver by her plate. ''A wedding invitation from the Comte de Quentin. He is to be married after the Easter season.''

The announcement galvanized Killian, sobering him instantly. ''The Comte de Quentin!'' Too late he saw the flash of triumph in the duchesse's good eye and knew that he had been baited. *Damn her,* he thought, *how can she know of that?*

The duchesse nodded. "Since your return from Nantes you have been different, *chéri*. Being a woman, I could reach only one conclusion: there is another woman involved. No, I should call her a girl. A woman does not tie a man's organ in knots. She uses it up!"

Her laughter was charming. "You must be honest with me. Is your *mal de coeur* caused by the virtuous betrothed of this petty comte?"

For a moment she thought he might reach across the table and strike her, so hotly did rage blaze in MacShane's eyes. Then, miraculously, the murderous look was gone, replaced by a wintry indifference to match the January wind.

Her spies had provided her with the name and description of the young daughter of the Irish officer who called himself Lord Fitzgerald. A shrewd intuition had put the pieces together. Jealousy burned in a white-hot flame as she thought of MacShane in the arms of the girl. What could a child know of giving a man pleasure? No doubt, MacShane had done nothing more than steal a few kisses before she snatched away her rosy lips. And he, as much a fool as any man, must think himself in love because the sweet meat of her virginity had been denied him.

The duchesse looked away, her bosom rising and falling quickly in her agitation. "She will disappoint you. All innocents disappoint the ones in whom they arouse passion. I disappointed my first lover."

Killian glanced at her and for the first time in many months genuine amusement warmed his features. "Did I disappoint mine?"

The duchesse smiled before she turned and saw his face. "You did not and you know it, you preening cock! But tell me about this young virginal goddess whom I should like to tear to shreds in my jealousy. Did she yield you her maidenhood, or do you lust for it still?"

Sparring with the duchesse had lifted the liquor fog from Killian's mind. If he gave away too much, piqued her bloodlust for conquest, he knew that Deirdre might well become the focus of the duchesse's rage. "Of whom do we speak?"

"Are you afraid to speak the name Deirdre Fitzgerald? Does the thought of her cause you pain?" she questioned silkily. "Melancholy does not become a man of your ilk, *mon cher*. Yet, I admit her attraction for you. The daughter of a nobleman of your native land, a lady who can converse with you in that heavenly Gaelic you so admire and will not teach me, she is a novelty for you. She, of course, is attracted to the *bête faroache* in you, my Irish savage." She smiled wickedly. She could well imagine the girl's reaction to Killian MacShane. She, who was wiser, more experienced, older . . . *older*.

For the first time in many years the duchesse felt the cool breath of uncertainty against her elegant neck. She must be very careful not to make a fool of herself in her display of jealousy. She sensed that Killian was not the sort of man to be amused by it, only annoyed. "So, if you must have her she shall be yours. Shall I have her brought here for you? You could use her as you wish and still return her to her home and her fiancé well before Good Friday."

"Generosity always has a price," Killian replied.

"*Mon cher*, you wound me." She faked a pretty pout. "I offer you, my favorite, a gift, a token of my esteem, and you would have me place a price on it." She looked down to hide the flash of annoyance in her eye. She had wanted him to snap up her bait, for then she would have been certain that his interest in the girl was carnal. "If, as you say, you doubt my sincerity, then you may name the terms."

Killian stood up, fully aware that he drew battle lines between them with the words he spoke. "If I were enamored of a lady, I would never think of asking my mistress to procure her for me." He hesitated as he saw her face register shock. Perhaps she deserved better. "The fault lies not with you, duchesse. 'Tis I who have changed."

The duchesse watched him until he reached the doorway. "If you leave my home, *mon cher*, I will never forgive you."

Without hesitating, Killian opened the door and walked through.

"*Zut!* The fool thinks he's in love!" she exclaimed to the empty room. And then she began to laugh.

She had had his faithful attention for nearly ten years, a young man who had brought her his virginity and loyalty like a knight from an age long dead. She was in her thirty-eighth year, wealthy beyond reckoning, an adventuress in a duchesse's clothing, a debauchee and a dilettante because it pleased her. What new challenge could life offer her once MacShane was gone?

She smiled and fingered the golden orb at her breast. "We are not yet finished, Killian MacShane, not you and I."

Deirdre Fitzgerald was to wed.

The thought lay heavily in Killian's mind as he rode out of the de Luneville courtyard and into the blustery winter night. The bright lacy snowflakes that jeweled his black cloak had turned the midnight to twilight, lighting his way toward the Rive Gauche, where he knew people who would give him a bed for the night.

Deirdre Fitzgerald was to wed.

He did not feel the cold. He had drunk enough whiskey to make him insensible, yet he rode upright, his muscles answering his slightest command. He felt more alert than at any time in the past six months.

Deirdre Fitzgerald was to wed.

Even in the small hours of the coldest night, life thrived on the Parisian streets. A *nymph du pave* hailed him in a throaty voice from a doorway as he passed, and his body answered with a dull throb that he did not heed.

Deirdre Fitzgerald was to wed.

This night was no different from any other night, he reasoned. He had been alone before and since he had met the duchesse. He had known fear and hunger, pain and loneliness. He had thought his life over more than once. He had been penniless before.

And yet there were virtues in these last months of his existence. There was no money left from the cashiering of his commission, spent in what had seemed pleasant diversions. He had learned more ways of curing a hangover than ever before. And, best of all, he was free of the troublesome dream that had plagued him for eleven years.

Why, then, did his heart ache? Why did he feel himself to be the most solitary creature on God's earth? Why was there this strange wetness on his cheeks?

Because Deirdre Fitzgerald was to wed.

Chapter Thirteen

Nantes: February 1703

The late afternoon sun lost its battle with the incoming storm clouds, its thin buttermilk light wavering and then disappearing behind the blanket of frozen gray. The bitter winds of winter rose, pelting the churchyard with hard pebbles of ice, but Deirdre scarcely noticed as she stared down upon the dark, damp mound under which her father had been laid less than a week earlier.

Even now it was difficult to believe that her father was gone. He had fought the last battle of his life as valiantly as any of those in the numerous wars to which his sword had been called. In the end, dysentery had done what the fever could not, draining his strength away until she had fallen on her knees in prayer for his release. Yet, when it had come, she was not prepared for the shock. She had not been able to reconcile the gray-faced, inert flesh that lay upon his bed with the man who had reared and loved her for the nineteen years of her life. That was why she was here now.

Deirdre knelt on the cold ground and pressed her cheek to the brown sod. ''I thought that you would take us home,

Da. You promised me again and again that one day you
would take us home. 'Tis no place for you here, buried in
foreign soil,'' she whispered as she stretched numb arms
over the width of the mound. ''You should lie in the
graveyard of Liscarrol with others of our family. 'Tis why
I've come, to promise you that I will take you home, Da.''

The wind snatched at her words, distorting the sound
and scattering it in nature's howl, but it did not matter to
her. She felt a stranger in this foreign land, more so in the
last six months than ever before. She was a stranger to her
family, even to herself.

One summer night in a hunting lodge had shattered her
carefree life. Contentment had turned overnight into a
restless hunger which had worsened with each day that
MacShane had not returned. She had not been worried
when he first went away. She had been as stunned as he by
the revelation of the passion that had sprung full-blown
between them. Perhaps he needed time to think things
over, she had told herself, but she had hoped, no, expected
him to return to Nantes and to her.

Only after Conall and Darragh returned to their troops in
late September had she begun to worry. If not for her
father's failing health she would have fled home in search
of MacShane, to face him and ask why he had not come
back when she knew that he loved and needed her as much
as she loved and needed him. But her father's health had
deteriorated quickly as summer slid into fall, and Lady
Elva needed her to help with the things that had to be done
for her father.

As the days turned into weeks and her father did not
improve, a strange fear for her safety overtook Lord
Fitzgerald. He wanted her wed. He demanded that she wed
before he died. Although he had never approved of Claude
Goubert as a suitor before, he suddenly asked for him,
expected him to visit, and finally announced that he had
accepted the young Frenchman's request for his daughter's
hand. .

As the winds howled overhead, Deirdre buried her face
in the chill ground. ''You should not have made me
promise to marry Claude. I did it for you, because it

seemed to please you and you were ailing so. Now I will
do what pleases me. Conall and Darragh are at war. 'Tis
only I who have a say in what will happen to me. You
must understand, Da. I need to go home. Please help me
to be strong, to do what my heart tells me I must. I will
not have you lie here forever."

When Brigid found Deirdre, her dark cloak was half-
hidden by the snow and her face was stiff with frozen
tears. *"Mavrone!"* she cried as she bent over the girl and
felt her cheek. "You're cold as ice, *ma alanna!"*

She scooped Deirdre up against her bosom and briskly
rubbed her cheeks. "You wicked, wicked lass! Why did ye
slip away? I'd have come with ye and seen to it that ye
were back inside before the storm!"

Deirdre opened her eyes, surprised to find herself in
Brigid's arms. "I fell asleep," she whispered through
chattering teeth.

"'Tis a wicked, wicked trick ye played on me," Brigid
scolded, but her voice was unsteady. "Ye could have froze
to death. If not for the *deeshy* lass, Fey, I'd never have
found ye. Up with ye now and come inside."

Deirdre allowed Brigid to prod and pull her to her feet.
"We're going home, Brigid. We're going home."

"Of course we are. Didn't I bring the pony cart for that
very reason?"

Deirdre raised her head and smiled as snowflakes tangled in her lashes. "Not this home. Ireland! I've just been
telling Da. I've promised to take him home to Liscarrol!"

Brigid nodded, not trusting her voice, and pushed Deirdre
toward the meager shelter offered by the back of the cart.
"In ye go, lass, and pull that blanket over ye." When she
had covered Deirdre with two additional blankets she
climbed up into the driver's seat and slapped the pony's
rump with the reins.

"Get home, ye great lazy beast!" she commanded the
small, surefooted pony. "Get us home before grief makes
the pair of us mad!"

*   *   *

Deirdre awakened to the curious sensation that she was being watched. The fine hair on her arms stirred as she opened her eyes to find dark eyes framed in black lashes regarding her intensely.

"I said ye'd nae die. I told her ye'd come round." Fey sat back and folded her arms across her narrow bosom. "I'll be after having me supper, then, seeing as ye've come back."

Deirdre glanced at the drawn draperies. "It is suppertime already?"

"Aye, and that famished I am, seeing that I've had little to eat and nothing to do but to watch ye these last three days."

"Three days?" Deirdre whispered huskily. "I've been abed three days?"

"That ye have, and old pisspot wailing and moaning fit for a banshee half them hours." Disgust colored Fey's tone. "There's better and quicker ways to end yer life if 'tis what ye were after."

"I'm certain there are. But I had no such thing in mind," Deirdre answered wearily, remembering why she had gone to the cemetery.

Fey shrugged. "Ye've missed naught. The house is that quiet, ye'd believe every one of them had died."

Deirdre closed her eyes, willing the grief to pass. After a long moment it lessened. Action must now replace the inertia of mourning. "Where's Brigid?"

"In the kitchen preparing another poultice." Fey made a face. "Should I fetch her?"

Deirdre shook her head and sat up, bracing herself as a wave of light-headedness swept over her. "I must get dressed. I must speak with Lady Elva."

Fey reached out to steady Deirdre as she swung her legs over the side of the bed. "Ye can nae do that! Old pisspot will have me head if ye set foot out of that bed!"

Deirdre shrugged free of the small hard hands that held her shoulders. "Oh, do release me!" she cried impatiently and slipped from the bed onto her feet. Her head swam but she ignored the dizziness. "Fetch a gown from there, and be quick."

Fey placed a hand on each hip. "I'm nae a servant!"

Deirdre blinked, fighting the boneless sensation that had invaded her body. "I beg your pardon, Fey." She looked up and smiled wanly, her dimples like caverns in her too-pale face. "If you do not help me, Brigid will come and tuck me back in bed and I'll be too weak to resist. But with your help . . ."

The trailing thought made Fey grin. There was little to stimulate an active child in this household. Since Lord Fitzgerald had fallen seriously ill, baiting Brigid had been her only release from tedium. "Which gown did ye want?"

"The black velvet," Deirdre answered. "And hurry!"

With Fey's aid Deirdre had dressed herself in gown and stockings and shoes before Brigid's footsteps were heard on the hall. With a resigned sigh, she lowered herself into the chair by the fire. When the door opened she sat with her trembling hands folded in her lap. "Good morning, Brigid, or is it night? I've not yet peeked through the draperies."

"Miss Deirdre!" Brigid exclaimed, all but dropping the tray she carried. "Ye're up and dressed! How did ye—?" Her gaze went to Fey, who stood defiantly by Deirdre's side, and her face flushed with anger. "Ye're the cause o' this. I should have known better than to trust the likes of ye!"

"Ye old bag!" Fey answered. " 'Tis a miracle the lady lives at all, what with ye pouring yer foul medicines into her!"

"Fey! Brigid!" Deirdre called, her voice softening on her nurse's name. "I am well, but very hungry. I would like soup, bread, and tea. And, Brigid, please inform Lady Elva that I would speak with her on a very important matter." She smiled beguilingly at her nurse. "Now, that is settled."

Brigid stared at her charge. Deirdre was too pale and too thin but the light of determination shone in her eyes, and Brigid was too glad to see her awake to scold her just now. "I'll prepare the soup meself. Cook's good for naught when it comes to preparing a proper broth. Ye must return to bed in the meanwhile."

Deirdre shook her head. "I will sit here a little longer. One thing more, is it morning or night?"

Brigid pursed her lips in disapproval of her patient's contrariness, then said, "'Tis mid-morning, and the snow is melting."

Satisfied, Deirdre leaned her back against the chair and closed her eyes.

Deirdre sat watching the porcelain clock ticking away the seconds of the morning as she waited in her father's library. Lady Elva was late.

A week had passed since Deirdre's defiant recovery. Unfortunately, her body had not been as sympathetic to her needs as Fey had been. The soup and tea had been rejected by her sensitive stomach within moments of consumption and she had been ignobly returned to bed by a frantic Brigid. For three days she was not allowed to raise her head from the pillow. Yesterday she had been allowed to rise and dress for the first time. If not for the visit from her father's solicitor the evening before, she doubted that Brigid would have consented to her coming down stairs even yet.

The sound of the door latch sent her out of her seat and to her feet.

"Deirdre, my love," Lady Elva said as she entered the room.

"Lady Elva," Deirdre responded, curtsying as she had when she was a child.

Lady Elva's progress across the room was slow and the reason for it struck Deirdre with amazement. Though her bodice was tight-fitted under her breasts, the waistline had been altered, raised, to accommodate the filling figure. "You're with child!"

Lady Elva smiled as she lowered a hand to her swollen middle. "Aye. 'Tis a son I hope for before Easter."

"I—I didn't realize," Deirdre replied, wondering at her ability to be so blind. "With Da ailing and— Did Da know?"

"Aye," Lady Elva answered softly, her eyes filling with unshed tears. " 'Twas a great consolation to him, you see. He had hopes of rearing the boy himself."

Deirdre came forward to embrace her stepmother. "If Da wanted a son, then he will have one."

Lady Elva framed Deirdre's face with her hands. " 'Tis not for you to be sad that he wanted a son, Dee. He often said that in you he had everything a father could want in a daughter."

"Whereas Conall and Darragh leave much to be desired," Deirdre finished smartly. "Aye, I'm grateful to hear that Da was pleased with me," she continued, retreating from the treacherous precipice of tears. "Come and sit. We've much to discuss."

When they were seated, Lady Elva said, "I know that your grief is as bitter as mine. But my future is planned, you see," and she patted her middle. "My confinement draws near and then the babe will require all my attention." She blushed suddenly and reached for Deirdre's hand. "That is not to say that I will not have time for you, my dear. 'Tis only that—"

"I understand," Deirdre answered. "You are right. Your future is settled and mine is not. 'Tis why I've wished to speak with you."

"I can guess your concerns," Lady Elva said. "You are young and eager that your marriage not be delayed. Very well. I've good news that should ease your anxiety." She offered Deirdre the parchment she carried. "The solicitor who came last evening informed me of your father's wishes for the dispersement of his estate. This is for you."

Deirdre took the paper and began to read. Her eyes swept over the writing twice before she raised her head "But this is a bill of sale for Liscarrol!"

"Aye, the castle and the surrounding lands as well," Lady Elva answered, quite pleased by the look of surprise on her stepdaughter's face. "I've been assured that the funds received from the sale will be more than enough to provide a generous dowry. That which is left can be used to purchase your trousseau."

Deirdre scarcely heard the last of her stepmother's

remarks. She stared at the paper in her hand, rereading each line. "It is not signed," she said at last.

"Nae. That must be done by you. Liscarrol has been deeded to you. 'Twas done years ago, at the time of your birth. Had your father not informed you? Well, perhaps not, since there was no need until now. Liscarrol was part of the wedding gifts your father gave your mother. She, in turn, deeded the land to you. Of course, as long as your father was alive the land was his. Now you are a landowner, Deirdre. How does it feel?"

Deirdre slowly shook her head. She did not know what she felt, besides enormous relief. Without looking up she asked, "To whom did my father wish to sell Liscarrol?"

"To your cousin, the one who has had the caretaker's duty of it these last eleven years."

Studying the sum offered, Deirdre said, "Cousin Neil must have fared well these years. The price named here is not a stingy one."

"Aye, your father was quite pleased with the offer. He had hoped to sell the land himself and present you with the gold. Had he lived, he would have—" She paused on a sob but she waved away Deirdre's touch of comfort. "Nae. Your father would not like me to weep so. I promised him I would not. 'Tis not good for the bairn."

She wiped delicately at the spilled tears and sniffed back the rest. "Where were we? Ah yes. While your wedding cannot be the grand affair we had hoped for, it can take place, say, within six months' time."

Deirdre looked at her stepmother. "I will not wed."

"Not right away," Lady Elva agreed. "But after six months of mourning, and if we're discreet . . ."

"I will not wed."

Lady Elva's smooth brow wrinkled in puzzlement. "There's no reason for you to wait the full year, unless, of course, 'tis your desire."

"I have no wish to wed Cousin Claude, now or ever."

Lady Elva made a small gasp. "My dear, your father would not wish you to grieve in loneliness forever." Her stepdaughter had done a very foolish and dangerous thing in going out into the snow to visit her father's grave. It was a sign that the girl was overwrought. "Let's save this talk of weddings for another time. Aye, I think that's what we should do."

She rose. "There's no hurry to sign the paper. The solicitor informed me that he will remain in Nantes for the next two weeks. He would prefer to take the papers with him when he sails for London, but if you are not yet ready . . ." Her thought trailed off as she received no response from Deirdre. She had reached the doorway when Deirdre finally spoke.

"I will not sell Liscarrol. If it is really and truly mine, then I shall go home, to Liscarrol."

Lady Elva put a trembling hand to her lips. "I knew I should have waited," she murmured to herself. " 'Twas too soon to burden the girl with her good fortune." To Deirdre she said, "We will discuss this again when you are feeling stronger."

When she was gone, Deirdre carefully read the paper once more and then with tears in her eyes she began to smile. It was an answer to her prayer. She would go back to Ireland, send for her father's remains, and bury him in Liscarrol's family plot, where he belonged.

She stood up. Now to find Brigid and tell her the news. They would have to wait until spring before making the journey, but they could make plans.

She crumbled the paper in her hand. She had no intention of selling even an acre of Liscarrol land.

" 'Tis nae a great amount," Fey commented. She picked up a bracelet and tested the gold with her teeth. "Sure'n 'tis gold, but the jewels is *deeshy*."

Deirdre eyed the small pile of jewelry with equal disgust. " 'Tis all I have. Unmarried ladies are not showered with valuable trinkets."

"Lady Elva's a married lady," Fey offered hopefully, her eyes on the small but fiery ruby in the ring she had slipped on her finger. "She'd nae know were ye to borrow a brooch or two."

"No thievery," Deirdre answered. Theft was the one constant battle the Fitzgerald household fought with Fey during those first months. The girl's tendency to be light-fingered had alarmed the entire family. Something had vanished from everyone, servant and master alike, before Brigid, suspicious as always, found the girl's horde in a loose floorboard under her cot. Only a closed-door interview with Lord Fitzgerald himself had broken her of the habit, for the most part. None knew what had been said between them, but Fey had remained by his side the last days of his life and even wept when she thought no one saw her.

Fey shrugged. "This lot will nae bring me what ye need." She waved a hand about the bedroom. "We could sell your clothes. Nae. What about yer horse?"

"I own no horse. I have the pick of the stable but none is mine."

Fey plopped belly-down on the bed. "Ask that Comte de Quentin for the money. He'll give it to ye. I've seen him mooning about these last months when he thought to get under yer skirts. Offer him a quick feel in exchange for what ye need."

Deirdre was too depressed to be properly shocked. "The Comte de Quentin will not be visiting here again. We are no longer engaged."

Fey braced her chin in her palms. "Truly? 'Tis a wondrous fool ye are!"

Deirdre looked across at the girl. Her hair had grown long enough to curl and pin up, making her appear the young lady of thirteen that she was; but the mutinous look in her eyes was still that of an eight-year-old ruffian. "What would you sell, if you were desperate for money?"

Fey considered this in all its possible variations. "Ye will nae let me steal. 'Tis only one thing left. I'd sell meself had I nae made a certain promise."

This time Deirdre's face registered surprise. "Sell yourself? To whom? Oh!" She blushed furiously. "I should say you will not sell yourself! Did Da extract that promise from you?"

Fey looked away suddenly, her lovely face marred by

fury. "MacShane asked it of me. Only, he's nae come back." She looked back at Deirdre. " 'Tis yer fault!"

The reminder of MacShane made Deirdre blush. She had not forgotten him—how could she—but she had been too busy these past days to give any consideration to the sinkhole of loneliness that lurked within her. "I do not suppose you know where he is."

Fey's expression shuttered over. "What if I did?"

Hope leaped shamelessly to life within Deirdre. "You know where he's to be found?"

Fey did not answer, would not even look up at her.

"If I knew where he was, I would write to him and ask him to come to see us," Deirdre said cunningly.

"He knows where ye are," Fey answered sourly. "Were he interested, he'd come back on his own."

Deirdre's smile dissolved. "You believe that he stays away because of me."

"Aye, because of what ye done and what ye did nae do."

"Why do you say that? We were quite—friendly before he left."

"And so ye were, lifting yer skirts and rutting on the floor like some tart." Deirdre's startled look made Fey grin. "Aye, I saw the pair of ye coupling in that cottage back of the garden."

Deirdre stared at the girl in shock. In all her worst fears it had never occurred to her that another soul knew what had passed between them. The thought made her feel ill. Anger and shame rushed the blood into her face. "You little sneak! You're a spy and an eavesdropper! Have you no shame, no respect for another's feelings! Go away! Go away!"

Fey backed off the bed, surprised that her revelation had so wounded Deirdre. "Had MacShane been me lover, I'd nae be shedding tears over the matter," she ventured boldly. "I'd nae be ashamed of it."

"I'm not ashamed." Deirdre blinked back the threatening tears. "I'm not ashamed."

"But ye'd have married that Frenchy comte," Fey

answered scornfully. "MacShane must have known ye'd nae be faithful."

Deirdre shook her head, but the truth of Fey's words could not be completely dismissed. "I wouldn't have married the comte to please myself, but to please my father. He was so ill, and the thought of my marrying gave him peace of mind. 'Tis why I accepted the betrothal."

" 'Tis one and the same," Fey maintained. "Married is married."

The truth of the statement appalled Deirdre. She had never imagined herself wed to Claude Goubert, only engaged. She had come very close to removing herself from MacShane's life forever. "Do you know why MacShane left?"

Fey chewed her lip. She did not want to answer. MacShane had been angry and protective of Lady Deirdre and the thought stirred Fey's jealousy. "Ye gave yerself to him and being a man he took what was offered. It did nae mean he wanted to be shackled with ye forever."

Deirdre said nothing.

"If I was to tell ye where to find MacShane, I'd have to go along."

Deirdre looked up at Fey's words. "You know where to find him?"

Fey hesitated. MacShane had probably forgotten that he had told her she could seek out employment in Paris with the Duchesse de Luneville. MacShane might not be in Paris but the duchesse might know how to contact him. "I know a place, but I'd have to see it to be certain 'tis the right one."

"Where is it?"

Fey had learned from experience never to give anything away. She looked down at the ruby glittering on her broken-nailed finger. "What's it worth to ye?"

Deirdre swallowed her agitation. "I will not buy the information from you. The ring is yours." So saying, she scooped up the remainder of her meager jewels to carry them back to the open box on the dresser.

Fey watched her in disbelief. No one gave away something for nothing. "He's in Paris. Only, I forgot the place exactly."

Deirdre nodded as she carefully placed her trinkets in the box. "Then we must go to Paris," she said softly.

"With nae money?" Fey scoffed.

"We must find some, " Deirdre answered.

The dream place was familiar, the stable yard of Liscarrol. Was it dusk or dawn? Pewter-lined clouds had shouldered their way across the sky, lending to the day an eerie twilight. Beneath the smoky sky, the green hills lay like frozen waves among the mist, stony-crested and green-sloped. Nearby, the last of the Liscarrol oaks groaned under the assault of the wind.

Deirdre lifted her face to the wind, gasping in the bog-scented air. This time the air raked her face with new intensity. The rain that stung her cheeks was colder than before.

The horse and rider appeared out of the mist, the rider's black cape whipped high over the horse's rump. There was determination in their flight but not panic. She could not help but admire the rider's skill as he rode down the long slope into the valley where she stood.

It was familiar, all of it, achingly familiar and yet new. There was joy as well as dread in his coming. When he reined in near her, she could not turn away or deny him. She ran toward him, her arms lifted in welcome.

As she expected, knew he would, he lifted an arm to warn her off. "Stay away!" he cried, his words clipped short by the wind. "Stay away in fear of your life, *mo cuishle*!"

This time panic did not jerk her into wakefulness. She ran after him; even as he turned and dug his heels into the horse's flanks she cried out, "Do not go! Wait! Wait for me. Killian! Killian!"

*   *   *

Brigid shook Deirdre until she awakened.

For a moment her gray-green eyes were misted by the vision, then gradually they cleared and a smile softened Deirdre's mouth. "I remember! I remember the dream, the one I thought I'd forgotten. 'Tis about him, Brigid! 'Tis about MacShane. He came to Liscarrol the first day I dreamed it! And later, aboard the ship bound for France, I dreamed it again! He was in trouble, terrible trouble, and he was afraid to let me help him!"

Brigid drew the younger woman against her bosom. "Aye, ye dreamed, ye've dreamed that dream every night of your life."

Brigid reached into her neckline and pulled free the stone on the string. "Do ye see this, lass? 'Tis a witchstone. I've put it under yer pillow these many years to keep the vision from driving ye mad, but the time has come when ye must face yer fate."

She picked up a cloth bundle that she had brought to the bedside. "I've been waiting this last fortnight for the dream to come full-blown to ye. Once last summer, I thought the time had come, but when MacShane went away, the dream faded. Now that you've remembered it, I will give ye this."

She carefully unwrapped the cloth to reveal an ancient skean, a dagger of Celtic design. In the candlelight, its keen blade gleamed blue-white but for the dull brown streak along one edge. The hilt was decorated in gold, enamel, bronze, and rock crystal with a huge amethyst stone at its center.

" 'Tis the talisman of the bloodred rose," Brigid whispered, awed by her own words. "None may fairly own it but a true child of the blood. 'Tis yers."

Deirdre drew back a little from the pagan artifact. "Mine? Why should it belong to me?"

Brigid smiled triumphantly. "The birthmark, lass. On your shoulder. 'Tis a very special sign. 'Tis the Bloodred Rose of Ulster. Ye were born with a powerful force at yer disposal, and the gift of sight to guide it."

Deirdre stared at the overly bright gleam in Brigid's

eyes and was suddenly afraid. "You do not mean that. 'Tis a jest."

Brigid's gaze slipped back to the light dancing along the skean's edge, her eyes unfocusing as a trance overcame her " 'Twas many years ago, more than ten times ten. A female child born, cut from the womb of a dead woman. A changeling she was, touched by the fairies with a red mark, the sign of the otherworld. She was the natural daughter of the Shane, the O'Neill of Ulster. The lass was hidden away, lest she do harm to others, or others to her. One day a golden-haired stranger came to Ulster and stole the lass's heart. She followed him to the Pale, and beyond. 'Tis said she saved the lives of the Butlers of Kilkenny and that because of her, the clan of O'Neill will never die."

She looked up at last. " 'Tis your fate, in the mark on your shoulder. Yer mother knew she carried a special child. 'Tis why she died so willingly. Born of a dead woman, do you nae see?"

Deirdre shuddered and pushed away the skean. "No. 'Tis a wretched story, that of dead women and marked bairns. I won't believe it. I'm not an O'Neill."

Brigid merely smiled. "Yer father was not of the O'Neill line but yer mother was a direct descendant of Meghan Fitzgerald O'Neill herself."

"Meghan?"

"The first to bear the mark. Her mother was a Fitzgerald, as ye are, and her father an O'Neill. Ask yerself: what name does the man ye love bear? MacShane! Son of Shane O'Neill, as any Irishman can tell you. With him the circle will be complete."

Deirdre pulled her knees up and hugged them protectively. "I dream of Killian MacShane because I love him. There's no magic in that."

"Aye," Brigid concurred. " 'Tis as ye predicted that day in the stable of Liscarrol. The fairies sent ye a black-haired lad for yer very own."

Deirdre shook her head. The dream of Killian had touched her deeply. It was as if he had just ridden away from her a second time. She did not want Brigid to claim a share in something so personal.

"Each time ye dream, ye have called out, 'Wait, wait for me.' What does he say to ye?" Brigid questioned.

"He says, 'Stay away, in fear for your life, *mo cuishle*.'"

Brigid sighed. "There's dangerous times ahead for ye. Would that I could aid ye, but ye must do this alone." She reached into her bedclothes, pulled out a small purse, opened it; emptied its contents onto the bed. Two dozen gold coins winked back from the bedding. "'Tis for yer voyage. Ye must find MacShane, or perhaps he will find ye. Ye must both return to Liscarrol or it will be lost."

Deirdre grabbed Brigid's arm as she rose to leave. "You cannot expect me to journey to Liscarrol alone. You must come with me!"

Brigid shook her head slowly. "There's Lady Elva with a child on the way. 'Twill come before the end of the month, there being a full moon then. I'm needed here. I've done all I can for ye, Deirdre Butler Fitzgerald. Ye must travel yer path alone. Do not fail yer task."

Deirdre snatched back her hand in anger. "You talk like a madwoman. What have I to fear at Liscarrol besides the English?" But Brigid did not answer; she turned away.

"Find MacShane," Brigid called over her shoulder before she closed the door behind herself.

"Aye," Deirdre whispered. She gathered up the coins Brigid had left behind. She would find MacShane.

Chapter Fourteen

The wooden wheels of the post chaise slipped and bounced over the narrow stone-paved street of Paris. Within it Deirdre moved a leather curtain and peered anxiously out at the night.

"Ye'll nae be spotting him in the street," Fey muttered. " 'Tis too miserable a night for strolling. Me feet are froze clean through."

Deirdre pulled the curtain closed over the chill February night. For nearly a week they had traveled the road that led from Nantes to Paris and both were thoroughly miserable and exhausted.

Deirdre groaned softly as they struck another jarring bump and wiggled about in hopes of finding a more comfortable position for her back. There was none. "I'm bruised from feet to ears!"

Fey snorted. " 'Tis me bum that's bruised. I may never sit again. Should have waited for spring."

Deirdre clenched her teeth as they were jolted again. That comment had served as Fey's answer to every wretched moment of their journey. From poor lodgings at inadequately provisioned posting houses to mud-clogged roads, which had cost them a wheel and half a day's journey time in repair, to the freezing cold that fur rugs could not defend against.

"You need not have accompanied me," Deirdre said righteously.

"Aye, and ye'd nae have found MacShane," Fey tossed back.

"Plague me no longer with that threat," Deirdre snapped. "I do not believe you know where he is to be found. I think you deceived me in order to make this journey."

"Sure'n, I wouldn't have missed so grand a time for anything!" Fey shot back caustically.

Deirdre turned to the girl, ready to answer her barb for barb, but one look at Fey made her pause. Fey's bonnet was powdered with dust, as was her woolen cloak. The weather was bitterly cold, and she knew her own face must be as pinched and her lips as blue as Fey's. They were cold, travel-sore, and weary beyond imagining. No wonder they were at each other's throats.

"We're nearly there," Deirdre said in a conciliatory tone. "Everything will seem better when we've had a decent meal and the warmth of a fire to melt the stiffness in our bones."

She reached out to pat the girl's arm but Fey drew back. "Keep yer words and hands to yerself. I'll nae soon be forgetting ye called me a liar!"

With a sigh Deirdre turned away. Some things were better left alone. She had far more pressing problems to solve. Unconsciously her hand tightened on the cloth-wrapped package inside the fur muff on her lap. She was in Paris. What now?

She had concocted many fine reasons to presuade her stepmother to agree to the journey, among them a letter from Conall inviting her to Paris. He was not, however, as she had suggested in the forged letter, open to the idea of accompanying her to Liscarrol. Nor had he found an honest man to take the job as Liscarrol's steward. In fact, he had no knowledge of her arrival in Paris. Anyone with a bit of guile would have seen through the ruse. But Lady Elva was too preoccupied with her confinement to look for lies.

Deirdre closed her eyes, knowing what to expect. It was

so simple. Each time she closed her eyes on this journey, MacShane was there, waiting for her just behind the veil of consciousness.

In her mind's eyes, his harsh features were made softer by desire. His mane of black hair had been brushed and curled, falling in smooth waves onto his shoulders. His smile intrigued her. As always, she felt a slow warmth spread through her from breast to belly as she concentrated on his mouth. It held a promise of a pleasure she had known for the space of a few short hours. She had tasted those firm lips, had felt their touch on her face, her shoulders, her breasts. She was not ignorant of bliss and the knowledge was a torment.

To be with Killian MacShane again, that was why she had come to Paris.

"Shall I ring, miss?" the footman asked when the coach had halted before the small house and he had jumped down from his perch.

Deirdre lifted the curtain and peered out. This was the place that Conall and Darragh had often told her would be the perfect place for her to stay if she ever visited Paris. It looked nothing like the charming townhouse that they had described. Rain fell in a waterfall over the porch from the slate roof, and heavy drapes at the windows obscured whatever light and warmth there might be inside.

"Aye, we are expected," Deirdre answered, but she felt less confident than she sounded.

To her relief the door opened almost instantly upon the footman's knock; and after a brief exchange of words, he came hurrying toward the carriage with a smile.

Minutes later, she stood frowning before the fire in a small, sparsely furnished but scrupulously clean room.

"Will ye nae eat then? 'Tis little enough that can be said for the French but they cook a fair meal," Fey remarked as she buttered a slice of the bread they had been given with their meal.

"I'm not hungry." Deirdre held her hands to the fire, her frown deepening. The hiring of the coach for the journey had cost her a goodly sum. The cost of lodgings had surprised her. Evidently what Conall considered modest prices was far different from her own estimation. At these rates, she could not afford to stay here more than a week.. That was little time in which to find a man in a strange city. Fey must be persuaded to act as quickly as possible.

"We must begin searching for MacShane in the morning," she said without glancing back over her shoulder.

"I do not know if 'twill be possible," Fey answered with a mouthful. "Me memory is still clouded."

Deirdre tamped down her impatience. "When do you feel that your memory will clear?"

Fey shrugged. She had exchanged her travel gown for a new wool gown and was feeling quite pleased with herself. After all, she had tricked Lady Deirdre into making the trip to Paris, a place she had heard about but never seen, and now she was within reach of MacShane. She could tell him that the lady was in town, but she would not do it until she had seen him, talked with him, and determined that he still wanted the lady. After all, Fey had seen how easily men were distracted by a pretty face. And she had grown these last months, was beginning to fill out in places that would be of interest to a man. "I need to rest, regain me strength. In a few days, 'twill be about then, I'd say."

Deirdre turned about to face her. "In a few days, my lass, you'll be seeking lodgings on your own. The money is nearly gone, and we have traveled a great distance." She took a step toward the girl, her patience slipping as worry and fatigue and hunger took their toll on her nerves. "If you have deceived me, if you have lied and dissembled, I will—will turn you over my knee and skelp you!"

Fey's hand paused midway between her plate and her mouth. She was not afraid of the threat, merely astonished by it. Then resentment reared up within her. "Ye cannot do that. I'll run away. Then what will ye do without me help?"

Deirdre's shoulders dropped in defeat. She put a hand to her throbbing head and closed her eyes. She was tired, too tired to argue. "I'm going to bed," she murmured and turned away.

Fey sat a long time after she had finished her meal, staring at the lovely lady who lay asleep in the bed in the corner of the room. She had been unkind. She squirmed in her chair, disliking the pricking of her conscience. She thought about apologizing but she knew the words would not come out right. No, there was only one way she could atone for her spite.

Without waiting for morning, she reached for her heavy woolen cloak, flung it about her shoulders, and slipped out the door.

Deirdre gazed up at the impressive facade of the grand chateau in trepidation. She glanced again at the paper in her hand to be certain she had not made a mistake. The address provided in the note Fey had given her that morning had meant nothing to her. She had been too shaken, delighted, and pleased to receive a note from Killian MacShane's own hand to think of anything but the fact that she was to meet him at seven in the evening. But this!

The house at 23 Chaussée d'Antin was really a palace. Inside the golden gates the carriageway turned from cobblestone to marble. The steps of the house itself led to gilded double doors carved in rococco fashion. Before the footman who accompanied her could alight and announce her arrival, the huge doors opened and a splendidly liveried doorman rushed down the steps to open the door of her carriage.

"Mademoiselle Fitzgerald?" he inquired politely, his accent mauling her name.

"*Oui*," she answered and accepted the hand he offered to assist her. Since she was expected, then Killian must be here. Fey had informed her with a broad smile that Killian was flourishing under the patronage of a member of the "Sun King's" court, but she had not suspected that his largess included a palatial dwelling.

The anteroom was hung with heavy sky-blue silk, the paneling intricately carved. But she was not allowed to linger there. The doorman turned her over to a footman in matching livery, and she was led up a flight of marble stairs to a pair of doors cleverly concealed in a mural that portrayed Louis XIV as Zeus upon Olympus. Unease moved within her as the doors were opened. Something was wrong. Killian could not be master of this splendor. Who was?

The huge octagonal room into which she stepped was draped in vivid sapphire silk interspersed with gold cloth drapery and carved wood.

"Mademoiselle Fitzgerald, your grace," the footman announced before closing the door behind himself.

At first Deirdre thought the room unoccupied, but then she saw the woman at the end of the salon. She sat on a gilded chair whose ornate back spread out behind her like a peacock's tail. In a sapphire silk gown, the skirts of which billowed out onto the pink marble floor like a great sea-wave, she sat with her hands folded and her eyes closed. Sapphires and diamonds of every size and cut glittered at her throat, her ears, her wrists, and fingers.

"Come in, mademoiselle," the lady said without opening her eyes.

Deirdre moved closer until she could see the lady more clearly and what she saw made her shiver.

The lady's face had once been beautiful; lily-white skin still stretched seamlessly over the elegant bones of one side of her face. A cruel lash had cut the left side of her face from hairline to mid-cheek.

Before Deirdre could compose her features, the lady suddenly tilted her head forward and opened her eyes and Deirdre could not still a gasp of amazement.

The lady's left eye was missing, and in its place was a glass orb set with a huge sapphire where her iris should have been.

The lady smiled. "Did I startle you, child?"

Remembering that the footman had addressed this woman as "your grace," Deirdre sank in a curtsy. "Forgive me for disturbing you, my lady. I am here at the request of Captain MacShane."

"Rise, child," the duchess said, her voice as cool as the night air.

Deirdre rose, keeping her eyes averted from the lady's face.

"MacShane has not yet returned. Will you not favor a lonely woman with your company? *Alors.* Does my ugliness revolt you?"

Deirdre looked up into the lady's face, quelling the trepidation she felt in staring at the cold sapphire eye. "You are not ugly, my lady. Indeed, you must once have been a beauty without comparison."

"You are too generous, *chérie.* But then I like generosity in youth. They have so much, do they not? Energy and hope; ah, to recapture what you have. That would be worth the loss of more than an eye."

The duchesse's gaze flickered over the younger woman as though taking in her appearance for the first time when, in fact, she had been observing her through her lashes from the first. "You wear black well. I would have expected it to dull your hair, but it sets if off like spun gold against ebony. I would counsel you, however, to exchange those dreary pearls for diamonds. A gentleman prefers a little ice with his fire."

The condescending tone rankled, and Deirdre forgot a little of her nervousness as she said, "You have the advantage of me, my lady. I am Deirdre Fitzgerald, daughter of the late Lord Fitzgerald of Liscarrol, County Cork."

"That would be Ireland, *n'est-ce pas?* You are in mourning, I presume. My sincere regrets. I, child, am the Duchesse de Luneville. You know of me certainly."

"No, your grace, I did not know to whose home I had been invited."

"*Vraiment?* MacShane shall soon hear of that! Have you known my Killian long?"

"Your Killian—?"

The duchesse smiled. "La! I see that Killian has been keeping secrets again. Naughty boy! Did he not tell you of me? *Non.* Of course he did not. Perhaps it should come from him, since it is him you have come to see." She waved a languid hand toward a velvet chair which had been placed near her own. "Do sit, mademoiselle, you fatigue me with your youthful energy."

Her legs felt like wood and her heart thumped irregularly in her chest as Deirdre crossed to the chair. *Killian and this woman!* No, she must not think that!

The duchesse's painted brows rose in amusement as she watched the young lady. "While we wait I will tell you a little about myself, because it pleases me. As you have said, I was once a beauty sans rival. I was but fifteen when the Duc de Luneville took me to the altar. I was too young, *chérie,* to know what utter boredom and disillusionment awaited me.

"So, what was I to do? I made friends, of course. The duc's companions were much more interesting than he. They had their vices and their mistresses to keep them company. From them I learned that I had two passions: a hunger for the pleasures of the flesh and a mad desire for chance.

"Do you gamble, *chérie*? You should not develop the talent. It is a madness of the soul, a searing hunger without satiation. I nearly ran through the duc's entire fortune before he died. Afterward I was free to indulge both my passions. I met many fascinating and dangerous people, men and women for whom the gamble of a life is nothing. One night I was feeling that hunger and had lost all my money. I made a bet which was accepted by the man who had become my lover a few nights earlier. He was a stranger, a Venetian, a wicked man who made love as he gambled: recklessly, passionately, uninhibitedly. It was he who gave me the idea. My eyes were my best jewels, he had whispered as we made love. He said they were more beautiful and precious than the sapphires they resembled because they were the only two in all the world."

The duchesse laughed. "Such horror on your face, *ma petite*. Have you guessed the end of my tale? You are correct. I lost the bet. I refused to pay, but naturally my Venetian lover was not a generous man. He hired thieves to take what I refused to part with. I am told that for a while he wore his prize about his neck in a golden globe."

Deirdre swallowed convulsively as she felt the duchesse's one eye on her.

The duchesse clapped her hands and a servant appeared at Deirdre's side with a crystal goblet of sherry.

"Drink it, mademoiselle," the duchesse commanded coldly "If you faint, Killian will accuse me of tormenting you and that will make him very angry with me."

Deirdre swallowed the liquid fire, grateful for its bracing warmth. She felt cold in every part of her body. She wanted to rise and leave, to run away, but the thought of seeing Killian kept her rooted in her chair, though she knew the duchesse had done her best to frighten her away. Yet, why should she have?

Deirdre lifted her head when she had drunk half of the sherry. "Does Killian work here?"

"Do not frown, *chérie*. It encourages wrinkles," the duchesse answered smoothly. The little guttersnipe had courage, she thought. "Killian, *ma chère*, lives here. When he first came to me, he was a very young, very sad, very confused young man."

She leaned forward a little, smiling with a warmth that did not soften her face. "You will not, I believe, think too harshly of us if I confess that, each bound up in our own sorrows, we sought diversion in each other's arms."

Deirdre remained silent but her insides had begun to churn. This woman, this duchesse, was Killian's lover.

"My—" the duchesse laughed, "*our* Killian is a very clever fellow. He gradually became indispensable to me." She eyed Deirdre with a mixture of amusement and pity. How innocent, how defenseless she was.

Deirdre held her condescending gaze. What good was caution in the face of utter contempt?

The duchesse nodded her approval. "MacShane has been a hunter too long. He should be ashamed of himself for stalking an innocent."

Deirdre stood up. "You may have known MacShane long, your grace, but you do not know him well. He is a good man. There is gentleness in him and a willingness to do good."

"Facts of which he does not relish being reminded,"

the duchesse cut in dryly. "*Enfin*. I love him, too. Oh, do not look so stricken, *chérie*. Is that not what we have been discussing all along? You love him. I read that in your eyes. When you say his name, I blush with embarrassment for your transparency. But perhaps only another woman who loves him could detect the passion so easily. Does Killian know of these feelings you have for him?"

"Yes."

"And still he left you," the duchesse mused. "*Alors*. I despair of him. Of course, he may change his mind when he learns that you are here."

Deirdre started. Suddenly she knew the truth. "You sent for me."

"But of course! I confess it." The duchesse shrugged. "Curiosity is another of the vices I permit myself. When your little maid came to my door and asked for Killian, I was intrigued. She has the manners of a whore and the guile of an alley cat, but she was quite willing to tell me who had sent her to find Killian. Do not blame her. I wrote the note myself, telling her that Killian would be informed. You must stay, for certainly Killian will return at any moment."

"No, your grace, I should not," Deirdre maintained stiffly.

"Should not? But why not?"

"Captain MacShane may have lived his life in France; but he is an Irishman, and he would not like it if he found me here."

"In the company of his mistress," the duchesse suggested, mirth nearly bursting from her.

"Where he has not invited me," Deirdre answered.

The duchesse's one eye narrowed. She had underestimated her rival. How delightfully surprising. And sad. If she lost Killian, she would lose him to this pretty, golden-haired child with eyes as pure as the waters of a lake. Strange how purity drew some men, against their natures, against their reason. Purity would draw Killian. She had always known that and feared it. Perhaps that was why she had tried so hard to make him hate himself. Self-loathing was an antidote to the search for salvation.

"Perhaps you shall win him. I wish you *bon chance, chérie.*"

Deirdre curtsied and turned away. Only then did she allow a spasm to cross her face. She felt cut to ribbons by the duchesse's rapier wit. It seemed almost as if she should be holding a hand over her wounds, so badly did she ache. Killian was this woman's lover. No, worse than that, he was kept by a wealthy woman for her to enjoy at her leisure. How could she have been so very wrong about him?

"One thing more, *chérie.* Killian is not the paragon you would believe. You have not heard the end, or the best part, of my tale. Would you not like to know how he fits into the story?"

Deirdre turned about, too battered to care that she must accept one last cut.

"I made him swear to avenge me on the Venetian." The duchesse lifted the golden globe which hung from the ornate necklace she wore. "The Venetian's eye was the color of tourmaline, I believe."

Blinded by tears and revulsion, Deirdre turned away with a hand to her mouth. She did not notice that the door had opened or that it was blocked. She ran headfirst into the man standing there and, lifting her head, looked up into the blazing blue eyes of Killian MacShane.

"You had no right, damn you!"

The duchesse shrugged under the assault. After the girl pushed past him and ran out into the night, Killian had gone after her, but her carriage whisked her away before his horse could be brought from the stables. Since his return he had been pacing and swearing but not directing a word at the duchesse until now.

"I thought to save you the embarrassment of turning out a former mistress," she drawled. "Would you have seen the girl?"

Killian paused in his pacing, his face livid. "That's none of your damned business!"

"Then, it is as I thought. You would not have brought her here. You did not want her to know who and what you are."

"Who and what am I?" Killian questioned dangerously.

The duchesse laughed in his face. "You're a drunkard these days, *mon cher,* and you are my own and only love."

"What? Will you give no credit to those who came before, those who came after, and even those who have occupied your bed these last months even as I reside here?"

"Jealous, *mon cher?* It becomes you." She stood and raised her arms to him. "The others, they do not count. They cannot match you, *mon amour.* And yet, perhaps you should be grateful to the ones who came before you. Because of them, I know how to please you best. And because of me, you know how best to please me."

"I know how to please any woman," Killian corrected brutally.

The duchesse smiled. "There, you are angry with me. I, too, should be angry with you. If there is another in your place it is because you have neglected me. Not once in seven months have you come to my bed." She walked toward him. "Do you think I do not burn, that I am not afire knowing that you lie across the hall, that your magnificent body is so close, and yet so far away? Why do you lock your door?"

She paused before him, running her hands over his shoulders and then down his chest to his waist. "Do you know what torture it is to want you . . . to want this?" Her hands closed over his manhood and she began kneading him gently through his clothing. "Come upstairs with me, my fine stallion . . . my splendid wild savage . . . my greatest and best love!"

Killian pushed her hands away and walked toward the door.

"Where are you going?"

"To find her," Killian answered.

The duchesse took a step toward him, one hand raised in pleading, but then she caught herself and straightened. She was a duchesse, not a whore. She would beg nothing more of him. He must come to her. "You do not know where to find her. I do."

Killian turned at the door. "Will you tell me?"

"You will come back to me," she said in full confidence. "This child, she cannot give you what you want, what you need. I have seen her. She is a soft, innocent creature who will give you her love and her body, but both will appall you with their sweet emptiness. You will come back to me. No one else on earth can take my place."

Her voice trembled, betraying the agitation she would have kept hidden from him. "You have a taste for wild fruit, for forbidden passion. You are hungry for more and yet you do not realize it. That is what drives you. You think you are tired of passion. You are wrong. You are tired of ordinary delights. There are elixirs which feed and magnify the passion in the blood. There are instruments of delight, carnal joys of the flesh which we have not yet shared. Come to bed. I will send for Jean. You will see. Have you never hungered for a man as you hunger for a woman's flesh? Jean knows how to please a man. You will be amazed and tantalized beyond your wildest dreams!"

Killian drew back from her flushed face and trembling lips, sickened as he had never been before by her. She was depraved, and the depravity was twisting her mind toward madness. He must escape her! He had known it for months. Yet, there had been nothing to flee to. Until now. "I will find her, with or without your help."

"I could have her throat slit before you do," the duchesse said, suddenly calm.

Killian turned back slowly, his face distorted by rage. "If you touch her, if anyone touches her, I will kill you myself, slowly, horribly, and I will see you in Hell after!"

The duchesse retreated a step, a hand clutched to the bauble on her necklace. She believed him, in that moment, believed him fully capable of following her even into Hell.

"Go then!" she whispered furiously. "Go and be damned!"

Killian watched her a moment, pity mingling with his rage and dulling it. "You saved my life. I will not forget that."

She made a movement of denial with her head. "I hate you, Killian MacShane! Do not think I will forget. She will bore you to tears within a week. Have her. I curse you with her! She is in the Rue Gallion, number twenty-three."

Deirdre had not believed that she was capable of so many tears. They came in great heaving gulps that choked her and soaked her bodice and made her throat and chest ache. And still they continued to flow. She could barely stumble from the carriage and up the stairs to her room before they flooded her face anew. When she found the room empty she was too grateful for privacy to wonder where Fey was. She threw herself across the bed and gave in to the great misery that threatened to drown her from the inside.

Killian had a lover, a beautiful, evil, wealthy duchesse who adored him!

No wonder he had spurned her interest from the first. How amused he must have been when she offered her innocence to him. Yet, he had taken it, taken it ruthlessly without even a promise to return. And she had allowed it. It had never occurred to her that he might be tied by circumstance or emotion to another. How foolish, how gullible she had been.

The gentle rapping on the door did not surprise her. It would be Fey. "Come in," she mumbled as she hastily wiped her face on a pillow.

The door opened and closed but she heard no footsteps. "I—I think I've caught a cold, Fey," she mumbled in a hiccupy voice. "I don't feel well. Would you mind fetching me a cup of tea?"

"If tea will cure your tears, then I will fetch it."

Deirdre sat straight up at the sound of that masculine voice. "Killian!" she whispered in amazement.

He stood just inside the doorway, his face dark, half-lit by the small fire blazing in the grate. He saw the tear streaks gleaming on her face and winced. "Do not cry over me *acushla*. I am not worth your tears."

Deirdre crushed the pillow protectively to her breasts. "Do not tell me what I may and may not do."

Her anger eased his tension. He had not known what to expect when he heard her sobs from the stairway. "You are very angry and very disappointed in me. I tried to warn you that you knew nothing of me," he said grimly. "I am a savage man, a dishonorable man, a whoremonger, and worse."

"Aye!" Deirdre whispered. "And I am the greatest fool who ever lived!"

"Nae, not a fool, only a young innocent who loved not wisely. But I do not understand what brings you here." A sudden chill went through him and his eyes raked the dark interior of the room for clues. "You are not in Paris as a bride? Certainly Monsieur le Comte could afford better accommodations?"

"What do you know of that?" Deirdre asked, caught off guard by his question.

"I heard you were to wed," Killian replied.

"You are mistaken," Deirdre answered. "I will wed no one."

"There were announcements of the engagement," Killian persisted.

"Did you receive one?" she asked tartly. "I am amazed to learn that Cousin Claude knew your whereabouts."

"I heard," Killian answered, thinking better of disclosing that the news had come from the duchesse. "There is no need to lie to me."

Deirdre pushed the hair back from her face with a trembling hand. "I was engaged; 'twas my father's wish. Now he is dead and I wish not to wed."

The news of her father's death brought an unexpected sorrow to Killian. "I had not heard. My sympathies, mademoiselle."

"Why do we speak French? We are Irish."

"What would you have me say to you, *acushla?*"

"Do not call me that!" Deirdre cried. "Go away, go back to your duchesse! I am certain that she waits for you. And you, you left my side to seek your fill of her! Go away and leave me to my shame!" Angrily she scrubbed away a tear that fell on her cheek. "Must you mock even my misery?"

"I did not come to mock you," Killian said gently as he moved toward the bed.

"Why then did you come? Did you think to explain to me something the duchesse forgot?"

"I imagine the duchesse told you everything that I would not have. And, that being the case, I have nothing to add."

Deirdre looked up at him but she could not see his expression, and his voice frightened her. It made her want to put her arms about his neck and cling to him and weep and beg him to love her. She looked away. "Please. Please go away and forget that I came."

"Nae, lass," he said as he sat down beside her. "A man cannot turn from the tears of a woman until he knows why."

Deirdre shook her head. "Must you have it all? Must you hear the words?" She raised her head, her tears streaming freely once more. "I came because I loved you. There, 'tis said. I loved you."

"Deirdre," he began, reaching out for her.

She eluded his touch. "No, do not touch me. I said I loved you. That was before. Now I feel nothing but shame and bitterness and anger."

Her voice lashed him with its pain, and he rose, unable to bear her dislike. "I have hurt you. I never intended that you would be hurt." He spoke mostly to himself, his voice low and sonorous in the stillness. "That is why I left Nantes. What was between us, it was impossible. We were strangers. There was nothing but pain and misery for you in being near me."

He turned back to her, his voice rising in intensity. "Do you see now what I tried to warn you of: you're bound for disappointment and unhappiness the more you learn about me."

"*Gom!*" Deirdre smoothed the last of the tears from her face. "'Tis no more pain than any woman suffers when the man of her choice does not want her. I'm not so great a fool that I do not understand that," she said in a surprisingly practical tone.

Killian stared at her. "Why have you come to Paris?"

Deirdre bit her lip. It seemed so foolish now. He would think her a greater fool, if not a madwoman, if she told him. "We have nothing more to say. Go away, Captain MacShane."

Killian stared at her a moment longer and then turned to reach for the door latch.

"Wait! You have not kissed me. 'Tis the thing I shall miss the most. Will you not kiss me one last time?"

Deirdre did not know why she had said it, and could not quite believe she had spoken aloud until Killian shut the door and came toward the bed.

He bent over slowly, giving her every chance to turn away, and then he placed his lips very gently over hers.

Her lips were cool and damp with salty tears and they trembled under his mouth's caress. For a moment he resisted touching her and then his hands found her arms and he lifted her closer and wrapped her in his embrace.

Deirdre held still under the gentle assault of his kiss, willing herself to remain apart and record this last moment of joy at his hands. But she could not remain apart. She raised her hands, tangling her fingers in the heavy black silk of his hair, and pulled him closer. She clung to him with her lips, cherishing his sweetness, his strength, and the wind of passion that his kiss stirred to life, and terrified of the moment when he would break away.

Her lips parted under his and the hot breath of desire escaped, the passion clean and pure that burned for him alone. She heard him gasp as if in pain and then she was crushed against him. She gave up resistance, going with him as he climbed onto the bed, falling back under him as he bent her to the mattress, their lips never parting but savoring the unexpected joy of the moment.

Killian ceased to think of what he was doing the moment passion gusted between them. He had not thought he wanted her, had not considered the danger of desire when he bent to touch his lips briefly to hers. Now he was lost as her lips clung to his, murmuring nameless, glorious delight at his touch.

Her hands were on him, her cool satiny hands, and then the whole length of her warm softness lay under him. She moved under him, slowly, slow-moving, heart-stopping, feeding and strengthening the terrible wild hunger between them. The gentle-tender motion of love changed, became a swift-moving, wild-rapid, storm-blown current of pleasure-agony that ended in a swift eruption accompanied by their cries of pleasures.

Neither of them spoke, yet each was excruciatingly aware of the other as they lay side by side, not touching but not drawing away. The fire hissing behind the grate was the only sound in the room as the minutes passed.

"I hate her," Deirdre said at last, her voice low and sad. "I hate her for loving you, for having you."

Killian sat up, cradling his head in his hands. What could he say? How could he explain? He could not.

"Now will you run away again?" Deirdre asked, emotion edging in over the serenity of the last moments. "A fine soldier you must be, *abu*, retreating at every challenge."

Killian smiled in the dark. The lady was more she-wolf than he had credited. "I have been praised for my courage in battle. They say I fear nothing and that is so. It is then that a man has his life, his fate in his hands. If he dies, he knows the moment and the cause. I care nothing for physical pain. With the duchesse it is the same. I was attracted to her, the danger, the violence, and I stayed because it was of my choosing. But this...this is different."

He turned to her and saw her eyes shining in the darkness. "You frighten me, *acushla*. When I see you, when I am near you, I am robbed of myself. How can I explain? You have bewitched me. I am no longer able to choose." His voice roughened with desperation. "Just now. What have we done? Madness! All of it! Madness!" He rose from the bed, unthinking that in doing so he exposed his nakedness.

"I saved your life," Deirdre said gently. "Yet you say you fear me."

"I fear the loss of reason," Killian replied. "If I am to believe the dream that haunted me until seven short months ago, then I have never had a choice in wanting you. Yet, in wanting you, in having you, I place you in great danger." He brushed the hair from his eyes. "A reasonable man would not put a thing that he desires in danger. And yet I am capable of doing that."

"By being here?" she questioned softly.

"By being here, by remaining here, and by allowing the duchesse to know that I am here with you."

Deirdre sat up, reaching for the modesty of cover. "The duchesse knows that you have come here?"

"Aye," Killian said grimly. "She knows or suspects, damn her, what my feelings are."

"And you fear what she may do?"

Killian heard the caution in her voice and understood her thoughts. He turned to her. "I do not care what she may do to me. I have told you, I thrive on a certain amount of danger; it piques my appetite. She and I are well matched. Do not look away from me, *acushla*. My concerns are not for myself. My fear is for you."

Deirdre stared at him, wishing that the room were not so dark. His expression was lost in the gloom and his voice was disconcertingly neutral. "You say you're concerned for me. How do you know that danger will not come even if you are absent from my life?"

"The danger is of my making."

Anger blazed in her face. "Then go back to the duchesse's arms. She will forgive you. I saw it in her eyes. She will punish you, but she will forgive you. She loves you."

"I have not touched her in seven months," Killian said.

The joy that flared in Deirdre's eyes was caught by the firelight and Killian felt something in him burst free. "Then you are free of her," she whispered low.

Killian stood very still, listening to the echo rising from somewhere deep inside him. Yes, he was free of the duchesse, completely. The lust that had bound them was gone, routed by the gentle touch of an Irish lass with eyes the color of a lough at sunset. "I will never touch her again, not in that way."

Deirdre let the sheet fall from her hand and it slid down to her waist. "Then I must be more selfish than she, *mo cuishle*, for I will never give you up!"

Fey congratulated herself as she climbed the stairs to the room she shared with Lady Deirdre. She had been below, chatting with the concierge and spinning such a sad tale of woe that the woman had promised them a room for two weeks for the price of one, which meant that she and Lady Deirdre could remain in Paris a week longer than expected. If Lady Deirdre respected Fey's talents more, she would have realized how simple it was to solve their problems. That was the lady's trouble; she sought the most difficult, if pious, answer to every question when most things were easily solved by guile and wit.

For instance, Lady Deirdre had not questioned the note that she had been brought. She had not asked how MacShane looked or even if he was well. She had not asked where he lived or what it was like. She had simply smiled like the silly goose she was and tried to keep back foolish tears of joy.

Fey smirked as she thought of what she had found. MacShane, despite his priggish prosing against sin, was the lover of a wealthy older woman. No doubt Lady Deirdre would return from the Duchesse de Luneville's residence humming a very different tune. Well, it served her right, thinking that all she had to do to have a man was want him.

"He'd have been mine had she kept shy of him," Fey muttered.

The sound of voices inside halted her outside the door to her room. She recognized Deirdre's voice at once. It took her longer to recognize the second voice, but when she did, her face drained of color. MacShane was inside, in bed by the sounds of it, with Lady Deirdre.

Fey turned away, screwing her eyes up until the tears could not escape. "Damn them!" she whispered huskily. "Damn them both!"

Chapter Fifteen

Killian lay on his back in the pool of morning sunlight, his hands folded behind his head. Had he ever been more at peace with himself? He could not remember it. A few short hours ago he had dreaded entering this room. He had expected to find inconsolable hurt, recriminations, tears, rage. He had braced himself to offer labored explanations, to endure more anger, regrets, and apologies, and ultimately to face Deirdre's rejection. It had not been like that at all.

He turned to gaze at the woman who lay next to him and contentment flooded him. She lay on her back, one arm thrown above her head, her other hand clutching the sheet that did not quite hide the rosy peak of one breast. She was asleep, unaware of his warm regard and of his feelings of love, of tenderness, protectiveness, and fear.

Fear was what had awakened him from the deep dreamless sleep of peace. Would she be there when he opened his eyes? She was. The peace had flooded back, only to wash away again. In its wake had come new concerns. Would she regret the night? No, she would not. She had come to Paris to find him. She had not told him so, nor was he so arrogant and conceited as to assume this. He simply understood her better now. She had no guile, no falseness, no protection of pride to keep her from seeking that which she desired. It was he, not she, who was humbled by her search. He did not deserve to mean so much to this lovely woman.

He smiled as she stretched, kitten-like, releasing the sheet. She was all beauty and warmth and softness. From the brilliant waves of her golden hair to the roses-and-cream complexion of her young body, she was all things sweet, pure, clean, and good. And she wanted him.

The joy of that knowledge was sweet-piercing to the heart of him. He did not know what love was. He had had little experience with it, but surely this serenity which swept over him as he gazed down at Deirdre, surely this was close.

I must marry her, Killian thought. Dear God! How would they manage? He had no income, no prospects, nothing to offer her.

Once more peace ebbed from him. He was nothing—no, less than nothing, because he had set out since the summer to ruin himself. The quest to drown his despair with whiskey had become the summation of each day's rising. He did not feel it now, but would it last?

Back and forth his emotions swam on the tidal action of his thoughts. He was bound to her, had been since that fateful day nearly twelve years earlier when as a green boy of seventeen he had given his life into the hands of a serious-eyed lass of seven. She had been there for him all along. At any time he might have presented himself to the Fitzgeralds and found the answer to his dreams. Yet, he had waited.

Because I was afraid.

Killian bent and touched his lips to her cheek. He was a danger to her but he understood now that he could not run from it. If he spurned her, he might set in motion events which would endanger her, and he would not know what they were or where they struck. If she stayed within his reach at least he would be able to defend her against whatever evils his nearness spawned.

"I have never feared danger, *acushla*," he whispered as

his lips moved to cover her mouth. *Dear God! Make me worthy of this love, make my arm strong enough to defend her, my heart courageous enough to join against all her foes.*

Deirdre awakened to his kiss. She knew only a moment's hesitation before welcoming the warmth of Killian's mouth and the fiery heat of his tongue. And then he lifted his head, and his laughter, free and easy, filled her ears.

She waited in patient confusion for him to explain himself, but he did not, and when he looked down at her once more, she did not mind.

His eyes had never been more brilliant. The summer sky was not so vivid a blue. But it was his face, softened by happiness, that made her heart contract in love. The deep lines were erased by his happiness, the solemn man replaced by the carefree man of her imagining. "I love you."

Killian's expression became serious. "Marry me."

Deirdre's eyes widened. "Yes! Yes, oh, yes, yes!"

"But it is madness!"

Deirdre tightened her laced fingers as she watched Killian's expression harden in anger. She had sent Fey on an errand in order that they might speak in private. She had been ashamed to the roots of her hair when she learned that the girl had slept on the floor outside their door while she and Killian shared the intimacy of the bed. Fey would not accept an apology or Killian's offer of renting another room for her. She had slipped away in sullen silence, and, for the moment, Deirdre was grateful. She and Killian had much to discuss.

"I must do this," she said quietly. "You may come with me or you may remain in France. I will go home to Liscarrol and bury my father's body in Irish soil."

"You'll never get through the English blockade. You have no papers. You're Catholic. You may not even claim ownership of Liscarrol under the new Penal Laws. If you do not sell it to this Protestant cousin of yours, you will be forced to forfeit Liscarrol, with nothing to show for your bravado.''

Deirdre shook her head. "I will not sell Liscarrol, nor will I lose it. I refuse to accept that."

"Because your nursemaid has fits and 'sees' the link between you and some wretched lass a hundred years dead?"

Deirdre refused to be roused. "Because, my darling simpleton, because I will do what I must in order to save my home. My home, Killian. Can you not understand that?"

Killian's face drained of its color. "Nae, lass, I cannot understand what I've never had. An orphan child calls no place home."

Deirdre rose to her feet and grasped one of his hands in hers. "I did not mean that, and you know I did not. Please listen to me. I have sworn that I will wed no man but you. Liscarrol will be your home as well as mine." She smiled a cajoling smile. "In truth, the moment we are wed, Liscarrol becomes yours. 'Tis my bride's dowry to you." A strange light came into his eyes, and his expression altered from one of anger to one of high speculation. "What is it, Killian?"

Killian shook his head, shuttering his eyes with lowered lids. "Why is this so important to you?"

Deirdre made a helpless gesture with her hands. "I cannot explain it. Have you never felt driven by needs that you cannot name?"

"Too often," Killian answered.

"Then?"

"Does this mean so much to you that you are willing to thwart me, even postpone our marriage, that you may call Liscarrol your home once more?"

"I would rather *we* called Liscarrol home," she answered lightly. Then, seeing that he was serious, she added, "Even if it meant we should never wed. I cannot explain, even to myself, but I must do this. I have waited for a man who would help me win and hold Liscarrol. That man is you."

Killian stared hard at her. "Then I will help you. But

you must swear, and think well on this, you must swear to accept me in everything that I do. You must not question or forestall me in any matter, regardless of how bitter or distasteful you may find it.''

"You frighten me," Deirdre answered.

"Aye, and I should. You will not like my methods, but I believe I know a way to save Liscarrol."

"What is it?"

"Nae, lass, you must trust with blind faith, if you are brave enough."

A gust of fear blew through Deirdre, a clammy gust that slid down her spine and eddied in her stomach. "You will not leave me?"

"Never that!" More kindly he said, "If you ever change your mind, if ever you wish to abandon the battle and return to France, I will cease at once and bring you back."

Deirdre nodded. "Then join the battle, my love. I am ready."

Killian looked down at her with a mingling of pity, tenderness, and horror at the bargain they had struck. Into "the valley of the shadow of death"; did she realize that that was what she asked for? No, she could not, not yet.

As for himself, once more he was called upon to champion another's desires. She had a use for him. That was not the same as love. All his life, people had found uses for his talents. From the monastery to the battlefield to the duchesse's bedroom, he had served wants not governed by his own needs. Something of his own—at last he had found it. But was loving Deirdre enough when her love for him was not enough for her?

He shook his head. He must not think like that. It would destroy everything. What Deirdre wanted he would stake his life to get for her. "We will begin by finding a priest, but before that I must make a call."

"Upon the duchesse?" Deirdre asked.

Killian's smile was tinged with irony. "But of course."

"Do not sell your soul for me!" she called after him.

Killian did not answer, for that was, in part, exactly what he planned to do. He needed work, and the duchesse had offered him the job of overseeing her smuggling operation out of Ireland. If the position was still open, he would find a way to persuade her to give it to him.

He shut his mind to the thought that he had lost once again the battle to govern his own future. Perhaps it was never meant to be.

PART THREE

The Return

All changed, changed utterly:
  A terrible beauty is born.

—Easter 1916
W. B. Yeats

A power of faint enchantment doth through their
beings breathe.

—The Fairy Thorn
Samuel Ferguson

Chapter Sixteen

Deirdre awakened gasping for breath, her heart pounding heavily in her chest. *Danger! Danger! Danger!* The word galloped through her thoughts in accompaniment to her pulse. Cold beads of sweat rolled down her forehead and others trickled down her spine, pasting her night rail to her back. Icy fingers of dread lingered as she gazed about frantically for the sight of familiar objects in the gloom. Still caught in the nightmare's grip, she recognized nothing. This was not her bedroom in Nantes, nor was it the room in Paris which she had rented for the past four weeks. The tiny enclosed space had no windows or light.

The sudden pitch and roll of the mattress beneath her made her grab the side of the bed with a squeal of fright. The room righted itself immediately and settled back into the shallow rise and fall that she had not been aware of until now.

She was aboard ship.

Memory came flooding back as she reached for flint and struck a spark to light the lantern that hung at the bunk's head. The ship was a Dutch merchant vessel bound for the Irish city of Cork. The golden flame of the lantern spread light before the retreating darkness and struck a warm gleam from the surface of the wide gold band on the third finger of her left hand.

Deirdre stared at her hand, happiness washing over her. That morning she had stood before a priest and wed Killian Mainchin Aodh MacShane.

Unease wriggled across the surface of her new calm. How strange that when her happiness was at its peak, she should awake shuddering in the grip of a nightmare.

She gazed uneasily at the dark corners where shadows lay piled high. Was she being watched? The darkness seemed alive, alert to her very breath. She pulled the covers up over her and pressed herself back against the bulkhead.

The opening of the cabin portal made her heart skip a beat. When Killian emerged from behind it she scrambled from the bedding and launched herself into his arms.

"Mo cuishle!" Killian exclaimed as he reached out to steady her, "you're shivering." He bent to catch a glimpse of her face. "What is it, *asthore?* Did something frighten you?"

Deirdre lifted her head reluctantly but did not relax her grip upon his waist. She felt very foolish as she gazed up into his concerned face. Would he think her a child or, worse, unhappy, if she complained of nightmares? "Aye, something frightened me. You were not here."

A frown of doubt furrowed Killian's brow. "Truly? Nothing more?"

Deirdre hugged him closer until her cheek was once more against his shoulder. "Is that not enough? I am a bride but a day. Am I not to be skittish, even foolish, when it comes to the whereabouts of my husband?"

"Aye, *asthore.* 'Tis reason enough." He was edgy himself, his mind full of the venture before them. In a few days they would be docking in Ireland, where the future was far from certain.

Deirdre raised her head. "Why did you leave? Did I do wrong to fall asleep? After all, we did, we had . . ." She could not finish as a knowing look entered his eyes.

"Aye, we did and we had, lass, and never was a man more satisfied than I," Killian finished for her, gentle laughter in his voice. His arms closed around her, lifting her feet from the floor. "But then there's a madness in my blood that never stays satisfied for long. I daresay you'll never be safe from me when there are quiet hours before us and you blush so rosily and look quite pleased by my lustful ways."

Happily embraced in his arms, she said, "Aye, I'm pleased by your lustful ways, as long as that lustiness is for me alone."

The laughter disappeared from Killian's face. "I've sworn my fidelity to you before God and man. Never you doubt it, lass. You must trust me or we're lost."

Deirdre gazed at his serious face and regretted her words. Over and over again during the weeks before their marriage he had looked at her solemnly and asked her if she had changed her mind. "Then you must trust me," he alwasy had said when she answered that she would wed him.

There were secrets between them. He would not tell her whence came the money for this voyage, nor would he tell her what he planned to do once they reached Cork. She did not know by what means he intended to secure Liscarrol for her. Despite that, she did trust him.

"I am jealous, 'tis a sad failing of mine, but trust you with my life I do," she said and reached up to capture his lips with her own.

She felt the familiar surge of desire run through his body, the tremor of tensing muscles, and marveled that she had the power to so affect this enigmatic man. In the weeks between their pledge to marry and the wedding, they had lived as chastely as any respectably betrothed couple. Fey had kept her company and shared her room until the morning of the wedding. And so this, their wedding night, had been as full of anticipation as any nuptial night, or perhaps more so.

As he carried her to the narrow bunk they shared, she savored the intensity of her own desire. It throbbed deep within her, pulsing in her breasts and loins, a longing to be soothed and assuaged by the touch of his hands and body.

When he laid her back onto the mattress he hovered a

moment above her. "Is it too soon?" he asked. To her amazement he blushed, his skin darkening in the lantern light. "I do not mean to use you hard. We have made love once this night. Perhaps we should wait. It is late, you are—"

Deirdre cut short his apology with a fingertip against his lips. "It is late, *mo cuishle*. We have made love once but not, I think, enough." She saw the hesitation in his eyes and reached for his hand curved on her waist and brought it up to cover the fullness of her breast. The heat of his palm upon her skin made her nipple tighten and it rose under his touch. "Do you not believe me?" she whispered, her voice husky with desire.

Killian stared down into the dark green depths of her eyes and felt the astonishment of her desire to his very soul. She wanted him—nae, she desired him with an intensity that matched his own!

There had been times in his life when he wondered if he was capable of this burning of the flesh for a woman that his comrades-in-arms had spoken of often and fondly. Never before had he experienced this tormented longing, this inescapable need to be with a woman, to see her, hear her voice, and know that she was well. Only in his dreams had he known ecstasy and fear—until now.

He smiled suddenly. How foolish he had been to doubt. Here, lying in trembling softness beneath him, was the very embodiment of that tangled skein of emotions called love.

"I believe, *mo cuishle*, that you are all that mortal man dreams of," he whispered as he bent and touched his lips gently to hers. "I love you."

Deirdre wrapped her arms about his neck, almost afraid that he would still pull away from her, but he did not. He stretched out beside her on the bed, rolling her toward him, and embraced her. They lay side by side for a long time, trading kisses and smiling at the desire that darkened their eyes and melted their inhibitions.

She had learned in a few short hours of lovemaking to follow his lead. When his tongue flickered lightly over her face she followed suit, tasting the saltiness of the sea on his cheeks, and knew that he had been walking on deck. She reveled in the sweetness of his breath upon her face, and when his mouth closed over hers again, she reached up and entwined her fingers in his hair. Her lips were no longer soft and pliant but swollen with desire.

Her body stirred under the firm, molding caress of his hand which moved leisurely back and forth from her waist to her neck. She moved to the movement of that hand, wanting it, needing it, letting it feed the blistering heat of desire that scalded her from shoulder to thigh. Her hand moved to the buttons of his shirt. She worked them awkwardly with one hand, whispering a curse when she could not loosen the third.

Killian rolled back onto his back, laughing. "Do not curse my garments, love. This is how 'tis done." With a casual but ruthless pull he ripped his shirt open as buttons scattered. "There, that is better," he said as he brought her hand to his chest. "Touch me, *mo cuishle,* touch me where you will. It is pleasure at your hands."

His chest was more pale than his face and hands, smooth and sleekly muscled. He was warm and hard, like the satiny flanks of a stallion. There was power, strength, and gentleness in him. Her hand trembled as it slid down into the concavity of his belly. Where his breeches gaped away, a sketch of black hair traveled downward in a widening path until it disappeared. Using both hands, she loosened the heavy belt buckle and rows of buttons that closed the placket of his breeches.

She had seen him in his nakedness before, briefly in the moonlight at the hunting lodge, but never before had he lay openly, swollen and ready, under her regard.

She stared at him a long silent time, so long that Killian finally overcame his reluctance to speak. "Am I so ugly then that you are struck dumb, *acushla?*"

She glanced up into his face, all the wonder and love of the moment in her eyes. "Nae, you are lovely to look at. I did not know that men were so lovely."

"No one has ever called me lovely before, lass." he said quietly with the wonder of it in his words.

She reached out to encompass him. "You're the most lovely thing I've ever seen. And this, is it so with all men?"

"What?" he questioned between gritted teeth, for she stroked him with an incredible amount of enthusiasm.

"This, this pouting of the flesh. Are all men so, so big?" she asked with nervous laughter.

Killian shut his eyes, caught between amusement and desire. "I would not know much of other men, *acushla*. As long as I please you, does it matter?"

Deirdre shook her head. " 'Tis only glad I am that I did not know before," she admitted shyly.

"Know what?"

"That you were so big. I would not have believed that you'd fit."

Killian gave up his effort to control his laughter and he wilted immediately in her hand.

"Och, look what's happened!"

Killian wiped the mirth from his eyes to find Deirdre gazing down at him in utter disappointment. She looked up doubtfully. " 'Tis ruined."

He touched her face, his thumb pulling her lower lip free of her teeth. "You may easily mend the damage, lass, with a kiss or two . . . or three . . . or four."

Later, when they still held each other as if the fruition of their desire had not yet been achieved, Deirdre stroked his face and smiled as her nails raked the blue-black stubble on his chin. "Man is a wonrdrous thing."

"Aye, and woman." Killian smiled down at her with all his heart in his eyes. "I love you, Deirdre Fitzgerald. You are my heart's desire. What is your desire, I shall get for you."

Joy suffused Deirdre. This man with secret corners and quicksilver moods loved her. Others saw him as a soldier, a dreaded man with a sword whose rage and relentlessness were legendary. None of them knew the man who shared her bed in these moments. They did not know his tenderness, his carefree laughter, his unguarded moments. It was there in his face now, a vulnerability exposed to her alone. He would do anything for her. If she asked him to turn around and take her back to France, he would. If she asked him for jewels and diamonds, no doubt he would find a method to produce them. The knowledge both pleased and appalled her. Out of love he would do as she asked. Reason warned her that if she overburdened that love he would come to resent her. She must tread carefully in her desires. He was no horse to be put through his paces. He would get and hold Liscarrol for her. What more could she want of him than that?

"Simply love me." Deirdre said it confidently but was no less amazed to hear his reply of "I do" because she knew that he did.

After a moment he slid from her and a chill touched her where their bellies were wet with sweat. A moment later, he was asleep, his head resting upon her left breast.

Deirdre strained with mounting excitement for sight of the city of Cork as the ship sped up the misty waters of Cork Harbor. Behind them, off the starboard bow, Blackrock Castle sat on the south bank of the river Lee. An English flag flew from the main turret, holding sway over the dozens of others which flew from the masts of the British naval vessels plying the waters before it.

"Redcoats!" Deirdre muttered. "How dare they ply Irish waters— *Ouch!*"

"Speak Gaelic no more," Killian commanded as he released her arm. "'Tis a French lass you are from now on."

Deirdre scowled up at him, rubbing her pinched arm. "You gave me a bruise."

"Let it be a reminder," Killian replied unrepentently. "I will not be disobeyed in this." He raised a questioning brow. "I am understood, *n'est-ce pas?*"

"*Oui, mon mari.*" She smiled at him. "But may we not speak English also?"

Surprise brightened Killian's face. "You speak English? Why did you not say so before?"

Deirdre shrugged. "You did not ask me, and it did not seem a talent you would prize."

Beside them but a little apart, a youth dressed in the velvet coat and breeches of a gentleman's ward watched as the handsomely dressed black-haired man bent closer to his bride to whisper words that made the lady's face turn pink. The youth turned away, hurried across the deck to the opposite railing and, face hidden in an arm, burst furiously into tears.

"Bitch! The cheap doxy! And him, as randy as they come!" Fey mumbled between sobs. Even now, when she had been so close that they could touch her, they were too wrapped up in their own pleasures to realize that she had sneaked aboard ship before it had left France.

A long miserable month had passed since the night she had returned to that rented room in Paris and found MacShane in bed with Lady Deirdre. She had never learned what had occurred at the home of the Duchesse de Luneville, but it did not really matter. MacShane had chosen to wed Lady Deirdre.

They did not want her with them. MacShane had said it was because she was a child and they were embarking upon a dangerous, uncertain future. She did not believe him. MacShane's interest in her had evaporated because he was besotted by love. Lady Deirdre's solicitous inquiries about her and her gentle words of sorrow that they must part had not blunted the rage of her knowing that she had lost MacShane.

They had paid her passage back to Nantes, and Lady Deirdre had promised her a permanent place in the Fitzgerald household. They thought her in a coach bound for Nantes at this very moment. They did not know that she had cut her curls once more, dyed the remainder with boot black, and bought a suit of young gentlemen's clothes and a ticket aboard the ship. It had been easy to avoid them on the short voyage. They had scarcely moved from their cabin.

"Ye may not pay attention to me now," Fey muttered to herself as she squeezed her pocketful of coins, "but there'll come a time when ye'll wish ye had!"

In her pain she had discovered an ally. The Duchesse de Luneville, too, disapproved of the marriage. It gave them a common bond and a common interest in the fate of Liscarrol and MacShane.

The duchesse was very generous . . . and very clever. She expected loyalty in exchange for her money. She wanted to know MacShane's every move, where he went and what he did and said. And if he should show signs of growing weary of his young bride, she wanted to know that, too.

Fey shrugged off the guilt of becoming an informer. MacShane had betrayed her. He deserved no more. She could look after herself. He must do the same.

Yet, as she gazed at the green and gray vista of the coast of Ireland, she could not help wondering what would become of them. Danger rode the soft wet breezes. The unease of the French crew in British waters was a near-tangible thing. This was a country in conflict, a land in subjugation. MacShane endangered himself by coming here. Perhaps she was not betraying him in spying on him. She might be saving his life by following him to Ireland.

That thought made her dry her eyes. If she was able to help MacShane, he would be grateful. He would not turn from her a second time. As for the duchesse, she was in France and they were in Ireland. What she did not know she could not prevent.

Fey smiled and wiped her nose on her velvet sleeve.

"What do you mean that I may not accompany you?" Deirdre questioned.

"Exactly what I say," Killian answered impatiently. "I must speak with the customs officials and it will be easier not to have you present."

"Why? Do you think I cannot speak for myself?"

"I know you will speak quite clearly for yourself," he muttered, "and that, my love, is what worries me." He reached for his tri-corner hat and set it on the golden-haired wig that covered his own hair.

"Why do you wear a wig?" Deirdre wrinkled her nose

in distaste. "You never wore one before. And ruffles, what is this?"

"A different style of armor," Killian answered obliquely as he adjusted the lace ruffles of his cuffs. "I am going ashore to secure our papers. Until then, keep yourself occupied by musing upon the fact that we have completed the first leg of our journey. Before nightfall you will have the sod of Ireland beneath your tread."

He did not wait for her consent but turned and left the cabin. After assuring himself of the papers in his pocket, he strode down the gangway onto the quay.

When the whitewashed walls of the customs house loomed before him, Killian took a deep breath and expelled it. He had chosen a difficult masquerade to play before the English. To be successful he needed to seem a mountebank, a charmer, a man of much ambition and very few scruples. He had bought his crimson velvet habit with that part in mind. He meant to be a visible, easily recognizable figure about the city of Cork. It would make his role as an interloper more plausible. He only hoped that Deirdre would never learn of the method he would use to gain their admission into Ireland.

"For Deirdre!" he muttered to himself as he set his hand on the door latch.

Two hours later, the English naval officer looked up from the sheaf of papers spread before him. "You are Killian MacShane?"

"I am," Killian answered in English with a heavy French accent. After lounging in the antechamber of the customs house while waiting his turn to be interviewed, he had become all he seemed: tired, bored, and eager to be gone from the place.

"And you are seeking to return to your home in Ireland?"

"No, monsieur." Killian tapped the paper on top. "As you read, I am French by birth."

"So it says," the lieutenant answered dryly, exchanging a sly look with his young assistant who stood nearby. "Your name is Irish and you claim lands once owned by an Irishman by the name of Fitzgerald. Does that not make you Irish?"

"Irish by heritage, French by upbringing and persuasion," Killian replied.

"That is no recommendation to me," the officer said coolly. "The French are our enemies. They aided the impostor James in his pretensions to the English throne. They stir up the Irish with promises of guns and aid. Daily we are raided by smugglers and pirates, many of them flying the French flag." He appraised Killian from head to toe and back, taking in his lavish attire and expensive wig. The distinct odor of rose water that emanated from him made the officer's lips thin in distaste. He was a simple man and disliked the excesses of the French. "I am inclined to deny your entry."

"Inclined but not determined," Killian answered smoothly. "You must follow the letter of the law. To that end I am not to be denied."

"You are a Catholic. That alone prohibits you from entrance into Ireland."

Killian's black brows arched in surprise. "Where does it say that I am Catholic?"

The lieutenant was not amused. "Do you tell me that you have renounced your faith?"

Killian seemed to appear embarrassed. "Must you word it that way? I would rather believe that the calling was never fully mine. A man of your experience must understand how the temptations of the flesh often hold sway over the pious psalms which would deny man his small vices."

"You are aware that we have strict laws governing the conduct of Irish papists? As a Catholic you are forbidden to enter a profession, hold public office, engage in trade or commerce of any kind. You may not purchase land or lease land, nor may you accept a mortgage on land in security for a loan, nor may you receive or inherit land."

"Your laws are quite strict, as you say. What, however, have they to do with me?"

The lieutenant's eyes flickered. "You are educated, that much is clear. An Irishman who sends his son abroad to be educated forfeits all his property—as does his son."

"I am educated, that is true. But my circumstances are not of the kind you describe. My mother went abroad after the death of my father—of cholera—in hopes of taking the veil. It was discovered there that she was with child. After I was born, she did become a nun and remained so until her death a few years later, when I was sent to be raised by monks. So you see, my father did not send me abroad, nor is it my intention to lay claim to whatever small holding he may once have held.''

''So you say. How do you propose to subsist here?''

''I have come to claim a small property inherited by my wife, which, as her legal husband, now belongs to me.''

''Papists may not inherit property.''

''That again,'' Killian murmured, allowing his annoyance to show through. ''Kindly show me whatever document you wish me to sign that I am not a traitorous villain bent upon spreading the papist cause throughout the land and I will sign it here and now.''

The lieutenant made a steeple of his fingers and pressed them lightly to his lips. ''You are eager to be gone from here, Mister MacShane. I wonder why.''

Killian gave him a knowing smile. ''I am wed but three days, monsieur. Were you to see my bride, you would know what spurs me.''

''Is she, your bride, Irish?''

''Yes.''

''Her father was a papist and a traitor loyal to James?''

''So it would seem,'' Killian agreed cautiously. ''But I own I did not know the man well. He had no liking for me, nor I he.''

''Why?''

Killian shrugged. ''Our views of the world and politics were different. Our views of the practicalities of life were also.''

''You quarreled?''

''We did.''

''Over the daughter?''

''What else?'' Killian smiled expansively. ''What father enjoys losing his daughter to a young vigorous man? We would not be wed now but for Divine intervention. The father died.''

''And you have come to inherit his lands?''

"I have come to claim my bride's dowry. I will not quibble with you, I am a, ah, how do you say *un chevalier d'industrie?*"

"A sharper," the lieutenant offered unhelpfully.

"Mais non! I am not a swindler. I live by my wits. In marrying I hoped to extend my livelihood into that of gentleman and landowner."

The lieutenant frowned. The man had as good as said that he had married his bride for her dowry alone. Well, it was no business of his. "You may not inherit unless you can prove that you are a man loyal to the English throne and a member in good standing of the established religion."

"How may I do that?"

The lieutenant looked again at his assistant with a slight smile. "It is not so simple a task as you may imagine. We are serious in the method of accepting converts. Many papists would perjure themselves for a shilling. Any man who applies for admission into the established Church must first undergo a period of instruction. Afterward he must submit himself to an examination. If satisfied with his devotion and piety, he will be given a certificate guaranteeing him to be a fit subject for baptism. Only then is a man entitled to full ownership of the lands which he seeks to attain."

Horror showed in Killian's face. "So much? But I shall be old and buried before the inheritance is legally mine."

The lieutenant's smile widened. " 'Tis up to you. If you should accept instruction, you will be given a temporary permit to reside in Ireland. If not, you must return whence you came."

"If I accept these, ah, restrictions, I will be allowed to pursue my claims?"

The English officer nodded. He did not like this man but there was no reason to lie to him. Before admitting the man into his company he had determined that Liscarrol was a small holding in the wilds of the west and of little interest to the Crown. "For the time it takes to assess your true feelings upon the matter of religion, you will be allowed to remain."

Frowning, Killian stroked his chin. Then a smile lit his face and he nodded. "So be it. What must I do first?"

The lieutenant withdrew a paper from his desk drawer. "Fill this out and then fill out a separate one for your wife."

Killian took the paper but his smile faltered. "My wife is not concerned with this."

"Surely she intends to follow in your footsteps?"

Killian raised his eyes and they gleamed with guile. "I am not so ignorant of your laws as you would think me. As my wife, she has no claim to anything she owned before the ceremony. She is young, innocent, sweet, and delightful. She may remain in happy ignorance of my deed which, in the truest sense, benefits her. She may not attend Mass, I have apprised her of that fact. Why should she be bothered with details of state which do not affect her?"

"You fear losing her," the lieutenant said baldly.

Killian nodded slightly. "Just so."

"If you become a Protestant, she may seek an annulment."

Killian shrugged. "What benefit could that be to her when it is I who own the land and your law permits me to retain it?"

The lieutenant looked away. He knew the man for what he was now, a cheat, a swindler, a rogue who had caught an innocent young girl in a fraudulant marriage for the sake of confiscating her property. The man was the lowest sort of creature and becoming a member of the established Church would not better him. The laws sometimes seemed greatly unfair, yet there was nothing he could do about it.

When Killian MacShane had signed the necessary papers and was gone, the lieutenant looked at his assistant. "I hope the land has gone to bog and the house has been razed!"

"Perhaps the smugglers will see to him," the assistant offered helpfully. "There's been trouble again in the west with the rebel O'Donovan."

"Just so," the lieutenant answered. "May the man make that devil's acquaintance."

Outside on the quay, Killian unwrapped his lace jabot and wiped his face.

Instruction in the established religion, how would he explain that to Deirdre? No, he would not explain it. She would not accept his deception as a condition of their remaining in Ireland, while he knew it was their only chance.

To his surprise, he realized that his hands were less than steady. He had won the right to remain in Ireland, but he had also placed his head in a noose which, if he slipped, would tighten and strangle him.

From the corner of his eye he saw a small figure dart between the legs of a red-coated soldier. As he straightened, the child came hurtling toward him. The soldier yelled for the boy to stop and lifted his musket from his shoulder. Sensing the danger in which the boy stood, Killian reached out to grab him by the collar, but the boy twisted free and Killian was left holding a small velvet coat.

The blast of gunfire on the crowded quay sent startled passersby fleeing in every direction with cries of fright. The boy disappeared around a corner with the scattering crowd.

For a moment Killian stood staring after the soldiers who ran past him. He smiled. They would not find the boy, of that he was certain. The child had seemed familiar, and then he realized why: the boy's antics reminded him of Fey as he had first seen her.

He looked down at the coat he held and his grin broadened. Perhaps in a year, if his plan succeeded, he would send for Fey. She was bright, courageous, and quite pretty, but she needed a heavy hand to keep her in line.

But first he had other business to attend to.

The duchesse had hired him to pursue and eliminate from her cache of smugglers those who were disloyal to her. Before they had set sail from Nantes, he had made himself known to one of her sea captains by presenting a letter from the duchesse herself. The captain had given him the name of a man to contact when he arrived in Cork. This man would put him in touch with the smugglers who worked the coastline between Ballydehob and Bantry.

Killian smiled grimly. The duchesse's spies were everywhere, it seemed. He was to be followed. He knew the contents of her letter because he had steamed it open ahead of time. She did not trust him. It was just as well. He did not trust her either.

Killian's features hardened as he reached the gangway of the ship. He did not like the idea of setting Deirdre among smugglers, but he had accepted the job because it paid extremely well and he had nothing to offer Deirdre without it. When in time he put Liscarrol on its feet, he would loosen his ties to the duchesse. Until then, Deirdre was better kept in ignorance in yet another matter.

"'Tis a smugglers' master, a swindler, and a groom I've become in the space of a week," he murmured to himself. "What more will the season bring me?"

Chapter Seventeen

Southwest Munster, Ireland

Deirdre shifted in her saddle to ease the pain in her lower back. The leather creaked as she moved, and Killian glanced around, his light eyes as distant and cool as the mist-laden day about them. She straightened her back immediately and kicked her mount to increase its pace but the weary animal merely continued to plod along, its hooves making sucking noises as it traversed the boggy ground.

"There's nothing to be gained by hurrying," Killian announced grimly, using English because they were not alone. "'Twill take hours until we reach Kilronane. We should have spent the night in Enniskean as I suggested."

Stung by his words, she allowed her weariness and hunger to answer for her. "Aye, and to your way of thinking we'd have done better to stay in Cork until summer. Or better still, we should have stayed in Nantes altogether!"

"Like a bairn, you see the wisdom of my suggestions too late to do us any good," Killian answered dryly.

Deirdre angrily pulled her hood forward to shut off the

sight of him. How dare he insult her before the company in which they traveled. He had not spoken more than three sentences to her the entire day and now he chose to fuel the animosity between them.

Killian did not speak again but suddenly dug his heels into his horse's flanks, and his mount lunged forward from a walk into a canter that quickly outdistanced her.

Snickering from one of the two men Killian had hired to protect them on the journey made Deirdre turn her head to glare at the offender.

The man nodded his shaggy head pleasantly and bared a mouth of rotten teeth as he said to her in Gaelic, '' 'Tis the *oinseach* sees the *amadan's* faults!''

"A wise head keeps a shut mouth!" Deirdre retorted in Gaelic and was gratified by the stricken look that overcame the man, who thought her ignorant of his language.

"Begging your pardon, mum," he mumbled and fell back behind her with his friend.

Deirdre's mouth tightened as she looked ahead. Killian was a dim figure in the distance, his outline darkened and blurred by the fine but persistent rain that had been falling since dawn. It was his fault that the man had dared to speak to her so. MacShane's callous treatment made them view her with contempt. Now he had ridden off and left her in their company like one of the sacks of meal in their provisions.

"He is angry, but so too am I!" she muttered.

No, she was not angry. She was cold, wet, and miserable. Why could Killian not understand how eager she was to see Liscarrol after more than twelve years' absence? For two weeks she had waited impatiently in the small dismal room near the waterfront of Cork while he busied himself with plans which he was very reluctant to share with her. In fact, he was reluctant to share much more with her than an evening meal and their bed.

Deirdre flushed, annoyed with herself for the delicious shiver of desire that ran through her at the mere thought of Killian in bed beside her. Each night he had thoroughly wiped from her mind the petty grievances that she had amassed during his long absences each day. One touch and she forgot everything but her need of him and their pleasure.

He had used their love as a blind against her inquisitiveness. He had answered her questions with drugging kisses, her inquiries into his daily business with seductive caresses, her pleading to leave for Liscarrol with the tantalizing beguilement of his body's touch. A fortnight had passed before she became suspicious of his actions. The realization of the truth had made her furious because she had become so willing a pawn.

As Deirdre watched his silhouette disappear behind a line of trees, she wondered how long Killian would have kept up the pretense that he had made plans for their journey had she not decided out of boredom to check on the traveling coach he said he had ordered. She had found that there were coaches readily available, not the waiting list Killian had told her of, and that had he not yet ordered one. They would not now be within a day's journey of her goal had she not ordered a coach herself and begun packing.

The cool wind of trepidation blew across Deirdre's conscience as she remembered Killian's reaction to her discovery. She had never seen him angry before, and it was a revelation.

"You have done what?" he had demanded.

"You lied to me," she had answered, too annoyed by his petty contrivances to notice at once the strange look that had entered his eyes. "You said there were no coaches available. There were. I ordered one of them. Though you seem enamored with the city, my husband, I am bored with Cork. We will leave for Liscarrol in the morning."

The hand that grasped her shoulder and spun her about had astonished Deirdre in its power. Then she saw his face. The bitter cold blue of his eyes, so hard and angry, silenced whatever she had been about to say. His features were stony, altering his countenance into that of a stranger. "You will cancel the coach," he had said low, his voice made more menacing by the tenuousness of his control. "You will cancel it and never *never* question my authority again!"

Deirdre shook her head in denial as the memory assailed her. In that moment she had been afraid of him. He had seemed for the first time the Avenging Angel of her brothers' stories.

If not for her moan of pain she doubted he would have realized how mercilessly his fingers dug into her skin. When he released her, he had seemed as amazed as she to see the red imprint of his hand on her skin above her low-cut bodice.

She touched her shoulder. The marks had remained there for hours, a silent reminder of the depth of rage of which he was capable.

And yet, he had been immediately contrite. Through her stunned surprise she had recognized the look of horror and then shame as he stared at the evidence of his anger. He had bathed her bruised shoulder in cool water and then kissed each mark. And though he had not said a word of apology, she understood and accepted the depth of his remorse.

Later, in bed, with the balm of satiation between them, he had sworn to her that he would take her to Liscarrol as quickly as possible. He had convinced her that a coach would be useless on the narrow boggy trails. They rode, leaving most of their possessions in Cork to be sent for later. There had proved to be wisdom in that.

Deirdre glanced back covertly at the two men riding donkeys and leading pack animals behind her. Killian had hired them for protection. Yet, the men he had chosen were singularly unsuited for the work. They were seamen; anyone could tell that by listening to them. They were unaccustomed to riding, could barely keep their seats on stretches of uneven ground. Besides that, they were rude and sly and made her uncomfortable when Killian was not beside her.

Once more she kicked her horse, digging in hard, and this time the horse went into a canter. Urged on by this success, she shouted and slapped the horse's haunches and the beast stretched into a gallop that sent her racing after Killian.

Killian heard the approaching horse and slowed his

pace, but he did not glance back. He had lost his temper with Deirdre again, a thing he had promised himself he would not do.

It was not her fault that the journey had been forced on him too soon. Yet, if she had not been so stubborn about leaving, he would not now find himself alone with two men whom he trusted less than he would a stray boar or wolf. They were two of the duchesse's smugglers and they did not yet trust him enough to allow him to leave Cork unescorted.

"Do you find my company so distasteful?" Deirdre questioned as she drew alongside him.

Killian did not reply directly. "If you are weary we will pause for a short while, but we must reach high ground before dark."

Deirdre caught her lower lip between her teeth. He had not even glanced at her. "You are angry."

"I am impatient with this wretched weather."

"And you wish both the elements and I would go directly to Hades," Deirdre finished for him.

Killian turned to look at her. Her face was damp and the bright curls that had escaped her hood were darkened with rain, but those things did not mar her in his eyes. "You are quite lovely when you're angry," he confided with the beginning of an intimate smile.

"Well, you are not!" Deirdre retorted but could not repress a return of his smile. "You are a most uncivil bore."

Killian was not fooled by her demeanor. There was hurt lurking in her eyes, hurt he had put there five days earlier. He looked away. He could not explain to her his reasons for wanting to remain in Cork. She had forgiven him for the bruises on her shoulder, but he suspected that other things might not be so easily forgotten or forgiven.

"I am a man accustomed to his solitude," he began as he stared straight ahead. "I've never needed to answer to another for my moods or actions. This business of being a husband, of caring for the needs of another, is new to me."

"I had not considered, my husband, what a burden I

must be to you," Deirdre answered. The tone of her voice made him whip his head toward her and he saw the golden glint of anger as well as hurt in her green eyes. "So I will relieve you of my burdensome presence!"

Before Killian could guess her intent, Deirdre urged her horse forward with a hard kick. He shouted at her but she gave no sign of having heard him as she galloped away.

"*Gom!*" Killian swore as his body tensed to give chase. The horses he had purchased in Cork were of poor quality, not the well-bred steeds Deirdre was accustomed to. The animal did not have the breath and stamina for a long gallop. He relaxed; she could not go far.

Expecting to be chased, Deirdre crouched low in her saddle until she nearly lay on her horse's neck. With all her strength she urged the horse on, up the slope of a hill and then down the steeper plunge of its far side. The wind raced past her, whipping her skirts and tugging at her cloak. It tore her hood from her head and dragged the heavy knot of hair from her crown and sent it spilling across the horse's shoulder.

The ride made her pulse beat hard and quickly in her ears but she did not care. It was the first exhilarating moment of the journey. As the green, granite-strewn ground stretched out before her, she inhaled deeply of the wet pungent air. It smelled of mud and wood and turf and . . .

She did not recognize the first unpleasant whiff as anything other than the stench of stagnant bog water. Ahead stood a lone oak, its dark skeletal limbs spread in welcome to the sky.

She tugged on the reins to slow her horse's pace but the animal was already tensing. It dropped from full gallop into a reluctant trot, tossing its head nervously as the unpleasant odor reached its nostrils.

With the back of one hand she brushed the tears of the ride from her eyes. The sight before her was so completely alien to her experience that she did not at first recognize what she saw.

Hanging from the lower limbs like misshapen sacks of grain were nearly a dozen bodies. The tree groaned under its burden, its heavy limbs moving imperceptibly as the dark forms suspended from it swung gently in the wind like ghastly fruit.

Deirdre opened her mouth and screamed but she could not turn her face away. She sat spellbound by the horror while her mind recorded the horror before her.

All her life she had heard tales of the atrocities of war, of murders and tortures that turned men like her father silent in the midst of a sentence, but she had never seen a hanged man.

The victims were men with blackened, swollen faces so distorted that she doubted they would be recognized by their own kin. One by one, she gazed at each in morbid fascination until she came to the last.

It was a small bundle, its arms and feet not bound like the others. Strung from a lighter limb, it spun dizzily in the wind, its swath of long black hair whipped into a pathetic banner for the girl it had once been.

The hanged girl was no older than Deirdre herself had been when Killian MacShane first entered her life. Her skin shrank against her bones. Had she, in helping Killian, come so close to this end? What evil could have marked so young a child for that slow torturous death? The horror of it still distorted the child's face as she seemed to cry out to Deirdre for release. Was there no one who fought for the girl's life? Would no one even cut her down?

Deirdre did not heed the cries of the men riding toward her. An anger stronger than fear replaced her revulsion. She was not afraid of death but abhorred the bullying cowardice of men who would hang a child.

Without waiting for help, she withdrew the O'Neill skean from its sheath on her saddle, tucked it into her belt, and dismounted. The oak was ancient and easy to climb but she was hampered by the heavy skirt of her riding habit. She had gained no more than a few feet when she was plucked from the trunk by a strong pair of arms.

"No! Stop! Let me go!" she cried. Enraged to be thwarted, she twisted and writhed to break free of the hands that held her back from her purpose.

"Dee, lass! Dee!" Killian commanded sharply as he struggled to contain her flailing arms and legs. He saw the silver flash of a blade in her hand, and when she made a downward slash toward his wrist, his soldier's training took over. He closed his hand over hers and gave her wrist a quick twist. With a yelp of pain Deirdre opened her hand and the weapon fell to the ground.

"Deirdre!" he cried as he spun her about.

For an instant Deirdre gazed unseeingly at Killian and then she became aware that it was he who gazed down at her with concern. "They hanged her! And no one would stop them!" she cried. She gripped Killian hard by the arms. "You must cut her down, Killian! You must!"

The anguish in her voice overruled the protest Killian was about to make concerning the foolhardiness of her actions. "Aye, Dee, I'll see it done. Go back to your horse." He turned to the men who had dismounted beside him and pointed to the body of the child. "Cut her down."

"Are ye daft?" the one called Sean questioned in amazement. "The English leave them as a reminder to the local folk. I know the law. Not till they drop from rot are they to be touched. Sean O'Casey will nae dance the jig for an English fiddler."

"Aye, we'd best be gone before the English return," the second man offered. "What with the lady screaming her head off, like as not the bloody English heard her as far away as Dublin."

There was sense in all they said, but when Killian looked toward Deirdre she was watching him. He lifted his pistol from his belt and cocked it. "Cut the lass down and bury her or you lie here and rot beneath her."

The men stepped back. They did not carry pistols. "You'd nae do it!" Sean challenged.

Killian leveled his pistol at the man's middle. "I'll not have my orders questioned."

"He means it, Sean," the other man whispered.

"Aye, I do mean it."

Sean swore under his breath. "Ye're nae better than the bloody English, but I'll be damned afore I bleed me life's blood for want of a burial!" He turned away and with a jerk of his head signaled the other to join him.

Killian put away his pistol as Sean shinnied up the oak,

a skean clamped between his teeth. After the body of the girl was cut free, Killian retrieved a flagon of wine from his saddle and brought it back to Deirdre, who had moved away from the protection of the oak into the blustery day.

He laid his cloak about her shoulders to shield her from the heavy gusts of spring rain and held the wine to her lips. "Sip it slowly," he cautioned.

Deirdre swallowed a little of the wine before she shook her head and backed away from him. She watched warily as he drank more freely before stoppering it. "I—I have never before seen a hanging," she offered in a low voice. She looked up angrily. "You must get rid of those men. They're inhuman. The sight of that poor wee bairn is enough to curdle the blood of any feeling man."

Killian considered her words. He had seen so much killing and death in his years that the simple matter of a hanging left him unmoved. Of course, he felt sorrow that a child had died on a gallows tree, but he was not horrified. "There are worse ways of dying," he offered as solace.

"Worse ways?" Deirdre echoed faintly. "How can you say such a thing? That—that poor lass was not above eight years of age. How can you be so indifferent?"

Killian bridled under her incredulous stare. "I'm a soldier, lass. I've seen more than you would imagine."

Deirdre clasped her hands tightly together. They felt like ice. "I have heard many tales of the horrible deeds that men in battle are capable of. Conall and Darragh spared me little. But if war has made you indifferent to the unspeakable crime that was committed here, I—I . . ." She could not finish. There was nothing to say if he could gaze upon the sight and feel nothing.

Killian saw the horror in her face but did not know how to help her. Death was a terrible thing, violent death a horror that each must face in his or her own way. Yet, he longed to reassure her, and he was grateful that she turned into his arms when he held them out to her.

"I am not indifferent, nor am I unmoved," he said quietly as he stroked her hair. "But I've learned that a man must spend his energies upon those things he can change.

My anger will not bring the bairn back. 'Tis done, Dee. You must forget it.''

Deirdre raised her head, her green eyes shining with tears. "Never!"

"What will you do, challenge the Englishmen you meet with your skean?" he questioned in sardonic humor.

"You stopped me from freeing the lass," Deirdre answered testily and pulled out of his arms. "You would have done nothing, nothing, had I not demanded it of you."

"Merde!" Killian turned and stalked away. There was no reasoning with her now.

"It might have been me twelve years ago!"

Killian turned back. So that was what had frightened her.

"She was helping to hide someone from the English," Deirdre continued. "That's why they hanged her."

Killian shook his head as he came toward her. "You cannot possibly know that, Dee."

Deirdre sidestepped him. "I know." She bent and picked up the O'Neill skean, carefully wiping away the mud with a corner of her skirt.

Killian watched her a moment longer before giving up and going to where the two men had begun digging in the soggy ground. It had been a strange day. Deirdre was overwrought with fatigue and anxiety. Of course she would be terrified by the gruesome sight she had come upon so suddenly. Things would be better when they arrived at Liscarrol.

"They could scarcely be worse," he muttered as the drizzle became a downpour.

The sun was setting when they rode into Kilronane, which lay in a valley between dark-shouldered hills. It had not taken long to bury the child's body, but the rain had continued well into the afternoon, making travel hazardous and progress slow.

With disappointment Deirdre noted that the village was nothing more than a cluster of dark, mud-walled, thatch-roofed huts. She had hoped to find the welcoming bustle of a busy community.

At the entrance to the village stood the remains of what had once been a church, one of many such relics from the Cromwellian years. The dim light of sunset softened the contours of the old church, making the ruin seem romantic and mysterious. As they moved toward the center of town, the faint acrid odor of a peat fire carried on the wind gave the only evidence that the silent huts were inhabited.

"Dark doings," the man riding alongside Deirdre muttered and drew his skean. Immediately his companion did likewise.

Killian reached over and grabbed the reins from Deirdre's hands and drew her horse to a halt beside his. "I do not like the looks of this place." He leaned toward her. "Stay here till I've roused someone. If we are attacked, ride straight back the way we came. I'll catch up with you."

"But I—" Deirdre began, only to have Killian move away.

"Stay with my wife," he ordered softly and pointed at Sean. He signaled the other man to follow him.

Killian walked his horse through the lane that divided the houses into two irregular rows, pausing at the last. It was no better built than the others but it was larger and longer, and though he could not read the sign which hung above the door he surmised that it proclaimed it an inn. "Stay mounted," he ordered his companion as he dismounted.

There was no answer to his first hard knock, but the hiss of a fire within was audible. "Open up!" he shouted. "We're not the bloody English!" It was a risk but one he felt confident in taking. The people of the village were afraid. What had they to fear but the English?

He heard the sound of bare feet scurrying across the earthen floor. The scrape of a bolt being lifted came next and then the rough-hewn door opened just enough to reveal a single eye. "Who are ye?"

"My name is MacShane and I've my wife with me," Killian answered in the outlawed Gaelic tongue, though the question had been put to him in English. "We seek lodging for the night."

He saw the bright eye move curiously from his face to his boots and back. "Ye've the look of an Englishman," came the answer, again in English.

"Would English dogs not demand rather than request their lodgings?" Killian asked in Gaelic and touched his coat pocket. "I've a coin or two for your effort." He heard whispers before the door was reluctantly dragged open.

A gaunt old man stood in the doorway, his back bowed by years of hard labor and his face permanently reddened by the sun. His shaggy hair was uncombed and a rope held his breeches about his waist. He was poor and dirty but the light of defiance shone vividly in his eyes. "There'll be nothing here befitting the likes of ye . . . sir." The last, deferential word seemed to have been dragged from him.

Killian looked past the man to the glow of the turf fire in the center of the home, around which a ragged woman and four children crouched. Smoke from the fire had gathered in the rafters where it curled in thin bluish white eddies. No wonder he had thought the village deserted. There were no chimneys.

His eyes quickly scanned the rest of the smoky interior. Along the opposite wall, long boards propped up by whiskey barrels at either end provided a bar. He looked back at the proprietor. "This is an inn. You are bound to give shelter to those who enter."

The smaller man bobbed his head once but his eyes were cautious.

Killian understood the man's apprehension. "Perhaps I should have said you should give shelter to those who can afford it." He took two coins from his pocket and held them out. "Will this buy four meals and two beds?"

The man's face altered so quickly that Killian nearly laughed. Money kept its virtue, whoever its owner. The innkeeper might detest him but his coins were welcome.

" 'Tis the Blessed Virgin brought ye, I'm thinking. Certain I am that ye're nae an Englishman to be parting with yer gold so freely," the man declared, grinning. "If it be true that there's a Mac before ye're name, ye've come to the right place and I'll gladly offer ye *didean*."

"The name is MacShane," Killian reiterated.

"Cuan O'Dineen is me name. 'Tis of nae use to me but to give the English cause to string me up beside the rest of the poor sodden bastards."

"The English have hanged men of your village?" Killian questioned quickly.

Cuan's gaze once more became suspicious but after a moment's reflection relaxed. "Saw the lot, did ye, coming in from the east?"

Killian nodded.

"Well then, enough said. Bring yer lady wife in. 'Tis a cool night."

Killian hesitated. Deirdre had sobered quickly from her hysteria but she was pale and frightened. If there was to be talk of the hangings, he would rather she not hear it. "Why were the men hanged?"

" 'Twas but a single man they came to hang," Cuan said grimly. "O'Donovan is his name. If ever a man was born to hang, 'twas him."

"I do not know the name; should I?" Killian questioned casually as the innkeeper pocketed the coins. But he did know the name. O'Donovan was the man the duchesse had sent him to find.

"Were ye a Munsterman ye would," Cuan answered. "Where do ye come from then?"

Danger glittered in Killian's gaze. "What does it matter? A man's travels do not denote his heart and home."

Cuan eyed him suspiciously. "Aye, but a man cannae be too distrustful these days. 'Twould not be revealing much to tell ye what ye could learn in any village between Bantry and Cork. O'Donovan's hunted by the English."

"He's a smuggler?"

Cuan grinned. "Were it only that, there's many an Englishman who would make him as safe as a babe in arms."

Killian filed that bit of information away. It might prove very useful later. "Then he must plague the English soldiery."

"That he does," Cuan agreed reluctantly. He looked toward his wife, who had not moved from her crouched position by the fire. "There's too many rumors about," he grumbled. "Bring in yer lady."

Killian pressed him. "Is one of the men hanging from the gallows oak O'Donovan? Were the others those who sought to protect him?"

Cuan's pale eyes lit up. "Protect O'Donovan? God rot their black hearts! 'Twas the English method of flushing him out. They swore they'd hang one man an hour until he showed himself, but they do not know O'Donovan if they thought he'd save another man's life with his own."

Killian thought back briefly to the dead man and a shudder passed through him. "Were they all of your village?"

"Nae. The English had captured a few of them on the road while chasing O'Donovan. 'Tis no secret Kilronane is his home. They took two of our lads when they came looking for him."

"Why the child?"

Cuan's gaze slipped from his. "Do nae speak of her! Ye've a lady wife chilling in the night. Fetch her in."

"I am not that thin-blooded," Deirdre answered from the doorway. "Do continue your explanation. I, too, would know why the lass died when able-bodied men such as yourself were there as witness."

Cuan gaped at the aristocratic-sounding lady in his doorway. Backlit by the dying light of day, she appeared in a golden halo that shone brightly through her hair. " 'Twas naught to be done for the lass. She showed an English soldier the sharp edge of her blade. Cut his wrist. He fair bled to death."

Deirdre remained framed in the doorway. "Surely there is more?"

Cuan muttered a curse but saw the look in MacShane's eye and did not turn his back on the lady. "She were a bastard, one of O'Donovan's. She thought they'd hang her Da."

"Why did you not speak up for her?" Deirdre persisted, a sharp edge in her voice.

"Risk me life for the likes of her?" Cuan lifted his hand toward his family. "I'd me own to think of."

Deirdre lifted her eyes to Killian's. "I will not stay in the house of a coward."

"Coward, is it? Coward!" Cuan cried, anger making him brave as he advanced on her.

Deirdre was not afraid of the little man. She drew her skean and held it so that the jewels in the hilt caught the fading light and glowed as warmly as if they had a life of their own. "You do not recognize me, old man, but you will remember a time when this village and all those within twenty leagues belonged by my family. I'm a Fitzgerald and I have come home to claim what is mine. The lass has been cut down and buried. Find yourself a priest and ask for mercy for your cowardice. Then go and erect a stone for the child at the mount near the oak."

Cuan stared open-mouthed as Deirdre turned and walked back out into the twilight. "That be yer lady wife?" he asked after a moment.

"Aye, I fear so," Killian answered grimly as he followed Deirdre out the door.

"Why did you do that?" he demanded when he caught up with her. "You've been unforgivably reckless in proclaiming your lineage and Catholicism to a stranger."

Deirdre turned to him. "You cannot expect me to sleep beneath the roof of a man who allowed that child to die."

Killian stared at her without pity. "Then know that there's not a roof within five leagues that will satisfy you."

Deirdre looked up at him with tears in her eyes. "How could they, Killian? How could they be so afraid?"

"They are not to blame entirely," he answered, and then despite his anger he slipped an arm about her. "They have nothing with which to fight back. A man needs daring and strong nerves to play a winning hand these days."

Deirdre wrapped her arms about his neck as he lifted her into the saddle. "Then we must be very cunning."

"Aye, like a wolf," Killian answered heavily. "There's the ruins of the church. Shall we bed down there?"

Deirdre nodded, too heartsick to care where they spent the night. Tomorrow they would reach Liscarrol and the culmination of twelve years of longing.

Chapter Eighteen

Deirdre rode toward the crest of the hill with an odd kind of excitement beating high in her chest. She had waited for this day for so long that she could hardly believe it had arrived. Much of the surrounding countryside was different from her memories as an eight-year-old, but it did not matter. She recognized the pale green tinge in the western sky just above the shoulders of the Shehy Mountains and knew that Liscarrol lay in the valley just beyond the rise.

There was an eagerness in her face that drew Killian's gaze to her again and again as they slowly climbed to the summit. In the soft morning light, the pale gold of her skin matched the shining crispness of her hair, which she had left uncovered under the rare near-cloudless sky. She was the embodiment of all that was young and unspoiled and vulnerable. His heart went out to her in hopes that she would not be too disappointed in the sight that lay ahead. He could not warn her not to expect too much. It would only spoil her happiness that he did not share her expectant joy.

When she glanced at him and flushed in surprise to find him gazing back at her, Killian smiled. He had been

warned in Cork that Liscarrol had been without a caretaker
for most of the last twelve years. He had even been able to
learn that the cousin left in charge had been elected first to
the Dublin Parliament and then appointed a position in
London. Liscarrol was isolated away from the main traffic
lanes and therefore was of little use or interest to the
English. No doubt neglect had made it uninhabitable.

He suppressed a sigh. Ireland was a land of the disinherited
and the supplanted. He had come only because of Deirdre.
Yet, when he looked at her as he did now, a tender, fierce
love gripped him. He loved her.

More than she loves me.

He pushed aside the thought. He had known that from
the moment she begged him to bring her here. When the
time came that she found bitter disappointment and tears
replacing her joy, he would be there to comfort her, and
that should be enough.

But it isn't, a voice inside him whispered. *You want all
her love and Liscarrol stands in your way.*

As the last few yards stretched out before them, Deirdre
rose in her stirrups and gasped in joy as the horizon
suddenly dipped into the verdant valley below.

A long silver thread of the river Bandon meandered
through the valley, glistening like a snail's track on the
dew-drenched green grasses. Atop a rocky rise on the
valley's floor where the river looped out below it stood
Liscarrol.

The granite fortress gleamed like a silver-gray jewel
with a cape of deep green ivy trailing from its wall.

"'Tis as I remember it!" Deirdre cried breathlessly.
"'Tis the same!"

She urged her horse through the narrow gap at the top of
the hill and began the steep descent.

Killian followed her, less impressed with the beauty of
the place. Deirdre's adoring eyes had not seen what had
caught his attention. The fields were empty of sheep and
cattle. Old rock fences were tumbled and tangled in
overgrown bracken and vines. There was no smoke from a
fire in or near Liscarrol, no sign of life at all.

Deirdre slowed long before she reached the castle.

Breathless but exhilarated, she forced herself to allow her horse to canter the rest of the way. As she neared the river that separated her from Liscarrol she smelled the wet, faintly fishy odor of the water and the pungent scent of the decaying rushes. She smiled as she gazed on the swift-flowing water. Her father had always boasted that beneath the green and brown rushing waters were the best salmon runs in the area.

Bees hummed in the new buds among the long grasses and a memory came back so quick and sharp that she sighed in pleasure. She had loved above all things to toast bread in the huge hearth of the Great Hall on long lazy evenings and spread the thick crisp slices with sweet fragrant honey gathered from Liscarrol's apiary. She wondered who had gathered the honey these last years.

Slowly, savoring the moments, she raised her eyes to the far bank. In the distance great common yews, like static green flames, lined the avenue that led from the river to the castle. She frowned as she noted the brown clumps of weeds which had invaded the lane. In her father's time the lane had been kept clear of grass and a fresh layer of stone had been added each spring. Away to the left of the stone-walled fortress where once there had been a flourishing orchard there were only leafless, black-limbed trees, their buds still tightly closed against the harsh spring.

"How do we cross?"

Deirdre looked up, startled to find Killian at her side. "There's a bridge down there," she answered, pointing down the bank toward the right.

She was surprised but grateful when he backed away and let her lead the way. He did understand, she thought. In spite of his disgruntlement he realized how important the moment was for her and would not steal from her the pleasure of entering her home first.

The stone bridge was missing more than one plank and the horses had to carefully choose a path across it.

"Cousin Neil must have few guests," she mused aloud. Killian did not answer.

Holly bushes had overgrown the boundaries of the bridge's far side, and for the first time she considered the possibility that no one lived at Liscarrol. She paused and turned to Killian. "I had not thought that we might arrive with no one to greet us."

Killian shrugged. "If your cousin is absent we will be spared the necessity of explaining our purpose. 'Tis easier to oust an absent host."

Deirdre smiled at him. "I would not oust Cousin Neil without ceremony. In any case, he will be welcome as long as he chooses to remain."

Killian looked back at the men who accompanied them; they lagged far behind. "Come, wife, let's secure our new home."

Deirdre nodded and urged her horse forward.

The ride was quickly accomplished. The carriageway's disrepair was more evident up close but Deirdre hardly noticed. It was the castle itself that made her gasp aloud as she slid from her saddle.

The stone walls were still firmly in place but the massive portal was gaping open on broken hinges and the glass in every window of the facade had been shattered. The few remaining pieces of furniture had been tossed from the doorway and lay splintered in a pile of ashes.

Anticipating her next move, Killian threw a leg over his horse and dismounted, but Deirdre was ahead of him, running with lifted skirts toward the house. She reached the steps and plunged into the dark interior. Her cry of surprise made Killian's blood turn to ice in his veins. He drew his pistol as he ran after her but before he gained the first step Deirdre reappeared in the doorway, her face livid.

"They've destroyed it! They've burned everything!"

Killian paused. "Who's burned it? Who's in there?"

Deirdre looked at him with a stricken look in her eyes. "There's no one here. There's no one at all. The house has been burned. Do you think Cousin Neil was attacked by the English? Perhaps they murdered him!"

Killian swore under his breath but caught himself before blurting out the truth. She looked so hurt and defeated when moments before the light of joy had shone in her face. He could not tell her that her cousin was not only unharmed but reveling in his friendship with her enemies.

He must not even be aware of the ruin Liscarrol had become, for he had been ready to buy it from Lord Fitzgerald.

"Look about you. Whatever happened here happened months ago. Your father would have heard had your kinsman been arrested. As for the damage, it could have been done by any *aulaun*. Or perhaps the English feared the abandoned fortress would offer shelter for the desperate and they burned the place as a reminder of their authority."

Killian amazed himself with his ability to spin the plausible, glib lie, but he was not sorry when he saw a little of the sorrow lift from Deirdre's expression. Her cousin was not worthy of the grief she suffered. He put an arm about her. "Let's look the place over."

They climbed the stairwell to the Great Hall. As Deirdre had said, a fire had been set inside the stone walls and not a single tapestry, carpet, or stick of funiture had escaped the lick of the blaze. The slate floor was littered with charred debris, but instead of the odor of soot and ash, the sharp, acrid stench of feces and urine stung their nostrils.

Deirdre turned to him with a hand held to her nose. "Why does the place stink so?"

Killian shook his head, then followed his nose until it led him to the archway of the small private chapel which had served as the place of worship for many generations of Fitzgeralds. There he found the cause of the stench. Piled more than three feet high in the middle of the desecrated chapel was a hill of sheep dung.

"The blasphemous swine!" Deirdre declared, anger percolating through her stunning disappointment.

"There's proof if we need it that the destruction was deliberate," Killian murmured to himself. "A spade and a strong back will soon take care of it," he continued in a louder voice. "Come, let's see whatever else awaits us."

Upstairs, the heat from the blaze had burst many of the windows. In each of the rooms on the upper floor new fires had been lit. In places where the flames had eaten through the heavy beamwork of the ceiling, the roof had collapsed.

Killian said nothing as Deirdre moved from room to room. He watched as bewilderment replaced sadness on her face, until finally a kind of weary resignation settled over her features as the extent of the damage to her beloved home revealed itself.

When at last she slumped against the archway of the minstrel's galley above the Great Hall and gave up to the tears she had held at bay, he remained apart. It was her grief and she would feel better for the letting of it, he told himself. Yet, when her sobs of bitterness, anger, and disappointment threatened to overwhelm her, he moved to enfold her in his arms.

"'Tis a sad business, this," he said low and tightened his arms as she began to pull away. "Nae, lass, do not reject me. You're grieving the past, but you must let go of it. We must return to Cork."

Deirdre lifted her tear-streaked face. "Leave Liscarrol? I will not. Liscarrol may have suffered but it's far from defeated. The walls still stand. It could be made new again with work."

"Aye, that it could," he agreed. "There's enough work to be done to keep a score of men working a full six months." With his thumb he rubbed a tear from her cheek. "See reason, *macushla*. There's just you and I. We cannot accomplish the task alone."

"I am not afraid of work." Deirdre felt better as she talked of a future for her beloved home, and her eyes sparkled with renewed hope. "The walls are sound. Half the roof remains intact. We can clean out the lower rooms first and live there while the new roof is built."

Killian said slowly, still trying to dull the blow, "From where do you suppose the money will come to buy the new materials and furnishings you desire?"

Deirdre frowned. "I had not thought of that."

"So I supposed."

"Are we so very poor then?"

Killian shrugged. More poor than she could guess. He had held a slim hope that Liscarrol might prove a productive estate, but there was nothing here but a blackened shell surrounded by empty fields. He could expect to receive no more money from the duchesse until he had found and dispatched the smugglers who were cheating her, and that might take him weeks or months. No, he could not provide Deirdre with funds for rebuilding, nor could he afford to keep her long in Cork. Pricked by his own lack, his sense of failure when she needed him, he turned surly.

"I am not a wealthy man. You are accustomed to comforts that a man like me has rarely known. I do not fault you for your soft hands and silken gowns, but it makes you unfit for the work you claim you would do. We will return to Cork at once. After the sale of Liscarrol's land, we will return to France where you may live comfortably from the proceeds of your inheritance."

"I will not!" Deirdre's chin rounded in determination. "I am not some simple-minded lass to be ordered about at will. You underestimate me, Killian MacShane, if you think me fit only for salons and ballrooms. I am fit for any chore I choose. As for money, I will hire a few of the local people on the promise to pay them in—in a few weeks' time."

Killian's laughter was nasty. "Who would work for a lady of no fortune or means?"

"I am a Fitzgerald," Deirdre replied. "That name counts for something in Munster."

"Nae, lass. You are an Irish lady, and that carries little enough weight these days. Liscarrol may be yours but you are without visible means of support. Where are your cattle, your sheep? Where are your tilled fields? And, were you to be so fortunate to possess them, do you think the English would allow you to keep them? The taxation alone would keep you a debtor. God's love, lass! Do you not know what has become of the country you say you love? Is it only through the rainbow mists of childish fancy that you see this place?"

He grabbed her by the arm and turned her to face the Great Hall below. "Look! What do you see? Filth! Decay! Neglect! 'Tis the end of a dynasty. The rule of your beloved Fitzgeralds is over!"

Deirdre twisted free of his grasp. Anger blazing in her eyes, she turned and slapped him.

Killian saw the intent in her eyes before she struck and

chose not to defend himself, but when she raised her hand a second time he lifted his arm. "Once is quite enough."

His voice was low, almost gentle, but the look in his eyes stayed her hand the second time. Deirdre blushed. She felt lightheaded with frustration and impotence. He was right, right in everything he said, and yet she could not, would not accept it.

"You knew what we'd find, didn't you? You knew! Why did you come with me? You did not want to come, you lied and schemed to keep me in Cork. Why did you agree to come to Ireland in the first place? You never wanted to do it. You could have stayed in France. What is it you seek?"

Killian moved a step away from her but his eyes never left her face. "I am your husband. We share everything."

Deirdre shook her head and loose strands of wavy blond hair swirled about her shoulders. " 'Tis a poor excuse, that. You do not share my pain, my anger at the damage that has been done here. You are indifferent. Liscarrol means nothing to you!"

"You are wrong, lass."

But Deirdre was not listening. She felt as though all her insides were tumbling. She braced herself in the doorway with one hand and swept the hair from her eyes with the other. "I will not leave here. Liscarrol is my home. I will live here until I die!"

Killian lightly rubbed his stinging cheek. Part of him wanted to shake her, to turn her over his knee, but another part of him admired her tenacity. She had a fine Irish temper but it would not solve her problems.

"You must know that the English will not sit idly by and watch you raise a fallen bastion of Gaelic dominance," he warned roughly. "If you find the means to breathe life into Liscarrol once more, you will only be making it an attraction for them. But, if you are determined in this foolhardy venture, I will stand by you."

Deirdre clung to the door frame, her insides churning. How could Killian look so coldly at her? She had thought he understood a little of her feelings for this place, but he did not. "I do not need your help. Go away, Killian MacShane. I rue the day I first set eyes on you!"

Killian watched her go. It was not a pretty beginning. He did not have the soft words a lady needed to hear. He had blundered through in a loud voice that had only made her angrier and more determined to remain. Yet, stubbornness was no substitute for reason.

For the first time since entering the castle he wondered what had become of the men accompanying them. Had they not found the bridge across the Bandon? A few steps brought him to the nearby window which looked out onto the front lawn. Sean and his companion were not there. Neither were they visible in the distance. They had disappeared.

He raised his eyes to the rocky outcropping of the nearest hill and saw a thin gray-white thread of smoke rising from a clump of trees. Unconsciously his hand touched the pistol he had tucked in his waistband.

"Mille murdher!" Deirdre muttered, imitating Conall's voice when he was at his most disgusted with her. "That man will not see reason!"

If Darragh and Conall were here they would not have been so unconcerned by the fate of Liscarrol, nor would they have been dismayed by the amount of work needed to restore it. They would have stood by her and helped her plan its reconstruction.

But as she walked across the floor of the Great Hall she could not help taking quick, sidelong glances at the wreckage about her. Killian was right, of course—they could not do all the work themselves. "But we can make a beginning!" With that in mind, she headed out through the main doorway and toward the stables.

Killian had been right, too, in his assessment of her lack of interest in money matters. It was not from her lack of experience with finances, however. With her brothers and father away most of her life and Lady Elva often in delicate health, she had taken responsibility early for the household accounts. She knew the cost of cheese and linen, a fair price for a keg of ale or a tinker's pot. She knew her own finances to the last sou, of which there were very few left, she mused ruefully. She was not extravagant. She had asked for nothing from Killian but passage to Ireland. Yet, she should have considered that he was not a wealthy man. He had been a soldier, but, unlike her brothers and father, he was not a nobleman and his wages must have been meager.

A pang of guilt made her stop and glance back at the gray somber walls of Liscarrol. Somewhere inside it, Killian was no doubt pacing and swearing. Even so, the glow of pride warmed her as she stared at her ancestral home. She was home, where she belonged. And, because she had married him, Liscarrol was now as much Killian's as hers. She would remind him of that.

The day had begun to grow cloudy. In the short space of an hour a dark band of rain had risen from the southwest. As she watched, it crested a distant hill, obscuring the ridge in a curtain of dark water. Pulling her hood forward against the cool air, she hurried across the yard into the low-roofed stable.

To her surprise, the stables had been left untouched. Other than the usual wear and tear of the seasons, the structure was sound and dry in contrast to the damp, lichen-plagued walls of the castle.

Lifting back her hood, she scanned the dark interior, surprised to find neatly swept stalls and half a dozen bales of hay stacked in the far corner. It almost seemed as if the stables were in use and empty now only because men and animals had departed for the day. But the tackle wall was empty of bridles and bits and no extra saddles hung from pegs.

"We will sleep here tonight," she said with satisfaction when she had completed her tour. Killian would see that she was uncomplaining and quite able to deal with the rougher aspects of their new life.

To make certain he understood her unshakable decision to remain, she reached for the long-handled wooden shovel that stood in a corner of the tack room. The least she could do was to begin by removing the offensive excrement from the chapel.

A rustling behind her made Deirdre turn back to the doorway where she half-expected to find that Killian had followed her. "I'm sorry I—"

No one was there. Through the open door the sky was darker than before and a gust of wind sent winter-old leaves scurrying into the stable.

"Killian?" Deirdre listened, certain she had heard footsteps. "Killian?"

The splatter of raindrops upon the ground outside began and ended abruptly. A blast of storm-borne wind whistled through the cracks in the stone walls of the stable, curling chilly fingers about Deirdre's body. She clutched her cloak together with her free hand and hurried toward the entrance. It would soon be dark and they had not made preparations for the night.

As she entered the yard she was surprised to see how swiftly and completely mist had come down from the hills to cover the land. Less than a hundred yards away, Liscarrol had become a gray-shrouded citadel with its balustrades flying wispy mare's tails of cloud.

The crunch of a twig nearby sent her spinning around, but no one stood behind her.

It was then that she heard it. The sound was faint but the rhythm was unmistakable. She turned to look toward the distant slopes of the Shehy Mountains.

It appeared out of the misty distances: the black specter of horse and rider. They swept down the long slope into the valley and disappeared into the low-lying fog. Yet, Deirdre realized that they had not vanished as the thunder of hooves grew closer, chasing the sound of her pounding heart.

Her hand tightened on the handle of the shovel but she was not afraid. She ran toward the place where she knew they would reappear. In his anger, Killian must have ridden off. But he had come back! Excitement pounded through her veins as she nearly tripped over a stone in her haste. She, too, had been angry, but all that was forgotten

now. He was so much a part of her that she could only
welcome him.

When they reappeared out of the mists, rider and horse
were so close upon her that she could hear their harsh
breathing above the muffled tattoo of hooves. The swift-
moving pair seemed not to see her, so headlong was their
flight. Just when she thought they would pass her by, the
rider reined in before her, his black cloak swirling forward
of its own momentum to cover him from shoulder to boot.

"Killian!" she cried. Dropping the shovel, she lifted
her arms to him as rain splashed down into her upturned
face.

The rider jerked back. "Stay away!" he cried, and
though his face was obscured by his hood she recognized
his voice. "Stay away in fear for your life, *mo cuishle!*"

"Wait! No! Killian!" Deirdre called after him, surprise
turning into alarm as he turned his horse. She grabbed for
him and caught the left stirrup. "No! Wait! Please! I'm
sorry, sorry, Killian!"

He looked down at her, his strangely light eyes the only
feature of him visible, and then he brought his hand down
sharply.

Deirdre released her hold instantly but it was a moment
later before the sharp sting of pain made her look down at
the back of her hand, and she realized what had happened.
A single bloody stripe lay diagonally across it. He had
struck her with his riding crop.

She looked up but it was too late. He was gone. Even
the sound of hooves was drowned by the sudden torrential
cloudburst that flattened thick cold raindrops against her
face. Killian had rejected her! Had struck her!

Tears formed in her eyes, obscuring what the mists and
rains did not as she turned and stumbled blindly for
shelter. Killian had been so eager to get away from her that
he had used a brutal cut of his whip to free himself. Was it
possible that he could be so angry in the aftermath of their
argument?

"What the devil! Are you truly and thoroughly mad!"

The rough anger in Killian's tone did not surprise
Deirdre as much as the fact that she was caught by the

shoulders as soon as she entered Liscarrol. She looked up, eyes wide in disbelief.

"Well? Will you freeze me with your silence?" Killian demanded as he took in the shocked look on her face. Then he realized that she expected him to still be angry. He smiled at her. "Come, we're not so civilized that a good fight should spoil a marriage of one month."

"Good fight?" Deirdre echoed in stunned outrage. "Good fight! You call this a good fight?" She lifted her injured hand to his face.

Killian looked first at her hand and then at her damp face with golden curls plastered to her forehead. "What's this? A token for me to kiss, perhaps?" He took her hand in his to bring it to his lips but she jerked it away before his mouth touched her skin.

"Do not play the courtier with me, you *spalpeen!* 'Tis the cut of your whip that mars my hand!"

Killian looked at her, frowning. "Cut of a whip? Deirdre, *acushla,* what cut?"

Too enraged to find words, Deirdre drew back her hand to strike him but she never completed the gesture. Her hand halted in mid-air as she stared at it. The skin was unbroken. Not a drop of blood marred its surface. It was smooth, unblemished, untouched.

She looked back up at Killian, a stricken look in her eyes. "You were riding in the hills just now."

"Never I was," Killian answered. His frown deepened. "Why do you say that?"

Deirdre bit her lip so hard that she tasted blood. He could have ridden away from the house and then circled back to beat her to the doorway, but how would he have remained dry? And dry he was, from his raven-black locks to the fine dry dust on his boot tips. Not even a cape would have prevented his feet from being wet. "What color is your horse?"

"What is the matter, Dee? You're shaking."

"Just answer me, confound you!"

Killian released her and looked past her to the yard where the early-spring storm spent itself on the surrounding countryside. He watched for a long moment, but there was no sign of man or beast in the violence beyond the door. "Were you frightened, chased, is that it? And you thought it was I?"

"I—I do not know." Deirdre buried her face in her hands. Was she mad? She had recognized him, knew his posture when he rode, had gazed up into those dearly loved blue eyes. It wasn't a trick of her imagination. It could not have been. The sting of the whip had been so real. She jerked her hand away from her eyes to look at it again. Bloodless. Smooth. Was she mad?

"Hold me! Please!"

Killian enfolded her tightly in his arms. "Of course, *macushla*." She was wet clean through. Where she stood a widening puddle was forming. "You're trembling! Won't you tell me what happened?" But Deirdre merely turned her head from side to side against the front of his coat as her hands tightened on his waist.

"Never mind. I've managed a fire." He nearly laughed as he thought how inappropriate a fire seemed in this burned-out hulk. But Deirdre was in no state to appreciate his humor. He lifted her off the floor and into his arms. "Come and sit by the fire to dry. You may tell me later what occurred."

"And you were certain that it was I?" Killian turned to look down at her. Huddled beneath his cloak, she crouched before the fire he had built in the hearth of the Great Hall while her clothes lay spread out on the floor to dry.

"I thought it was you," Deirdre replied. Now that she was dry and safe, her story sounded like childish babble in her own ears. "I suppose the blow startled me so badly I imagined the blood." Even as she spoke, the back of her hand stung and she rubbed it, but there was no welt.

She raised shamed eyes to her husband's face. "I am not mistaken. If it was not you then it was someone else. I saw him. He spoke to me." She dared not add, *in your voice*. "I touched his boot. He was real."

"Could it have been Sean or the other man? They had disappeared. Could one of them have frightened you?"

Deirdre hunched her shoulders. "It was not either man. I would have recognized them." She left unrepeated that she had recognized *him* as the stranger. She looked up. "Where are the men?"

Killian shrugged. "We've been deserted."

"Our clothes? Our food?"

"I saw the pack animals running free just before the storm blew in. I will search for them at first light."

Deirdre lowered her head once more. None of that seemed very important at the moment.

Killian considered the possibilities. Deirdre was unaccustomed to hard travel. Liscarrol's devastation had been an unexpected blow to her dreams of a triumphant return home. Perhaps she had fallen asleep or simply been daydreaming. His mouth thinned. It was not difficult to think of a reason why she would cast him as a villain in her reverie. After all, they had quarreled repeatedly during the last days. They were newly married.

The thought carried Killian's attention back to the cloak Deirdre wore. Underneath it she was naked. On the five days' journey from Cork they had had no privacy to indulge their passion, which ran like wildfire beneath the battles they fought. The thought of her warm and soft and his made him stand in his breeches, but he did not move toward her.

He had heard it said that gently bred girls often took time to adjust to the married state. Lovemaking had come naturally to Deirdre but that did not mean it had not frightened her. They had parted on angry words. Perhaps she had seen someone and thought it was he coming to apologize.

He crouched down beside her. She was young and heartachingly beautiful. At her brow frizzly curls had formed, glowing amber in the firelight. They stirred with her every breath, dancing firelight along their shimmering coils. He reached out to stroke the golden fall from her crown to the dark damp ends that touched the floor, and strands curled about his fingers and clung like seaweed. "I think, *mo cuishle,* that you are very angry with me."

"No." Deirdre shook her head slightly. She did not look up from the fire, nor did she move away when his hand moved to stroke from hip to knee the length of her thigh outlined by the wool of her cape. She was weary and still a little frightened by what had happened.

"Then you will forgive me?" Killian whispered, leaning close to place the words into her ear with kisses. He felt the trembling of her thigh under his hand and smiled. He might not have a courtier's understanding of ladies but he did know how to reach the woman in Deirdre. *"Madilse,* of the sweet thighs. How I have missed you."

Deirdre closed her eyes. "I have missed you, too."

Heat wound its way down into his loins as his hand continued its gentle stroking. He had been harsh with her too often in the last days. He wanted to bring her gentleness and pleasure. "Do you forgive me?" he repeated.

Deirdre moved her head slightly and he was not certain whether the gesture was a shake or a nod. His caressing began again, his hand gliding up the gentle curve of her thigh, slipping up, over and under the full, ripe curve of a buttock. "We are wed a full month, *mo cuishle,* yet when I touch you I cannot believe that you are mine. I cannot remember your touch, that you have lain beside me, beneath me. I forget the taste of you, the feel of your flesh enclosing mine. Tell me, *madilse,* the source of your magic that each time is like the first."

Deirdre trembled inside as his hands moved to lift her cloak back from her breasts and laid it out on the damp floor. She thought of the dry shelter of the stable as he pressed her back until she lay on her woolen cloak. She remembered the sweet grassy smell of aging hay as the odor of rot and mildew stirred in the air about her.

And then she ceased to think of anything but Killian.

She breathed in the pleasant musky odor of his skin as he pressed her body down under his. She touched his black silky hair, threading her fingers through the smoothness. She felt first his hot breath on her cheeks and then the warm pleasant taste of his lips on hers.

It had been too long, she thought as she helped him shed his clothing. It had been less than a week and yet a lifetime. He was right. This passion between them did not have an ending. It fed on itself; each time it brought with it both a momentary satiation and the pangs of a new hunger of anticipation.

Beginning and end, that is what he is for me, she thought as he slid deep within her. *We are one. Inseparable. The arguments and harsh words, they mean nothing. They cannot divide us. The years could not keep us apart, nor distance or circumstance. We were pledged long ago. Here, at Liscarrol. We are one now. We will be together always. Always.*

Killian awakened to the unpleasant sensation of water trickling across his shoulders. He turned from his side to his back, but another cold wet drop struck him on the shoulder and slid across the slope of his chest to drip into his armpit. He opened his eyes.

It was dark. The fire had died. He reached for Deirdre but she eluded his touch. Stretching forward, he groped for her until he was nearly flat on his belly. She was gone.

He was on his feet in one agile movement. "Deirdre?" he called softly. He found his breeches with a foot and pulled them on. His boots were nearby.

"Deirdre!"

The darkness was stifling but as his eyes adjusted he realized that the night beyond the broken doors and windows was brighter. He found his pistol, tucked it into his belt, and headed toward the light, drawn by it as he suspected Deirdre had been.

The rain had ceased. A hard, brilliant disk of moon shone in stark white contrast to the last of the black clouds streaming past it. He looked around the still yard bathed in a milky-white glow.

"Deirdre!" Silence answered him. He hurried toward the stable because that was where she had gone earlier in

the day. When he stood framed in the stable doorway he
thought he saw movement at the back. "Deirdre?"

Deirdre turned to face him, saw him outlined in sharp
contrast to the night, but she did not answer. She recognized the shape of his torso, the hard shoulders and broad
chest, the set of his head, the swirl of long black hair
hanging free . . . but she no longer trusted her sight.

She had been dreaming again. The dream had awakened
her and drawn her here, away from Killian's side. Now she
understood her confusion of the evening before. Brigid had
been right. The rider had been a specter, a vision she had
first experienced here, in this stable, just before Killian
MacShane had come into her life. It had invaded her
dreams for years, always awakening her in fear. It had
come to her the evening before, more real than dreams
should be. Was this the dream again?

"Deirdre?"

"What you want of me?" she asked softly. Brigid had
warned her to be careful, that danger lay ahead. Was this
the danger? Or was it madness? "Who are you?"

Killian could not see her but he heard the plaintive cry
underlying her words. "I am no vision, *mo cuishle*. Come
and kiss me and you will know it."

Deirdre took a reluctant step toward him. "You will
disappear," she said accusingly.

"Nae, lass, I will not," Killian answered.

Deirdre moved forward silently on bare feet. She had
not dressed completely, for most of her clothing was still
wet. When she stepped into a slat of moonlight she heard
his gasp of surprise to find her clothed only in his shirt.
That gasp of manly interest convinced her as nothing else
could have that this was Killian. He was real.

She launched herself at him and found the solid warm
muscles of his chest and shoulders with her hands. He
lifted her by the waist as his mouth swooped down on
hers.

"You are real!" she exclaimed in laughter bordering on
tears.

"More dreams, Dee?"

"No, no dreams," she whispered and kissed him again.

She did not want to think of what the last hours had portended. For now she wanted only to be held close by the man she loved.

She saw them too late. They appeared suddenly in the eerie moonlit yard, half a dozen hulking shadows. Before she could gather breath to scream, the shadows were upon them, wielding skeans and *sgains*.

Killian saw the horror on Deirdre's face too late to dodge the blow that stunned him. His knees buckled even as he reached for his pistol. His fingers numbed and the pistol fell, useless, to the ground a moment before he sprawled face-down at Deirdre's feet.

"You killed him! You killed him!" Deirdre screamed as she dropped to her knees beside Killian, but the two men grabbed her by the arms and lifted her back.

"Let me go! Let me go, you sneaking *aulauns!*" She twisted and jerked, but she was pinned between them.

She glanced from one to the other, but they wore hats and their faces were blackened by soot, and she knew she would not recognize them again. She began to tremble but not in fear for herself. Killian lay absolutely still at her feet. "I do not know you but I will, you *mac mallachtans!*"

"Ach, now, colleen, there's nae need to be abusing us with such talk," one of the men answered. "We've nae murdered yer man. Get him, lads."

Two of the men bent and lifted Killian until he sagged like wet wash between them. His head rolled on his neck and a low moan escaped.

"There," the leader said. "He'll come to nae harm, providing he has the right answers to give us."

"Where are you taking him?" Deirdre cried as they dragged Killian from the stable.

The leader turned, his teeth gleaming in the moonlight as he smiled at her. "Fear not, *ceanabhan*. We've orders nae to harm him . . . or ye, more's the pity. Ye've a sweet look about ye, and a man being a man could nae wish it otherwise."

He came toward her until the smell of onions and ale from his warm breath assailed her. "Ye'd nae be doing yer lad harm by offering his captor a *pogue*."

Deirdre drew back from him as far as her pinned arms would allow. "'Tis a *polthogue* I'd be offering ye, were me arms free!" she answered.

"There's an answer for ye, Cuan!" said the man on her right.

"Shut up, ye great lout!" The leader took Deirdre's chin between his calloused thumb and forefinger. "If ye care for yer man's life, ye'll have heard nothing, *nothing!*"

Deirdre bared her teeth. "I know the direction of the house you keep and the name you use, Cuan O'Dineen!"

Cuan regarded Deirdre steadily. "Ye've brave words but no brave arm to protect ye, Lady Fitzgerald, if that in truth be yer name. Only we do nae fear the name any longer, and ye may as well learn it now as later."

As he dragged her chin forward to grind his lips against hers, Deirdre braced herself on her left foot and brought her right knee up sharply, the way Conall had taught her, and slammed it up between his legs.

Cuan fell with a strangled cry of pain, and in their surprise Deirdre's captors loosened their hold. She twisted and jerked, gaining her freedom. She flung herself into the dark space where Killian's pistol lay unseen. Her hand closed over the butt as the scuffle of men's footsteps sounded beside her and she rolled onto her back and lifted the pistol with both hands. "Stand back or I'll shoot!"

The men paused, their shapes black silhouettes against the moonlit doorway. "Step back! Into the doorway!" she ordered as she rose to her knees.

"Now, lass, ye would nae want to point that at a man," she heard Cuan say, but his two companions did not seem so certain and they did as she asked.

"If a man of you comes near me again, I will put a hole in him," Deirdre said, gaining her feet.

"If ye murder one of us, the rest will hang yer lad."

Deirdre did not doubt him. They had dragged Killian away. She could not expect them to release her husband unharmed if she shot one of them.

"Ye'd best keep quiet, lass." Cuan straightened a little but kept one hand covering his groin. He pulled his forelock and then gave a defiant laugh. "I will say this, ye

Fitzgeralds always were quick on yer feet.'' He turned and limped out into the night with his silent companions.

Deirdre stood irresolutely, the pistol wavering in her hands. She had lost. Killian was gone and the men with him. What could she do? She knew not a soul in the valley. Even if she had, she could not be certain who was friend and who was foe.

Even as she thought of them, she heard the pair of horses she and Killian had ridden gallop away, urged on by the cries of the men who had accosted them. She was trapped in a burned-out hulk of a castle. She was alone. All she could do was wait.

Carefully she uncocked the hammer and lowered the pistol. When the last of the voices died away in the distance, she walked quietly back into the gray stone fortress of Liscarrol.

Chapter Nineteen

"Faith! That's a fine ugly look to give a man what's saved yer life!"

Killian sucked in a quick angry breath as the filthy blindfold and gag was ripped from his face. As he worked saliva into his dry mouth, he looked up at his captor. The man was huge and as shaggy as the native cattle which still roamed the countryside. Long hair, tufted eyebrows, mustache, and beard all flowed together in a wild matted tangle of fiery red. Tufts of orangy hair sprouted on the ridges of his shoulders, which were bared to the chill by a sleeveless leather waistcoat, and a heavier, darker mat of hair crested his chest and rode the curve of his gut where the waistcoat gaped open for lack of buttons. A wide leather belt kept a brace of pistols snug against his belly and held up breeches black with grease and wear. In his right hand was the skean with which he had cut Killian's bindings.

Killian looked down and carefully spat to one side.

"There ye are, lads, a gentleman, this one!" the giant of a man declared. He thumped Killian hard on the shoulder. "What will ye be saying for yerself, gent?"

"I give my name freely to any man who asks it, but not

to those who hold a dagger at my throat," he replied in a voice that sought neither to antagonize nor to assuage.

"Ye show little fear for a lad within an arm's length of losing his life."

Killian looked about. He was in a stand of trees, probably the patch of forest he had seen from the minstrel gallery of Liscarrol. The man standing over him was the only one made visible by the small campfire but he could hear the breathing of others. His gaze swung back to the huge man. "Where's the lass?"

"The lass? What lass?" the man asked and burst into laughter.

The giant moved his dagger until the point of it rested in the hollow of Killian's throat and his eyes narrowed until they were nothing but silver slits of light. He pricked Killian's skin but withdrew the point almost before Killian realized he had been cut.

"I keep it sharp so, for skinning rabbits," the man explained as casually as though he talked to a bairn, and stuck the dagger in his belt. "Yer woman's as safe as when ye left her side."

Killian felt a warm trickle at his throat and knew it was blood. "Where is she?" he asked again.

The giant swung about, roaring a command into the darkness, and a man moved haltingly forward into the ring of firelight. "Tell him about the lass!" he demanded.

The slight man in black face said, "Yer lady's well, for all she aims her knee more recklessly than 'tis right."

Killian almost smiled as the reason for the man's hobbling sank in. Deirdre had defended herself well. "You did not harm her?" he questioned.

"The lass kicked his balls back into his belly," the giant answered and waved the man aside with a thick arm that nearly knocked him off his feet. " 'Twill be some days afore he can harm any lass the way you mean."

Killian turned to the leader. "Why have you brought me here?"

"Ye're here because ye've come to claim lands that are now mine. I'm giving ye a chance to explain yerself, for I heard little that made sense from the pair of lickspittles ye had in tow.''

Killian now knew what had happened to his men. ''What did you do to them?''

The giant shrugged.

''Would your name be O'Donovan?''

The man's eyes widened an instant before his laughter boomed through the campsite once more. ''I like ye, MacShane. Ye've courage.''

''My name's MacShane,'' Killian said, ''but I'm certain that you learned more than that from my men. What should interest you is the reason I am here.''

''And so it does.''

''Your patroness is disturbed by certain rumors which have reached her ear.''

O'Donovan grinned. ''Is she now? And would that patroness be the *colleen dheas* up at the old castle?''

''That lady is my wife.'' Killian locked gazes with the taller man. ''She is my business and no other's.''

''More's the pity,'' O 'Donovan answered. ''Well. You're here now, so speak.''

Killian shook his head. ''Come to Liscarrol in three days' time and I will welcome you as a guest.''

O'Donovan grinned. ''Ye've a fine way with words for a man who has naught to say in how matters are settled. I may yet slit yer throat. I've been of a mind some little while that such as us owe nae allegiance to a French lady who profits more than we from our sweat.''

''You will always need ships to carry your contraband,'' Killian answered casually. ''Murder of a merchant's employee will keep others from dealing with you. Even profit has its limitations to beguile. There are many smugglers, few ships. Merchants may easily find smugglers of more even temperament.''

O'Donovan scratched his belly. He liked MacShane better and better. He did not panic. ''Mayhaps there'd be a place for ye with me. Ye've a glib tongue and manners that the English admire. Yer share of the profit could be handsome, if ye work out. Think on it before ye spurn O'Donovan's offer.'' He signaled to someone in the dark, roaring, "Where are ye, Teague? God's Death! The man's nae about when he's needed."

Killian stiffened at the name, and an instant later his disbelieving senses had proof of his suspicions as a slight, pale-haired young man with a sad narrow face stepped from the darkness.

"So ye'll be knowing we're nae all ignorant braggarts, here's the schoolmaster among us. He's a cousin who goes by the name of Teague. Talk to him, MacShane, and see the sense of throwing yer lot in with O'Donovan."

Killian stood up, taking in at a single glance the painfully thin figure of his childhood friend.

"The men respect him," Teague murmured as dawn turned the sky pink. Killian and Teague had talked for more than an hour, but nothing was settled. "His methods may not be mine, but a man cannot measure himself against another unless his accomplishments are as great. The people are behind him. They respect O'Donovan."

"The people fear him, and you and I know that is not the same," Killian answered and set aside the empty bowl that had contained cold porridge. With a fleeting pang of conscience he remembered that Deirdre had spent a miserable night without food of any kind. "What you have told me, good Father, is that O'Donovan is rabid for the blood of the English; and when he cannot have it, he bleeds his own."

"We are at war. These are hard times. Our people must protect their own."

"But not the jackals that hide among them," Killian countered, his voice dropping even lower. "Men like O'Donovan live only to fight. I've met their sort in every battle, fought both beside and against them. When they have no enemy, they invent some quarrel among themselves. How can you, gentle Teague, defend him?"

"You've been gone some while," Teague answered softly. "The English are squeezing the life's blood from the land. Ireland must be rid of the English. If we must kill, then so be it. We will kill and kill again until there are none of them left and the land belongs to us once more!''

Killian eyed his friend in astonishment mingled with pity. ''You have changed, Father, or do O'Donovan's men know you for a priest?''

''They do.''

''And do you pray for them and urge them on with vengeful sermons against the Pope's enemies?''

Teague stiffened. ''You come close to blasphemy in your tone, MacShane. Not so long ago I asked you to come here with me to do spiritual work and you would not. Now you are here. Allow me to advise you in this matter.''

''Be Deirdre's friend, for 'tis certain you cannot be mine,'' Killian answered. He had his own method for dealing with O'Donovan that no other man could be party to.

''I do not understand.''

Killian smiled suddenly. ''I am wed since last we met. Aye. My wife lies alone in the roofless castle beyond this wood without food or blanket. If you would be a friend, go and help her.''

'' 'Tis little enough to ask, Killian, but I will promise.'' Teague hesitated, his brow furrowing. ''This lady of yours, is she pious?''

''She is not a woman of the streets, if that is what you mean, Father. She's a Fitzgerald, daughter of a lord. Had I not a man's view of the world, I would believe as she does that the work of the Sidhe brought us together.''

''The fairies, your lady believes in fairies?'' Teague asked in shocked tones.

Amusement brightened Killian's expression. ''Were you to hear the full tale of our courtship, you might wonder at it yourself. But that's a chat for another, happier evening by the hearth. Liscarrol belongs to her and she'll fight the English or the devil himself to retain it.''

''There are those here who would help her fight the English,'' Teague reminded him gently.

''Aye, and get her hanged in the bargain!'' Killian rounded angrily. He eyed the priest hard. ''Many a good man has come to a bad end for a good purpose.''

"O'Donovan has done good for the people."

"Then you can be certain there's a purpose in his generosity. A man who would allow his own child to hang in his place, well, what will that man not do to preserve his skin?"

The priest was still and white. "The village folk were frightened. They would blame any evil on O'Donovan to excuse their own weaknesses. O'Donovan encourages the stories because they gain him a certain amount of notoriety and respect wherever he goes."

"And fear. Do not forget the power of fear, Father," Killian answered.

"You have not been here long. You will understand in time."

Killian looked at the priest's flushed face and avid gaze. "You came to feed the Father's flock, not raise rebellion."

"To feed the flock here in Ireland one must first throw off the oppressor's yoke!"

"Do not feed my wife this brand of theology," Killian said flatly. "I will not have her stirred by brave words that cannot be followed by equally brave deeds."

"Of course," the priest replied. "If she is gently bred, she would not understand in any case. It might do as well if you sent her back to Nantes immediately."

"She is not so gently bred as that," Killian answered with a chuckle. "Even if I were to threaten her with a beating, she would remain until she sees an end to Liscarrol."

The priest blinked. "'Tis strange how you phrase that. Since I came I have heard talk of the return of the old guard, of the rising of Liscarrol. An old wives' tale, to be sure, but one would hope it does not reach your lady's ear."

"What tale is that?"

Teague hesitated. "'Tis bound up in the old religion and best forgotten, but I will tell you. It began just before the Bastard Queen Elizabeth conquered the north. From the clan O'Neill there was to come a savior of her people, a beautiful lady with the mark of the otherworld emblazed on her skin. The first visitation is said to have taken place in Leinster a century and a half ago. I remember hearing the tale as a child. The lady was a Butler, but she was said to have been the natural child of Shane, the O'Neill of Ulster, and her mother was the daughter of a Fitzgerald chieftain. She became known as the Rose of Ulster.''

The priest's cheeks reddened as he hurried on. "She was marked from birth with a bloodred mark on her cheek. Legend says she saved the Butlers in their quarrel with one of the Bastard Queen's men. The Butlers now deny her existence; but tales have a life of their own, and so it has been handed down among the common folk."

"What has this to do with Liscarrol?"

Teague smiled. "You were nae born here or you would not need to ask. A few years before the English victory at Kilkenny in ninety-one, the then Lord Fitzgerald took as his wife a lady from the house of Butler. 'Twas rumored she was a witch. I never saw her, but they said she was a black-haired beauty with strange eyes that changed color like a lough when cloud and sunlight play on it.''

Killian smiled at his friend's wistful tone. The priest was still a man.

"She bore Lord Fitzgerald a child, and before it was born she proclaimed that her child would be the next fairy woman of the O'Neill line. A daughter was born. I know nothing of the child other than that she fled to the Continent with her family in ninety-one.''

"And . . .?" Killian urged when the priest fell silent. "And you fear that my wife's return to the Liscarrol will stir old superstitions?''

"Perhaps. But then I fear too easily." The ghost of a smile flitted across his features. "You've nothing to concern yourself with unless she bears a rose birthmark on her cheek.''

"Nae. 'Tis on her shoulder."

The priest choked. "What did you say?"

"Deirdre has a lovely rosebud mark on her left shoulder," Killian replied and then erupted in laughter. "Shame, priest! You should be above superstitions of the bog and Sidhe!''

The priest stood up. "You find humiliating me a pleasant pastime."

"Nae. But go and see my lady for yourself. She is a lovely golden-haired lass with eyes that change color like the seasons reflected in a lough. You will find her charming, spirited, and loyal to both the true Church and Ireland." Killian sat forward suddenly, his humor gone. "But do not tell her your tale of fairy women. She feels too strongly about Liscarrol for my tastes. I would not have you stir her head with fancy."

"I will say nothing."

"You will take her food and wine? She has gone these last two days without."

"Aye, I will see to her good care, MacShane."

"Tell her I love her."

The priest looked down into MacShane's strong face, the defiance for once in abeyance before the more tender emotions of love and concern.

Teague shook his head slightly. He could not imagine the joy that Killian found in a woman's arms. The pleasure, yes, the release of urges he, too, had felt. But the rush of feelings that colored Killian's words were reserved in him for the moments of ecstasy he felt in prayer. "So you have found your place at last. 'Tis glad I am for you."

When Teague was gone, Killian sat staring at the fire. Teague's final words had stirred the old unrest within him. Deirdre was his heart. Where she was, there he would be. But something of his own, that measure which a man must have in order to exist, where was that place to be found?

The answer came to him gradually, a feeling that he had long denied because it carried with it inherent dangers and great risks that he no longer found acceptable. But it was real, and as he allowed the thought to enter his mind, he knew that it had been waiting for his acknowledgment all along.

He was a part of Deirdre as she was a part of him, and Liscarrol was a part of them both. Liscarrol had brought them together. If it would keep them together, he must

hold it. He would fight not because Deirdre wanted it but
because it would be his home, something he had never
had.

Deirdre paused in her work to lean against the handle of
the wooden shovel. It was nearly noon of the second day
and Killian had not returned. The knot of fear in her
middle tightened painfully. Perhaps they were not coming
back. Perhaps they had only said that to make her wait,
remain inactive, until their tracks were securely covered.
Perhaps Killian had resisted them, or had tried to escape,
and been killed. How long would it be before she knew?
How many days should she wait before going for help?
And, if she did go for help, how would she know whom to
trust? Cuan was one of the abductors. How many other
people of the countryside would be his followers? If she
made a mistake, she might find herself taken captive or
murdered. And if Killian did return and she was gone, he
would not know where to search for her. That fact alone
had kept her from running away at first light.

Her hand moved to Killian's pistol, which she had
tucked in the jacket of her riding habit. She had learned as
a child how to load and prime a pistol and the lesson had
come back as she had checked the loaded weapon. Yet,
she was alone, and two balls would not stop half a dozen
men. She had no supplies, no food, and if Killian did not
return soon she would have to go for help.

"No! No! I must not brood about it!" she said aloud. If
he were dead, she would know it, feel it, and she did not
sense his death. She must wait, and work while she
waited.

She turned and viciously dug the shovel into the last of
the pile of manure that had filled the small chapel and
heaved it onto the makeshift litter she had fashioned from
a scrap of drapery that had not burned. She had been
working since the morning mists parted, taking with them
the breath of moisture too fine to call rain. Her back
ached, but at least the pain took her mind off the gnawing

in her stomach as she dragged pile after pile of manure out into the yard and dumped it in what had once been the orchard.

Every new sight at Liscarrol made her heart ache. There was not a single piece of furniture undamaged, and seeing the once ornate plasterwork ceilings blackened by smoke and whitened with lichen filled her with sorrow. There was so much to be done that she began to doubt whether the task before her was one she could ever accomplish, yet she could not stop.

When the last of the dung was gone, she found still intact a stave-built piggin in which she could carry water from the river. She cast piggin after piggin of water onto the slate paving stones of the chapel until the room was flooded. Each trip was a goodly hike, but Deirdre did not dwell on that. She thought only of accomplishing something fine before Killian returned. She would not run away from Liscarrol. She had waited too long to return to give up so easily.

By noon, sweat rolled freely down her back and between her breasts, and her bodice stuck to her as she knelt on the chapel floor and scrubbed it with handfuls of plaited straw. She had long ago removed her riding jacket, skirts, and corset, working only in her shift and petticoats. She had no ribbon to tie her hair, and so it tumbled down her back and across her shoulders, sticking in curls against her damp arms and neck. She had become inured to the stench of dung, but the pain in her back had grown worse.

"Keep working, Dee, me lass," she muttered to herself. "You may not have been accustomed to menial labor ere this, but Liscarrol needs strong backs and clever hands more than silk skirts and pretty faces."

"Amen!"

Startled by the voice, Deirdre looked up sharply to see a tall but slight man standing in the chapel entrance. He stood with hands folded before him, but she glanced at the pistol on the far side of the room where she had laid it beside her clothing and muttered a French curse. She rose to her feet and reached for the shovel, which was nearby.

"Who are you and what do you mean by entering my home without an invitation?"

Teague O'Donovan gazed at the young woman before him in rapt amazement. A mass of tumbling golden curls framed her face and shoulders. There was noble blood in her, he thought, though she was dressed as poorly as the lowliest bond-maid. Framed in the golden halo of sunlight pouring through the broken chapel window, she appeared a creature more of myth than reality, and he wondered fleetingly if Liscarrol was a favored place of the fairies.

He did not mean to think of it again. If not for Killian's curious phrasing, he would not have remembered the tale of the fairy women of the Fitzgerald clan.

"You are Lady Fitzgerald," he said without preamble.

Deirdre nodded slowly. "How do you know me?"

Teague dipped his head to shield himself from her gaze. Her eyes were too bright, too beautiful for a man such as he to look upon. But he understood now the look on Killian's face as he had spoken of this woman. "You are the lady wife of Killian MacShane?"

The pretense of haughtiness dropped from Deirdre and she moved toward him, her shovel poised to strike. "You are one of them! You took my husband! Where is he?"

Teague shook his head. "Nae, lady. I am not one of the men who took your husband, but I have seen him. He is well."

Deirdre bit back the angry words she had been about to speak, but she could not keep the scorn from her voice. "If you are not one of them, how is it you have seen my husband?"

Teague hesitated only a moment before producing the prayer book and rosary from his pocket. "I am a friend. I am one who is hunted with bloodhounds and who lives not in fear but in constant hiding from the Informers."

"You are a priest!" Deirdre dropped the shovel. "Oh, Father, you must help me!"

Teague took the outstretched hands she thrust into his when she reached him. Blinded by the fierce blend of joy and fear on her lovely face, he looked down at her hands only to flinch as he saw the raw, oozing blisters that had broken open on her palms. "But you're bleeding, dear lady!"

Embarrassed, Deirdre pulled her hands free. "Forgive me, Father. I will wash."

"Nae, child. There's no shame in the results of honest labor in the Lord's service. I will help, and when we are done I will bless this place, making it as holy as it is clean."

"Tell me first of Killian," Deirdre replied, flushing under the priest's gentle regard.

Teague nodded. "He worries that you are terrified at being left alone."

"I was terrified that he might have been killed," Deirdre answered. "For myself, I am well enough." To give lie to her assertion, her stomach grumbled loudly.

"I have a cure for that," Teague said, smiling shyly at her. "I have orders to feed you."

"You have orders?" Deirdre echoed. "I do not understand. Why is Killian not with you? Are you truly his friend, or only a spokesman for the men who dragged him away?"

"I come in peace as a friend to you both."

"That is not a definitive answer," Deirdre replied. "As a man of God you cannot stand on the side of thieves and murderers."

"You speak harshly of that which you do not understand."

"I know what I have seen and what I have learned to believe is true."

Teague turned away from her vibrant anger. Though he could admire her beauty as one did an exquisite sunset or flower, she was curiously lacking in sexual appeal for him. She was as headstrong and determined as a man, but neither her beauty nor her will unsettled him. Her gaze did. She snared him with her green eyes, pulled him toward her in a way that spoke of unnatural power. She had eyes that sought to see into a man's soul.

The priest lifted his eyes, his gaze straying to the bared skin of the lady's left shoulder.

A bright crimson mark lay on the pale skin, its convoluted configuration the shape of a perfect rose.

Teague shut his eyes tight, murmuring a prayer of protection against spirits, but when he opened his eyes again she was still before him, her sea-green gaze clouded with concern.

"Are you ill, Father?" Deirdre asked, surprised by the sudden pallor in his thin face. "You look as if you'd seen a ghost."

"Your mark. How came it upon you?"

Deirdre turned to look at her shoulder and blushed a fiery shade as she realized that she stood before a priest in only her petticoats. With a belated sense of modesty, she snatched up her jacket. "Forgive me, Father. I expected no one."

"Your mark," he repeated. "How did it come about?"

"The mark on my shoulder? Why, I was born with it. 'Tis the kiss of the fairies to mark their own," she said airily, repeating what Brigid had so often told her as a child.

To her amazement, the priest fell back a step and crossed himself. "What is it, Father? What have I done? You do not take me seriously? I am a good and faithful Catholic, I promise you."

"I must go!" Teague cried, backing away from her. "I brought you food. And I will see that Killian is released, but you must leave here. Times are hard and men are desperate. Some will sell their souls to protect what little they have. You must leave before the word spreads."

"Wait! Father!" But the priest was gone. She heard his canvas-wrapped feet pelting down the stairwell.

She paused when she reached the doorway of the house, for it was obvious that something had frightened him and he would not heed her pleas. What had she done that would scare off a priest?

Before she could further ponder his strange actions, she noticed the aroma of boiled beef wafting through the air, and she turned to find a reed basket set before the hearth. Inside it she found oatcakes, a slab of butter, and a few scraps of boiled meat.

She ate with her hands, and though the beef was almost too tough to chew, the oatcakes were damp, and the butter was sour, she ate with relish until the twist in her stomach eased.

Killian sat with his back to a tree. His arms had been stretched behind him, around the trunk, and bound. His feet were tied at the ankles, and a thick knot of cloth had been stuffed into his mouth, and a gag had been tied to keep it in place. He was alone in the forest. His captors had melted away just after dawn like shadows retreating before the blaze of the sun. It was mid-afternoon, and the wretchedness of his situation was borne in full upon him.

He turned his head as a bee buzzed past. Spring was beginning. Through the brown moldering leaves at his feet poked the tightly curled tips of fronds. A rare red squirrel darted around the corner of a nearby tree, its feathery tail flicking nervously before it disappeared. If not for the fact that he was bound to a tree he might have enjoyed the idyll, Killian thought.

But he was bound. The blood had drained from his arms until they were numb, and his shoulders ached where his arms were wrenched in their sockets. O'Donovan had not said when he would return, only that he hoped his "guest" would prove more tractable when he did. It would be torture to be left for a few days. And, of course, that is what O'Donovan intended.

Killian swallowed his anger, gagged on the cloth in his mouth, and coughed, straining against his bindings until tears started in his eyes. He gagged, fighting to catch his breath, but he could not. His chest heaved, and blood pounded in his temples and behind his eyes until tears flowed onto his cheeks. He was choking to death.

The slipping free of his arms from the tree did not register with him at first. Instinct directed him to tear the gag from his mouth before he realized that he had been freed.

He gasped for breath several times before the pounding of his heart eased. "Teague, rot you, why do you not show yourself?"

"Mayhaps because 'tis not Teague who saves ye," came the answer in a light boyish tone.

Killian whipped his head around, but no one stood beside the tree. He reached down to work the knots at his ankles, saying, "Show yourself or be damned!"

"Kind words for a savior," came the teasing reply. "Shall I leave ye then?"

"Do as you like," Killian answered grimly.

High feminine laughter filled the silence of the glade. "Ye looked a fine sight, trussed up like a swine to the slaughter."

Killian stilled, the last knot momentarily forgotten. "Fey?"

Fey leaned around the tree trunk. "Well now, and here I'd thought ye had forgotten about wee sad Fey. And she, thinking ye would nae welcome her coming, nearly passed ye by."

Killian took in at one full glance the thatch of dark hair once more sawed short by a dull blade, the boy's jacket and breeches, and the distinctive smell of fish. "What are you doing here, lass?"

Fey grinned and pocketed her skean. "Do ye care, seeing as how ye were in need of a friendly face?" She gazed contemptuously about the unoccupied area. "Left ye quick as that, has she? Well, no matter. She weren't worth the trouble ye took with her, and that's a fact."

Killian jerked the last knot free and rose to his feet, only to have the sting of returning blood to his lower limbs make him grab the tree for support.

"Ye're growing slack and fat as a slug." Fey observed in malicious delight. "If that's what taking a wife does to a man, I'll nae have one."

"You'll not have in any case, lass," Killian reminded her.

Fey turned crimson beneath her mop of hair. "Ye know what I mean!"

Killian took a step and then another, testing his legs. "I won't say I'm not glad to see you, but I wonder how it came about all the same." Fey set her mouth in a familiar stubborn line. "So, keep your secret. You came when you did and that's enough for now."

Fey shrugged. She owed him nothing and that was what she would give him. "Where are yer companions?"

Killian cocked a black brow. "How do you know that I had companions?"

Fey shrugged again. "Like as not, ye didn't truss yerself up that way." She grinned suddenly. "Did yer lady wife grow tired of yer simpering and leave ye as a gift for the wee folk?"

"Deirdre!" Killian set off at a run, calling over his shoulder, "Come with me!"

When she realized that Killian was leaving her behind, Fey ran after him cursing a blue streak. Always it was the same: he thought of no one but Lady Deirdre. "When 'tis I who saved yer bloody life, ye *spalpeen!*"

Deirdre saw him a moment before she recognized him. She had been resting, gazing out from the minstrel's gallery at the patch of forest beyond the river, when a man suddenly appeared. He was shirtless, his black head an inky spot against the soft green grass as he sprinted across the valley toward the bridge which led to Liscarrol.

"Killian!" Deirdre dropped her makeshift broom and hurried down the narrow, worn stairwell to the main floor. She gained the front yard before she remembered the pistol she had left on the windowsill, but she cast the thought of protection aside as she continued her headlong flight.

The early-afternoon sun had broken through the clouds, lighting the day in a soft golden haze that deepened the greens and sharpened the gray walls of Liscarrol. Killian spied first the golden head glittering brightly as it bobbed up and down between the hedgerows. Even before she gained the bridge, he knew it was Deirdre. As she clambered across the dilapidated planks, setting them rattling underfoot, he called out a warning; but Deirdre did not pause, and a moment later she was on the far side of the river, running toward him with her arms outstretched.

The moment his arms closed about her and she knew that Killian was safe and well, a contrary anger rose up within her. Before he could even kiss her, she was pushing free of him.

"You! Where have you been?" she cried.

Killian smiled at her, his laughter barely contained as he reached for her a second time. "Come, lass, will you not kiss your husband?"

She sidestepped him, slapping his hands away. "You miserable, ungrateful man! Can you think of nothing but your own pleasure? And me so worried about you I nearly died."

Killian's brow furrowed as he searched her flushed face. "You were not harmed? They promised me you would not be harmed."

"They promised you, did they? And what other pleas- antries did you exchange that kept you away these two days?" She brushed away the tear that dared to dampen her cheek. "Had I known you were dealing with gentlemen I'd nae have been worried at all!"

"Dee," he coaxed as he reached for her once more. "Poor lass, you've had a time of it, worrying about me and frightened half out of your wits at being alone."

"I was not frightened," Deirdre lied and folded her arms across her bosom. "I was angry and worried, I admit." Against her will, her gaze strayed to his bare chest where fine black hair clung in damp curls to the sleek- muscled contours. It was a fine chest, she thought fleetingly as she dragged her eyes away, but not so fine that it would make her forgo her anger.

Killian's gaze, too, had wandered; to her bare arms and the décolletage of her bodice, over her petticoated hips to her bare ankles and feet. His eyes darkened. "You are undressed. Where are your clothes?"

The abrupt tone turned Deirdre's complexion bright red. She opened her mouth but closed it with a snap and turned on her heel to stalk back toward the bridge.

A grin spread across Killian's face as he watched her walk away. There was no denying that he had feared the worst for her. To find her perfectly sound had come as a shock. He well understood her irrational anger. The senti- ment had risen within him also as relief had turned to chagrin.

He caught her just before she reached the first plank and encircled her about the waist and swung her off her feet and into his arms.

Deirdre glared at him. "Put me down, you great brute!"

Killian bent to nuzzle the warm damp skin of her neck. "You were frightened for me. I'm sorry, lass."

Deirdre kicked her heels and pressed her hands against his chest to hold him away from her. "Put me down!"

Killian looked at her, reproach in his eyes of vivid blue. "Dee, lass."

Deirdre's hands curled into the furring on his chest. "You left me for two days!"

"It could not be helped."

She drew her hands away. "You should not have allowed them to take you."

An ironic smile curved Killian's mouth. "Much as you may not believe it, I have no great desire to be apart from you, lass. As for not besting my foes, you should remember that a man is at a wee bit of a disadvantage when his back is to the door and his senses are filled with the tantalizing nearness of his bride."

Deirdre looked up to see that desire had expanded his pupils, but she was not so easily appeased. "You do not look as though you tried very hard to resist."

"What did you desire, bloody wounds and blackened eyes?"

"Aye!"

"Nae, lass," Killian murmured warmly, nuzzling her neck once more.

"Put me down this instant!" Deirdre commanded sharply, but oddly enough she reached out to encircle his neck with her arms.

"*Mo cuishle*," he murmured thickly into the hollow of her throat.

"Now!" she answered less steadily.

The grass was lushly green on the riverbank. She sank into it as easily as into a feather tick when Killian lowered her onto the ground. He was smiling at her, a new cocky grin that she had never before seen on his face.

"You're very certain of your welcome," she challenged.

Killian did not answer. Instead he reached for the row of tiny bows on her bodice.

Deirdre giggled. "We stand in fearsome company. What if you're attacked again?"

Killian opened her bodice and plucked loose the lacing that held her corset closed.

"You would not?" she whispered in scandalized tones.

The corset parted as easily as her bodice and he brushed one rosy peak with a finger. "You're an uncommon lass, Lady Deirdre. Not many a gentlewoman would bare herself in the open light of day, however hotly passion runs in her veins."

Deirdre tried to close her bodice but he caught her hands, laughing at her outraged face. "Lass, lass, do you not yet know when a man's delighting in your wantonness?"

"Release me, you *spalpeen!*"

Killian threw a leg over her until he straddled her waist. "Does it shame you to want a man so?"

"I do not want you, Captain MacShane. You're too conceited by far. Killian? Do not—Killian!"

His cheeks were dark with whiskers and they lightly abraided her skin as he tenderly suckled her. Deirdre shut her eyes against the pleasure as a shameful blush warmed her skin from cheeks to belly. His actions were shocking, reckless, scandalous . . . and very, very exciting. As his lips moved from her breasts to her abdomen, she felt his hands on her thighs raising her petticoats.

"Can ye nae manage a place of shelter that ye must be rutting under a bush?" questioned an exasperated voice.

Deirdre squealed in fright and tried to throw Killian's weight from her but he would not budge. He looked up, more startled than frightened, for he knew the owner of the voice.

Fey stood a few feet away, her hands on her narrow hips and a look of pure disgust on her features.

"Fey, lass," he greeted with a lopsided grin as he lowered Deirdre's petticoats to a more respectable level. "I apologize. I had forgotten about you."

The truth of his statement did not have the desired effect. Fey turned on her heel and stalked away.

Killian looked back at Deirdre. "I fear I hurt her feelings."

Deirdre watched the girl's retreating back. "We both did," she answered quietly, "more than I had realized until now."

She did not question why the girl should be here in Ireland. The answer of how did not seem important for the moment. Fey had crossed an ocean and the reason was as plain as the look that had been in her eyes as she gazed at them sprawled in the grass. The girl was in love with Killian MacShane.

She looked at her husband and put a hand to his cheek. "I think perhaps we should rise, my love."

"We have not finished," he answered with a prodding reminder.

She smiled and tweaked his nose. "*Musha,* my love! If we rise now, I've no fear but what you'll rise again later."

Chapter Twenty

Deirdre paused in her sweeping to adjust the strips of linen that Killian had wound about her palms to protect them from further blisters. She smiled as she remembered the look of horror on his face when she told him of her labor. He had been impressed, she could see, but a little ashamed that his wife had taken on such a menial task. After berating her for damaging her hands he had strictly forbidden her to work. That had been three days ago. Since then she had cleaned the solar room on the upper floor, carted away most of the debris from the Great Hall, and cleaned the plasterwork of the small chapel, while Killian worked to repair the roof on the third floor. When he finished they would finally be able to sleep in a private room, away from the tense silence of their guest.

Deirdre glanced at Fey, who lackadaisically moved her broom over the slate floor without accumulating any dust. The girl rarely spoke and when she did it was with a dagger-point gaze which rebuffed any attempt at friendliness.

The rumble of Deirdre's stomach reminded her that Killian had gone to check the rabbit snares he had laid in the grassy fields beyond the river the day before. Food was their most constant problem. If they were lucky, they would have roasted mountain hare for supper.

The sound of heavy boots in the hallway brought a smile to her lips before she raised her head. "You're back so quickly. Did you have luck then?"

The smile froze on her face as a man moved to fill the doorway. He was huge, larger even than Darragh or Conall. And hairy. Bright red hair sprouted from his head and chin, ran in tangled skeins down his massive forearms, and curled forth on his half-bared chest. A pistol was stuck in his waistband but something more surprising riveted her gaze. The jeweled hilt of the O'Neill dagger, lost when her horse disappeared, was sticking from his belt.

"Forward, the lass is, and without the bashful eye of a maiden." Laughter bellowed forth from the giant. "*Musha!* Had I known I'd be made so welcome, lass, I'd have come all the sooner."

A flush of embarrassment flooded her face as she met his leer, and she gripped her broom handle in both hands. "And who would you be, that you enter this house without knocking?"

The big man smiled expansively and lifted both arms wide. "Why, yer neighbor, lass, come to welcome ye."

Deirdre saw now that he held a brace of pintail ducks in one hand and a reed basket slung over his other arm. "There's ale inside," he said, lifting the basket higher. "Butter and oakcakes, and honey as well."

Deirdre did not answer though her stomach turned over at the thought of bread and honey; and when she glanced at Fey, the girl was looking at her with interest for the first time in three days. "We've little enough to offer a guest," she began carefully, her eyes on the doorway beyond the stranger. "My husband will return at any moment. You may deal with him."

He walked toward her, his jack boots ringing on the slate tiles. "I've an eye for a winsome lass and ye could do nae better than to make friends with Oadh O'Donovan."

Deirdre's mouth was suddenly dry. She had heard that name before, in the tavern in Kilronane. This was the man

the English soldiers sought, the man they had tried to flush
out by hanging others, including his own child.

O'Donovan's smile widened until it seemed his face
would split under the pressure. "I see ye've heard of me."

Deirdre quickly quelled a shudder at the ghastly memory
of the child. "Aye, I've heard of you," she answered
stonily, "and none of it was to your credit."

O'Donovan's red brows peaked above his nose. "Ye
know the name O'Donovan and have no fear in the hearing
of it. 'Tis a rare one with so much courage, for all I'm
known for a soft spot for the lassees."

Deirdre lifted her broom. "You're not welcome here,
O'Donovan." She sent Fey a beseeching look, but O'Donovan
caught it and turned to the child in breeches and coat.

"Here, lad. The ducks are nae half so fine till they've
been plucked and gutted. Take them into the yard so the
feathers will nae fly about yer mistress's head."

To Deirdre's dismay Fey took the proffered ducks and
basket and with a last smirking glance turned to leave the
room.

"Fey!" she cried, but the girl ignored her. O'Donovan's
triumphant grin provoked her too much for her to repeat
the plea for help. She squared her shoulders. "You've
come to the wrong place for pleasure. Take yourself to
where there are willing lasses."

"Now there's a saying, lass, that there's no unwilling
lasses, only untutored lads."

"They lied," Deirdre maintained stoutly, but her hands
trembled slightly on the broom as he continued toward her.

"Ye're more than passing fair, *colleen dhas*, but ye've
nae the look of a *bean sidhe*."

"Why do you call me that?" she asked. Her eyes darted
toward the window. Had she seen a man crossing the
bridge?

"They told me ye were a daughter of the Sidhe. Where
are yer fairy companions, then?"

He reached for her, but Deirdre twisted away, bringing
her broom handle down hard. It cracked in two where it
met the hard bone of his shoulder. She twisted away but he
swung her around by the shoulder to face him.

"Let me go!" she said through gritted teeth and brought her knee up sharply.

O'Donovan was adept at sidestepping such a blow and her knee harmlessly struck his thigh. "A fine try, lass, but Oadh's nae so slow or careless as Cuan O'Dineen."

Deirdre stilled. Cuan had been with the men who captured Killian. He was one of O'Donovan's comrades.

"Aye, I know what ye're thinking, lass, and ye're right. Yer man and I have crossed paths afore."

Deirdre had not been listening to his words, only watching for the moment when he tensed for action. She was not the daughter and sister of soldiers for nothing. When his grip tightened to draw her close, she went limp so that her weight was suddenly full against him. Her right hand closed over the hilt of the O'Neill skean and her left sought his pistol. An instant later she flung herself away from him with all her might.

She came free with a suddenness that left half the bodice of her blouse in his hands as she tumbled backward onto the floor. Her left elbow struck the slate with a painful jolt, and the numbing pain made her drop the pistol.

"Och, lass, ye're a fighter, and that's the truth of it!" O'Donovan declared cheerfully as he threw away the torn cloth. "Mayhaps there's more of the Gael in yer blood than I'd allowed."

He glanced at the skean she clutched. "Ye would nae cut a man, lass. Ye've nae the stomach for it."

Deirdre flashed her weapon. " 'Tis an O'Neill blade and one that would not fail its owner."

To her surprise, a puzzled look came into the huge man's eyes. An instant later a stricken look replaced it and he fell back a step.

"The mark!" He wiped his mouth with the back of a hand and then pointed at her shoulder. "I said I'd nae believe until I saw it for meself."

Deirdre glanced quickly at her torn sleeve and the rose mark revealed through the rend. The priest had reacted the same when he saw the mark. She looked up. "What does this mean to you?"

" 'Tis the sign of the otherworld," O'Donovan replied,

making with his fingers the sign to warn off the spirits. He was not a religious man, and found the mealymouthing piety of men like his cousin Teague O'Donovan worthless, but he was an Irishman. The Sidhe was strong in the wilds of the west. Living in the bogs and mountains of Munster, he had seen things more astonishing than the pitiful miracles that Christianity proclaimed but could not produce to order. "I did nae know ye for a *bean feasa*," he said defensively. "And 'twas no insult I offered ye in wanting to kiss yer lushmore lips. Ye'll nae be holding it against me?"

Deirdre glanced once more at the doorway and joy lit her face. "Killian!"

O'Donovan swung about to find Killian standing behind him with his pistol drawn.

"MacShane, lad!" he greeted expansively. "And looking as well as ye might. I was just welcoming yer lady wife."

To Killian's surprise, relief flickered in the man's gaze. His gaze swung from O'Donovan to Deirdre and his features hardened as he saw her torn clothing. "You've a curious method of conversation, O'Donovan. I do not believe my wife approves of it."

O'Donovan shrugged. "Ye cannot blame a man for amusing himself when the temptation presents itself. 'Twas only to pass the time till ye arrived."

Killian eyed him casually. "Is that what it was?"

O'Donovan glanced at the still angry young woman and then at her mark before his gaze slid away. "I'm nae a man to overstay his welcome." He sidestepped toward the door. "Liscarrol has fallen on hard times, anyone can see. I brought ye just now a fresh brace of ducks and drink enough for both ye and your lady wife."

Killian frowned as he regarded the huge man. Where was O'Donovan's bluster, his swagger, his evil temper? And why was he watching Deirdre as though he expected her to turn into a wolf and bite him? "And here I thought you'd come to see me."

O'Donovan nodded, his gaze continually flicking back and forth between the two. "Ye outfoxed me, that ye did, MacShane. And I've had another thought on the matter of our business dealings.'' He grinned. ''Half for you, half for me and the lads.''

Killian's frown deepened. ''For a careful man, you're damned careless with your speech. Come out to the stables. We've kept my wife from her cleaning long enough.''

''You cannot mean to entertain him, even if it is in a stable?'' Deirdre asked.

''Dee, my love, kindly keep your sweet mouth shut,'' Killian answered and pocketed his pistol. ''O'Donovan?'' He gestured toward the stairwell.

''He's the man the English seek!'' Deirdre challenged.

''Thank you, Dee, for the announcement, but we've no Englishman to interest in the matter,'' Killian replied in the same maddening tone.

When they were gone, Deirdre tucked the O'Neill skean into her waistband and bent to pick up the ruined broom. With a mutter of disgust she cast it aside. How dare Killian behave toward that depraved creature as though he were some country squire who had come calling. What business dealings could they possibly have together?

From the corner of her eye she saw Fey on the stairs. ''Just one minute!'' she called as the girl tried to sneak up the stairwell.

Fey paused and swung about. ''What will ye be wanting then?''

''Why did you run away and leave me?''

''When?'' Fey questioned in a bored voice.

''You know very well when—when O'Donovan came.''

Fey shrugged. ''I did as I was bade.'' She looked up quickly, a flash of enmity in her eyes. ''Ye've said I do nae do as I'm told often enough. Ye do nae think I hear ye whispering to MacShane in the dark. Well, I do!''

Deirdre blushed. Much of what she and Killian whispered in the night was too private to be repeated in the daylight. ''I've never said a harsh word against you, and well you know it. I've even taken your part against Killian.''

''Ye've nae need to take me part against MacShane. If he's angry, he's right!''

Deirdre regarded the girl's flushed face anew and what she read there appalled her. The girl hated her enough to wish her harm. "You think a great deal of MacShane," she said softly.

Fey's mouth tightened into a silent knot.

"You told me once you wished you were old enough to attract his eye. You still do, do you not?"

Fey dropped her gaze to her boot tips.

"And you hate me for being the lass he loves."

Fey's gaze swung upward in sharp wariness.

"I do not blame you," Deirdre continued. "I would hate as well any other woman Killian chose to love. 'Tis a bitter thing to love a man who does not love you back."

"Shut up! Shut up!" Fey cried, flying from the steps with her fists raised. "Shut up talking about MacShane loving ye!"

The force of her body nearly knocked Deirdre from her feet. She flung her arms about Fey, pinioning the girl's arms at the elbows to keep the pair of them from toppling to the floor. Fey did not stop struggling. She kicked Deirdre's ankles and beat her back with hard small fists, but Deirdre held on until Fey turned and sank her teeth into her shoulder.

With a gasp of pain, Deirdre flung the girl from her.

"Ye do nae deserve him!" Fey raged, her chest heaving up and down and her eyes blazing. "Ye did naught to earn his love when 'twas me who saved his life!"

Deirdre's own heart was pumping like a piston and her ankles throbbed too much for her to think of the wisest, most mature thing to do. She reached out and grabbed Fey by the shoulders and shook her as hard as she could. "You will never, never hurt me again! Do you understand?"

Tears burned in her eyes and she gulped back a sob as she released the girl. "Have you learned nothing of manners in the year you've lived with me? What is to become of you if you go about biting people and bruising their ankles whenever you are angry."

Deirdre paused suddenly, stunned by the triviality of her words. She spoke as if to an unruly but well-reared child, not a cast-off orphan who had killed a man before her thirteenth birthday. "Fey, Fey," she murmured as she sank to the floor in defeat.

Fey watched her a moment in silence, wondering if Deirdre would faint, but she merely wiped away a tear and sat staring at the floor.

"Ye'll be telling him what I done," Fey said after a long silence.

Deirdre shook her head. "It doesn't matter. O'Donovan did not hurt me."

"But he might have," Fey replied.

"Aye," Deirdre answered wearily.

"And 'twould be me fault. MacShane should know."

Deirdre looked up. "Then you tell him."

Fey jumped. "Me? Why should I?"

"Because it would be the grown-up thing to do."

Fey screwed up her face and spat a string of colorful Spanish epithets she had learned at the dockside of Nantes. "Ye bloody stupid cow!" she finished. " 'Tis always the same. It's 'be a lady, Fey,' 'be sweet, be pleasant, be good, be stupid, be quiet,' be what everyone else thinks I should. But it does nae mean I do not feel things. I love MacShane and ye took him from me!"

The raw pain in those words made Deirdre wince. "You are wrong, Fey. I do not think you are too young to love." She swallowed her pity. Fey did not want or need it. "I know what it is to be young and in love. I loved MacShane the first moment I set eyes on him and I was but seven."

Fey glared at her in frank disbelief.

" 'Twas here, at Liscarrol, we first met. He was a tall but scrawny lad of seventeen, hiding in the stables. The English were after him, you see, and he was bad wounded." Deirdre's lips turned up in a winsome smile. "I thought him the bravest, dearest lad a lass ever saw." She turned to Fey, who was watching her with a guarded expression. "I did not learn his name, nor he mine, and we parted within a few hours of our meeting; but I knew even then that I would love him forever."

She met the girl's dark-eyed stare. "I did not win him from you. He was always mine."

In astonishment she watched Fey's lower lip begin to tremble and one thick tear slide free from beneath her heavy fringe of dark lashes. Though she expected a rebuff,

Deirdre held out a hand to the girl. Without hesitation, Fey flung herself into Deirdre's lap and burst into tears.

"I am sorry, Fey," Deirdre said gently as she stroked the girl's heaving back. "As one woman to another, I am sorry."

"It—it hurts—so bad!" Fey murmured between hiccupy sobs. "I hate loving!"

Deirdre bit her lip. "I know. Loving can be hard, but it can be wonderful, too. There'll be another man for you."

Fey lifted her head, her expression hostile once more. "There wasn't another for ye, ye said so. Why should there be another for me?"

Deirdre silently cursed herself for her poor choice of words. She had complicated the matter. "I did not say that I would never have loved another man if MacShane had never returned to me. I said I would have always loved him, no matter what."

Fey's expression soured. "Ye do nae want me to keep loving MacShane."

Deirdre stroked the girl's short dark curls into place. "That would be very foolish of me. MacShane loves you, too."

Fey backed away from Deirdre, suddenly ashamed of having sought refuge in her arms. She stood and tugged angrily at her wrinkled jacket. "Do nae lie to me. I am nothing to him."

"You do not believe that," Deirdre answered reproachfully, "not after all he has done for you."

Fey sucked in a breath as her temper teetered dangerously on the edge of renewed rage. "He cares, does he? Then why did he leave me behind in Nantes when I'd have gone on foot to Paris to be near him? And why did he pack me off to Nantes the moment ye were wed? So he'd have none of me about to bother him, that's why!"

"We hurt your feelings," Deirdre murmured mostly to herself. "We did not mean to, Fey. We both wanted you to be safe."

"Ye wanted me out of yer life. Ye do nae need me." Fey braced her hands on her hips. "As well I do nae need ye. But take care that one day ye'll nae wish I'd return."

"Return? Where are you going?" Deirdre rose to her feet as Fey marched away. "Fey?"

The girl turned, her back stiff with indignation. "I'm not staying where I'm nae wanted. I can go the way I came."

"And how was that?"

The question startled Fey. " 'Tis none of yer affair."

Deirdre saw the guarded look. "You could not afford passage to Ireland. Who paid your way?"

Fey shrugged. "I did nae steal anything from ye."

"*Merde!* Did I suggest it?" Deirdre exclaimed angrily. "I give up. Go your own way. You will not be my friend, and neither will you allow me be yours."

"What's this? Full-scale war?"

Deirdre turned an angry face at Killian. "And you, you're no better than she! Keeping company with murderers and rogues. Next you will tell me they did not kidnap you! Go to the devil!" she ended with a stiff-armed shove that foiled Killian's attempt to embrace her.

When Deirdre had marched out of the house, Killian turned a speculative eye on Fey, who stood spread-legged in the middle of the hall. "What did she say to you?"

"She told me to go back to Nantes," Fey answered, her face stiff with dried tears.

"Did she?" Killian mused. "Well, perhaps she's right. You are in danger. Have you thought what might have happened had Deirdre been here alone or if you had been? If you had not thought quickly enough to take the ducks and come running to me, he might have raped the pair of you before I knew he was here."

Fey's sullen expression did not alter. "I can look after meself. 'Tis your lady wife what wants a talking to."

Killian nodded at the wisdom of the suggestion. "I will see to it. You've a born talent for self-preservation. I'm certain Deirdre will thank you properly for saving her when she has calmed."

"I do not want her thanks!" Fey spat. "I did nae do it for her!"

Before Killian's puzzled expression, Fey turned and ran up the tower stairs.

"What is the matter with the women in my household?" Killian grumbled, only to frown deeper as his words lingered in his mind. *The women of his household.* Two months earlier he did not have a household. Two months earlier he did not have a pair of women in his keeping.

"Gom!"

The duchesse expected him to rid her of O'Donovan, but she did not want the smuggling ring she relied upon dismantled; therefore, he could not simply kill the man. If he hoped to remain at Liscarrol in some measure of safety, he would have to wait patiently until he had proved himself among O'Donovan's followers to be a better, more profitable leader than O'Donovan had been. That would take time. Meanwhile, he must find a means to make Liscarrol into a livable home for his wife and himself.

Killian looked about. Deirdre and Fey had cleaned away the last of the lichen and bracken from the interior walls. The Great Hall was nearly ready for a coat of plaster, but from where was the money to come to buy it? How was he to make Liscarrol self-sufficient?

"I am a soldier, not a farmer," he grumbled. Yet, he needed the skills of a squire to set his new kingdom to rights. He needed cattle and sheep and a garden just to maintain the basics of life. Then there was the need for chairs and tables . . . and a bed.

Though she had not complained, he knew Deirdre must be weary of sleeping on a slate floor covered with rushes.

He thought of the ship that O'Donovan had told him about moments before. A French ship, loaded with brandy and silks, furnishings and tobacco and other goods bound for the thriving blackmarket of Dublin and Waterford and Wexford. The ship would be making an extra stop off the coast near Bantry Bay, and he had been invited to accompany O'Donovan and his men to see how the smuggling of wool and beef was accomplished. The incident of the morning had shown him that Deirdre should not be left alone without means of protection. He had declined.

Killian swore again as he strode toward the door. He had not finished checking his snares; but if they supplied no better catch than the first ones, the inhabitants of Liscarrol would once more be dining on watercress and wild onions.

On the front steps he found the pair of ducks lying where Fey had dropped them when she went running to fetch him. He bent and retrieved them, smiling as thoughts of roasted duck replaced watercress and boiled onions. O'Donovan had mentioned a basket as well. He looked about until he saw it standing inside the doorway. The contents brought a huge grin to his face as he opened the small barrel of ale and drank deeply.

O'Donovan's generosity was out of character, Killian mused when his thirst was slaked. Such a man would not feed his enemies. O'Donovan wanted something.

Killian remembered the outrage on Deirdre's face as he had led O'Donovan out of the house, but it was O'Donovan's reaction to her anger that intrigued him more. The huge man was eager to be out of her sight. Why should that be?

As he replaced the barrel, Killian thought again of the French frigate and her lovely cargo the smuggler had teased him with. He was not averse to the idea of owning a few bottles of French brandy, nor did he think Deirdre would turn up her nose at a French silk gown. Taking Deirdre along was out of the question, as was leaving her behind, so that was that.

"Next time," he murmured to himself in consolation.

Killian heard them first, but Fey was the first to react. She jumped up from her pallet by the smoky fire and on soundless feet went down the stairwell to peer through the ax-made gashes in the main door.

It was nearly dawn, Killian decided as he slid his arm out from under Deirdre and carefully laid her head on the rushes that served as their bed. When she did not stir, he silently followed Fey's path to the door.

Fey looked up as the heat from Killian's body touched her skin. "'Tis two score or more of them," she whispered in a sleepy voice.

Killian bent and pressed his eye to the spot she had used. The sky had lightened to shades of gray as night faded and mist began to rise. At first he saw nothing, and then they appeared, irregular dark figures against the lighter gray mist crossing the valley beyond the river.

"What do ye think?" Fey questioned in his ear.

Killian put a finger to her lips but she jerked back as though his touch burned her. He glanced at her in surprise, but the room was too dark for him to clearly see her expression.

The first sounds on the bridge broke the early-morning silence as the loose boards creaked and bucked under the weight of many hooves. Killian looked out again, alarm tingling through him. It sounded like a full mounted battalion crossing the failing bridge. He had not seen the mounted army through the mist.

Almost immediately a low bawling filled the morning air, followed closely by another and another. Not soldiers and horses. Cattle! And, by the sounds of them, they were stampeding.

"O'Donovan!" Killian straightened. A herd of cattle would easily stove in the main doors which had been hacked from their hinges.

He grabbed Fey by the arm and dragged her so quickly across the floor that her feet scarcely touched it. "Upstairs!" he cried as he flung her up the first stone steps. Without waiting to see if she obeyed, he turned and raced across the floor to Deirdre.

Awakened by the ever-increasing din, Deirdre sat up just as Killian reached her. "What is happening?"

He did not reply but lifted her to her feet by the shoulders and pushed her toward the stairway. "Upstairs! Hurry!"

Deirdre resisted the hands on her shoulders. "But I'm not dressed! Wait! Where's my shift?"

A colorful curse accompanied Killian's actions as he scooped her up and ran the rest of the distance to the stairwell.

Fey looked back from her perch at the window with a smile that dissolved as she saw Deirdre in Killian's arms.

Deirdre slid from Killian's embrace, blushing furiously. "He would not allow me to find my clothes," she answered, but, as usual, Fey turned away before she finished.

Killian recorded the discord between the two, but their differences were not as important as what was occurring below. He walked over and looked out.

"The cattle have been turned away from the house,"

Fey informed him casually. "There's herdsmen with them and dogs."

"So I see," Killian murmured as he looked out.

In the yard below were several dozen cattle, and more were pouring over the bridge into the yard. The shaggy coats of the ancient Irish cattle mingled with the smooth black and white hides of the newer breed of milk cow. Killian's gaze shifted to the men who whistled and prodded the cattle to the accompaniment of their dogs.

They wore the knee breeches and short coats of common laborers. Some wore hats and cloaks, others went bareheaded. There was a single woman among them; her long cloak swirled about her ankles as she approached the house. A call from one of the men, little more than a hiss really, made her turn back. They huddled together, voices barely a hum as they spoke to each other.

Deirdre moved to Killian's side and tugged at his shirt sleeve. "Who are these people and why are we hiding?"

"We are not hiding. I'm sizing up our guests," he answered; but his gaze never left the pair conversing below. "You will allow that they have the better of us in numbers."

Deirdre nodded but she had begun to shiver. " 'Tis dreadfully cold, Killian. I need my clothes."

Killian regarded her almost absently. She was lovely in her rose and cream nudity, he thought with a swift but fleeting rush of desire. He stripped off his shirt and handed it to her and then turned back to the window.

The pair in the yard parted. The woman started toward the stables but turned off just past the corner of the house.

"What rooms lie at the rear of the castle?" Killian questioned, for he had been too busy repairing it to thoroughly survey the place he now called home.

"The kitchen," Deirdre answered. "But there's nothing in there to attract a thief. The pots and pans are blackened with age and riddled with rust. Nothing else remains." When she finished the last button she moved to his side and peered below.

"Why, it looks as it did when I was a child," she exclaimed in a voice that made Killian's brows wing upward. "I loved to watch the herdsmen gather our cattle before they went into the mountains for *booleying*," she explained. "We had over a thousand head, nearly a complete recovery from the days of Cromwell." She spoke the hated name low, as if he were some monster from Hell to be conjured by the mere mention of his name.

" 'Tis nae a bloody party in the yard below," Fey answered roughly. She appealed to Killian. "Will they rush the house, do ye think?"

Killian shrugged, never taking his eyes off the scene below. They were very suspicious attackers. They seemed to be paying no attention at all to the house. Liscarrol had been abandoned for some time. Perhaps this company of wandering herdsmen assumed Liscarrol was theirs to occupy for a night or two. There was evidence in the stable and in the yard that cattle had grazed here recently. For all its dilapidation, Liscarrol offered a sound, dry place against the rain and mists. And, if his suspicions were correct, these people were the only folk in the area with whom he could be certain that O'Donovan had no contact.

Killian straightened. " 'Tis time I greeted our guests."

"You will be careful?" Deirdre asked.

Killian looked at her with a quizzical expression. "Careful?" In his entire life as a soldier no one had ever asked him to be careful. Cautious, yes, and clever, and quick. "Careful," he repeated, and then, as though it were a private joke, his laughter echoed back up the stairwell down which he disappeared.

"A bloody stupid thing to say that was," Fey grumbled.

Deirdre shot the girl a venomous look but she held her tongue and started down the stairs behind Killian.

Fey jumped to her feet. "Where do ye think ye're going?"

"To stand beside my husband," Deirdre replied and hurried down the steps.

Killian paused in the hallway long enough to assure himself that his pistol was primed.

The morning was as gray as old sheets and as damp as drizzle could make it. He stood on the top step and waited patiently until the first man noticed him. To his utter amazement, the man merely looked at him and away, continuing to prod the young heifer he guided toward the main herd. The next man who saw him tipped his cap respectfully and then he, too, continued on his way.

"You," Killian called in his carrying voice. "Come here."

The third man looked at his companions; though they stopped to stare, neither of them spoke. Reluctantly the hailed man came forward.

"A good morning to ye, m'lord," the man said hesitantly, his cap quickly snatched from his head.

"Who are you?" Killian demanded.

"Colin," the man replied. "We brought them back, just as we promised, and three dozen more besides." The man indicated the cattle behind him. "We lost a few to the English; but like as not, the eating of stolen cattle killed them, and more's the pity then that we could nae have crammed the lot down their miserable throats!"

"I see," Killian answered. "The cattle belong to Liscarrol," he ventured, and was rewarded with a broad smile and nod from the man. "Who told you we had returned?"

The man appeared puzzled for a moment but Killian was too good at reading men not to notice the quick flexing of his hands on the brim of his cap. Whatever the man chose to answer would not be the full truth.

"We saw movement," the man began in an embarrassingly poor attempt to lie. "Folk hereabout suspected 'twas ye who had come home, m'lord."

"Do you recognize me?" Killian asked in surprise.

"For truth, I do not," the man replied. "The Fitzgeralds of Liscarrol were fair and freckled to a man. But 'tis nae business of mine should the raven show up in a flock of swan, m'lord."

Killian's lips twitched. Was that how he appeared, a raven among the swans? As for the lie, he would not press the man now. "What am I to do with the cattle you return?"

The man frowned again. "Do, m'lord? Sure'n a man may keep his cattle any place he chooses. The bloody English haven't taken away his rights to that, yet!"

"Thank you, Colin. In the meantime, will you and your lads be good enough to remove them to the bog field beyond the river?"

"O'course we will," Colin replied jauntily. "Anything ye want, we can do. Ye'll nae hire better herdsmen anywhere in the county, and that's truth worth the hearing.''

Killian let the matter of hiring pass for the moment. He could not afford to hire an empty bucket, but the cattle needed to be moved from his front door.

''What do they want?'' Deirdre asked as she stepped up beside Killian.

A quick appraisal of her showed him that she had pulled on her own clothing before showing herself. He smiled. ''Your cattle have come home, Lady MacShane. 'Tis all the matter that confronts us today. There'll be milk for supper and butter for breakfast.''

Deirdre gazed with widened eyes at the sea of cows streaming past.

''Are they truly ours? All of them?''

''So they tell me, sweet wife, and I am not of a mind to question it.''

''There'll be money to be had from the selling of some of them,'' Deirdre said thoughtfully.

''Aye, and leather and beef, sparingly,'' Killian agreed.

Deirdre turned on him a full smile. ''We are rich!''

''We are the owners of a respectable herd,'' Killian amended, but he smiled as broadly as she. The fortunes of the MacShanes appeared to be changing.

Deirdre suddenly sobered. ''Will O'Donovan reive the herd?''

Killian shook his head. ''Oh, we may lose an animal here and there to his thieving band, but O'Donovan's not a herder.'' Unless the cow was aboard a smuggler's ship, he doubted O'Donovan could give it a second look, but he was not about to tell Deirdre that.

Deirdre yawned broadly, using a hand to cover her mouth, then she looked at Killian with an impish grin that made the most of her dimple. '' 'Tis dawn. 'Twould seem time for the milking to begin.''

Killian knew she was hungry. He was hungry. ''Milk and onions?'' he suggested with a cocked brow.

Deirdre made a face. ''Milk and milk!''

*   *   *

"Sheep. Sheep would bring us a greater profit and require few men to tend them," Killian mused aloud as he sat on the floor and drew a figure on a slate with a charred stick. Two days had passed since the return of Liscarrol's cattle and in that time he had been busy planning their future. "Wool can be our regular crop with lambs for market thrown in on occasion." He smiled to himself. The French were especially fond of spring lamb. Then, too, sheep were more easily concealed than cattle, and the wool gathered from shearing was more easily disposed of than milk and cream. He would take half his wool to market, the other half he would sell to the duchesse.

"I did not suspect that you possessed a head for business," Deirdre replied when she had drained the last of the milk from her wooden cup.

"I do not," Killian answered, "but any man of sense can see that a thundering herd of cattle is more likely to catch a greedy eye than a distant, elusive flock of dirty sheep."

"Milk cows do not thunder, my love," she answered. "They are among God's most sedate creatures."

Killian smiled as he looked at her milk-mustachioed face. "I stand corrected. A field of slovenly, contented cows is more likely to cause us trouble. I have talked to the herdsman named Colin, and he tells me that the cattle have been kept from the English by hiding them in the hills of the Shehy Mountains and that their milk suffers from the poor grazing provided by the winter hillsides."

"The milk tastes as rich and sweet as top cream to me." Deirdre licked her upper lip with a long sweeping action that caught her husband's attention. "Honey! I want to bring the honey bees back. Can we repair the hives very soon?"

"We will repair everything in time, *acushla,* but repairs require workers and workers must be paid. That is why I must go to market."

Deirdre's face brightened. "Market? May I come? I need new gowns, even just one, and shoes, and a brush and soap and—"

"And many other things that cost money which we do not have," Killian finished for her, his face darkening. "I am a poor husband, lass. You've much to tax me with and little to praise me for."

Deirdre looked at him in surprise. "Do I complain?"

"God no! And that is little to my credit." He rose in a single fluid movement. "You sit in rags on the floor like the lowliest of peasants with a cup of thin milk for your daily meal and I do nothing to change it!"

Deirdre rose to her feet, shaking out the dirty folds of her ruined riding skirt. "I may not be in the height of fashion, sir, but you once told me you did not think much of ladies, those in particular who needed wooing with soft words and deeds."

"Did I now? I must have been in a temper," Killian said, his eyes fastening on the work of her fingers at the buttons of his shirt, which she wore in place of her ruined blouse.

"Aye, you were that," Deirdre answered, her fingers prodding the final button open. "You had just discovered that Fey was a lass." She began pulling the blouse from her shoulders, and though she smiled she did not look up at him. "I was furious with you for being so rude, but I could not help but be jealous that you had kept a lass in your room the night through."

"Jealous?" Killian questioned without interest, for she had begun loosening her corset and he, too, realized that they were on this rare occasion alone. Fey had gone to check the rabbit traps.

"Aye. Jealous. I had spent years learning the very manners which you were throwing back in my face." She lowered her corset slowly until he was gazing at one of his favorite sights. "Since then, I have given up my fine schooling as it is not to your liking."

"You, however, are to my liking," Killian answered with a grin as he took a step toward her. He lifted her chin with a finger and gazed smiling into her eyes. "You've no reason to be jealous, *mo cuishle*," he said, his brogue caressing each word. His hands fell to her naked waist. "As for your manners, they suit me fine, lass."

"You mean because now I have none," Deirdre replied

and laughed up into his face. "You've turned me into a shameless lass and, what's more, I like it!"

"There's none to compare with you, and that's a truth." His hands rose to cup her breasts. "No, you're not so shameless as you may think. You please only your husband, and that you do quite amicably."

"Is that a compliment?" Deirdre questioned doubtfully. "It makes me sound so, well, matronly."

Killian chuckled. "Should we be lovers, forbidden by your father even to speak? Would we snatch secret moments, steal kisses and cuddles? Nae, lass, I do not see myself as a pining swain to your vanity."

"My vanity, is it? And what would you be calling the conceit that causes you to think I would consent to snatch even one secret moment with you?" Deirdre watched his face crinkle into lines of laughter. The lines of worry had disappeared for the moment, forgotten as they dallied in a game of love. As he bent to kiss her she gazed deeply into his eyes. The pupils had expanded to nearly eclipse the bright blue irises and the image of herself was clearly reflected in those dark depths.

He loves me, she thought exultantly. *He thinks of nothing but me in this moment and I will cherish every instant of it.*

His mouth was warmly persuasive on hers, and as she spread her palms across his chest she knew a moment of perfect peace. Too often in recent weeks they had been at odds. Now, for this moment, they were in perfect harmony.

The woman who entered the Great Hall was surprised but not amazed to find a half-nude young woman in the arms of the new owner of Liscarrol. This would be the lady wife of whom she had heard but had not seen. She waited politely at the door for the embrace to end, a steaming kettle in one hand and a trencher in the other. But when it seemed that this was the beginning, not the end of a moment of pleasuring, she cleared her throat loudly, for she was impatient to be gone and the pot was heavy.

Deirdre gasped and turned away so quickly that Killian bumped his chin on her head and groaned as his tongue crunched between his teeth. He turned his head toward the intruder, pulling Deirdre close to hide her breasts against his chest.

"I did nae mean to intrude, m'lord," the woman said humbly, "but 'tis a matter that will nae wait." She held up the trencher. " 'Tis *cabaiste Scotch* and a rare treat it is in this weather. And there's mulled wine come from an unbroken bottle found in the kitchen."

"Thank you," Killian said over his bruised tongue. There was no reason to ask where the wine had really come from. He had searched every inch of Liscarrol looking for anything left intact. A bottle of wine would never have escaped notice. "Set them by the door."

The woman did as she was bade and then turned back with a smile for the young couple. "May yer wife come to the birthing bed afore Samain. 'Tis easy to see she's a bonny lass." The woman paused, her broad pleasant face paling visibly.

"What ails you, woman?" Killian asked.

The woman pointed a finger at Deirdre. "I was told the truth of it, but, well, a body must see. I'll go now," she added as she turned and hastened out the door.

"What was that all about?" Deirdre questioned.

Killian looked briefly at her shoulder, remembering Teague's tale of fairy marks, and shook his head. Once Deirdre, too, had believed in fairy magic. They were both better off without the reminder.

"I do not know. Simple folk are often embarrassed before nobility. Perhaps she realized her blessing was out-of-place."

Deirdre looked down at her exposed breasts pressed full against his coat and then up at him. "Out-of-place? Hardly, my love, when you're as lusty as a bull!"

To her delight and amazement a bright pink flush suffused his cheeks a moment before he bent and kissed her.

Chapter Twenty-one

Deirdre lay awake in the dark. The dream that had been absent since their first night at Liscarrol had come back. Her palms were clammy and her heart pounded in long heavy strokes that shook her body. He was out there, waiting. She could feel him drawing her from her bed and yet she was paralyzed with fear. Killian lay sleeping beside her but she did not reach out to him. She did not want to tell him that she believed a specter that looked just like him waited beyond the door. He would think her foolish or mad, or both. Yet, the impulse to learn if it was true was too strong to resist.

She rose, the chill of the night reaching out for her as she walked barefoot toward the door. Killian and two of the herdsmen had set the great doors on new hinges. The bolt was heavy but the door opened easily once it was lifted.

It was not yet dawn; but the mantle of night was green-tinged at the edges, and phosphorescent mists illuminated the path of the dark river and veiled the mountains. She crossed the yard toward the stable, knowing that this was where the specter would reveal himself. She remembered the last occasion. He had been more real than fantasy. She had touched, had felt the solid reality of his leg and boot. He had been a lover enticing her toward him, and then a demon striking out at her. The back of her right hand tingled at the memory of the whip's lash and she rubbed it against her skirts. She should turn about, should flee the desperate phantom who had sought her out over and over through the years, but she could not.

The stable was not empty. From inside came the faint glow of a turf fire about which were curved the sleeping bodies of the herders and their families. Deirdre paused in the doorway. The phantom would not be here. He would come out of the mists down the mountains. She waited, her back to the night, but the only thundering she heard was the pumping of her heart.

A minute passed. Two. Five. The night was still, holding its breath against the first stirring of dawn.

In relief mixed with disappointment, Deirdre turned back toward the house. She had been so certain, so confident that someone, something, waited for her in the violet and gray darkness.

The figure came out of the mists to her right, a frail wraith in woman's clothing.

Deirdre froze, her blood chilling.

The creature came forward slowly, limping as she carried a ragged bundle in her arms. Her face was in shadow and Deirdre had the unsettling impression that the apparition was faceless. "Who are ye?" it cried in a strangely thickened voice.

Deirdre fell back a step.

"Who are ye!" she repeated in a desperate rasp.

"Lady MacShane," Deirdre murmured.

The creature paused, half in shadow, its bare womanly shaped legs showing white as candle wax in the twilight. "Be ye a Fitzgerald of Liscarrol?"

Deirdre nodded slowly. This questioner was not a part of her dream, nor had it ever been.

The creature leaned toward her from the waist and thrust her bundle forward. "Ye must help me! Heal me! Ye've great powers, *bean sidhe!* Help me save me child!"

Deirdre fell back another step. Though she knew the

herders slept in the stable behind her and could be summoned with a single loud cry, she whispered the words, "I do not know you. I do not know what you want of me."

The woman moved forward awkwardly, her limp more pronounced. "Ye do know! 'Twas said the powers of sight were yers. See me, *bean sidhe!* See me and heal me!"

As she stepped from shadow Deirdre saw that a hood had cloaked her face, but when the hood slipped back a visitor from Hell stood before her.

The face was distorted beyond recognition. The brow, chin, and jaws were swollen to twice normal and blackened. The right eye was lost in the bulge of distended flesh, and her mouth was smeared into a permanent grimace of pain. The odor of rotting flesh wavered sickeningly from her.

Deirdre gasped in revulsion and clapped a hand over her mouth as she spun away from the nightmare.

"Bean sidhe!" the creature called as Deirdre ran toward the house. "A blessing!" came the last feeble cry that was more a wail than speech.

Deirdre did not feel the stones that bruised her feet as she ran across the yard. She was in the grip of a nightmare more terrible than any she had yet dreamed. There were tears in her throat clogging the screams that percolated up from her terror. The door seemed an eternity away, and the pause between each heartbeat became longer than the last until she thought she would burst with frustration before she reached safety. Then, mercifully, the cold stone slabs of Liscarrol's steps were beneath her feet.

She pushed the door wide with both hands, sending it crashing against the wall with a force that reverberated throughout the great house as she reached the stairwell.

Killian was on his feet in an instant but before he could speak, Deirdre had thrown her arms about him.

"Hold me! Hold me!" she cried frantically, climbing his legs until he held her off the ground.

"What is it? What has happened?" Killian demanded as he felt deep shivers ripple through her. "Is someone outside? Were you attacked?"

Deirdre shook her head wildly, her nails digging into his

back as though he would disappear if she relaxed her grip. "Nothing! Nothing!"

Fey lifted her head from her pallet and said groggily, "She were dreaming again. She did it often in her father's home. Like as not, she's had another dream of the *púca*."

"It was not a dream!" Deirdre cried, only to realize the implication of what she had said. "'Twas a nightmare," she added lamely.

Killian lowered her to the ground and brushed back the tangle of hair from her face with a gentle hand. "Dreaming again? Like the last time? Was it me this time?"

Deirdre shook her head, refusing to look up at him. "'Twas a different dream."

"But it frightened you just the same."

She nodded.

"Well, there'll be no more nightmares. I'll see to that." He picked up his cloak, which had served as their blanket, and wrapped her in it. "Come sit by me while I stir the fire. 'Twill be light soon. The days are lengthening. 'Tis spring, and summer cannot be far behind." He continued to speak in the same light tone as he settled her beside him and tucked her under his arm.

Deirdre opened the cloak to share the warmth with him and then wrapped her arms tightly about his waist as she laid her head against his chest. The solid, even rhythm of his heart was the most welcome sound in the world. Yet, she could not completely shake the quiver of revulsion she felt for the grotesque figment of her imagination. What were these dreams which plagued her? Was Brigid right, did she have powers over which she had no control? If that were so, why should they come to her? What could they mean?

When he could think of nothing more to say, Killian began to softly whistle a tune. One became a second, and before the third was finished he felt Deirdre slump against him and knew that she had fallen asleep.

He did not think of sleeping again. He had too many matters on his mind. He had sent two dozen of his best milk cows to market with Colin's son, Enan. If they brought him the money he expected, he would at last be able to provide some measure of comfort for Deirdre.

He bent and brushed a kiss across her forehead. No wonder she had nightmares, living in a drafty, windowless ruin. He was still amazed that she smiled at him with such love. Many another lady would have run home in tears to her parents, but Deirdre stayed and remained hopeful that their lives would change.

Killian smiled suddenly. Some things would change immediately. If he was forced to eat one more serving of *cabaiste Scotch*, he knew he would explode. Cabbage hearts and onions with sour cream were not a thing of which to make a steady diet.

"Tomorrow, *mo cuishle*, you will have salmon," he whispered. He had seen the first of the fish in the river that morning, a single flash of silver beneath the green-brown waters. The spawning season would soon be upon them and the bounty of the season would augment their diet.

"What do you mean by saying they're gone?" Killian demanded angrily.

"They was taken, m'lord," Colin's son Enan mumbled, his head hung low.

"Who took them?"

"An Englishman named Glover. He says 'twas ag'n the law, an Irishman selling his stock at the open market."

Killian stared at Enan until the boy began to shake, but his black scowl was not for Enan but for his own thoughtlessness in the matter.

The boy was too miserably ashamed of his own poor accounting to be silent. "I should have gone into town to check afore I drove 'em in, but there wasn't supposed to be English gentry at the market." He hung his head again. "I forgot about the Discoverers."

"Call them spies! The slunk-back weasels who profit from depriving upright men of their livelihood should not be dignified with a title," Killian answered sharply. "So, I am to be served with a Bill of Discovery, am I? And until then my cattle are locked away.''

The boy nodded miserably. '' 'Twill be a week or so, I'm thinking. They must send to Cork for the magistrate.''

''Well then, I must do something in the meantime. I will not wait upon the pleasure of the local authorities.'' Killian dropped a heavy hand on the boy's shoulder. ''Find O'Donovan for me. Do not begin a lie, lad. I know you know how he's to be found. I do not ask you to betray that confidence. I ask that you get a message to him that I must see him at once.''

When the boy was gone, Killian went to the chapel where he kept his pistol in the niche that had once housed the Blessed Host. He had secreted the gun there along with the powder and shot he had had on him when they lost all their other belongings. He had no alternative but to go with O'Donovan to meet the French smuggler. His share should be enough to keep Liscarrol supplied until he could find a way out of the Bill of Discovery.

''What are you doing?''

Killian looked up and smiled at Deirdre. ''Going hunting,'' he said shortly and pocketed his weapon.

Deirdre licked her lips nervously. Killian had left her side before she awoke at mid-morning and she had not immediately sought him out. She had not been seeking him out at this moment, but now that they faced each other she knew she should say something. What could she say about her actions of the night before that would neither sound foolish nor yet be a lie? ''I slept well,'' she began uncertainly.

''And glad I am to hear it,'' Killian replied smoothly. Deirdre's eyes were downcast and her cheeks were too pale for his liking, but he was determined not to mention the events of the night before if she did not do so first.

''I believe I must have been walking in my sleep during the night,'' she added softly.

''So it would appear,'' Killian answered. What had she seen before daybreak that frightened her so much that she must keep it a secret from him? Always before, even when she had thought that he was the horsemen who had struck her, she had come running to him with the accusation. "You are feeling better now?" he asked.

"Aye." Deirdre raised her head and made a small helpless gesture with her hands. "I feel so foolish." She looked at him solemnly. "We are yet a little like strangers to each other."

Killian nodded. "But we shall learn, *acushla*, we shall learn. We have time."

Without him saying so, she knew that that was his answer to her need for privacy just now. He was satisfied that she could not tell him everything. In time, when she felt stronger, she would confide in him. Perhaps she would even reveal what Brigid had told her of the legend of the ancestor.

"I will be gone for a few days." Killian curved an arm about her waist and turned her toward the door.

"Where are you going?"

"To slay a dragon for my lady fair."

Deirdre slanted a doubtful gaze at him. "You must be bored beyond reckoning. Conall and Darragh would not have been half so patient. They always kept their visits to Nantes short so that they would not grow so ill-humored from lack of activity that they would bicker with Da."

"There, you see, you know me better than you think," Killian answered, grateful that she had not taxed him with questions of where and why he was going.

He smiled above her head. "A gift rarer than pearls, a complaisant wife."

"I will not ask you where you go, only that you return, and quickly." Deirdre kept her head lowered. She did not want him to see the selfish tears that stung her eyes. He deserved to do as he saw fit. She mustered her brightest voice as she said, "Does the dragon guard a great fortune?"

"I devoutly hope so!"

She looked up in amazement. "You would not do anything wrong?"

Killian stopped and pulled her against him so that she could not see his face. "I would not do anything to harm you. If I flirt with danger, it is because it pleases me. Do you understand that?"

Deirdre nodded. She did understand. "How could I
not . . . a woman with soldiers for family?"

Killian bent and kissed her quick and hard before
releasing her. "Colin and his family will help you. Give
me a few days. I will return."

Fey struck at the tall grasses by the river with a stick.
MacShane had gone away and, not only would he not
allow her to accompany him, he had asked her to look
after Lady Deirdre.

She swung viciously at a newly sprung nettle plant,
neatly loping off its head. "*That,* for the care I'll be giving
her!"

She hunched her shoulders, dissatisfied with the vague
unease her feelings caused her. She had never before
regretted her feelings, only used them as valid reasons for
her actions. She could not give up her jealous dislike of
Lady Deirdre, not when she had MacShane's love. Their
talk had not changed her feelings in the matter, just made
it painfully clear to her how utterly hopeless her feelings
for him were.

She looked up as rooks' cries sounded overhead. On
graceful expanses of shiny black wings, the flock swooped
out of the sky and settled in the hedgerow which grew up
near the bridge. Their raucous cries and preening irritated
Fey. She wanted to be alone with her dark thoughts.
Without really thinking about it, she ran screaming toward
the birds, beating the hedge to drive them off. They took
flight immediately, all indignant cries and flapping wings.

"Are ye that daft, lass?"

Enan appeared suddenly at the end of the bridge and
came toward her, his face flushed with anger. He snatched
the stick out of her hand and broke it over his knee. " 'Tis
certain ye know nothing of the ways of the Munster. The
man who claims a rookery on his property is a man folk
respect. If the birds are run off, a man's luck will leave
with them."

Fey stared at the gawky young man. In the month that

his family at been at Liscarrol, he had not spoken a single word to her. Now he spouted rebuke.

Her chin jutted out. "I can do as I wish!"

"Not when it endangers another man's luck," Enan answered promptly. He shook his head and dislodged a reddish shock of hair which dipped across his brow and into his eyes. He pointed a finger at her. "Look at ye, strutting about in a man's breeches when ye should be properly dressed in skirt and shawl. Aren't ye ashamed?"

His words made Fey even angrier. "Ashamed? What would ye be knowing of anything, ye whey-faced cow herder!"

"I know a lass when I see one," he answered, his jaw jutting out to match her own.

Almost unwillingly Fey noticed that his chin bristled with fine golden whiskers. He was a head taller than she, and though his shirt hung shapelessly from his shoulders, those shoulders were broad and sinewy. He was not handsome but not ugly, plain-faced but for his bright blue eyes.

For reasons she could not understand, her observations made her even angrier. She turned away and picked up a new stick and began deliberately to lop off the heads of the yellow-leafed plants which grew near the water's edge.

Enan watched her in frowning disapproval for a moment but he said nothing until one leaf flew up and then drifted down into the water.

"Och! Stop!" he cried and reached out to grab her wrist. "That's *bainnicin!* Ye'll poison the fish!"

Fey lurched away and then swung her free fist up to strike him hard on the nose. With a yelp of outrage, Enan clapped a hand over his offended nose. " 'Tis bleeding," he cried accusingly.

Fey jumped back as he bared his teeth in anger, and her feet slipped on the slick grass that sloped down to the water. With a squeal she flung her arms out to catch her balance, teetered a moment uncertainly as she continued to slide backward, and then fell spread-eagled into the river.

Enan watched her flounder a moment, waiting for her to right herself, but suddenly he realized that she was not

staying afloat very well. She could not swim. With a curse
of disgust he flung himself into the water after her.

"Ye damn stupid bitch!" Enan yelled near her ear as he
caught her by the collar. "Ye could've drowned, and how
would that have looked for me? 'Drowned the lord's ward,
did ye, Enan?' Like as not they'd have hanged me over the
small loss!"

Fey allowed herself to be dragged toward the shore, too
limp with fear to protest. When he loosened his hold, she
panicked and grabbed him too tightly about the neck.

"Leave go!" Enan cried, shoving her away and scrambling onto the bank. Only then did he remember that she
could not swim and had sunk beneath the surface again.

Wading back into the waist-high water, he reached in
and grabbed the wrist of the figure floating just below the
surface. "'Tis the last time I'm sav—!"

Fey suddenly broke water near the riverbank a few yards
away, spewing water and curses in equal portions.

Enan's rosy complexion turned ashen as he looked down
at what he had drawn toward him. He almost released his
unwanted catch, but a part of him told him he should not.
When he looked up again, Fey had gained a slippery
footing on the bank. "Get me Da!" he cried. "Hurry!"

Fey turned back, annoyed to be shouted at when she had
already nearly drowned. "Get him yourself, ye fu—! Oh
God!"

Deirdre turned about in surprise at the pelting footsteps
on the stairwell. An instant later, Fey appeared on the
second floor, streaming water from every part. "Ye must
come! There's a woman! A woman drowned! Enan's
fishing her out! Come!"

Deirdre hurried after Fey, a prickling of fear along her
spine. Killian was not yet two hours gone and already
there was trouble. What should she do? What was expected
of her? She had not thought of the responsibilities Killian's
absence had placed on her, only the loneliness his going
had brought her.

When they reached the bridge, others were there before them. Colin stood in the reeds with Enan while his wife and companions stood behind. "What's happened?" she called from the bridge.

"A poor bedeviled soul is drowned," Colin called back. "Do you know her?"

Colin shook his shaggy head. "Nae! And there's not a man among us would forget if we had."

A cold salt-tinged wind, blown miles inland from the shore, enveloped Deirdre. "I'm coming down."

"Nae, m'lady. Ye won't want to do that, I'm thinking," Colin's wife answered, and a murmur of assent from the others echoed her words.

Deirdre paused at the edge of the bridge. In truth, she did not want to look upon a drowned stranger, but it seemed the appropriate thing to do, the thing her father or Killian would do. What if the woman were known locally and inquiries were made about her? She should have a description of the hapless soul.

"Ye shouldn't want a look, m'lady," Colin cautioned when Deirdre stood beside him.

The upper half of the body was covered by Colin's coat and Deirdre smiled at him in thanks. "I appreciate your concern, Colin, but as my husband is not here, it is my duty."

Colin shook his head and reluctantly bent down. "One quick look and I pray ye'll nae regret it," he said and lifted the coat.

Deirdre did not scream. She could not. It was the face of her phantom. In a few short hours the water had bloated the face until it was nearly featureless. Yet, the ravages of disease clearly remained. A huge tumor had swollen one side of the woman's head and begun eating away at her cheek, lips, and chin.

Deirdre whirled away, a hand to her mouth. The phantom had been real. "Send for the priest."

"What priest would that be?" Colin's wife asked cautiously.

"Do not play ignorant with me," Deirdre snapped, her heart beginning to slow. She turned to Colin's wife. "I know there's a priest about. He's related to O'Donovan. He came to see me my first day here. Send someone for him immediately."

"He won't bury her," Colin's wife stated flatly.

"Why not?" Deirdre questioned.

"Because she's drowned."

"What possible difference could that make?"

"I saw her when they dragged her out. A lass like that, what man would have her?"

Deirdre understood. "You think she took her life?"

The woman nodded once. " 'Tis a mortal sin, that."

"But none of us know that," Deirdre answered. "She might have slipped in the grass in the dark of night with none to see and none to hear her."

"I slipped in just now," Fey offered glumly, but when Deirdre turned to offer her a smile of thanks for her support, Fey looked away.

"Send for the priest. We will let him decide. Until then, wrap her in what you can find and have a man dig a grave in the old cemetery."

" 'Twas the French pox done that to her," Deirdre heard Colin's wife whisper to her son. "Ye want to be shy o' that sort."

Deirdre bit her lip to keep from shouting at the woman. The victim's face had been distorted by a tumor. Her brothers had been fond of relating all the details of their visits to foreign places, both the beautiful and the gruesome. In Spain they had seen whole communities where people with disfigurements of the body, tumors and diseases of every sort, gathered in hopes of miracle cures. The woman had been dying of such a disease.

She came to Liscarrol seeking my help, Deirdre thought with a shiver. *Why my help?*

Had she killed herself when she was refused, or had she simply drowned because her legs were crippled and—

"The bairn!" Deirdre swung about suddenly. "Did you find the bairn?"

"What bairn, m'lady?"

"The woman had a child with her, a babe in arms."

"How would ye be knowing that, m'lady?" Colin questioned in amazement.

"Because I saw her," Deirdre blurted out before she could think better of it. The men exchanged glances and Colin's wife moved back a step, crossing herself.

"Begging yer pardon for asking it, m'lady, but when would that have been?" Colin asked.

Stung by his open skepticism, Deirdre was about to reply when she realized how her answer might sound. The woman had drowned during the night. If Deirdre was the last to have seen her, she might become suspect or accused of mischief. Killian had told her she could not be too cautious or too careful. She might be a noble lady but she was also Irish and Catholic. There were those who would use any excuse to get rid of her, she was certain.

"There was a bairn. I know it. Look down stream, half a mile if you must, but search. The bairn might have been saved." She turned quickly and started up the slope to the bridge and no one said anything more.

Before she had crossed the bridge a cry went up from one of the men and Deirdre turned to see a man in the reeds along the bank holding aloft a dirty ragged bundle.

" 'Tis a bairn right enough!" he cried. "A lad it is! And alive!"

Deirdre retraced her steps hurriedly until she was staring at the pinched, ill-fed face of a fair-haired baby boy. She took him from the man, who was glad to be released of his burden. "I knew it!" she whispered, cradling the babe gently. "Poor wee lamb. You've come close to losing all this morning." She turned to hold the child out for the others to see but they backed away from her, their faces averted. Deirdre turned angrily to Colin. "What is wrong? 'Tis only a babe."

" 'Tis a miracle," Colin's wife murmured and crossed herself, and many of the others followed suit.

Colin looked at the young woman with eyes as wide as a child's. "How did ye know about the bairn?"

Deirdre looked into his bemused face. "Is it not enough that I did?"

He reddened and nodded. "Ah well, the lad thinks so! We'll be sending for the priest then."

Fey ran after Deirdre, too intrigued to keep up her resentment of MacShane's wife. "How did you know?" she asked breathlessly.

Deirdre glanced at the girl and decided the truth was best. "I saw the woman last night in the stable yard. I thought she was a ghost. She was terribly disfigured. I wish now I had told Killian the truth. He might have found her and saved her life."

Fey's mouth went askew. " 'Tis nae so good as the tale Enan's ma will tell." She smiled at Deirdre. "They think ye've the gift of the Sight, and 'twas that that saved the bairn."

Deirdre shook her head. The very thought of it made her feel cold. "Foolish talk."

"Is it?" Fey kicked at rock. "Brigid would nae say so." She had Deirdre's full attention now. "Ye did nae think of me listening that night Brigid fell down in a fit. Ye were too concerned with old pisspot to think of me in me bed sitting and watching. Brigid said ye had the Sight and the mark proved it. And here ye've found a bairn what should have drowned by all rights. Ye'll nae be changing their minds." She jerked her head back toward the riverbank. "Only I'm nae so gullible as the rest." With that she turned away.

Pausing in his labor, Killian wiped the sweat from his brow. It was chill on the sea, the dusk painted with cold shades of purple and gray, yet perspiration squeezed from every pore with his exertions. He and O'Donovan would be working under cover of night, emptying the hold of the French smuggler into the numerous fishing smacks that were tied up alongside it like piglets suckling a sow.

"Ye must work for yer supper here, laddie!" O'Donovan called down jovially from his position on deck.

"Getting too old for it, are you?" Killian called back.

"I've done me share over the years, done me share,"

O'Donovan answered. "Why do ye nae chuck yer shirt, MacShane? 'Twould be cooler."

Killian looked up with a grin. "And have you steal it?"

As O'Donovan roared with laughter Killian relaxed and went back to work. He bore certain scars that he showed to no man. Once he had been afraid of Deirdre's reaction to the lash marks he bore. The first time they made love, in Nantes, it had been too dark for her to see him properly. But, the night they loved again in Paris, she had put him at ease.

"You're a proud man," she had said. "I'm not so surprised you bear scars as a result. 'Tis no shame in them, but I own I would kill those who did this to you."

Killian smiled as he lifted another hogshead. Her kisses had seared his skin as surely as the lash had, and with them he had felt absolved, freed, of the stigma of having been sold to the galleys.

"What's got ye grinning like a man in his cups?" O'Donovan called down once more.

"The thought of all this lovely wine in my cellar," Killian answered.

Four hours later he sat at the captain's table and surveyed his companions. Ventura, the captain, was not known to him. He looked past Ventura to the first mate and steward. His gaze moved on to O'Donovan, who had drunk enough brandy to float this tub, and then to Cuan O'Dineen, who watched them all in stony silence.

"There you are. Your cargo in trade for mine," Ventura said as he handed the slate of inventory past Killian to O'Dineen. As Cuan reached for it Killian clamped a hand over his wrist.

O'Donovan gave him a startled look from beneath his bushy red brows. " 'Tis always Cuan who reads the cargo list."

As O'Donovan's eyes narrowed, Killian realized that the man was not nearly as drunk as he had appeared. Perhaps it was his way of watching without being watched. He released Cuan's arm. "Let him read it, by all means." He looked at Cuan. "Read it aloud."

Cuan frowned over the slate a moment, then thrust it at

Killian. ''Ye read it aloud. I've nae finished me brandy.
And be sharp, MacShane. Ventura's a man who loves
money nae less than we.''

Killian glanced at the captain, expecting a smile of
agreement, but the captain's face was blank, as if he had
been surprised by Cuan's gesture. ''With your permission?'' Killian said, and Ventura nodded slowly.

Killian glanced at the list. It contained what he might
have expected. Rum and molasses, bottles of brandy and
French wines, silks and velvets were listed on the duchesse's portion of the tablet. Irish butter, hides, wool,
flannel homespun, and *slaucan* were listed on the Irish
side. He read it again, to confirm that he had missed
nothing, and then looked up. ''It seems in order, but isn't
something missing?''

O'Donovan and the captain exchanged glances. ''What,
lad?'' O'Donovan questioned through a huge yawn.

''We unloaded at least twice as many crates as there are
listed here. And why aren't the kegs of butter and hides we
loaded listed?''

O'Donovan shrugged. ''Prices vary from month to month
so we added a bit to make up the difference. Ventura owed
us a bit from his last cargo. Now we're even again.''

Killian dropped the slate back on the table. Smuggling
was too risky a business for even the most honest of men
to be granted credit against goods owed. Ventura might
sink, be caught, or give up the trade before he could
deliver. Cash and barter were the only methods of payment.

He turned to gaze at the swarthy captain. ''Does the
duchesse know that you accept credit in her behalf?''

''Base-born bastard!'' Ventura swore and stood up.

Killian accepted with equanimity the man's baleful stare.
He was much more interested in the sleight-of-hand going
on between the first mate and the steward. He cocked his
pistol under the table. ''I would not do that,'' he said
softly, his gaze hard on the first mate's face. ''I will kill
you and have a shot left over for your captain.''

O'Donovan wheeled about, glaring at the pistol the first
mate had pulled. ''Have ye completely run mad?'' he
roared. He tore free his sword from its scabbard and

brought the flat of the blade down across the man's wrist.
The man yelped in pain and the pistol fell to the floor
where Cuan quickly scooped it up.

"Get him out! Out afore I kill him!" O'Donovan
roared. "Cuan, take the captain and crew up on deck till
I've finished me meal."

Shoving the captain and first mate before him, Cuan led
the men out of the cabin.

"A fine display," Killian said, his expression implaca-
ble. "I will keep my pistol drawn, you understand?"

O'Donovan wiped his sword blade on his sleeve and
shot it home into the scabbard. "Well now, laddie," he
began expansively as he reseated himself, "being as ye're
one of us, I'll be telling ye the truth. There's naught to do
with the duchesse here. The surplus goods are mine, and
what I exchanged them for is me business alone."

Killian laid his pistol on the table. "Weapons and
ammunition?"

"Aren't ye the cleyer lad!" O'Donovan grinned but his
eyes were cold. "Ye're of a right mind for the trade, ye
are."

"You smuggle weapons?"

"Aye! I have done so for some little time," O'Donovan
agreed pleasantly. "And a nice tidy sum it earns me, too."

"You arm the Irish?" Killian questioned.

O'Donovan squinted to bring Killian's face into view.
"I would nae have thought ye a partisan in politics,
MacShane. 'Tis the porridge of men like O'Dineen. I say
take what ye can from the present and let the future rot. If
the fools are set on fighting after the battle's lost, then *bad
cess* to them, I say! A man's entitled to find his death any
way he chooses."

Killian considered this. "That is a dangerous philosophy."

"Aye," O'Donovan answered and leaned back in his
chair. "I consider ye a clever man, MacShane." He
paused to pour a long swallow of brandy down his throat
before continuing. "But there's something a clever man
often forgets. He's nae so clever but there's others about as
clever."

"A threat," Killian said softly.

"Nae, lad, a warning. There's English looking for ye concerning a matter of cattle ye tried to sell on market day, I'm told."

"You informed on me."

O'Donovan shrugged. "The English are sorely tempted to hang me every once in a while. Fresh meat keeps them occupied."

"You bastard."

"Aye, that I am, God rest me mother's black soul!" He waved a hand. "But to yer problem. It could blow over, the business of the cows. But were ye to be found smuggling ammunition to the rapparees, well now, a man couldn't rightly talk himself out of the hangman's knot behind that, I'm thinking."

Killian's face was as granite. "Would murder not be simpler?"

O'Donovan chuckled. "Nae. I listened to you and there's sense in what you said. The duchesse would nae like ye turning up dead, and I've need of her ships to do me business." He gave Killian a sly look. "The men we captured the day ye came to Liscarrol were full of news. They said you were the duchesse's new man, come to take over the Irish trade." Killian said nothing. "To my way of thinking, we could work together and both profit without the duchesse knowing the difference."

"I could kill you and take my chances," Killian answered.

"But ye won't, MacShane, because if I die, ye die; and your lady wife will be left to face charges of being a smuggler's bride, my men will see to it. I would nae want to see her lovely neck stretched upon a gibbet. O' course, she might pixie her way out of it. She has the mark, and a man cannot know the power of a *bean feasa*. But, being that ye love her, ye will do nothing."

Killian carefully reached for his pistol. "Have you informed on me already?"

"Only the cows," O'Donovan answered, seemingly indifferent to the gun Killian held. "'Twas only to be a wee demonstration of me power. I did nae think ye'd discover me weapons business so soon. Now, well, ye must deal with me or else."

"Who else have you informed on?"

O'Donovan seemed not to hear the question. "Liscarrol has been mine these last years. Did ye nae wonder that the stable stands so well against the elements when the rest was rack and ruin? We keep our supplies there between smuggling runs. Lost a few the lads to the English a short while ago but the rest are as eager as ever." He grinned. "The hangman's knot cannot long dull the gleam o' gold."

Killian felt the bile rise into his throat but he thrust the feeling aside. "Why did you let the English hang your child?"

O'Donovan glared at him. "The lass was a sad mistake, but I had naught to do with it."

"Am I free to leave the ship and take one of the smacks back to Ireland?"

O'Donovan nodded. "Every bit of it, lad. And good luck to ye! Ye'll be needing it!"

Killian stood up, grinning broadly. "*Bad cess* to you!"

Chapter Twenty-two

"He's an ugly little brute," Fey observed from her position at Deirdre's shoulder.

"He is not. Dary's quite a handsome lad . . . for his age," Deirdre answered. She added the last qualifying phrase somewhat doubtfully, for the child they had fished from the river three days earlier was much too thin for her liking. No chubby pink cheeks or dimpled chin for him. His tiny face was sallow and withered like an old man's, and his ribs were visible through his skin. "Mrs. Mooney says that he will need a month of proper fattening before he resembles one of the cherubs."

"Mrs. Mooney should know," Fey answered. "She's a great cow, she is. Them udders of hers could suckle a calf!"

Deirdre looked up in disapproval. "Can you say nothing that does not torment, ridicule, or injure?"

Fey shrugged. "He's ugly and she's fat. 'Tis the truth, nothing more nor less."

"Mrs. Mooney graciously consented to come and live at Liscarrol with her new baby that Dary might have milk. I think she deserves a great deal of respect and courtesy. You nor I could do what she is doing."

Fey smirked. "Do ye think ye will grow as great and round as Mrs. Mooney when MacShane's seed has taken root? And yer udders, ye'll need a wheelbarrow like Mrs. Mooney!"

Deirdre turned back to Dary. "One day your mouth will get you into trouble from which no one will be able to save you."

Fey watched her fuss over the wizened babe a moment longer and then swung away toward the door. No one had time for her anymore. As much as she hated to admit it, she missed Deirdre's company even when they did not speak. Now, with the babe in the house and MacShane gone, she might as well not exist.

She walked out into the yard, considering what she should do. She still had enough money to return to France. Darce's death would be forgotten now. She could go back to Nantes and . . . and . . .

She kicked viciously at a stone and yelped as she stubbed her toe.

"*Oinseach!* Why'd ye do that!"

Fey looked up, her dark eyes blazing. "Go away, ye cow-eyed *bosthoon*!"

"Still as evil-tongued as ever," Enan said sourly. "Were ye a proper lad, I would have me licks on ye."

Fey lifted her fists. "Would ye try now?"

Enan's lips twitched. "I'd never strike a lass."

"Well, I've nothing against striking a big stupid lad," Fey cried, and with one well-aimed fist she landed a solid blow to Enan's middle.

She heard his *oooph* of surprise but he did not double up under her blow. He merely sucked in a great breath of air and then expelled it as laughter.

"Ye've a fair hook there, but I'd nae advise ye to do that again," he said when his laughter subsided.

Fey looked at him doubtfully and then, shrugging, dropped her fists. " 'Twas me best punch," she admitted begrudgingly. "Learned it from a Portuguese seaman."

"Did ye now? And were ye his doxy?"

Fey stiffened. "I was not!"

Enan shrugged. "I just wondered, what with ye dressing

like that. Me ma says only doxies and such wear men's britches in public.''

"What yer ma knows would nae fill a thimble," Fey shot back.

For the first time Enan's expression hardened into anger. "I will thank ye to keep yer mouth respectful when ye speak of me ma, or, lass or no, I'll make ye sorry ye ever spoke!"

The usual mutinous look marred Fey's features as she said, "I do nae care if ye never speak to me again." She spun on her heel and marched away.

She was surprised that he followed her. She had struck him, insulted his mother, and made him angry. By all rights he should never speak to her again. She spun around just before she reached the bridge. "Why do ye follow me?"

Enan shrugged, his slow, almost shy smile making the most of his ordinary face. "Ye're a strange girl, that ye are. I'm nae so attracted to lasses as lasses go. But ye, ye stomp about in them boots, swaggering enough to make a bull blush, and where ye go, ye spread anger and bad feelings. I've a cause to wonder why ye're so miserable.''

"'Tis no business of yers," Fey answered, but she was a bit unnerved to have herself summed up so poorly.

"Me ma says—" He eyed her warningly before he continued. "Me ma says 'tis only one thing can make a lass so miserable for so long and that's a man. Did ye lose yer beau?''

"I've nae beau and never have." Fey turned away but not, she knew, before he saw the blush creeping into her face.

"Me ma says yer foster mother could get yer beau back, were she of a mind. There's charms and potions known only to a *bean feasa* that can make a lad fall in love with the lass what wants him."

"She would nae help me," Fey answered in a small voice. "She's won him for herself."

"'Tis MacShane ye love?''

She did not mean to say it; it just slipped out; and Fey cringed instinctively against the laughter she expected to accompany her admission, but she heard nothing. After a moment she unhunched her shoulders and looked up at him.

Enan was staring at her, his bright eyes wide in amazement. "Ye love the master? *Mavrone!* 'Tis a sad thing, that. Only, tell me, why would ye be wanting him?"

Fey's mouth fell open. "Are ye mad? He's strong and fine and brave and kind and—"

"And old," Enan finished with a self-satisfied grin. "All them qualities are good ones, but what's to separate him from many another, like meself, for instance."

"Yerself?" Fey questioned scornfully.

Enan blushed but he held his ground. "I said, for instance. I'm nae a beauty but I do not put the rooks to flight. I'm strong. Saved ye from drowning, didn't I? And I'm brave and kind, when necessary."

"And young," Fey finished in derision.

"Young and healthy," Enan amended. "Well?"

"Well what?"

"What's wrong with me?"

Fey eyed him coldly. "I do nae love ye."

"How would ye know?"

Fey's dark brows winged up to disappear behind her bangs. "That's a fair stupid question even from ye."

Enan's cheeks reddened even more but he would not quit the field. "Ye say ye love a man that belongs to another. Ye say ye love him for qualities I possess, and then ye say ye don't love me but ye do love him. 'Tis easy to see who's the stupid one."

"MacShane doesn't make fun of me," Fey fairly shouted at him.

"Ah well, he has me there. He's the better man, I see it now."

Fey kicked him in the shin with her boot and he howled; but when she tried to run away, he let go of his ankle and gave chase, catching her before she had gone more than a few steps.

"Let me go! I'll scratch yer eyes out!" Fey cried as he hauled her backward against his long slender frame.

His hand on her waist turned her about until she looked

up into his laughing face. "Well now, I'm a brave man and nae so afraid of a few scratches." He ducked his head quickly and suddenly his mouth was on hers.

Too stunned to move, Fey remained still under his kiss. Even when he lifted his head she stood staring up mutely at him.

"Is that the way of it, then?" Enan questioned in mild surprise.

"Way of what?" Fey asked.

"To shut yer lovely mouth, *colleen dhas*. A *kippeen* or a *pogue*, I did nae know which it would take to do the trick." He grinned cockily. "'Tis glad I am to know ye prefer kissing."

Fey balled up her fists but Enan gave her no chance to use them. He dragged her slender body once more against his, and to the surprise of them both she lifted not fists but gently curling hands that cradled his head and brought his mouth down once more on hers.

Fey did not know much about kissing; but she had watched Deirdre and MacShane at the exercise often enough to know that it was pleasurable, and she was not disappointed. A cow herder Enan might be, but he knew a thing or two about kisses. When they finally broke apart, she was smiling and he was gazing at her with new insight.

"Ye're a fair fey creature," Enan said huskily. "But I would nae grieve over MacShane any longer. Ye've a beau, if ye want." He glanced down at her. "But only if ye wear skirts like a proper lass. I do nae want the countryside thinking Enan Ross is sweet on a lad!"

Fey stared at him, not knowing what to think of the strange emotions tumbling through her. If she did indeed love MacShane, how could Enan's hot hands and warm kisses make her feel giddy and happy and hungry for more?

She pushed out of his arms and he let her go. She lifted her chin. "I do nae need yer charity. Keep yer kisses!"

As she turned and walked away, she heard his gentle mocking laughter and knew that he knew what she had felt in his arms.

The sound of horses was faint but both of them turned

together as the pounding rode the wind toward them. Enan recognized them first. "English!" he cried and grabbed Fey by the wrist, dragging her after him. "Go to the house and tell Lady MacShane. I'll call me da and the others. There's trouble in the wind!"

Fey did as she was told, but Mrs. Mooney was there ahead of her. Deirdre turned with a worried frown to her as she entered the Great Hall. "Did you see them, too?"

Fey nodded. "Bloody red coats and all. Enan says it means trouble."

"Perhaps it's my cousin Neil," Deirdre answered. "Killian wrote him to say we married. Perhaps he's come for a visit."

"With English soldiers?" Mrs. Mooney questioned doubtfully.

Deirdre sighed. "I don't know. Whoever it is, we must greet them. I wish Killian had returned."

The two other women shared her wish.

"Ye'd better give Dary to me," Mrs. Mooney said, reaching out for the boy. "And I would nae mention him to the others, yer ladyship."

"I mean to ask about the lad's mother," Deirdre replied. "She may have worked for someone they know. She would be easy to identify. I want her tombstone to have a proper name."

"Were ye to get her proper name, ye'd lose the lad," Mrs. Mooney warned sternly.

"To his relatives?" Deirdre questioned.

"Yer ladyship," Mrs. Mooney answered with a barely contained sigh, "do ye nae know the law? An orphan child, be he Irish and Catholic, can be fostered only by a person of the Protestant faith. They will take him away from ye, as if he had nae suffered enough."

Deirdre shook her head. "Certainly that is not the case. He would be brought up to be a Protestant."

"That he would, and so much the worse for us all," Mrs. Mooney answered as she turned to leave.

Deirdre looked at herself and shook her head. "I look frightful. Cousin Neil will think me without any accomplishments at all."

"What accomplishments would he like?" Fey asked sourly. "There's nae a harp or violin about. We've nae china or crystal. We've little enough food and ye'll nae be sharing my portion with a redcoat."

Deirdre arranged her hair with the comb that Killian had whittled for her. She had only a few hairpins and no mirror with which to check the results. She turned to Fey. "Will I do?"

" 'Tis too good for the English," Fey answered and stomped off.

With that dubious compliment in mind, Deirdre straightened her jacket, which she had hastily buttoned over her poorly mended gown, and gave her faded riding skirt a final twitch.

The sound of horses approaching drove all thoughts from her mind as she went to the door.

Dismay was Deirdre's first reaction as she gazed at the yard of red-coated soldiers. There were a full dozen of them and none of their faces were familiar. Certainly her cousin was not among them. As the officer dismounted she folded her hands to wait, and another thought came to her. They were dirty and their horses were lathered; these men had ridden far and hard. Perhaps they were chasing some luckless soul who had broken one of the many laws of the land.

"Good day to you, ma'am," the officer said in English as he approached.

"Good day," Deirdre answered in English.

"You speak English," the young man answered, his face beaming. "Good luck, that. My Gaelic is poor at best. Would there be a man by the name of MacShane living here?"

"I am Mrs. MacShane," Deirdre answered, her voice as cool and crisp as the spring air. She gave him a single piercing glance. "Why do you clutter up my yard with your horses and men?"

The young officer looked as if she had shut the door preemptorally in his face. "Begging your pardon, ma'am, but I've come on a matter concerning your husband. May I speak with him?"

"No."

The answer left him little to work from. "Why not?" he asked weakly.

"Because he is unavailable," Deirdre replied and started to close the door. If the English sought Killian, it meant that he was in danger.

"We've a warrant for him," the officer called. "We have a right to search."

Deirdre turned around slowly. "As I believe the English are responsible for the present state of my home, you will permit me to be astonished at the thought that there may be something of interest you left behind. The third-floor ceiling has caved in. There is not a stick of furniture. As for tapestries and draperies, we have none. You will find nothing." She turned away once more.

"We look for something more substantial," the officer called after her.

Deirdre turned back. "What, may I ask?"

"Black cattle, Irish cattle."

Deirdre smiled. "You may find them on any hill or in any valley of the county, sir. Cows are notorious for their roaming habits. However, not a single cow resides inside my residence. You have my solemn word on it."

The murmur of laughter among his men cost the officer a little of his composure, and Deirdre smiled an acknowledgment of her small victory.

"Are you Catholic, ma'am?" the officer questioned sharply.

"Are you a fool, sir?" Deirdre replied promptly. "Or perhaps you have not heard, since you English change your laws more often than your clothes, Catholicism is all but outlawed in Ireland."

The young man's pleasant face stiffened. "You have not answered my question, ma'am."

"Nor do I intend to," she replied. "It is not yet against the law to *be* Catholic, sir, only to practice the religion. Is that not so?"

The officer nodded his head reluctantly.

"Then I am not bound to answer. I do not see that it matters, if cows are your business."

"Your husband, ma'am, he is a Catholic?"

"Did you not hear me?" Deirdre asked impatiently.

The officer pulled a parchment from his coat. "I have a document here, signed by one Killian MacShane. This is a petition for instruction in the established Church. What do you know of this?"

"No more and no less than you say," Deirdre answered evenly, but she was suddenly very nervous. What madness had Killian undertaken? The established Church? That was the Church of England!

"He attempted on last market day to sell a number of cows which he claims belong to him. A Discoverer brought a petition against him because he has not yet received his certificate of acceptance into the true faith. What do you know of that?"

"The cows, do you mean? They are ours. As for Discoverers, whatever that is, I know nothing. Please feel free to help yourselves to the well before you leave." Deirdre turned toward the door, feeling like a weather vane in a gale.

"We're searching for a priest hereabouts. One Father O'Donovan."

Deirdre turned slowly to give herself a chance to think. When she faced the young officer she could see nothing but the image of a tiny, helpless corpse. "The only O'Donovan of my acquaintance, and I admit that it was after the fact, is that of a tiny lass left hanging from the branches of a huge oak near Kilronane. If that was your handiwork, sir, I hope your mother lives to hear of it and you live to regret it!"

The young man turned as bright a shade of red as his uniform. "I had nothing to do with that, ma'am."

"But you know of it, sir, you know of it. And you did not cut her down. For that I will never forgive you!"

This time Deirdre managed to reach the door and slam it firmly behind her. She sagged against it, but every sense was alert as she listened to the men beyond the door. At first she heard nothing, and then, mercifully, came the sounds of retreating horses.

"Well, who'd have believed it of ye," Fey exclaimed in

genuine delight from the step of the stairwell on which she sat.

Deirdre smiled at her as she came forward. "I was rather good, wasn't I? Just like a play." She smiled and then burst into laughter, and to her delight Fey joined her and they embraced.

"Mavrone! Was that a near thing!" Mrs. Mooney cried as she entered from the rear door.

"I did nae understand it all, but I heard enough," added Colin's wife, Mrs. Ross. "Yer ladyship, ye were a wonder!"

"Thank you. I only hope I've shamed them enough to keep them away for a few days. Killian must hurry home." She did not add that it was more imperative than ever. If he hoped to fool the English with that piece of paper that he had signed, he was wrong. They would come again. She smiled uncertainly at the woman who held Dary, wondering just how much any of them understood. The respect she and Killian had among these people was tenuous, and a mistake might ruin it. "Put Dary to bed, Mrs. Mooney. I'll be out in the orchard. It appears a few of the trees may survive with a bit of care."

"I'll take him," Fey volunteered, scooping Dary from the woman's arms. "He's still ugly," she said after a quick look at his sleeping face, "but he's nae so ugly as Enan!"

It was an hour after nightfall before Deirdre heard the faint sounds of boot steps outside. She rose from the floor and reached the door just as a knock sounded.

"Killian?" she called softly, her hand poised on the crossbar.

"It'll be Colin, yer ladyship," came the reply.

"Come in, Colin," she said when the door was open, but he shook his head.

"Ye'll be having a visitor of another sort below in the kitchen, yer ladyship. A particular kind of visitor, if ye take my meaning."

"Father O'Donovan?"

"*Mister* Teague O'Donovan, if ye would, yer ladyship."

"Of course, Mister O'Donovan," Deirdre answered, chastened by this gentle reminder.

"If ye'll unbolt the servants' door, he'll be on the stairwell. I'll be keeping an eye on the far side of the river." He jerked his head toward the distant hill where a faint glow in the trees marked the English soldiers' camp.

"He should have waited a few days until they were gone," Deirdre said.

"Would ye have a man the likes of Teague O'Donovan afraid of an Englishman's shadow?" Colin asked. " 'Tis enough he came after they were gone. Bolt the door and know that none will come through it except if Colin Ross has given up his life."

Deirdre shut the door with a shiver. Colin's tone had not been one to mock. He was deadly serious about the danger in which Liscarrol lay this night with a priest being within its walls. Two months earlier she would not have believed such precautions were necessary. Now she knew she had come home not to the Ireland of her memory but to a land touched by the flames of prejudice and passion and faith.

She opened the rear door to admit a man who looked even thinner and more ragged than she remembered. "Father," she whispered, and bent her head to receive his blessing when the door was safely shut and bolted.

"Bless you, my child," Teague O'Donovan answered, briefly touching her hair. "Why have you sent for me?"

"Come and warm yourself by the fire, Father, while I tell you." Deirdre indicated the way. "There's buttermilk and porridge left from dinner."

The priest shook his head. "There's many a more deserving man who goes without this night. I will offer up my sacrifice for them."

Deirdre slanted a curious look at him. "But, Father, that will not feed the hungry, and it does waste the precious food we have. Is there no joy to be had in this land from even the simplest pleasures?"

"Only a daughter of the aristocracy, Lady Deirdre, would speak so carelessly of the poverty and misery of those beneath you."

Deirdre's eyes widened. "I am of noble birth but that does not make me an uncaring tyrant, Father. 'Profess not the knowledge . . . that thou hast not,' " she quoted daringly in Latin.

Stung by her adroit turning of his gentle rebuke into seeming gratitude, Teague could only stare at her for a moment. Then he remembered the mark upon her shoulder. This woman was not like others. Perhaps that fact kept her from feeling awe before one of God's chosen . . . or perhaps it enabled her to see through his piety to his weaknesses.

Deirdre regretted her words as soon as she had said them. This was not Darragh or Conall that she could throw his insults back in his face. "Father, forgive me. I meant no disrespect."

"I will sit by your fire and eat your food that we may share the community of spirit," he answered at last.

As he sat cross-legged before the hearth with a bowl of porridge in his hands, Deirdre told him of the drowned woman and her son. Afraid that he would misunderstand her dreams, she omitted her reason for walking Liscarrol's grounds that night, and spoke instead of being frightened by the woman's sudden appearance.

When she was done, the priest nodded his head slowly. "It is as Colin Ross told me." He looked up from his bowl. "But what of the magic they claim you performed?"

"Finding the child? But I have explained. The woman was ill. She told me she wanted me to help save her child. It was not magic but reasoning to expect that the bundle she carried was a bairn." Deirdre spoke earnestly. "I might have been wrong. If I had been, there would be no talk of magic."

"The woman came to you, asked for your help. Why *your* help?"

"I don't know," Deirdre answered uncomfortably, because she was beginning to remember the woman's words.

"Did she think you could remove her ailment?"

Deirdre started, though the priest had spoken in a low tone. "She seemed to think I could," she said slowly, wishing she did not need to speak at all. "I do not know why. She addressed me as *bean feasa*." She hung her head, feeling guilty though she knew she should not. "I have never claimed any power; I have done nothing to make anyone think such a thing."

"You've done enough," the priest remarked obliquely. He hesitated a moment, remembering MacShane's warning that his wife must hear nothing of the old legend, but MacShane was not born or raised on the sod, Irish though he might be. He could not understand the depth of feeling and respect accorded ancient beliefs. If the lady were to be sincere in her repudiation of her heritage, then she must understand it fully.

"You have a mark upon your shoulder," he began, his eyes hard upon her face. "There's a legend about such a mark. You know of it?"

Deirdre nodded reluctantly. She could not lie to a priest, though she had omitted some of the truth in her story. "I know a little, not all."

"I did not believe the tale of your return until I saw the mark myself, and it is as legend predicted." He paused, feeling the night's chill though the fire glowed healthily. "You are the second to bear the mark. I will tell you what I have heard about the first."

When he had finished repeating the story he had told Killian, Deirdre sat with her arms wrapped about her middle. She felt faintly ill, as though some ague would soon be upon her.

"The mother came to you with her babe because she had come to me and I could not cure her. She was dying and she knew it. No worldly power could save her, and I do not claim for myself powers reserved for God."

"Neither do I!" Deirdre answered. "Father, believe me, I have spoken to no one of the legend, showed no one the mark."

"And yet Mrs. Ross has seen it," the priest replied.

The memory of the woman entering in upon her and Killian as they were about to make love came back to Deirdre and she blushed. "She came upon me suddenly, while I was dressing."

The priest finished his porridge in silence. Only then did

he speak. "Why have you sent for me, to find a home for the orphan bairn?"

"Oh no, Dary can remain here. I want you to baptize him, if his mother has done so not already."

Teague O'Donovan felt the breath of fear on his neck. "That I will not do."

"Why not?"

The priest shook his head, rising. "Folk believe the bairn was saved from drowning by fairy magic. His mother died under dubious circumstances. Until it can be proved that magic had no part in these events, I will do nothing."

Deirdre rose indignantly to her feet. "You are a priest. You cannot fear the fairy boughs and straw charms of simple people."

"I do not fear them. But I will not be a party to abetting their beliefs. The saving of the bairn could be a devil's trick. I'll not be drawn into it."

"Baptizing Dary will make him a child of God. How can you be certain that it was not God's doing? Could He not have worked the miracle of sparing the baby's life to demonstrate the goodness of His spirit? Why must goodness be questioned as the devil's tricks?"

Teague shook his head. The lady made sense, so much so that he feared to glance at her again. If she was as pure of heart as she seemed, she could be a formidable ally. Yet, he must be careful, wary.

"If you will come to Mass when next I am in the valley, and take the Host, I will baptize the bairn then."

"I will," Deirdre agreed enthusiastically, but the priest was already moving away from her toward the door through which he had come. "How will I know where to find you?"

"Mrs. Ross will bring you." he answered over his shoulder and slipped out into the night.

"You're home! You're home!" Tears of relief blurred Deirdre's vision as she was caught up in Killian's arms and swung around in the yard.

"Aye, Dee! Home!" Killian hugged her hard before setting her back on the ground. She gazed up at him, her green eyes as bright as the first patch of spring shamrocks in the valley. Her face was thinner, Killian noted in concern, and those lush green eyes were ringed with dark crescents of worry and discomfort. The hands he held in his were thickened by blisters and the beginnings of calluses. She was still beautiful, but how long would that beauty remain if she had to live like a wild thing in the west country of Ireland?

Deirdre put a self-conscious hand to her hair as he continued to stare at her. "Have I grown ugly, or have you forgotten entirely what I look like, you've been gone so long?"

"I've forgotten nothing, Dee," Killian answered in a voice roughened by emotion. "I'm sorry I've been away so long."

"More than two weeks!" Deirdre complained and tugged the black whiskers at his chin. "You've grown a beard. Where have you been?"

Killian smiled suddenly. "Bartering, lass, like any gypsy you see on the roads." He turned to show her the pony cart he had ridden into the yard. "I've gifts from so far away you'll never guess them all."

Deirdre looked at the brimming cart for the first time. "Where did you get the money for the cart and the pony?"

"Bartered for them," Killian answered, and then with his hands on her shoulders he pushed her gently toward the back of the cart. "Stand here and see what I've brought you."

As she watched, he slipped a knife under the knot that held the canvas cover tight and then threw back the cover. There were so many things piled in the cart that she could not take in everything at once. The item that captured her attention first was the largest. "You've bought a bed!"

"Aye, that I did. 'Twas time we had one. I've grown weary of that slate floor. It wears like the very devil on a man's knees."

"You don't sleep on your knees," Deirdre answered as

she ran a hand appreciatively along one long branch of black bog oak that was a bedpost.

"Sleeping's not the only thing a man does in bed," Killian answered and was pleased to see her blush. "My first several sons shall be born on this bed."

"First . . . several," Deirdre echoed in faint dismay.

"Aye, and we'll have a lass or two to round out the number," Killian added.

"Look! Is that velvet? It is! My velvet gown," Deirdre cried in delight as she pulled it free. She turned to him. "You've been to Cork."

"Aye, so I have. There are wools, velvets, and even a silk gown," Killian answered. "I brought a pair of chairs and a table. They're not as fine as those you're accustomed to, but they'll do."

Deirdre's face was wreathed in a huge smile. "Aye, they'll do, Killian MacShane. And so you'll know, I love you!"

Killian folded his arms across his chest in satisfaction as she filled her arms with the gifts he had claimed as his share of the smugglers' horde. He had pleased her, and that's all he had wanted. Later he would tell her how his trip to Cork had forestalled the Bill of Discovery against him. It was quite amazing what a few cases of French brandy could buy. His cattle were to be released and the petition dropped. As for the rest of his adventure, the less she knew, the better. O'Donovan's threat was real, and the investigation he had begun against the man must not leak out.

"Leave the rest for Colin and Enan to bring in," he said as he took the bundle from her. "You have yet to show your husband a proper welcome."

Deirdre smiled saucily at him. "I thought you did not want to wear out your poor knees."

Killian grinned at her over the pile in his arms. "And so I was thinking on my journey home. You're not to know but there's ways, lass, of pleasing a man that don't wear out his knees."

Deirdre colored to the roots of her hair but she hurried after him as he strode toward the house.

"It doesn't need a great mind to know where they're going and what they'll be doing when they get there," Enan Ross exclaimed from where he stood watching in the doorway of the stable.

"Shut up!" Fey glowered up at him. "Ye do nae know everything."

"I know enough to please a lass, were I of a mind," he answered cockily.

"Yer mind does nae come into it," Fey shot back. "And as for the lass who'd choose ye to bed her, she'd must have a mind smaller than me *loodeen.*"

"I could prove ye wrong, were ye nae so afraid of me loving ye," Enan said as he reached out for her.

"I'd rather eat turf!" Fey cried and swung away from him.

Enan smiled as he watched her walk across the yard. His ma was wrong about her. Were she a loose girl, she would have succumbed to his blandishments long ago. It had been two weeks since he had fished her out of the river, and she had done no more than allow him to kiss her on one occasion. But he could wait. She was just beginning to blossom into womanhood. When her hips filled out and her hair grew in, she would please him right enough. Already her breasts had begun to jiggle as she walked. Aye, he would wait, for he was barely fifteen. There was the widow beyond the valley who had once proved to him that he was a man and might again, if he brought her a gift. When Fey was ready, he would make a proper bride of her.

"Never fear, *madilse!*" he called after her. " 'Tis proper wed I'll see ye!"

An hour later Deirdre's head lay on Killian's bare chest, her naked thighs riding along either side of his waist. "You were right, my love. There are other ways."

Killian slowly opened dreamy eyes. She sat up astride him, the thick, billowy golden cloud of her hair blanketing her shoulders. "You are more beautiful than life."

Deirdre laid a finger against his lips. "No, never say that. It is unlucky to think yourself too pleased with life." She shrugged. "I myself am only moderately pleased."

Killian frowned. "Did I not satisfy you, lass?"

"Aye, you did," she answered, her eyes softening as she gazed down at him. "You please me so much it frightens me."

"Why?"

Deirdre wet her lips, suddenly shy. "Because . . . because no matter how much you please me, I always think of what the next time will be like. That is greedy, ungracious. I feel I want to gorge myself on you, to never let you rise, ever. Do you understand?"

Killian nodded, unable to voice the deep emotions that her words roused within him. He raised his hands to her shoulders, resting them lightly there, and then brought them in slow descent down over her collarbone to her breasts, which he squeezed lightly, eliciting a soft open-mouthed gasp from her.

He would not tell her today, could not. Was it selfish and perhaps cruel to know what he must say to her and yet wait, allowing her to give in completely to the joy of the moment? He could not believe so, not when she looked down at him with a passion that made him melt and grow hard in the same instant. They needed this day, these hours, to cement a loving that must withstand a parting.

His hands moved to her waist and he lifted her slightly to bring them together, reveling in her sigh of joy as he slid within her; and then he forgot all but the glory and magic of their union.

Killian glared at the glossy surface of the bog-oak table at which he sat with his supper, not lifting his eyes until he thought he had some measure of control over his temper. "You sent the English soldiers packing without so much as a cup of water?"

Deirdre's chin jutted out. "There's no reason to shout. I did what seemed necessary."

"As you did with the child and sending for a priest. God bless, woman! You might have gotten yourself arrested for any or all of those things!"

Deirdre stood up and folded her arms across her chest. "I did what I thought was best. Were you here, you might have chosen to do else. But you were not here."

"I've explained—"

"You explained nothing, nor did I ask you to," Deirdre cut in. "You've been roaming about, doing who knows what, and I do not complain about it. But you will not shout at me under my own roof!"

Fey looked up from her perch on a wine barrel. "The pair of ye sound like fish mongers!"

"Stay out of this!" Deirdre and Killian cried in unison.

Fey rose. "Well, that's telling me, I'm sure. Scream at each other and wake the bairn, for all I care. I'll nae rock him to sleep again." She stomped off.

Killian suddenly changed color. "The bairn. I forgot he was actually here."

Deirdre gave him a blighting look. "You were too busy shouting to think of him. His name's Dary, at least for now. Mrs. Mooney's a fine wet nurse. Later we may find another home for him."

"You'll do that now," Killian said grimly.

"Why should I? I'm capable of looking after him."

Killian raised his head. "You won't be here to look after him after tomorrow."

Deirdre gazed at him in shocked surprise. "Why not? Where are we going?"

"*You* are going back to France," Killian said in clipped tones. "Don't even question it. 'Twill do you no good to rail at me. Back to Nantes you go until I say you're to return."

Deirdre was not about to argue. She was so taken aback that she could think of nothing whatever to say for a moment. "Why?" was all she said in the end.

"Because Ireland's not a safe place for a lady. Look at you, playing the wife of an impoverished farmer with no crops and fewer cows. The crop of blisters on your lovely hands are all we've to show for our months here. You have nothing to wear, less to eat, and now a babe on your hands that could cause you to be arrested. Oh, we're a fine pair, we are!"

"I thought I looked rather well," Deirdre said primly, forcing Killian to look up at her.

After a thorough scrubbing she had donned the dark wine velvet gown Killian had brought her. It shone vibrantly against the smooth skin of her neck and bosom, and she felt beautiful for the first time in months.

"Aye, you warm my heart, Dee, but that's the very reason I must get you away. There's trouble. If the English came once, you can believe they will come again."

"What will you do to pacify them?" Deirdre questioned innocently. He had told her of the Bill of Discovery and how he had escaped it, but he had not mentioned the petition she had been shown by the soldier seeking admission into the English Church.

"What I must," Killian muttered.

"Does that include collusion on the loss of your soul?"

Killian turned cold inside. "Who told you?"

Deirdre's eyes flashed. "Why did *you* not tell me? Why must I hear of your schemes from strangers? Do you not trust me?"

Killian stood up. "I wanted to spare you that."

"What, the fact that my husband is capable of blithely turning his coat without turning a hair? *Mille murdher!* I am not a child to be protected from the matters of adults."

"It has nothing to do with that," Killian roared, drowning out the end of her speech. "This is not a parlor game or a romp, Dee. Our lives may hang on every action we take or refuse to make. The green meadows and hills filled with quiet times and sweet tunes are gone. Can you not see that every man, woman, and child who calls himself an Irishman is fighting for his very survival?"

"I'm not too good to fight for mine," Deirdre answered stoutly.

"No, Dee, you're not. But I cannot think on what might happen if you lose." Killian turned away, amazed by the unsteadiness of his voice. For years he had faced the danger of death or maiming. It had never frightened him, never fostered within him this stark cold terror that the thought of losing Deirdre brought to mind.

Deirdre came up behind him and put her arms about his

shoulders. "Perhaps I have been foolish or careless, but not out of ignorance, my husband. I see what war has done to my home, what unjust laws and greed have done, but it is my home. I wanted you to make it yours."

Killian stood still within her embrace. He felt as cold and rigid as the granite peaks of the Shehy Mountains. "I want to keep you safe and I do not know if that is within my power. Whatever I have done, or will do, I do it for you."

Deirdre leaned her forehead against his back, smiling through the tears that had risen. "Two months ago you said you did not know how to be a good husband. You have learned, my love."

Killian turned in her arms and Deirdre caught in his eyes the gleaming of tears which would not fall. "You will then trust my judgment?"

"Only if you do not ask me to leave you," she answered.

Killian sighed like a bellows and then the beginnings of a smile lifted his mouth. "It would be like you to return as quickly as I sent you away."

"Aye. Like bath water thrown into the wind, I'd rebound with unpleasant swiftness."

Killian hugged her so tightly that she moaned. "Then you must at least promise me you will not leave Liscarrol or speak to anyone until I have settled matters with the authorities."

"Very well, my love."

"And under no circumstances are you to be seen with Teague O'Donovan."

"What of the Mass and Dary's christening?"

Killian's expression became one she had seen only once before. "If you set one foot out of this house without my permission, I'll wedge you into one of these wine barrels and ship you to the duchesse!"

Deirdre stiffened. "Mention that woman's name again and I'll be the one sealing *you* in a barrel!"

Killian bent his head and kissed her. "The matter is settled."

"Aye. For now," Deirdre murmured.

Chapter Twenty-three

"Lady MacShane, 'tis to be a fine new moon rising just before daybreak," Mrs. Mooney said as she laid a wooden plate of oat bread before Deirdre. "There's nothing quite like a Sabbath moon. A body could do worse than to rise to greet a morning moon."

Deirdre looked up in surprise, for Mrs. Mooney had seldom spoken to her in the weeks since Killian's return, and then only when he was not present, as he was now. A single quick nod of the woman's head confirmed what Deirdre suspected. Word had come that Father Teague would be saying Mass at daybreak somewhere nearby.

"Thank you, Mrs. Mooney. Where do you think would be the best view of such a sight?"

"Och, for a young body such as yerself, 'twould be no great journey to take the path to the top of the mountain beyond the river. Following the right shoulder would bring ye to the top for a grand view."

"That sounds like a great deal of exercise for a small reward," Killian said between a bite of oat bread and a sip of buttermilk.

"Perhaps for you it is," Deirdre replied genially. "But I

have not stretched my legs in a great while, I am cramped in every limb. I miss horseback riding most of all.''

Killian gave her a quick warm smile. "Then take the pony."

Deirdre could not hide her surprise. "Do you mean it?"

Killian nodded. "Would I deny you a rare fine moon rise?"

"Will you come with me, Mrs. Mooney?"

The woman nodded and turned away.

"Then 'tis settled," Deirdre announced and picked up the first piece of her supper.

"Be careful, *mo cuishle,*" Killian added in a low voice.

Deirdre glanced at him suspiciously but his expression was bland. "Of course."

The night dragged by so slowly that Deirdre could barely lie still in bed. She was glad that Killian slept so heavily and soundly beside her, for he would have guessed that she was up to no good had he been aware of her restlessness.

Finally she heard a scraping in the room below and knew that Mrs. Mooney had been awakened either by Dary or by Colin's wife, Mrs. Ross. Moving as quietly as possible, she slipped out of the bed and was immediately enveloped in the icy breath of darkness. She had placed her clothes on the floor beside the bed so that she would not need a light, and she dressed quickly, adding a woolen shawl over her velvet gown.

"There ye be!" Mrs. Mooney greeted in a loud whisper as Deirdre descended the stairs. "I was about to come up for ye."

"Will you lace me up the back before we go?" Deirdre asked, lifting her shawl.

Outside, the pony had been bridled and a blanket thrown over his back, and Colin held his head while Enan lifted her onto the animal's back. "Would ye want to be holding wee Dary, yer ladyship, seeing as ye're riding?"

Deirdre nodded and took the child Mrs. Mooney held, folding her woolen shawl over his thin garments. "Will Mrs. Ross be coming too?"

Colin shook his head. "His lordship will be waking

before we return and wanting his breakfast, no doubt. Sila agreed 'twould be she who stayed. We must go, yer ladyship, or 'tis late we'll be!''

It was still dark when they set out, but during the twenty minutes of traversing the valley the black gloom gave way to a blue-gray twilight. Thick white wisps of mist hovered over the path of the river and circled the tops of the trees to the south. As they began to climb, Deirdre finally ceased to shiver with cold. Dary stirred in her arms, his face a pale blue amid the covers.

"Today we're making a good Catholic of you," she whispered as she held him tighter. "You must live up to that honor, my *bouchal*, for 'tis certain a number put themselves in mortal danger for you."

The pony's hooves sounded sharply in the silent morning air, each a distinct *click* upon the granite stones as they climbed.

When at last they reached the shoulder of the hill, the morning sky was bathed in pastel shades of blue, mauve, and rose beneath the deep green sod of the surrounding countryside.

Deirdre did not realize they were not alone until she looked back over the rise and saw other dark shapes like themselves climbing the hill. For an instant fear gripped her, but as she pointed them out to Colin he merely nodded.

"That'll be the O'Dineens and the O'Donovans," he whispered low.

The "church" was nothing more than a deserted hillside, the altar a simple crucifix set up on a huge boulder laid on its side by time. It was a mean and demeaning place for this holiest of rituals, and she wished fervently for the graceful archways and stained-glass windows of a real church.

She did not recognize Father Teague among the dark knots of men and women clustered together, nor, she noticed, did any man speak to another as they took up their positions before the makeshift altar.

Deirdre knelt in the grass with the others, feeling the sharp prick of heather stubs through the velvet of her gown, but she did not give voice to her complaints. Lowering her head, she breathed deeply of the air tinged with salt from the sea more than fifteen miles to the south.

Slowly she began to relax and gradually she took up the ancient psalm that had begun at the far side of the congregation. No one had to warn them to sing softly, but that did not dim the beauty of the tune or the fullness of belief that surrounded her.

If only Killian had come, she thought fleetingly, ashamed now that she had not told him what she intended to do and asked him to join her.

The Mass began without preamble. Suddenly a man in cassock appeared before the altar. He emerged from the crowd and never turned back toward them during the service. When the moment of distribution of the Host came, he pulled his hood forward over his head and stood with his face in shadow. But for his voice intoning, "Corpus Christi," he might have been no more substantial than the sooty shadow he cast on the dew-drenched grasses.

Following the others, Deirdre knelt before the priest and extended her tongue for the Host.

For an instant the priest did not move, the Host held suspended by his fingers, and Deirdre raised her head to look at him. And then the Host was in her mouth, and he was moving on down the line of kneeling supplicants.

She rose and turned to walk away only to catch her breath in awe.

The moon had risen in the east, a silver crescent illuminating the surrounding clouds tinging their edges rose.

The fragile instant of beauty, of colors and light, went as quickly as it came but not before Deirdre absorbed the moment forever in her memory.

How wrong she had been. The canopy of the heavens was a more lovely and fitting setting for God's work than any manmade beauty ever could be.

This was why she had come home, to be a part once more of the wild, ever-changing beauty of a land whose heart was not its monuments or its politics but the natural constant vibrancy of its nature and the people who loved it more than bread and hearth.

When the moment came for her to step forward with Dary, she did so proudly and without fear that she would be recognized. If there were spies on this hillside, they could do nothing now. This moment belonged to the honest, God-fearing souls who had risked their lives to be a part of an outlawed worship of God. If only Killian were here the moment would be perfect.

The priest did not look at her as he performed the baptismal ceremony and Dary was named Dary Finian Fitzgerald, given in foster care to Lady Deirdre Fitzgerald MacShane.

It was over quickly, and before she turned away from the altar the faithful had begun to disappear into the mists below. The touch at her elbow surprised her and she turned back to face Father Teague.

He had lifted back his cowl and his fair hair hung in damp strings before his brow. " 'Tis a brave but dangerous thing you've done, taking in an orphan bairn without name or lineage. Any of the folks gathered here this morning would have raised him.''

"But would they have loved him?" Deirdre asked softly.

Teague looked at the woman before him, seeing past her beauty for the first time to her spirit, and he understood why Killian had chosen her. "May God go with you, Lady MacShane,'' he said in blessing.

"And you, Father,'' Deirdre answered.

The trek home was accomplished more quickly than the journey out; and when Deirdre sat beside Killian, who had waited to share her breakfast, she could hardly contain the joy that filled her.

"You look especially lovely this morning,'' he remarked as he gazed at her. "Was the view that fulfilling?''

"Aye, and more,'' Deirdre answered.

"Good, then you will have a memory to take with you.''

Deirdre shook her head. "I have said I will not go.''

"You have said a great many things, Dee, but I wonder if you will truly disobey the wishes of your husband?"

Deirdre reached out across the table. "Do not force me to go. Please, Killian. I will be discreet as a mouse. No one will even know I'm here."

"Not even when you attend Mass on a moonlit hillside?"

Deirdre gasped. "You knew!"

Killian nodded grimly. "I am not a fool, *acushla*."

"Why did you not say so and spare me the need for deception?" she retorted.

"Stubborn," he muttered. "That is why I have decided that you must go to safety. You risk too much, even for my taste."

"You might have come with me," she said low.

"But I did." His hard-featured face was inscrutable. "Who do you think stood at your back while Dary was christened? Who led your pony home?"

"Enan," she answered faintly.

Killian shook his head. "Enan went ahead to stand watch while Mass was said."

"But you were here when I entered," Deirdre protested.

"Two doors," Killian offered coldly. "So, you are not so clever, Dee, and I cannot spend my days spying upon you. You will pack today and we will leave for Cork in the morning."

Deirdre stiffened at the rebuke. He was packing her up and sending her off as though she were a naughty child or a faithless wife. "What will you do?"

Killian shrugged. He had yet to make his move against O'Donovan, but his weeks of spying had uncovered dangerous information that could hang the smuggler. "I've an interview with the authorities. When I've proven myself a loyal subject to the English Crown, I will return to Liscarrol. I must find a way to make a decent living before I can consider sending for you."

"That could be months!"

"So it could," he answered heavily.

Deirdre looked at him incredulously. This cold man was the one she had met in her father's kitchen, had encountered again the day Fey was discovered to be a lass, had faced in

Cork the morning she challenged his deceit about the journey to Liscarrol. Each and every time she thought she had his measure, he confounded her. He had lied to her once; he was doing so again. "Did you take an oath of loyalty and embrace a new religion in Cork?"

To her surprise, Killian seemed not at all affected by her words. Except for the shuttering of his gaze by heavy black lashes, he did not move. "I have not, but perhaps I shall do both," he said in a curt voice.

"I cannot imagine myself wed to a turncoat," she answered defiantly.

Killian leaned toward her, his face set in lines of anger and some indefinable torment. "Another Bill of Discovery may soon be brought against me. If it is found that Liscarrol exceeds the number of acres a papist is legally entitled to, the land will be confiscated unless I swear my loyalty to the English throne."

Deirdre shook her head. "I do not care! As much as I love Liscarrol, I love you more. If we must leave, then let's do so together."

The speech knocked the force from Killian's anger. It was the one thing he had never expected to hear from her. The one desire that had never left her, even when she had followed him to Paris, was her wish to live at Liscarrol. His love had not been enough to dissuade her from the goal. It was too much to expect that she had suddenly changed her mind. He must not read too much into her words, he cautioned himself. He must not.

"You speak out of anger and anxiety." He covered her hand where it lay on the table but his voice was relentless and hard. "I will not lose Liscarrol. It will remain yours as long as I live to hold it!"

Deirdre reached out to him but he was on his feet. "So, you will pack and be ready at first light." He strode toward the door. "I must see to a few things. We will talk again at dinner."

Deirdre sat a moment in stunned sorrow. He was sending her away, and, barring an act of outright defiance on her part, she must accept his decision.

"His lordship's got the right of it. Ye should be safe away afore trouble returns."

Deirdre looked up to find Mrs. Ross at her elbow. "I do not agree, Mrs. Ross. And another thing, Captain MacShane is not a lord."

The woman stared at her a long moment before saying, "And yet he's the look and sound of a lord; and being that he's snared the heart of a lady, 'twould seem he's earned the respect of the title."

Chastened by the woman's words, Deirdre's cheeks burned. "I learned long ago that a man's estate is seldom a fair measure of his worth. My husband is a MacShane, and there was a time when a clan name was enough for an Irishman."

Mrs. Ross smiled. "Aye, 'tis enough for me. Will ye need me help in packing, yer ladyship?"

Deirdre sadly shook her head. "I will do it myself. Where is Fey? If I am leaving, she must go with me."

Mrs. Ross's expression soured. "Well that she should! Me Enan's a shade too fond of the lass for me liking. She'll be hanging about, watching him at his chores, while himself struts before her like a cock in the barnyard."

The rest of the morning passed in uncanny quiet as the promise of a beautiful dawn turned into a steady downpour that grayed the sky and hills and valley until the view from the windows of Liscarrol was that of a single, vast, colorless expanse.

When Fey returned at mid-afternoon she was unusually subdued; and though they did not speak of it, Deirdre knew that Killian had informed Fey that she was to leave Liscarrol also.

Dusk came quickly, changing the pale grayness to smoke and laying deep purple shades among the shadows.

The heavy pounding at the door came only an instant before Mrs. Ross appeared from the rear of the house. "That'll be Oadh O'Donovan himself," she announced loudly and then melted away as quickly as she had come.

Killian smiled briefly at Deirdre as he rose from their evening meal. "Better than a hound, that woman."

"Och! 'Tis a devil of an evening to be abroad,"

O'Donovan announced when he was shown into the Great Hall. Rain streamed from his cloak and ran in rivulets from his bare head. "Will ye not be offering a man a seat by yer hearth, MacShane?"

"That depends upon the reason for your visit," Killian answered, blocking his path with a wide-legged stance.

O'Donovan looked over Killian's shoulder to where Deirdre sat. "A good evening to ye, lass. Will ye offer a neighbor a dry spot out of the rain?"

"Lady MacShane will do as I wish," Killian answered for her. "What brings you here on such a night, O'Donovan? Have you come to bait your trap?"

O'Donovan's brows rose in amazement. "*Musha!* Would I then be knocking and paying me respects?"

"Perhaps," Killian replied, but he stood aside.

O'Donovan stomped his feet and swung his sodden cloak from his shoulders, dropping it on the slate floor. His gaze moved greedily over the contents of the table as he came forward. "It would nae come amiss, a piece of that bread, la—yer ladyship."

Deirdre pushed the bowl toward him with two fingers, refusing to serve him. As Killian stood by, he helped himself and ate two large pieces of oat bread in as many bites. When he reached for the third, Killian's hand shot out and moved the dish from under his grasp.

"I did not invite you to dine. Tell me why you're here, or go the way you came."

O'Donovan's pale eyes gleamed in the meager light. "So, 'tis to be that way. Fair enough. I came to warn ye that English soldiers are once more in the valley."

Killian met his sly gaze with a wintry look. "You bastard!"

"Well, that's fine thanks! Did ye think I would nae come to warn ye if they were after ye? As they're nae hunting ye, I thought ye'd care to know that, too. There's nae pleasing some." He straightened himself to his full height. "And ye can be certain there'll be no more warnings."

"Who are they after?" Deirdre questioned as the two men glared at each other.

He turned a wide grin on her. "Ye being a daughter of

the Sidhe and an early riser on new-mooned Sabbaths, I thought ye would know. There're hounds abroad asniffing and abaying for blood.'' He leaned toward her. ''Who's blood do they howl for, *bean feasa?*''

She realized several things at once: that O'Donovan knew of her journey to the hillside Mass; that her fear of spies among the communicants had been a legitimate concern; and that O'Donovan's news was connected to the event. ''The English hunt a priest.''

O'Donovan chuckled with glee. ''There! Did I nae say you'd know the answer? And not just any priest. 'Tis a certain scoundrel going by the name of Teague O'Donovan.'' He winked at Killian. ''The English have it on good authority that he's a smuggler as well as a rapparee.''

''But that cannot be true!'' Deirdre shot to her feet. ''He's a kind and gentle man whom I doubt is worldly enough to understand the full peril in which he stands. That's true, isn't it, Killian?''

Killian watched O'Donovan. There was a trap for him in this, he could smell it. But when and how would it be sprung?

O'Donovan rubbed his bearded chin. ''I will be going now, for a man knows when he's outstayed his welcome.'' He started toward the door but then turned back. ''A last word to ye. I would nae open me doors to another knock this night.'' He stared pointedly at Killian. ''Cousin Teague is of a mind that he has friends among the local gentry. I would nae want ye to be hanged for harboring a criminal.'' With his cloak flung carelessly over his shoulder, he descended the stairwell.

''What does he mean?'' Deirdre questioned when Killian bolted the door and returned. ''Will Father Teague come here?''

''No,'' Killian replied curtly. ''That he will not!''

As Deirdre watched, he drew his cloak from a peg and settled it about his shoulders.

''What are you doing? You can't be thinking of trying to find Father Teague.''

''That is exactly what I'm planning to do,'' Killian replied. He took his pistol from his belt and began reloading it. "You will not be aware of it because there's been no time to tell you, but Teague and I are childhood friends." He looked up from his work with a small smile. "But for a chance encounter with a wild-haired lass of seven, I might be wearing a cassock like his today."

"Why did he not tell me?" Deirdre felt faintly betrayed by both men.

"I would not allow it. Teague is a man of odd temperament. He's a dreamer, a fanciful man of strong ideals but little common sense. No man in Munster would trust O'Donovan; but Teague has, and how his cousin has betrayed him."

Deirdre gnawed her lip. She did not understand all that Killian told her, but one thing was vividly clear. "So you will risk your life to save Father Teague."

It was a statement requiring no answer, so Killian said nothing. O'Donovan had known he would, too. That was why he had brought the news himself. No doubt he hoped the English would catch the priest and the owner of Liscarrol together and hang them both.

"You might be killed or at the very least arrested. If you're caught, you will be charged with abetting a priest."

Killian looked up again, his work finished, and slipped his pistol back into his belt. His expression was grim. "Why did you not think of that the morning you sneaked away from me to attend Mass? What I do, I do with your knowledge."

"It makes it no less dangerous," she said.

"No," he answered unhelpfully and belted on his sword.

"Let me go with you."

Killian looked up sharply, as though she had struck him with a stick, and then his expression turned gentle and he shook his head. "No, lass."

"I'm a fair shot," Deirdre insisted. "I've held the English at bay once already. You'd have been proud of me."

"So Mrs. Ross said," he answered with a warming grin.

"Mrs. Ross said?" Deirdre echoed. "She's never had a pleasant word to say to me in all these months."

"There you're wrong. You quite astonished her that particular day, and don't think the whole valley doesn't know of it. Not a week past, Cuan O'Dineen offered his respects to you for your fine accounting with the soldiers. Do not allow it to go to your head, however. I, for one, was not amused."

"Perhaps Father Teague will come to us if we wait," Deirdre offered.

"He will not. I know where he is."

"Where is that?"

Killian gazed at her and said, his voice cool, "There are things a man may not tell even his wife."

"You do not trust me!" Deirdre said stiffly.

Killian turned away. " 'Tis not a matter of trust. 'Tis a matter of survival, and not only our own." He turned to Mrs. Ross, who had again appeared in the Great Hall. "Stay here. Stay quiet. And keep the doors locked against all comers until I return."

"Aye, yer lordship," she answered as she opened the door to allow him to depart.

"He did not even say goodbye," Deirdre murmured forlornly.

" 'Tis no reason," Mrs. Ross answered with a knowing gleam in her eyes. "He's nae going away. He's riding out a bit, 'tis all."

"Riding?" Deirdre questioned, but Mrs. Ross was already halfway across the room and did not turn back.

Deirdre hurried to the stairwell and climbed to the second floor, where the view from one window was that of the stable.

It was that short space of time between twilight and nightfall when the world is purple. The shape that bolted from the stable into the night was blackness itself against the softer, dusky violet darkness. A swirl of black cape over the horse's flank gave the pair a nightmarish quality.

For an instant Deirdre stood rooted to the spot as horse and rider galloped out over the bridge and into the valley. She did not need to see the rider's face, nor did she need the answer to the question of where the horse had come from. She simply knew, and the knowledge made her blood still in her veins. The rider hidden beneath the black-winged cloak was Killian, the rider of her dreams.

She did not cry out or even hurry down the stairs. She dressed quickly but methodically in her riding boots and heaviest wool gown before tying a woolen mantle across her breasts and binding her hair back with a strip of cloth. She reached for the ancient O'Neill dagger last, slipping it into her waistband.

When she reached the first floor she saw Mrs. Ross. "Mrs. Ross! Send your husband for Cuan O'Dineen. Tell him that Father Teague has been betrayed and that English soldiers have come for him. My husband has ridden out to warn the priest, but he must not stand alone. Tell Cuan 'tis his moment to clear himself with me in the matter of the hanged child. He'll know what I mean."

"Where are ye going, ma'am?"

"To find Killian. O'Donovan will betray him, too!"

Beyond the bridge, the valley quickly gave way under his horse's hooves to a steep climb. It had ceased to rain in the few short minutes between O'Donovan's departure and Killian's own, but the difference was negligible, he decided as the thick mists clung and ran down his exposed face. His cloak drew heavier with every moment, and the boggy ground sucked noisily at his horse's hooves as it struggled up the climb. Killian held the horse with an easy rein, allowing it to pick its path by instinct over the dark, rock-strewn ground.

He knew where to find Teague, thanks to Colin Ross's quick eye. Colin had seen the priest climbing the hill just before dark. It was known that on nights such as this, the priest chose to sleep in the open, offering up, like some ancient monk of old, the night's discomforts as penance.

"Gom!" Killian muttered as his mount slipped and nearly went down. If not for the need for speed, he would have left the horse behind. Colin kept it in the hills, pasturing beside the cattle. It was an advantage that only he and Colin were aware of, and one that might foil

O'Donovan's plot. For Teague to elude the soldiers he would need to be mounted, as they were.

The wind whipped his cloak mercilessly, promising more rain before long. As he reached the shoulder of the hill, Killian reined in his mount and stood in the stirrups to search the area. Behind and below him Liscarrol stood like a block of black stone. Before him the hill curved gently away to the right and rose toward another, higher crest to the left. He followed the slope to the right, riding through the soft wet air toward the granite outcrop that had served as an altar a few weeks earlier.

The sound of a horse slowly picking its way across the ground nearby pulled Teague O'Donovan from his prayers. No one ever came up to visit him on these nights unless there was danger. He rose slowly to his knees from a position of prayer in the mud and saw a rider approaching. He waited, kneeling in the shadow of the huge stone, knowing that if he did not move the rider might pass him by without ever detecting his presence.

The rider paused, twisting about in his saddle. "Teague O'Donovan," the rider called out softly as he looked blindly around.

Teague lifted back the cowl of the heavy robe he wore and rose to his feet with relief. "Here! MacShane!"

Killian threw a leg over his saddle and slipped to the ground before the shadow that was the priest. "The English know you're abroad. You must take my horse and ride south!"

Teague put a hand on Killian's arm. "How do you know? Have they been to Liscarrol?"

"No. Oadh O'Donovan came."

Teague nodded slowly. "Then there's time. I thank you for the warning, but I do not believe I could be safer than I am here in the open with the rain and darkness to cover my tracks. By morning, it will be as though I never passed this way."

"Thanks to your kinsman, you will nae have the luxury of the night. O'Donovan's a Discoverer."

It was a foul thing to call a man, even an enemy. It was an insult few would suffer at a kinsman's expense. When

Teague did not decry his statement instantly, Killian knew he was believed.

"How long have you suspected him?" Teague asked quietly.

"He's a thief, a coward, and a murderer. I suspected him of everything," Killian said.

Teague shook his head again, though he knew it could not be seen. "I, too, wondered. Recently there's a malignancy to the air when O'Donovan is near."

"Aye," Killian replied. "O'Donovan will have given them directions here. I've brought the horse. Take him west until you reach Bantry Bay. There are men there who will take you across to France."

Teague fell back a step. "They will betray me. They are O'Donovan's men."

Killian squelched the prick of annoyance at the quaver of fear in the priest's voice. "Think, man! Would O'Donovan tell them of his dealings with the English? They'd murder him if they knew he'd betrayed even one of them, and he has. I've learned much there these last weeks."

Fear trickled down his spine like rain. "I am not a brave man, MacShane. I do God's work because I fear not to. Perhaps He despises my good deeds because they are a product of my fear rather than my faith. If I remain, fear rattling my teeth in my head, perhaps then He will disdain me no longer."

Killian loosened a string of oaths that made the priest in Teague shy away. "Damn you for a martyr! But you'll not be so on my property."

He ripped his cloak from his shoulders as he continued. "What do you think the English will do to my wife and the others if you're found on Liscarrol land? Will you have their murders on your conscience because you fear you're nae brave enough to suit your impression of a warrior priest?"

He stripped off his jacket and then his shirt, throwing them at the priest's feet. "Take off your robe and put on my clothes. Do it, damn you, or I'll throttle you myself!"

Because he had never been able to defend himself

against MacShane, Teague stripped off his robe and began replacing them with Killian's finer garments.

Killian slipped on the sodden, malodorous robe made of unwashed wool and muttered an oath as shivers of cold raced across his skin. " 'Tis like old times, Teague, when we were lads shut behind the monastery walls. I feel the weight of my sins hard upon me. Let us hope they do not catch up with me this night. I do not relish greeting Saint Peter in a monk's disguise."

To Teague's amazement, Killian laughed, low but easily. "You were always the brave one among us," he whispered.

Killian grinned. " 'Tis because I feared that nothing would ever happen to me, locked behind those cloistered walls."

"While I feared constantly that one day they would open and eject me," Teague admitted bitterly. "You're the better man."

Killian sobered. "How can that be when God chose you? You've taken the harder road, Teague; I've no doubt of it. And if saving you goes a little way toward mitigating the harm I've done, then you've that to your credit besides."

Teague stared through the dark at his childhood friend, humbled and flattered in the same instant. "Your lady wife, I misjudged her. I thought she'd come to stir up the ancient beliefs. I—"

"Tell her yourself, another time," Killian said tersely. "Give me your boots."

"I wear none," Teague answered.

Killian considered relinquishing his but changed his mind as he thought of covering the rocky, boggy ground on foot. Bending over, he began to rubbing his boot soles with a sleeve of the robe.

"What are you doing?"

"Giving me boots your scent," Killian answered. "Your robe should lead the hounds my way once they pick up your scent from this spot."

"What will you do if they catch you?"

Killian chuckled. " 'Twould be more than O'Donovan hopes for, but in less than an hour I will be safe abed beside my wife while your robe lies on the bottom of the river, weighted by stones. The hounds may lead them to Liscarrol but they won't cross the bridge.''

The daring plot made even Teague smile. ''Perhaps you, not your wife, has a bit of magic. I'd nae have thought of that.''

''It has yet to work,'' Killian reminded him as he pressed a gun in the man's hand and pushed him toward the horse. ''Ride back to the crest of the hill and then turn west, over Nowen Hill, toward Bantry.''

Teague looked down. ''You'll be in my prayers every day of my life.''

''Live long, then, Teague, for I've need of Divine forgiveness,'' Killian retorted cheerfully and slapped the horse's rump.

''Bless you, my son!'' Teague called back as the horse moved back up the hill.

''Ride, Father, like the hounds of hell pursue you,'' Killian murmured as the man and horse disappeared into the night.

Deirdre lost sight of the rider after he crossed the bridge, but some sixth sense sent her up the side of the hill where Mass had been said. It seemed not unreasonable that Father Teague might still be nearby. But she had none of the advantage of daylight or guides or a pony. As she traversed the rocky ground on foot she hoped she would not become hopelessly lost.

''*Merde!*'' she swore as she stepped up to her ankle in a muddy hole for the third time.

Rain was falling again, a soft steady hiss that drowned out the small sounds of the night and made her view of the ground before her even more difficult. Her woolen skirts greedily soaked up the brown water until they dragged at her like weights and her back began to ache from the strain. As if in mockery of her misery, a star occasionally winked at her from a break in the clouds. She waded on, arms outstretched to keep her balance.

She knew she should turn back, that an irrational moment of surprise had brought her out on a very dangerous night, but she could not shake the bond with her dream. It had ridden at the edge of her consciousness for as long as she could remember. She had not been asleep this time, had not even been daydreaming. Killian had been real. She had seen him leave.

Finally the crest of the hill loomed ahead, its irregular stone shape a welcome sight. And then she heard the rumble.

The wind whipped up suddenly, whistling past the stone tor and raking her hair back from her face. In its wake, the wind carried the thunder of hooves.

The specter appeared out of the gloom of night, suddenly cresting the hill and then plunging down it directly toward her.

Deirdre stopped, her heart pounding in rhythm to the hooves, and she lifted her arms with the cry, "Wait! Wait!"

Teague O'Donovan expected to encounter no one on the hillside. Killian's warning had come soon enough, he told himself. But suddenly there was a figure blocking his path, waving its arms and crying out in alarm.

"Stay away! Stay away!"

He tried to rein in, but the horse, frightened by the sudden voice before him, reared and then plunged on down the hillside.

He did not see the figure again, but the chill in his veins told him that he had seen one of the *Daoine Sidhe*. He rode on, crossing himself and praying fervently that he would never again encounter one.

Deirdre lay in the grass a long while, her eyes open to the night. She did not feel pain. The horse's hoof had caught her a glancing blow. By all rights she should have been trampled to death. Once more she had encountered her dream. Yet, this time it had been different.

She stared at the sky above her, at the many stars spangled behind the thin veiling of scattered clouds.

It had not been Killian.

The rider had turned to her at the last moment, his head

gleaming palely in the gloom. The man had been fair-haired. It could not have been Killian.

The faint squishing sounds of footsteps nearby brought her alert. Her heart in her throat, she stared at the dark sky, wondering if she would be discovered. But the footsteps passed by in the rapid rhythm of a person on a journey elsewhere.

When the footsteps died, she sat up only to gasp in pain. Her shoulder! The horse had not missed her entirely. She forced herself upright, gritting her teeth as the pain knifed down between her shoulder blades. Very carefully she moved her hand, then bent her arm at the elbow, and finally lifted her arm, sobbing a little when she realized that her shoulder was not dislocated.

Moving stiffly, she rose to her feet. There was no point in going on. The rider and the footsteps had convinced her that the hillside was too dangerous a place to remain.

She made her way down much more quickly than she had made her way up, using Liscarrol as a beacon. The rain had ceased again, and this time the starry night held its own against the wind-borne clouds.

Deirdre did not stop until she reached the river and saw the figure of a man standing in the tall grasses that grew along the bank. Too afraid to cross the rickety bridge lest it creak under her weight and alert the man of her presence, she crouched behind a rock and waited, her teeth aching from clenching them against the pain in her shoulder.

As she watched, the man pulled a robelike garment over his head. Was it Father Teague? She nearly called out but fear held her back. She heard him shuffling about in the dark and then a short silence followed. He repeated his actions several times and then he stood. She heard a gentle splash followed by a second, louder one, and she knew that he had dived or fallen into the river.

She waited, shivering in her damp clothes, until she heard a scrambling sound on the far bank and realized that he had swum across. He was a dark hump moving up the riverbank and then he disappeared.

Every muscle in her body protested as she rose from her

crouch, but then she dropped back again as another shadow detached itself from the river's edge.

Deirdre rubbed her eyes with a weary hand. Was she dreaming? Was she delirious, or did Liscarrol swarm with spies and secrets?

When she lifted her head again, she was surprised to see a man on the bridge, sauntering across its creaky surface as though he were an expected guest. It was too dark to see his coloring or clothing.

Once more she rose painfully to her feet. If she could just reach the house, the turf fire, the warmth of Mrs. Ross's porridge, she would never disobey Killian again. Her thoughts were childlike and she knew it, but she hurt so much, was so tired and frightened. When she was a child, there had been Da and Darragh and Conall to keep her from making mistakes. Perhaps Killian was right. Perhaps she should go back to France where she would not cause him any more anxiety.

Her cheeks burned, but the rest of her body felt icy cold as she hurried across the bridge. Mrs. Ross waited inside, she told herself, but as she neared the castle the shiver worsened until she heard the strange sound of her teeth chattering.

Something was wrong. The very scent of danger was in the air. Had the black-cloaked rider appeared in the yard before her now, she would have sighed in relief, for it would have been preferable to the feeling of clear and present danger that puckered her skin and made her stomach quiver.

She backed away from the front door. *Not that way,* her instinct whispered. *Too quiet. Too still. Something is wrong.*

She glanced at the darkened stable in the distance but there was no sound, no sign of life. Colin and the others had disappeared. If the English soldiers had come, it would be impossible to hide the fact. The danger lay somewhere else.

Where were the two men she had seen? Who were they?

As another draft of anxiety swept her, Deirdre reached for the O'Neill skean, pulling it free. Brigid had warned her of danger, and she had thought that the danger was bound up in her phantom horseman. Now she was no longer certain of that fact.

Keeping in the shadow of the castle walls, she made her way to the servants' entrance in the rear. The kitchen was dark. Mrs. Ross had finished for the night. Deirdre crossed the floor, her heart beating frantically against her ribs.

The opening to the narrow stairwell yawned menacingly before her but she stepped in after only a moment's hesitation and began to climb. As she reached the second floor she heard voices coming from the Great Hall and with a leap of joy she recognized one of them as Killian's. She tucked her skean away and would have stepped into the room had not a second voice stopped her.

"So Cousin Teague's safe away. Och! 'Tis sad news, I'm thinking. The English will be expecting to capture a priest. O'Donovan's never steered them wrong yet."

O'Donovan!

"What will you do?" she heard Killian reply in his most careless of voices. "Conjure one from thin air?"

"Strange, yer saying that, for 'tis exactly what I will do, laddie. It came to me at the riverbank that one man or another, who's to tell them different?" There was a pause while something was flung upon the floor.

"Teague's robes. You followed me," Killian said.

" 'Twas a bit of luck, that. I was spying on the castle in case Teague came back with ye. A clever disguise. 'Tis what put me in mind of another trick. Ye're of a similar height with Teague, for all he was as thin as skimmed milk. The English want a priest; I will give them *you*."

As Deirdre heard Killian's laughter, chills raced along her spine. She pressed herself to the wall. A cold breeze yawned up past her and she turned to look down the stairwell but it was too late. A blackness rose up before her and a hand pressed the scream back in her throat.

"You forget I'm a married man," Killian said.

O'Donovan chuckled in return. "So ye've come to Ireland with a wife? Who's to say different if I tell the English 'twas a trick to cover yer papist preaching ways? Bring a wife and nae man looks for the priest in that. The English will look at one another and wonder that they had

nae thought of that deception before. Clever? Aye,
O'Donovan's a clever man. Did I nae tell ye so?''

"I'll deny it."

"Sure'n ye will, but the English believe in law and
order. They'll be wanting a confession before ye ever
come to trial. Torture's a terrible thing, I hear. Ye may find
yerself believing the truth of the charge before ye know it.
Not every priest's a man of iron and honor. Some go to the
stake with their heads high, others cry as pitifully as any
wee bairn. 'Tis the same with thieves and smugglers
and—''

"Discoverers," Killian offered.

"Well now, I'd nae be knowing that sort. Still ye should
know, none in the valley will testify for ye. They'd be
confessing that they know the identity of a real priest, and
for that they'd hang.''

"You seem to have thought of everything."

"I'll be taking that as a compliment. Come the morning, I'll be telling the valley that 'twas ye who were the
Discoverer, and O'Donovan did nae more or less than best
ye at yer own game!'' He chuckled at his own cleverness.

"What of my wife?"

O'Donovan shrugged. "I'm nae a man to bother the
Sidhe, but she's a clever sort and could make trouble. She
seems a high-strung lass. Who knows but what the news of
yer arrest will nae make her mad. One mad lass drowned
outside her door a few weeks past. I would nae be at all
surprised were yer wife to fling herself in the river and
drown herself dead!''

"She'd be a stupid bitch to do that. Ye're growing lax,
O'Donovan. The lady was spying on ye.'' Cuan O'Dineen
stepped from the stairwell, pushing Deirdre before him
with a hand still clapped over her mouth.

"Deirdre!"

O'Donovan swung his pistol toward Killian. "Do nae
bestir yerself, MacShane. The lady's right as rain, isn't
she, O'Dineen?''

The smaller man gave a single ominous bob of his head.

Deirdre strained against the hard hand gripping her, but
Cuan whispered low, "Yer husband's a nervous man.

'Twould nae do for him to get his head blown off for lack of manners on yer part.'' Deirdre stilled. ''Aye, better, yer ladyship.''

''Hurt her and I'll kill you,'' Killian said softly, his gaze swinging between the two men.

''Such heat,'' O'Donovan said mockingly. '' 'Twould sound better were ye properly dressed, MacShane. Yer lady wife is blushing with shame to see ye standing as God made ye.'' He kicked he robe with his boot toe. ''Put it on, lad. May as well wear it now as later.''

Killian bent to pick up the sodden garment. O'Donovan had found him before he could dress after his swim.

O'Donovan swung about as voices came from the yard below. ''That'll be the soldiers.''

''Nae, that'll be our people,'' Cuan O'Dineen answered.

O'Donovan swung toward Cuan with a startled, angry look. ''They were told to keep to their homes tonight. Any man out will be hunted by the English.''

''There's talk abroad, Oadh,'' Cuan said slowly, solemnly. ''Talk of treachery.''

''Of course! Did I nae tell ye the English are hunting Father Teague?''

''So ye did, but ye did nae say why.''

O'Donovan pointed at Killian with the barrel of his pistol. ''There's yer answer. He's a Discoverer. Ye were the one to alert us to his coming. Well, I've been keeping watch.''

Victory beating high in him, O'Donovan found the final damning stroke as he pointed to the sodden priest's robe on the floor. ''There's proof, if ye need it. He tied stones in the cloth and heaved it in the river. I suspect he's killed poor Father Teague, played the hound's part for his English masters.''

''That's a lie,'' Killian answered calmly but firmly.

A shadow appeared in the stairwell behind Cuan and became Colin Ross. Behind him another figure appeared, revealing itself as his son Enan.

''Did the others come?'' Cuan asked over his shoulder.

''They've come,'' Colin answered.

''And the other one?'' Cuan pressed.

Enan smiled. "Safe away."

Deirdre was released so suddenly that she lurched forward, but a steadying hand caught her from behind. "There's nae need to be afraid," Cuan said behind her. "I have only one thing to ask ye, Lady MacShane. Who's the Discoverer?"

Deirdre stared at O'Donovan. He was perspiring, the sweat running freely over his big red face. She thought of his fear, for she had known a good measure of her own this night. And then she thought of the pathetic bag of skin and bones that had once been a child, a child dead because of Oadh O'Donovan. "I do not know if he is a Discoverer," she said softly, "but I know he set the English on Father Teague."

"Go to your man, Lady MacShane," Cuan said. "Go to him and stay beside him."

Deirdre started toward Killian but he held up a hand. "Stay away, *mo cuishle!*"

"What's this?" O'Donovan roared. "Nae man orders me prisoners about."

Cuan stepped forward, a skean in his hand. "There's a traitor among us, Oadh, a traitor who's lain on his belly among the flock, awaiting and awaiting. He kills only when the shepherd turns his back to scan the distant hills for the enemy."

"MacShane," O'Donovan said with a grin.

"Nae, Oadh. The wolf among us wears our wool, eats our food, kills his neighbor. The Discoverer is you!"

O'Donovan wet his lips nervously. It took a few moments for Cuan's words to fully sink in. "Ye do nae know what ye say. MacShane's the man ye want. The English will come and take him away."

"The English want O'Donovan the smuggler and rapparee. Ye've done enough murdering among yer own," Colin Ross said in a harsh voice. "There'll be nae more of it!"

O'Donovan turned his pistol on the knot of men. "Ye can prove nothing."

"We've yer own words to hang ye," Cuan answered. "Didn't I hear ye just now, boasting to MacShane how ye've the ear of the English? How is it, Oadh, that ye've never been caught unawares?''

''I'm more clever than the rest,'' O'Donovan boasted; but his hands had begun to sweat, and his forehead gleamed in the firelight.

''Not clever enough,'' Enan Ross shouted and stepped forward. ''We met Father Teague on the road. He was wearing MacShane's clothing, riding MacShane's horse. A man put the English on his trail this night. You! Discoverer!''

O'Donovan paled at the accusation, his eyes turning panicky until he realized that the boy held no weapon.

''*Gommach!* Ye know less than a beetle on a dunghill. The English will hang MacShane, and that'll be an end of it.''

''There'll be an end,'' Cuan agreed. ''Open the doors, lad.''

O'Donovan turned his pistol on Enan as he backed toward the stairwell that led to the third floor, repeatedly wiping his mouth with the back of his hand. ''Ye're making a mistake. 'Tis I who brought prosperity to ye! Who helps ye smuggle in the goods that keep yer bellies filled and yer women and children clothed?''

But they were not listening to him. Someone else had thrown the bolt on the front doors and the sound of many footsteps was heard on the main stairwell.

''They've come for ye, Discoverer!'' Cuan announced.

O'Donovan fired the pistol at Enan. It was a desperate, hopeless measure, yet he hoped it would give him time to gain the stairs to the third floor. But, as he turned in to the dark turret, a knife flashed out, slashing him across the cheek, and he fell back with a cry of horror.

Fey leaped from the stairwell with an unearthly cry as she ran to where Enan had fallen.

The others were on O'Donovan instantly, and he was dragged backward onto the slate floor.

''Not here!'' Killian had said nothing since he first saw Deirdre in the doorway. Now his voice cut across their fighting and the men turned to him. ''Take him out! I will not have my wife's home defiled!''

They gathered O'Donovan's flailing arms and legs and

lifted him screaming above their heads as they carried him down the stairwell and out into the night.

"They will kill him!" Deirdre cried.

Killian enfolded her tightly against him. "Aye. May God rest his black soul."

Deirdre turned her face into the hollow of Killian's left shoulder as a bloodchilling scream rose up beyond the door. Another followed it, and then other, weaker cries that were soon drowned out by the shouts and oaths of the mob.

Killian's hands came up to cover her ears, and Deirdre closed her eyes, concentrating on the strong, slightly rapid rhythm of his heart beneath her ear.

It was over quickly. The noise ebbed away until the night rang with silence. After a long moment Killian's hands eased their tight hold, but his face was hard as he gazed beyond the open doorway.

"Now there's only the English to deal with," he murmured to himself.

Chapter Twenty-four

Dawn came stealing softly over the gray-walled castle as if aware that its sleepless inhabitants feared its coming. Killian had been gone two days.

Deirdre stood at the window of the chapel, staring out at the lightening sky. Killian had left shortly after O'Donovan had been taken out. That was two days ago and no word had been heard from him since. Hard tight shivers quaked through her. The people of the valley had killed O'Donovan with their bare hands. And the fault was hers.

Because of her a man had died. The thought had kept her awake two nights through. Neither fear for Killian, nor Fey's hysteria over Enan's wound, nor her own aches and bruises could long keep the thought from her mind.

The fact that she had not known what they would do to him did not excuse her part in it. She had seen the look in Colin's eyes when he had asked her to name her Discoverer. If she had hesitated, said she did not know, or simply refused to speak, would O'Donovan still be alive? What power did she possess that they believed her so readily? Or had they always known and been too afraid to act? Had they used her as their excuse to do what they otherwise would not have done?

She now understood Father Teague's words to her the first day he had come and seen the mark on her shoulder. People were weak and easily frightened. Times were hard and men were desperate. Some, like O'Donovan, were willing to sell their souls to keep what little they had. Had the people of the valley turned to her, believing that she represented a power older than that of rosary beads and crucifixes, to help them escape the yoke of O'Donovan? If that was so, then she must leave here, must leave Liscarrol.

She gazed at the new greenness on the hillsides as the sun shed first light on the new day. Spring was well under way. Liscarrol was beginning to recover from years of neglect. In the distance, Liscarrol cattle lowed softly in anticipation of the morning's milking. With the crop of wildflowers budding there would soon be honey as well as milk flowing in the valley, but she would not be here to enjoy it.

She turned as footsteps came up behind her.

"Enan's awake and ye must come and see him," Fey said. Her face was bloated with two sleepless nights of worry, but there was a genuine smile on her face. "His ma says he'll heal."

"Of course he will," Deirdre answered. "We told you so the first night."

Fey grinned at her. "Aye, ye did. But Enan's a stupid lad. He might not have heard ye. Ye must come and tell him that ye've had the word of the Sight that soon he'll again be plaguing the milk cows with his cold hands and clumsy touch."

"Do not speak to me of the Sight!" Deirdre cried. "I will not have you speak of it ever again."

Fey cocked her head to one side. "Ye're a *deeshy* lady. The others can talk of nothing else. 'Twas ye, they say, give MacShane the idea of trading his clothes with the priest and who sent the word abroad that the English had come for the priest. 'Twas ye who knew O'Donovan was the Discoverer."

"That's not true." Deirdre shook her head. Everything was confused and turned upside down. She had known none of those things. "All I've done was point O'Donovan out to be murdered."

"Aye, that, too," Fey agreed. "And a grand thing it was!" She hesitated. "Once I did nae like ye much, but ye saved MacShane's life, and Enan's, too, so I'll nae be holding me grudge against ye any longer."

Deirdre nodded, too moved to speak. A week ago she would have laughed for joy to hear those words from Fey. Now she was too near tears.

"Ye'll be coming down, to see Enan, I mean?" Fey prompted.

"Aye."

Fey smiled once more, looking prettier than ever, and Deirdre realized she had put on a gown for the first time since she had arrived at Liscarrol. "You look very pretty," Deirdre said with a faint smile.

Fey looked down at herself and shrugged. "'Tis on account of Enan. He thinks 'tis only proper for a lass. He is weak now, so it doesn't matter. When he's up and about, I'll be putting on me breeches again. 'Twould be safer, I'm thinking."

"He's coming! MacShane's coming!"

The cry from below sent both Deirdre and Fey rushing toward the window.

"There he is!" Fey cried in delight as she hung over the sill. "And no soldiers with him!"

Deirdre reached the stairwell first, her satin slippers sliding over the well-worn stones as she raced round and round in descent.

As she hurried out of the house she wondered how many times in the future she would do this, run to greet the man she loved. *Perhaps never again at Liscarrol*, she thought with a sinking heart. Then so be it. As long as she met Killian each time, she would wait for him wherever he wished her to be.

As Killian watched his wife running across the yard, he was torn between pleasure and anger. She had no instincts for preservation where he was concerned. From Colin he had learned that she had gone out after him the night he went to warn Father Teague, heedless of danger.

When she launched herself into his arms, all the worry
and weariness that had raked him compounded into unrea-
soning rage.

"Let go of me, you damned silly bitch!" he roared, too
shaken by the conflicting impulses of relief and fear for her
sake to remember this once his soldierly reserve in the
open.

He grabbed her by the shoulders, intending to shake her.
Instead, his lips were suddenly against her in a hard,
ungentle, punishing kiss that quickly melted his anger and
left him gasping in the throes of an emotion stronger than
rage. "You might have been killed!" he hissed at her, his
voice colder than the wind.

Deirdre reached out to touch the hair at his temple. "I
thought you would be killed. Until the last moment. And
then Cuan and the others came. And, and..."

Killian caught the hand stroking his left temple and
squeezed her fingertips hard. "You're shivering!" he accused.

Deirdre lowered her head. "I cannot bear it, Killian!
Because of me a man is dead."

Killian frowned. "O'Donovan, do you mean?" She
nodded. Killian bit his lip. Too often he said the wrong
thing to her, trampling her sensibilities with his practical
view of life. "You feel guilt. Why?"

"Because of me a man is dead," she repeated.

Killian chose his words carefully. "I would rather think
that because of you two men live." He raised her face to
his. "You saved me, *mo cuishle*, by sending for Cuan.
And you saved Father Teague, too. Cuan and Enan met
him on the road coming here that night. He had taken the
wrong turn and would have run straight into the hands of
the English soldiers. So you see, there's nothing to grieve
about."

His logic was so comforting that she wanted to accept it,
but it seemed cowardly to do so. "The others think I've
the gift of the Sight and that that was what directed my
actions."

"How do you know it didn't?"

Deirdre's eyes widened. "Surely you don't believe?"

Killian smiled at her. "What does it matter, *acushla?*

The people of the valley owe you a great debt, and if it pleases them to make a daughter of the Sidhe of you, let them, I say. 'Twill be certain protection for Liscarrol as long as we remain.''

Deirdre shook her head. ''I did a stupid, stupid thing in going after you. I suppose that was what the dream warned me of. If I had remained here, I would have been here when you came back, and we might have overpowered O'Donovan; but I was too stupid to do as you ordered. Nae, I must go about tripping in bog holes and being chased by phantoms.''

Killian caught her by the arms. ''What phantoms?''

Deirdre nearly smiled. How foolish and innocuous it all seemed beside what had occurred following that incident on the hillside. ''The dream did not frighten me that night, though I've bruises this time to prove that it ran me over.'' She looked up at him. ''But it wasn't you. You did not say the words, did not look right. Your hair is as dark as a raven, while his hair was light.''

''What are you talking about?''

Deirdre laid a hand to his cheek. ''I saw you ride out, on the black horse, as you had in my dream.''

Killian sighed. ''Who else saw me?''

''No one. I sent Colin for Cuan and then I went after you on foot, but I lost my way on the hillside. It was then the phantom appeared and nearly trampled me.''

Killian shook his head in wonder. ''That was no phantom.''

Deirdre grew very still. ''Who was it, Killian, on the hillside?''

He smiled. ''That was Father Teague. I had given him my clothes and my horse. The English didn't find him. He was transported safely across the Channel before dawn.''

Deirdre gripped Killian's hand between hers. ''I'm ready to leave Liscarrol, too. I love it, but I love you more. I will go anywhere you say, but I beg you to go with me. Either we stay together or we go together.''

As Killian looked down into her face he felt the conviction of her words register in his heart. He believed that she would willingly, happily leave Liscarrol if he asked it. She loved him completely. She always had. How foolish he had been to be jealous of a pile of stones. With Deirdre and Liscarrol he had found the things he had searched for all his life: a home and love of his own.

He bowed his head and fervently kissed her hands. "I love you," he said huskily. "I cannot promise you safety. I cannot promise you security. I cannot even promise you a life of plenty. But I will keep Liscarrol for you, whatever I must do!"

"Because I have asked it of you?"

"Nae, lass, because it has become as much mine as yours, and I've a need for a place of my own."

Deirdre smiled at him, feeling the weight of her guilt and fears drop away. Killian considered Liscarrol his home, and just maybe, together, they might keep it. "Will you continue to steal for me, as you have done before?"

Killian lifted his head, his expression ravaged by emotion, to find her smiling at him. "You guessed about the smuggling?"

Deirdre shrugged. "My father was many things, including a man fond of French tobacco and brandy. He traded with those who offered the best prices. He said, ' 'Tis an honorable profession for an Irishman if it bedevils the English!' "

Killian broke into a grin, lifting the lines of worry from his strong face. "I do believe O'Donovan had your measure. He said you'd the spirit of a buccaneer." He sobered suddenly. "You'll need to develop your instincts for survival, though, if you mean to stay."

"I've a rather sharp nose for it already," Deirdre answered lightly. "I suppose a few more months in Ireland will see to the refinement of it."

"Then we will stay," Killian said firmly.

Another thought struck Deirdre. "What of O'Donovan? And shouldn't we expect the soldiers to come looking for a priest?"

Killian sobered. "Nae, lass. I've taken care of it. 'Tis where I've been. I've turned Discoverer."

Deirdre put a hand to his mouth. "Don't say that, not even in jest."

Killian stared at her, and there was nothing of gentleness

or humor in his eyes. "I had to get rid of O'Donovan's body. I took it to the English soldiers who had camped for the night in Kilronane and handed it over. I told them I had killed him because he was a rapparee and had threatened my life if I remained in the area. Thanks to a persuasive conversation with Cuan, I could tell them where they would find a cache of weapons that O'Donovan had stored away. I said that I was a law-abiding citizen and that as long as I remained at Liscarrol there would be no rebellion of my making."

"Killian!"

"Listen to me, Dee. The time for fighting is over. My soldiering days are done. I want nothing more than to raise a family, not rebellion. My deception gained me a good chance of doing just that. If in the future I must resort to more deception or outright lies, I will do so with a clear conscience."

He thought of his bargain with the duchesse, but this did not seem a good time to bring the lady's name into the conversation. He would tell Deirdre later, when he had time to explain, that he had also found a local English magistrate with a fondness for French silks and brandy who had promised him protection in his smuggling activities in exchange for a portion of his goods.

"We must live in the times in which we are placed, Dee," he said quietly. "Will you live here with me?"

Deirdre looked into his face and knew what he asked. Theirs would not be an easy life or a tranquil one, but if they chose they could live it out here, together.

"I hear there are laws forbidding a Catholic son from inheriting land from his father. What shall become of Liscarrol once we are gone?"

Killian grinned at her. "Well now, I've plans to become an old, old gentleman farmer with a herd of great-grandsons running me mad in me later years. By then, the laws may have changed."

"'Tis devoutly to be hoped!" Deirdre answered.

Killian caught her to him and held her tightly. "I swear you'll have no regrets on my account!"

"'Tis well enough, my love, for there are certain to be

regrets over other affairs.'' When Killian looked down at
her in surprise she smiled. ''I had a talk with Fey some
weeks back about men and loving. She's loved you from
the beginning, you know.'' He nodded. ''Well, I told her
she could not have you and suggested that she might find
someone else, but I did not expect she'd take my advice so
quickly to heart.''

''What do you mean?''

''Did you not notice that Fey waited to show herself the
night O'Donovan threatened to hand you over the English?
She did not come to your aid or mine.''

''She acted quickly enough when Enan took O'Donovan's
shot,'' Killian replied. ''Och! You do not mean—!''

Deirdre nodded. ''Fey's in love.''

''But she's just a wee lass. . . .''

Deirdre's expression softened with a knowing womanly smile. ''Lassie's grow up.''

''Indeed they do, *mo cuishle*,'' Killian said, gathering
his lady wife into his arms again.

GLOSSARY

1. *Abu*—Boy; "our boy."
2. *Acushla*—Little darling.
3. *Alanna*—Child.
4. *Amadan*—Male fool.
5. *Asthore*—My beloved.
6. *Aulaun*—Lout.
7. *Bad cess*—Bad luck.
8. *Bainne*—Milk.
9. *Bainnicin*—Irish spurge: yellow-green plant with corrosive juice. Used by unscrupulous poachers to poison the water to "catch" fish.
10. *Bean feasa*—Wise woman.
11. *Bean sidhe*—Woman of the otherworld; fairy woman.
12. *Bête farouche*—(F.)—Savage beast.
13. *Bodach*. Clown.
14. *Booleying*—Pasturing cattle or sheep in the hills in the summer months.
15. *Bosthoon*—Blockhead.
16. *Bouchal*—Boy.
17. *Cabaiste Scotch*—Stew of cabbage hearts, onions, and sour cream.
18. *Cailin deas*—Pretty girl (colleen dhas).

19. *Ceanabhan*—Blossom of the bog.
20. *Daoine sidhe*—Fairy people.
21. *Deeshy*—Small.
22. *Didean*—Aid, shelter.
23. *Dilse*—Love.
24. *Fain* or *Fainne*—Legendary warriors of ancient Ireland.
25. *Faolan*—First name meaning wolf.
26. *Geersha*—Girl.
27. *Gom!*—Exclamation.
28. *Gommach*—Fool.
29. *Kippeen*—Cudgel or stick.
30. *Loodeen*—The small toe.
31. *Lushmore*—Nickname of foxglove blossoms, deep pink.
32. *Mac mallachtan!*—"Son of a curse!" Wicked person.
33. *Macushla*—"My darling."
34. *Madilse*—"My love."
35. *Ma girsha*—"My girl."
36. *Mavrone!*—"My goodness!" (exclamation).
37. *Mille murdher!*—"A thousand murders!" (Exclamation of surprise or indignation.)
38. *Mo cuishle*—"My darling."
39. *Mo stor gal*—"My bright star."
40. *Musha*—"In truth!"
41. *Ochone*—"My goodness"; "oh dear."
42. *Oinseach*—Female fool.
43. *Pogue*—Kiss.
44. *Pothogue*—A blow.
45. *Raumach*—"Rubbish!" (exclamation).
46. *Rapparee*—Irregular soldier, guerrilla fighter.
47. *Samain*—Irish name for moon; Hallowsday, November 1.
48. *Sidhe*—Fairyhost
49. *Skean*—Irish dagger.
50. *Slainte*—"Health!" Irish toast.
51. *Slaucan*—Sloke: seaweed favored by Spanish as edible treat; part of smuggled cargo.
52. *Slieve*—Mountain.
53. *Spalpeen*—Rascal.
54. *Sthronsuch*—"Lazy thing!"
55. "The Sons of Aislui"—Ancient folktale made famous by Yeats's "Deirdre of the Sorrows."

56. The Wild Geese—Name given to the thousands of Irish soldiers who left their homeland to fight in the armies of the Catholic countries of Europe in seventeenth and eighteenth centuries.

57. *Wirra*—"Oh!"

27 million Americans can't read a bedtime story to a child.

It's because 27 million adults in this country simply can't read.

Functional illiteracy has reached one out of five Americans. It robs them of even the simplest of human pleasures, like reading a fairy tale to a child.

You can change all this by joining the fight against illiteracy.

Call the Coalition for Literacy at toll-free **1-800-228-8813** and volunteer.

Volunteer Against Illiteracy. The only degree you need is a degree of caring.

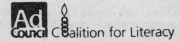

Ad Council Coalition for Literacy